DRIVEN TO THE HILT

The Deepest Cut

Copyright © 2017 by D. G. Lamb

Calyse Publishing
www.driventothehilt.com

ISBN 978-0-9993-2750-0 (paperback)
ISBN 978-0-9993-2751-7 (e-book)
ISBN 978-0-9993-2752-4 (Amazon e-book)

Driven to the Hilt: The Deepest Cut

Cover Design by Sheridan Lamb
Cover Art by David Lamb

Printed in the United States of America
First Edition

Author's Note

WAIT!

    Don't demand a refund! Those extra blank spaces in the first sentence are *supposed* to be there.   Here's the deal:

    The unusual spacing is a part of what I have come to call Dynamic Formatting. In a nutshell, it is the use of visual elements to convey additional information within the printed word. I come by this honestly: my father was a high school art teacher and his help with my drawings in elementary school started my lifetime enjoyment of art. I even ended up with a degree in Art. *(long story, for another time)* Bottom line? I don't claim to be an artist, but I do often see things in a different way.

    So, you can see one of the primary manifestations of Dynamic Formatting with the very first sentence. I put in additional spaces as a substitute for lapsing time, as in, the more spaces, the longer the pause in phrasing. I almost always do this within the context of dialogue, both in conversations and character's internal thinking. To my eye, and internal ear, the spacing produces a rhythm as you read, a pacing that further describes the exchange and more completely presents the characters.

    Dynamic Formatting also uses multiple fonts. Now I am not the first writer to do this. More recently, Brandon Sanderson used a different font in a very limited way (for a single character) in his Stormlight Archive series. However, I first saw it done on a larger scale in Terry Pratchett's Discworld books with the use of some variation of a tombstone engraving font whenever his character DEATH spoke. When I immediately knew who had begun speaking in a surprise appearance by DEATH in one of Pratchett's books, it occurred to me that this device could be used even more extensively by authors to create similar and additional effects.

    So   I have set the base font as Times New Roman, which includes all of Joshua's speaking and thoughts (it is his story, after all), but Arial is in place for any dialogue by any minor character. Now for other major characters, I have selected specific fonts with an eye to enhancing character presentation, while also maintaining

Author's Note

readability (frilly cursive fonts are a real pain to read, *IMHO*). The alternating of fonts also eliminates much of the need for dialogue identification phrases, such as: he replied, she said, George answered, etc. Getting rid of such filler words speeds things up for the reader and creates a more natural flow in the verbal exchanges between characters.

Finally, there are times I have used spacing to create a dramatic effect. I have done this sparingly, so as to avoid taxing the reader. Perhaps you will feel I have failed in that effort. Or you may just be a traditionalist, like my son ("That's what commas, ellipses, and dashes are for, Dad"). Or maybe, by the end of the book, you have found that Dynamic Formatting works for you and you like it. Whatever your reaction, go to driventothehilt.com and cast your vote! There is also a comment section for any feedback you may have about the book in general. I would appreciate your thoughts and ideas.

Cypress Grove

September 12, 2119 ESD

◄1►

He wouldn't lie to me.   But   he **has** *to know where he got it.*

snick snick snick

The steady rhythm of her chef's knife matched the beat of the rousing closing number from the musical, *Octavia's Curiosity*. Rachel allowed the knife's syncopation with the music to calm her so she could think about why he was being evasive. *After all, he can always tell me exactly where he's been in New Cincinnati.* Then it came to her and she bit back an audible sigh of relief. *Of course!   He wants to keep it secret so he can surprise me with other bargains before we launch the Café.*

snick snick.

Relieved to have an explanation, Rachel paused to survey the evenly spaced cuts with satisfaction and then rotated the small square cutting board and began a cross cut on the slice of tomato cube.

snick snick snick

Rhythm reestablished, she sought to infuse Joshua with some of her own restored celebratory mood.

"So, Joshua, where are you going to spend your free time this afternoon?"

"Oh. I don't know.   Ah   I   uh- haven't really thought about it yet."

snick snick snick   snick snick.

He always has plans for free time figured out in advance. So, **that** *was a flat out lie. What is going on?* The dicing done, Rachel straightened up and looked at Joshua with a deepening frown. He closed the door to the small cabinet refrigerator, having just replaced the remainder of the tomato cube in its Stay Fresh pouch. When he turned to face her, his eyes widened with innocence. *Too wide.*

Not wanting to over-react, Rachel picked up a spatula and turned to the SlipStone sauté pan, his recent birthday present to her and the object that had started the entire exchange. She pulled back the cooked edge of the "fused" eggs while tilting the pan to spill the still uncooked layer of pale yellow mixture onto the now exposed grey-speckled surface of the pan. She then sprinkled the just cut glistening red cubes over half of the omelet, quickly followed by matching white squares of already diced onion cube. Immediate cooking demands satisfied, she pulled in a long slow breath through her nose and spoke as she exhaled.

"Hank, please stop the music."

Rachel turned to her son as their household computer paused the morning playlist. His eyes spread open again, not with feigned innocence, but in apprehension. Her heart twisted at what she saw. *He's still so young.* His eleven-year-old face was open and vulnerable, miraculously not showing the scars from all that life had already put him through. *And yet, he's not my little boy anymore.* His upright posture and tendency to meet people's gazes with his green-grey eyes combined with an above average height and athletic build to create the impression of a 13- or 14-year-old. His short hair was mostly her auburn, but had red highlights from his father. *David.*

It hit her in a flash: powerful arms encompassing her from behind, gently squeezing away her self-doubt, his warm breath flowing against her neck-

"Mom?"

blink   the small curve of her husband's smile shifted into a soft melancholy   blink   his face transformed into her son's, his youthful features slightly twisted in puzzlement. The last blink brought Rachel back to the lies. A hollow ache thrummed in her chest as she tried to recall when the defiant lying stage of child development typically began. *Surely not this early.* Not for the first time, she wished her psych minor had provided more *practical* knowledge.

With effort, Rachel nipped the blooming self-pity and strengthened her resolve to discover the truth. "What's going on with you, honey? You've been in a mood ever since we got up this morning. That is so unlike you, especially on such a special day." A wave of guilt washed over Rachel, spawned by what she had not told Joshua about their "special day." She thrust aside the self-reproach to refocus on her son and his dishonesty, her tone both firm and imploring, "What do you need to tell me about my birthday present?"

She watched Joshua twist and look away as he struggled with the need to choose. Then his jaw clenched, he straightened upright, and looked right into her eyes, determination pulling down his brow. *That's just the way David looked when he came to a decision.* Her eyes did not mist up this time at the thought of her dead husband. Rachel pulled in another deep breath and was just about to press for an explanation when his words came out in a rush.

"I bought your pan on The Avenue."

Rachel felt her face harden.

Joshua hastened to add, "But it was hardly UpAve at all."

"UpAve? You're already using the street slang from   *that* place? Joshua, I told you to **never** go there!   You know all the stories about The Avenue!   Don't you know those people will hurt you, Son?   You cannot trust people like that. They will *use* you."

He pressed on. "I was on the corner off the Avenue and I saw a big sign that said 'Kitchen Sale.' I   I couldn't find anything that I could afford anywhere else, so...," he spoke softly to his feet, "I went there." His whisper lifted into the aromas that filled their cramped living cubical, "It was just the second store from the end."

The pleading in his voice tugged at her powerful need to be a "good" mother and she had to resist the urge to enfold him in a reassuring embrace. The matter-of-fact voice of Rachel's mother slid through her head, "Colonists must be as hard as the frontier they want to conquer and mothers must raise their children accordingly." This rationale had been pronounced every time punishment was dispensed, which had come just as frequently as praise. However, that balance of high expectations and constant encouragement proved to be much harder to strike with her son than with her students.

Rachel shrugged off the unproductive line of thought. *It doesn't matter anymore. I'll never teach in New Cincinnati again.* Besides, a critical piece of the puzzle was missing, something else that did not ring true. She could almost grasp it,   but-   Rachel sniffed.

The smell of browning egg mix pulled her back to the omelet. She pointed to a bowl on the counter, "Would you please hand that to me?" After spreading the previously browned sausage among the diced tomato and onion cube, Rachel looked up to find Joshua already extending another ingredient dish. Exchanging bowls, she distributed the meager amount of grated cheese. With a deft hand, Rachel folded the omelet and then turned back to her expectant son. She had decided on an educational approach, as was so often her way.

"Lying is still wrong even if you think something valuable will come from it. You obviously thought it was acceptable to break a rule **and** lie to me because doing so allowed you to get me a very nice gift. That's called   using the ends to justify the means." She tightened her lips to prevent a smile as her son frowned in concentration and silently mouthed the phrase to himself, committing it to memory. He obviously knew what came next.

Rachel's head tilted forward and she looked up through her eyebrows. "Instead of having free time this afternoon, you will research and write a paper on the concept of the 'ends justify the means,' to include its origins and ramifications for moral philosophy. Hank, you may cue Joshua with the name Machiavelli later today if he asks, but nothing else."

"Yes ma'am, provide the name Machiavelli if requested, but otherwise render no assistance on the topic of 'the ends justify the means.' "

Her son held a very neutral expression. *He thinks he is getting off light. And maybe he's right. But I still need to get breakfast done and not be late for my first day of work at the Silver Lining Diner.* She raised an eyebrow. "We shall see what else comes of this after I read your essay and see what you've learned."

Rachel distributed half of the omelet to each of the plates Joshua had already set on the counter. He carried them to the table top that slid out from the cabinet between their Vertabed couches. As had become typical for them, they both paused to savor the first bite, taking a long moment to slowly chew with half closed eyes. After swallowing, they shared a contented smile. The ritual reminded her of how much closer they had become since David's death. Rachel was again overtaken by the sudden fear that her son was growing up and would soon be leaving her. She fought back the discomforting thought and smiled.

"Pretty good, especially considering its all lab food."

"*Really* good, Mom."

"Just think of what it will be like with *fresh* ingredients." Rachel waved her empty fork at their surroundings, "This will all be worth it once we get the Homehearth Café up and running."

Joshua gave a half smile in response, but said nothing. *He can't bring himself to say it. My God, how he hates this place!* Rachel bent to her breakfast to hide the guilt that once again flowed over her. Even with their current low rent, what she already earned cooking at the Lunch Factory, and the additional money from her new morning job, it would still take an entire year to even approach the minimum startup costs for their own restaurant. Rachel winced slightly at the follow-up thought that they really needed another six months past that. *One thing at a time.*

She had almost finished eating when the missing puzzle piece unexpectedly clicked into place. Rachel looked up at Joshua as he speared his last bite, "So, just how big was this discount The Avenue merchant gave you?"

Joshua looked up, blinked in confusion, and frowned, "Fort- no, ah *60* percent off."

"Wow. 60 percent off! That's a really good deal."

His face relaxed, "Yep. I thought so too."

"Hmmm, let's see, 60 percent off of 16, that would be six UDs and ah 40 cents, right?"

Joshua's eyes began darting around the room like a cornered animal, "Would it? I ah 16? That sounds like a lot. I don't think I'm n-"

"I *know* how much the SlipStone pans cost, Joshua, and I *know* how much spending money I give you. Where did you get the extra money?"

His face contorted in anger. "Why can't we just eat breakfast without you giving me the fifth degree?"

"It's the third degree and I *still* need to know how you made the extra money."

"OH.　　Okay,　　so do I need to write something about *that*, too? Hank, remind me to write an essay on the third degree."

"OK Joshua, I'll remind you to write an essay on 'the third degree' later this afternoon."

They sat frozen, Rachel in disbelief and Joshua glaring, with the tension mounting in the expanding silence. Finally, Joshua looked at the speared bite of omelet and eased his fork back to the plate. With hands in his lap, he looked up, but said nothing. That, of course, would not stand. Rachel's mouth set into a thin determined line.

"Son?"

It was her turn to be thrown by a change in topic.

"Mom. My Orson 150 is　　*really*　　old.　　The clock rate on the processor -　Ok.　It's just *really* slow, right?　So　that's making it harder and harder for me to compete."

Her jaw dropped in disbelief. "Joshua,　*please*,　don't tell me you've been gambling with stickball again."

His face told her before his words, "I just want to help with the Café Fund, Mom."

"We *both* know that has *definitely* not worked out well before." Rachel felt the flush of anger on her face. "I do **not**　want to come home and find you like **that** *ever again!*"

Joshua was incredulous. "But　*that*　was such a long time ago!"

"Not nearly long enough for me."

"Mom. I'm a lot more careful now. I never bet so much that someone would want to fight after losin-"

The flat of her palm hit the table with a smack. "Joshua! I　*will*　*not* *have this!*" Rachel pushed herself up and bent closer, "You will **not** bet on stickball!　Ever again, Son!"

Driven to the Hilt

Joshua also rose in frustration, his eyes glistening and his words loud, "This is *so* unfair! *You* are always telling me that I have to be more grown up, to be *responsible*! And I *am*! I *always* try to do like you say, to act like the 'man of the house.'"

Rachel's mouth went slack, her shoulders sagged, and she thumped back into her chair. "I I have *never* said that, Son. It was something your father always said when he went on deployments." A hollow pain filled her eyes, her words were sad and wistful, "Actually, it was one of the few things we disagreed on."

Joshua's eyes opened wide in rage and defiance. His words came out hot,

"Yeah? Well, Dad was right and I wish *he* was here..."

Rachel stared at the unspoken words that almost shimmered in the air between them and silently finished the sentence *instead of me.*

The gut punch had driven the air out of her lungs. Rachel blinked rapidly, trying to understand what had just happened, surprised when a hot tear dropped onto her check. Through watery eyes, she saw awareness spread across Joshua's face and he dropped his head in shame. She forced herself to breathe and searched for something to say, something to repair the rift, praying that this would not stand between them. What came to mind did not feel adequate, but it was what she felt at that moment. She hoped it would be enough, even while she feared it would not.

"Joshua, there is *no* amount of money *anywhere* that is worth the risk of losing you."

His bent head nodded as he whispered, "I know, Mom."

Rachel rounded the table and pulled him in tight, his short cropped hair brushing the underside of her chin. His heaving shoulders and the feel of his fists clutching the back of her undershirt transported her back to when they had first learned of her husband's death. Joshua's face had burrowed into her stomach as she had searched the faces of the two Merchant Marine officers outside her front door, trying to find evidence that this was some training exercise, a grossly inappropriate joke, *something* other than the

The Deepest Cut

plain words they had just spoken. All she saw was pity. The reason it was not sympathy became clear when the senior officer informed her that an investigation into "the incident" had been initiated. She had held her son close until their sobs had subsided. When she had finally closed the door on the long empty porch, she had absolutely no comprehension of the pain that investigation would bring. *And still brings.*

Hand gently stroking the back of Joshua's head, she realized he was no longer sobbing. She kissed the top of his head and felt a squeeze in response. With a sigh, she stepped back, leaving one hand on his shoulder, while the other hand replaced a stray strand of long auburn hair behind her ear. Raising both eyebrows, she put a whiff of mischievousness into her voice.

"Well, I guess it's true what they say."

His red rimmed eyes did not move, but she knew he had just rolled them in his mind. *He knows there's a lesson coming.* Still, the corners of his mouth curved up as he provided the obligatory response, his voice carrying only a hint of exacerbation, "What do they say, Mom?"

"Oh,   I don't know.   I was just thinking of that famous Greek poem."

An outright smile came just prior to Joshua's exaggerated sigh. "What famous poem, Mom?"

"Well, I don't remember all of it, but it was about Cupid getting stung by a bee. He ran to his mother, the Greek Goddess of Love, and let's see, then it goes:

Spreading all his fingers he
    Sobbed to Aphrodite:
'Mother, little is the bee,
    But its sting is mighty!'
Then the Queen of Passion smiled,
    And she answered merely:
'You are small yourself, my child,
    But you wound severely.' "

Rachel cocked her head and gave her son a sideways look, along with a

Driven to the Hilt

slender smile.

Joshua's eyes were somber, but his return smile was genuine. "That's a good one, Mom."

They were not back to where they had been when they had awoken that morning, but Rachel felt it was much improved. She gave a single nod, but her glance at the time displayed on her minisheet made her jerk in alarm.

*"Oh my! Is it **that** late?"*

She pulled her silver chef smock off of its hanger and began shrugging it on over her wicking undershirt. As she finished buttoning, Rachel gave Joshua an apologetic, but firm look. She was relieved they had reconciled, but *We both know I have to follow up on this.*

"So. You will do your chores and your homework, but you will *not* have your outside free time this afternoon. We'll discuss this further when I get home from the Lunch Factory. I'm sorry, but that's probably going to be around four or five, because I'm pretty sure I'm going to be covering for Aliss today." She leaned forward and put a hand on the side of Joshua's face, "Son, I know you don't like it here. Neither do I. But I'm working this second job so we can get out of here even quicker. Before you know it we'll have enough in the Café Fund and then wh-"

knock knock

Rachel let her head loll forward and muttered, chin on chest, "Purrr fect."

"Just don't answer, Mom."

knock! knock! knock!

She looked at Joshua with resignation, but then straightened up with resolve. "He will *not* force me to be disrespectful and he will *not* make me late for my first day at the Silver Lining Diner!" She took three steps to the front door and yanked it open.

Mr. Donald stood posed with one hand on the door frame, the other held across his waist so that his still dripping umbrella could hang from his forearm. His expectant grin faded when he saw that she was already dressed for work. Still, his eyes traveled down and up her trim body once before he spoke. "Just stopped by to check on y'all 'n see if ya needed anything."

"Oh? Well, then I'm a bit surprised you don't have your tools with you, Mr. Donald. Or are the gaskets for the faucet *still* on back order?"

"Please, *please*, Rachel. Call me Roree." He tugged the lapel on his shiny blue jacket, gave a quick pass over his slicked back black hair, and leaned forward, his grin returning as he peeked past her with a noisy sniff, "Smells *wonderful* in there! Did I miss breakfast?"

Rachel shrugged into her slicker. "Yes, Mr. Donald, you did. Now, I need to leave for work, so excuse me, please." She placed one foot over the threshold with palm extended forward and waited, head cocked in expectation. Once the property manager had retreated, she completed her exit and whirled to face Joshua, surprised by the intensity of her son's glare at Mr. Donald.

"Joshua." His eyes softened as he refocused on her. "No stickball today." Then she gave Joshua The *Look*. "And Son, do *not* go on The Avenue again."

"OK, Mom."

Rachel let go of the door and watched it close on her solemn son. Then she set out at a brisk pace and began to mentally review the list of ingredients, item prep, and construction procedures for the breakfast dishes at the Silver Lining Diner. She was halfway to the end of the covered walkway before Mr. Donald caught up.

"Rachel! Let me escort you to work this morning. I can keep ya safe and we kin get better acquainted along the way."

Rachel came to a brisk stop and pivoted to place her pursuer under earnest regard. "Mr. Donald. I am *really* striving not to be rude, but this is my first day of work at a new job and I do *not* have time to stroll with you and chat." She then speared Mr. Donald with The *Look*, "And *please* believe me when I say, I am *quite* capable of protecting myself. So if you will excuse me."

She spun and resumed her high speed walk, grateful to hear Mr. Donald's sputtering response fade with the increasing distance. She began reviewing the current menu at the Silver Lining Diner, considering possible

Driven to the Hilt

changes and seasoning substitutions. Rachel had some definite ideas about how to build the Diner's reputation over the next year and a half, and with it, her own as well. However, as she left the NorthPoint housing project behind, she found that she just could not maintain her concentration on the task. The world felt somehow not quite *normal*, as if it had stepped back to watch her.

Rachel reminded herself that it had been a very emotional start to the day. She gave her shoulders a quick shake and strode with renewed purpose into the light rain.

The Deepest Cut

◄2►

Thunk!

Joshua stared at the closed door with its pattern of dull red anti-rust primer, his resentment shifting to rest firmly on Mr. Donald. *Another thing he'll probably never fix.*

The thought that he would be seeing the same unfinished patchwork when the lease was up started a slow spiral into depression. Joshua dropped onto the end of his Vertabed and flopped back onto the couch, eyes wandering over the bare metal spots where the paint was peeling off the ceiling. *He hasn't even scraped any of it.* His mounting despondency was halted by an echo of his mother's words *Whenever you are feeling down, find something to do.* He lifted his head and looked at the breakfast dishes and omelet pan. With a sigh, he rose from the Vertabed.

It was not long before Joshua surveyed a clean kitchen. As usual, he did feel better for having forced himself into action, but a glowing coal in the ashes of his resentment prevented him from giving credit to his mother. The thought of her brought the unresolved question of what he was going to do later that afternoon. His mind shied away from the problem and Joshua implemented another of his mother's aphorisms *Put it on the back burner.* He smiled at the memory of his mother placing a pot of spaghetti sauce on the back of the cooking pad and hours later showing him what needed to be skimmed from the surface. Of course she had *loved* that the saying came within the context of cooking. His smile became a frown when he remembered he was angry with her. He pulled the legs from his sheet case, propped the computer tablet up next to his school supplies on the pull-out table, and got to work.

The page of math problems took some time, since he was not allowed to use a calculator and had to show all of his computations. As for vocabulary, he just had to be sure and tell his mom about an instance where he had used the word of the day in a conversation. Joshua also spent over 45 minutes reading and taking notes for history. The chapter covered

Earth's prior attempts at cross-cultural governments. Although the report on Sweden's Citizenship Riots of 2071 was not due until the following day, he went ahead and created an outline. Joshua no longer complained about studying history, knowing it would just bring his mother's inevitable response, Those who don't know history are doomed to repeat it. Still, he could not quite understand how knowing what had happened on Earth 50 years ago helped him now.

Regular homework completed, Joshua stared at the screen of his sheet and forced his thoughts to the "punishment essay." A quick search of the GlobalNet produced several summaries of the historical critiques of *The Prince*. Despite his annoyance at having to write the paper, Joshua was fascinated to learn that over time, different writers had reached a variety of conflicting conclusions about what Machiavelli intended to say in his famous book. Still, he knew what his mother expected. So without a great deal of thought, he culled various quotes and references that supported her view that the ends should never justify immoral means and strung them together. Finally, satisfied the essay would serve its purpose, Joshua glanced at the time on his sheet. *Wow! Not even 11 o'clock. I guess getting up early has its perks.*

A mischievous smile stole across Joshua's face. It stayed there the entire time he researched the third degree on the GlobalNet and as he wrote the one page summary on the phrase. The smile became a grin as he dictated on the 1931 Wickersham Commission's conclusion of the widespread use of pain to illicit confessions in the United States. *There's your history, Mom!*

Joshua leaned back to savor a sense of completion. Instead, the dingy, faded walls seemed to press in on him, intensifying the gloomy silence of the tiny apartment. Then it hit him: the intense smell of rotting vegetation from The Swamp. On their first day, as they searched for space to put things in the tiny apartment, Joshua's mother had wrinkled her upturned nose at the aroma and laughed that it was the last place they could live before actually moving into The Swamp itself. The joke spoke to the truth that the back of their unit literally faced the dense jungle that surrounded New Cincinnati. The dark conviction that there was little to lose stoked the

The Deepest Cut

ember of Joshua's resentment still glowing from his mother not letting him contribute to getting out of the NorthPoint housing project. Joshua looked over at the large wedding photo that rested on the writing desk by the front door. *Dad would have let me help out, as long as I was careful. And I'm very careful now.*

Decision made, Joshua stowed the pull-out table, swept and mopped the floor, and changed into his stickball clothes. After wolfing down a simple sandwich for lunch, he was on a fast stroll away from NorthPoint. The walk in the light rain among the drab and grimy industrial buildings left little to do but think. A flush of doubt slowed Joshua's pace, but he replaced his mother's face with his father's, seeing him assume a pose and drawl in his not-very-good John Wayne imitation: "A man's gotta do, what a man's gotta do." The image renewed Joshua's determination to follow through on his decision, but as he transitioned into a newer section of the city, a flood of other negative associations assaulted him: the shocking news of his father's death, the lingering whispers of his betrayal, the ostracism that had cost his mother her teaching job, trying to stretch the value of every single penny to its absolute limit, their relentless slide down the social ladder to the worst slum in the colony, his mother's disgust for their leering new landlord, and...

...it all vanished when the sunlight touched his face.

Joshua stood transfixed by the sensation of heat on his cheek *from the sun!* He followed the golden beam's path back up to where it gloriously streamed down from a small patch of sapphire blue sky, the sun just peeking over the hard golden edge of the covering cloud. He marveled as the mists separated to reveal the upper slopes of Mount Lipsig looming to the north of New Cincinnati. He squinted against the sparkling explosion of sunlight reflecting off the metallic microfibers embedded in the Permacrete monorail posts. Joshua was amazed he could actually see the train sliding up the silver monorail strand that curved above the dense jungles surrounding the colony. Several large rusty horizontal gashes in the mountainside marked the extensive mining operations, the reddish earth in sharp contrast to the surrounding verdant vegetation. But the magnificent view paled in significance to what had just happened: for the first time in Joshua's life, he had *felt   direct   sunlight* on his face.

Fingertips explored the unfamiliar heat on his skin. The clouds shifted, the warmth faded, and an upward glance warned that the moment was coming to an end. Joshua's eyes returned to the nearby slopes, greedily taking in how the jungle's endless variety of greens almost glowed, providing such an invigorating contrast to the rain streaked grey-brown walls of the surrounding warehouses and abandoned residential projects that had once been filled with company miners.

A flash of light from a turning ore car pulled Joshua's eyes back up the mountainside. Vapors rose from the surrounding treetops and joined with descending clouds to choke out the lush vista. He looked up to his right at the shrinking blue opening. An approaching roiling darkness angrily overcame the last patch of azure and joined accumulating mists to reclaim the rare view of the mountainside. *It's over.*

He glanced up at the oncoming wall of charcoal clouds. As they intensified the gloom, Joshua's eyes returned to the dark green tree tops on the rising mountainside. Like most occupants of New Cincinnati, he did not often think about spidervipers. The mysterious carnivores had settled into the collective societal psyche to become a universal certainty that certain death awaited anyone who might venture into the surrounding jungle. However, with the surrounding forest just rendered vividly real, it was easy to imagine the spidervipers scurrying under the jungle foliage, looking for victims to strike with their fang tipped tongues.

Joshua shuddered away his skin crawling fear. Trying to reorient to his immediate surroundings, he caught the eye of a young woman blinking as if coming out of a trance, still smiling from having witnessed the singular event. She wore one of the new transparent slickers that allowed the fashion conscious to display their high sense of style even when outside. The curve of her mouth straightened out as she glanced over Joshua's shoulder. He turned to see a businessman speaking to a head suspended over the thin black leather case held flat in his hands. *Ooh, that's a Nebula Vivid 3-D projector case!* Joshua knew this from having recently

researched sheet cases for his birthday. Of course, 3-D projectors were not
in the family budget, but that had not stopped him from looking. Like any
other 11-year-old, he stayed up on the latest in technology.

The man had just said something about exclusive rights and the
following silence made it clear that the floating head's response was being
channeled through a wireless earpiece. A groan escaped Joshua as he
realized the reason for the woman's frown. The man had used his sheet to
video the rare direct sunshine and would now likely make *20, no   50
times* what Joshua could make from winning bets at a pickup stickball
match.

A rare flash and immediate crack of thunder from just outside the city
caused everyone's heads to swivel toward the approaching bank of purple-
grey clouds. Joshua recalled one of his home school reports, when he had
learned that despite the perpetual cloud cover, thunderstorms were
uncommon for New Cincinnati because the climate rarely produced a
sufficient temperature differential between cold and warm fronts. Then, as
if on cue, everyone bent their heads back down to the meshed pedway,
their focus three feet in front of the next step of their interrupted journeys.
The young woman was already passing him in the opposite direction when
Joshua turned from the coming rain and proceeded deeper into the city. His
initial excitement to tell his mom about actually seeing sunlight was soured
by the missed opportunity to contribute a significant amount to the Café
Fund.

He headed out of the slums toward Sunny Day Square, an entire block
complex of tenement apartments recently refurbished and reclaimed for
company miners. The first wave of rain slapped against his back and
Joshua's mood darkened with the overtaking thunderheads above him. He
had walked less than a block before a picture of his mother came to mind.
She looked at him with hands on hips, head cocked, and eyebrows raised.
*OK, Mom.   I'll say it   What a **promising** day!* Despite the internal
sarcasm, some liveliness returned to Joshua's step. *Speaking of which,* he
savored the feel of the new custom fit Nova HiTop Clingers on his feet.
There had been just enough cash to pay for the stickball shoes. Joshua
looked down at the grey and black Clingers with a smile. The specially

formulated rubberized plastic that formed the soles of the shoes allowed for greater traction on the stickball court, a helpful attribute on street courts with no protection from the rain. Skipping across the pedway as he made his way toward uptown, Joshua hummed the happy birthday song to himself as large raindrops assaulted his back with renewed vigor.

Moments later, Joshua came to a corner and looked up at the signpost across the pedway. His gut twisted as he recalled his mother's look when she realized he had come to this place. The right half of a street sign hung on a rusty wire, occasionally tapping against a cracked security camera case that also dangled from the light pole. It stated simply: Ave. And whatever the maps said about the official name, that was what everyone called this stretch of pedway: The Avenue.

Standing at the beginning of the DownAve end of The Avenue, Joshua looked UpAve through the 12 intersections that stretched further to the North, where it terminated only a block from The Swamp. He took in the shops lining the pedway along each side of The Avenue, with their brightly colored neon signage and flashing lights. Halfway UpAve, he could see where makeshift structures began to encroach upon the pedway, home to vendors who didn't care about zoning regulations and set up their businesses wherever space was available and they had the will to fight for their existence. It reflected a spirit of competition that was literally cutthroat.

Joshua's eyes were drawn to the second storefront on the left: Harlison's General Store. The 'Kitchen Sale' sign had been replaced by 'Clear Slicker's HERE – *CHEAP!!!*' He recalled how terrified he had been to even step on The Avenue, much less go into one of its stores. Despite having survived that foray unscathed, he had absolutely no desire to explore farther UpAve. Everyone knew of the predatory spidervipers lurking in the jungle surrounding the city, but with The Avenue, the dark menace that hung in the air was personal. It came from an accumulation of the whispers and oblique hints of unspoken evil acts that had taken place there, from the look of fear and reproach that came over people's faces when The Avenue was even mentioned.

Joshua pivoted away and crossed the pedway to head south. He picked up his pace when the feeling of being watched did not fade. Half a block away, a glance over his shoulder revealed nothing unusual, but the sense of that something bad was about to happen persisted. It was intense enough that he considered abandoning his quest and heading back to NorthPoint. Then came a vague memory of his faceless father, wordlessly holding his bicycle after an elbow bruising spill. *NO! Toughen up!* He could almost feel the same glow of approval that had come from his father when he had climbed back on that bicycle five years ago. Still, it took an entire block of dodging past startled and then annoyed pedestrians before he shook the sense of approaching doom.

And then he saw the sign.

◄3►

Pixel Pages!

The holographic sign of the ad-kiosk extended out from a building halfway down the block on the other side of the pedway. Joshua skipped his way through the sparse foot traffic and slowed as he approached the first window, dragging his toe on the wire mesh to make a satisfying BRRRrrrrrt sound. He pressed up against the window, taking in a life-sized cutout of a muscular man with no shirt, one knee to the ground, holding up a woman in his arms *Yuck!* The curvy lady with blonde hair was laid back and looking up at the man with equally long hair, one hand on his face, one laying limp on the ground. *Why are they always trying to lie down?* Joshua slid his forehead and palms across the window to the next display and found   a collection of Self-Help book covers. *BOORRRing!* But he hit the jackpot on the next display *Sci-Fi!!*

Joshua examined each of the book covers one by one, savoring the exotic artwork and story teases. The last cover depicted Jake Smith, hero of the Shooting Stars series, crouched behind a rock on a yolk yellow beach, energy pistol in each hand, about to take out two multi-limbed aliens emerging from purple tinged waters. Joshua sighed. He had sworn off downloading e-books onto his sheet, unwilling to pay the two dollars for such first releases that could go to the Café Fund. *Just have to wait 'til it hits the Cloudbrary.* He sidestepped to the last window, only to find a hodgepodge of uninteresting adult titles. He snapped a quick salute back to Jake before resuming his cross city trek.

As he skipped the pedway, his thoughts returned to the fantastic feel of the sun warming his cheek. That reminded him of   *Something, but what?* He struggled to grasp the elusive thought. Then he had it: *Coconut Custard ice cream!* He remembered the sunlamps at the Sky Creek Mall, where in happier times, his parents had taken him once a month for a single scoop of ice cream and to soak up some vitamin D from the sunlamps. Joshua pictured the interlocking ion shields atop slender poles, diverting sheets of rain into streams of water where the domes intersected, eventually

forming musical waterfalls that cascaded down throughout all three levels
of the Mall. Every hour, the sunlamps would dim for lasers to dance
brilliant colors off the domes of water in syncopation to music. However,
most of the shoppers came for the imitation sunlight rather than the visual
spectacle of lasers on the weaving waterfalls.

A loud horn jarred Joshua from his recollection. He looked down
through the woven wire surface of the pedway to the solid motorway one
level below. Two drivers were out on the vehicles only roadway, each
making their case for right-of-way. Joshua pressed on in a heavy drizzle.
He decided against taking the time to buy an insurance policy cover story,
since his mother rarely came home early when she covered for a co-
worker. *Besides, I'm on a mission.*

Joshua was careful to search for pickup games in different parts of
New Cincinnati to keep his abilities unknown. He ran only a slight risk that
he might see anybody at Sunny Day Square who knew him. Primarily
occupied by the families of miners, the residents had some money for nicer
equipment, but also possessed a more lax attitude about their children's
attendance at the public schools. This meant there should be some games
going during the day, which also meant an opportunity for profit.

Joshua pulled around the lance that had been hanging from the harness
built into his slicker. He examined the nicks and worn spots along the
meter long shaft, which resembled a golf club with the head cut off. His
Orson 150 was almost three generations behind the typical street baller
lance, putting him at a distinct disadvantage. To start generating significant
money for the Café Fund, he *really* needed an updated lance.

Joshua had become very, *very* good at stickball. He had a knack for
anticipating the movement of the "ball," which was a crimson sphere of
light created by a multitude of intersecting low intensity lasers. This ability
was critical when other players tried "bouncers" off the "uppers." More
often, though, Joshua's opponents were catching on to his skills, making it
a challenge to win money off of side bets. Forced to wager smaller
amounts, his profits were reduced when he won, which was still almost
always the outcome. This was partially due to what he called "slowtime."

In a recent interview, Ninian Thite, captain of New Cincinnati's semipro stickball team, the SpiderVipers, had spoken about getting "in the zone," when the action slowed down so he could see the entire field. Joshua had also experienced this sensation during particularly critical plays, but he never knew when it would happen and he could not initiate it or control how long it lasted. Whether "in the zone" or "slowtime," the ability allowed Joshua to be competitive with older players, who had more money to bet. Fortunately, it had been occurring more frequently of late.

The rain began pounding down with greater intensity. Feeling the day slipping away, Joshua did not pause under the rain arches as did most of his fellow pedestrians. The decorative archways that occasionally spanned the pedways were created to provide shelter from more vicious downpours and were more frequently encountered in the wealthier neighborhoods of southern New Cincinnati. In this newer part of the city, most rain arches were built by advertisers "as a courtesy to the hard working New Cinncy Citizen," with the "totally unintended" outcome of also creating more virtual billboard space.

Jogging out of the downpour into the next rain arch, Joshua smiled at the last few seconds of a Carly's Sandwich Shoppe commercial, proclaiming with big, bold red letters the arrival of the new "Ham" version of their very popular "Squarewiches." The thin sandwiches were a stack of square components that were produced in the food labs: flat bread, processed meat food, and a red and a green "veggie" slice of compressed tomato and lettuce cells. Of course, the surface of the bottom piece of flat bread had Vitamayo, a spread that contained a measured portion of vitamins and supplements. *Yuck! Nothin' like Mom makes.*

Joshua stepped out of the rain arch into a cascade of water. A brisk walk around a corner and he spotted his objective from under the dripping edge of his slicker hood: a monolith made entirely of a yellow tinted Greystone. *Ah, Sunny Day, I get it.* He jogged the remaining distance to the entrance tunnel, where he stopped, took a deep breath, and "made" himself older. He had learned through experience that if he wanted a shot at playing with the older players, he had to project a more mature attitude. Being an only child made this a bit easier because almost all of his conversations over the last four years had been with his mother, who *never* spoke down to him.

The stickball court stood to the left as he emerged from the access way. *Wow, nice set up.* From the entrance to the courtyard, it looked like a giant glowing tissue box, the bottom two thirds a soft white and the top third a muted fluorescent orange. Striding closer, Joshua noted the fine mesh of light beams created by hundreds of low intensity lasers in each of the six 12-foot-high metal projection poles, one set at each corner and two at center court. *That's impressive!* He usually played on courts with wider spaced lasers, like a chain link fence, and almost always with some missing lines in those light "walls." The light clarity of these lines also spoke to the newness of the lasers. And that meant a quicker processing CPU, which reduced some of the disadvantage of Joshua's older lance. Joshua smiled at the lack of cracks on the rubberized surface of the court and then looked up at the large ion shield that shed the heavy rainfall to nearby gutters. *That looks like it's permanent!*

Two three-player teams were using the court, just as Joshua had hoped. He headed around the bleachers nearest the tenement interior wall. A smattering of spectators sat in the stands, with only a few in the same age range as the boys currently running the court. *Perfect. Shouldn't have to wait too long to play.*

He met the stares from the too young players with a flat confidence, but did not hold them too long, because after all, they might be future teammates. When in a new venue, he usually needed to join a few games with younger players to first showcase his skills. If lucky, he would fill out a team for free; if not, he might have to buy in for a few cents. He could not remember the last time this strategy had failed to eventually get him in the mix with the older players.

Joshua spotted the bowl sitting atop the metal CPU cabinet between the back of the bleachers and the dirty yellow wall of the tenement. His optimistic mood evaporated when he looked into the bowl to see six quarters waiting for the victors of the current game. *Quarter ante? You have **got** to be kidding!* The typical buy in for a street game was a nickel, sometimes a dime for nicer facilities. *This court **is** nice, but not worth a soggin' quarter. Mop it, I'm gonna have to find another game. And I*

Driven to the Hilt

thought that sunbeam had been a good *omen.*

He turned away and almost bumped into the girl staring at him with an intense frown.

◄4►

Tifinity zeroed in on the tall boy and headed in his direction. She could not quite figure his age. His face looked young, but he was taller than she was and carried himself with confidence. When she saw his expression after looking into the ante bowl, she knew she would have to say something. Experience had painfully taught Tifinity that whatever she said would probably be the wrong thing, but she could not let him leave without at least trying. It had been three days since she had played a game and she would *not* give up without a fight. *That's for **damn** sure!* She stepped in front of him as he turned away from the bowl, forcing him to come up short.

"What's the matter, too rich for your blood?"

He raised his eyebrows and Tifinity berated herself, *Stupid! You want him to join your team, not get pissed and leave even quicker.*

Despite her antagonistic opening, he responded, "Yeah, well, a quarter *is* too rich for me. I don't usually pay more than a dime."

She could tell by his frown that her sudden attempt at a smile was not helping, but she pressed on anyway. "It's a *really* nice court," she tempted, "Madison high def projectors and we just installed an 893 TSW processor. Shines real bright."

"So I see," the boy nodded, looking over at the court, "but   "

Tifinity interrupted, "The quarter covers a best-of-three. So really, it only costs," *I **hate** muckin' math,* "uh,   less than a dime a game." She was flustered by his smile.

"Well, only if you play all three games."

He started to step by her. *This ain't working.* "I'll pay the other 15 cents!" she blurted out, prompting him to stop. His uncertain look was not encouraging, so   *Might as well try the truth.*

"*Look,*   I got Hareld over there who'll join us, but if you don't pony up, we're goin' to be stuck here watching," Tifinity jerked a thumb toward the court, "*them* for the rest of the day." As she waited, her limited powers of

Driven to the Hilt

persuasion tapped out, she again wished she could cry on demand like other girls, although *I don't think it would work on this guy.*

After Tifinity endured a long moment resisting the urge to fidget under his stare, the boy stuck out his hand and gave his answer.

"Okay." Then he flashed a secret smile, "Even though it's *exorbitant,* I'm in."

Exor bit what? This kid is haulin' weird, but   Not wanting to let him off the hook, Tifinity gripped his hand hard and pumped it up-and-down once. "Deal!"

"But I'll pay the full 25 cents," he added.

OH!   She shrugged nonchalantly. "OK. If you want."   Her prior desperate offer *would've about blown the bank.*

The tall boy stepped up to Hareld and held out his hand. "Hi Hareld, I'm Joshua." He then turned back to Tifinity, "And you are?"

"Tifinity," as she brushed by him to be the first to drop her quarter in the bowl, not sure whether she should shake his hand again along with the revelation of her name. Besides, she had no desire to hear what she knew would come next *Like ALWAYS!*

"Oh, like To Infinity and–"

"Look, we have a deal, right?" She jabbed her finger at the bowl.

"Uh, right."

Two more quarters clinked into the bowl and they all headed to the stands to watch the conclusion of the current match. The new boy smiled in appreciation as one of the older players made a double bouncer off the Uppers, the red sphere first hitting the orange ceiling and then bouncing off the middle of the orange upper wall. The ball nicely led his teammate, who had sprinted behind the younger team's defenses.

"They're good! Who's the point?"

"Marcus."

"Friend of yours?"

Hareld's snort cut off short under Tifinity's glare. Her sideways glance caught the boy's troubled expression *Don't blow it now!* "They tend to use a Phoenix defense. The call sign to switch from zone to man is 'blue.'"

The boy nodded. "Good to know. And as my Dad always said,

'Defense wins games.'" He winced as a shot from the younger point guard went wide and the red ball winked out as it passed through the white plane of light that made up the lower eight feet of the court walls. The larger boys transitioned to offense again. "Looks like Marcus prefers a Heidleberg offense. That only works if the point is good enough. We'll have to work on him."

"Oh, *I will*, don't you worry."

"You want to go man? Maybe you and Hareld have played a lot together, but…"

Tifinity knew she was glaring again, but could not stop, which made her jaw clench even tighter. Of course, it was true that some variation of a zone defense *would* be better than man-to-man. The fact that the boy was right only served to make Tifinity's teeth grind harder. He looked to Hareld for back-up just as the musical bells signaling Match point echoed off the yellow wall behind them.

They turned to watch Marcus exit the court with a confident smile. *Oohh, oohh, look at me! King of the Court. You're such a soppin' ass!* Tifinity heard the tall boy's "That was a nice shot" from behind her as she stepped off the bleachers and headed away from the green Home half of the court, and more importantly, away from where Marcus exchanged congratulations with his teammates in front of his "cheerleading" squad. As she walked, she pressed in the code on the control buttons recessed in the end of her lance handle to initiate warm up mode. Tifinity had just stepped onto the Visitors' blue half of the court when his grating voice called out.

"Tiff! Such a surprise! What's this? You found some fresh meat with enough coin to let you play? *Awlright!* Looks like this is gonna be a BANNER day, boys! See ya in 10."

Tifinity kept her back to Marcus as he strolled off the court and began catching practice balls launched from different sections of the far wall, then whipping them into the goal. She was soon joined by her teammates, who wisely said nothing and fell into the routine sequence of warm up drills. As always, Tifinity relaxed as they rotated through the various approaches toward the goal, taking turns presenting a maximized defense shield, passing to teammates, and shooting at the 3′ x 3′ goal with the circle in the center. *The boy is pretty good, in drills at least.* Tifinity lost herself in the familiar warm up maneuvers and the next ten minutes passed quickly.

Tifinity's mood of contentment evaporated as she crouched in her orange start circle and watched Marcus jauntily bring the ball up court. *I'm going to wipe that smirk off your face!* He faked a pass to his left and had started a cut to the right when he made a loud grunt *That sounds SO good* as both of Tifinity's fists, holding her lance parallel to the goal, drove into his chest. A long buzzer sounded as Marcus picked himself up off the court.

"Whoa, Tiff! Startin' off by givin' us a point? That's real generous of you, I must say!"

"You ain't made it yet," she snarled through gritted teeth. Stepping into the penalty box while Marcus awaited the Penalty Pitch, Tifinity saw the new boy's look and tried to explain, "Just trying to get his mind off the game, like you said." He did not reply as the point dinged for the green home team. Tifinity headed out to the point position circle for the post-penalty reset. *I don't care what he thinks!*

Eight minutes later, she stood panting, faced with a grinning Marcus in full defense shield, unable to get a shot. The tall boy had intercepted a bouncer, fed her a fast break, but Marcus had beat her down court. *I'm going to slap that smile from here to-* A chime sounded and the red ball disappeared. *What the?* Tifinity whipped around to see the new boy's back as he walked toward their goal. Hareld shrugged and headed back also. *If he thinks he can waste one of our four timeouts this early in the match and not hear* Tifinity stopped, breath forced out by what she saw on the scoreboard above their goal. They were behind 7 to 2. It was not so much the score as the fact that she had completely lost track of it.

As soon as they huddled in front of their goal, the tall boy asked, "What's going on?"

Tifinity just looked at him. *Another boy trying to boss me around.*

The boy did not relent, "I don't know if you just want to get close to this guy 'cause you have a crush on him or what-" Hareld could not contain the guffaw this time, even in the face of Tifinity's scowl.

The Deepest Cut

The new boy took a breath and tried again, "Look, *you're* the one who said you and Hareld could compete with these guys and convinced me to throw in a quarter. Now that may be hauler's wages to you, but my family can't afford to lose that kind of money." The boy lowered his voice, "This is your court, but if you want to play point, *play point*." Before Tifinity could formulate a response, the 10 second warning buzzer sounded and they all headed back towards the illuminated orange reset circles just behind their blue quarter court line.

Tifinity did her best to focus on setting plays and passing the ball, noting that the boy rarely missed whenever her feed gave him even a crease at the goal. While this increased their scoring, they could not narrow the gap. All because of *The Famous MarcOSpin*. He would approach, stutter step and then spin past the defender. What created the problem was that he could spin in either direction with equal ease. As Marcus advanced toward her, Tifinity could tell from his grin that Clydel and Rynk were again spreading the defense and he was coming again with the *MarcOSpin*. The only way she had found to stop it was to guess a side and hope for the best. Thus far she was 0 for 4. *Aaah, going   left!   Dammit!* Marcus spun away from Tifinity as his three girl cheering section on the front row shouted, "MAR CO SPINNN!!" Tifinity got her feet crossed and sat down hard on the court. The point was uncontested. She almost did not accept the new boy's hand, extended down to help her up. As they turned to take point reset, she almost did not hear his soft whisper.

"He stutters twice before going to his right, three times when he goes left."

Sure enough, the boy was right. In spite of her distraction from counting the steps on the next two plays, Tifinity still broke up the spins and forced Marcus to pass. She could not describe how good it felt to hear the MARC OO SPinn sputter to an embarrassing stop as she stymied the "Famous" move. *Bite that, girly girls!* Only silence greeted the third attempt, when Tifinity anticipated in time to draw a charge call.

With the score now at 12 to 9, Marcus decided to change tactics and held up three fingers as he crossed mid court. He clearly looked to pass to Clydel, who was being guarded by the new boy. Clydel broke toward midcourt, easily moving past *Dammit, wake up, you–* The boy had stepped behind Clydel's break and not only avoided the pick from a waiting Rynk, but with a long stretch of his lance, intercepted the throw from Marcus. He then sprinted straight toward Marcus, with Rynk striving to catch up from behind. Without looking and at the very last second, the boy flicked the ball to his left, and then made a lightning quick stepout to his right so perfectly timed that Rynk stumbled and lost control of a lunge obviously intended to sandwich the boy with Marcus. Instead, they were unprepared for the sudden void and collided, rebounding into separate heaps, lances rattling on the court. The flicked ball sailed toward a startled Hareld. Having followed up the steal automatically, he had really only loped up court to watch the action from the side. He was so unaccustomed to being the target of a pass, he almost missed the wide-open goal.

Tifinity grinned when Marcus cursed at Rynk, whom she could see held his tongue only with great effort. But she also saw him acknowledge a signal from Marcus, which he then passed on to Clydel. She knew they would now start collapsing on the newcomer to contain his play. Tifinity also acknowledged, at least internally, that her inability to stop Marcus from scoring had been the real problem. *Not anymore!*

For the next two plays she focused *everything* on matching up with Marcus, which she did successfully now that she could neutralize *The Famous MarcOSpin.* Tifinity also kept perfect lance discipline to prevent committing a foul. Even though the Green Team maintained their lead from the goals off Marcus' passes, at least he was not the one who had scored and brought them to game point. Tifinity swelled with pride at seeing the frustration cracking through her rival's arrogance. The crack became a shatter when their next attempt to take down Joshua failed.

It was 12 to 14 as Tifinity pushed up court with the ball, now looking for opportunities to pass the ball to Joshua. Marcus shouted "BLUE" as she snapped the ball crosscourt, leading Joshua in his break for a corner shot, which he had thus far only missed twice despite the extreme angle. Her puzzlement turned to dismay as Clydel stretched out in a dive toward Joshua's knees. She could not believe they were using "The Trip," especially since they were at game point with a two-point lead. But then,

Marcus was not the forgiving type and games had never before been this close.

"The Trip" was technically legal as long as the falling player touched his lance to the court before making contact with the opposing player. It was intended to allow for the not uncommon event of players stumbling and falling to the court in the absence of body contact. Clydel's shouted "Oh no" was unconvincing as he pressed his lance to the court to avoid the foul and immediately rolled to take out Joshua's knee. Tifinity watched in amazement as Joshua's weight-bearing right foot snapped up to avoid Clydel and his left leg snapped forward to step on the space that Clydel's head had just vacated. Impossibly, Joshua had simultaneously switched the lance to his left hand and precisely placed the tip to catch Tifinity's pass. Immediately his left arm came cross body, releasing the ball in stride less than a foot from the white end wall, to flash across and disappear into the goal with a ding, as his momentum ran him outside the court to flatten up against the tenement wall.

There was complete silence as he turned, jogged back onto the playing court, and stretched down his hand to Clydel, "That was a hard fall. You okay?"

Clydel had the decency to blush as he accepted the help up off the court floor. "Yeah, I'm okay."

The astonishment on Marcus' face transformed to fury as he called a timeout. Tifinity chuckled at the sound of Marcus and his teammates trying to argue without speaking loud enough to be heard. She nodded when Joshua observed, "Well, at least we've made a game of it."

Tifinity had allowed herself to think they might even win, when the first game ended. They had forced the shot clock down to two seconds when Marcus made a diving shot that just slid into the upper left corner of the goal. Although the defeat was especially bitter for having been so close, Tifinity thought she heard a slight hollowness in the self-congratulations of Marcus and his teammates as they approached the applauding female fan section in the stands.

Having made the winning shot and allowed time to bask in the praise of his admirers, Marcus had regained his swagger by the beginning of the second game. He pressed forward across midcourt shouting, "Tower, Tower!" and Tifinity knew what was coming. She leapt at just the right moment with lance held high, but she just was not tall enough. Marcus had extended his arm in a "skyhook," just getting the ball over the upper edge of Tifinity's shield to take a 1 to 0 lead. While his "Good try" actually sounded sincere, the pat on the top of Tifinity's head constituted a serious breach in sportsmanship.

Joshua did not allow this to go by unchallenged. "Come on. Your play is too good for that kind of cheap shot."

Tifinity's anger prevented her from seeing that Marcus actually appeared slightly embarrassed. Her attempt at retaliation was obvious as she drew a flagrant charging call on the next play. Not only did Tifinity fail to knock Marcus off his feet with the charge, she heard him say loudly to Clydel, "Just like clockwork," as he walked over to take his penalty shot. Knowing he was using her anger against her only made her more infuriated. The ding of the penalty shot and the fact that her play had given the Greens a 2 – 0 lead caused all the accomplishments from the first game to evaporate as Tifinity's rage took over.

Before she even got back to the point reset circle, the tall kid called another timeout. As they formed a huddle, his words were soft, but heavy with conviction, "Listen, I *get* it. The big boys don't let you play. It's not fair and they deserve to be taught a lesson."

Hareld muttered, "Yeah, like *that's* gonna happen." He leaned back with hands up to ward off the glares from both of his teammates.

Tifinity had not expected Joshua to come even closer, but she refused to step back as he leaned in nose to nose.

"So, do you want to get in a few more hits on this jerk, or do you want," his voice lowered to a growl, "*to win?*"

Tifinity glared back, but finally snarled, "I   want   to   *win.*"

The boy searched her eyes for a few extra seconds, nodded, and then turned to Hareld. "They really don't have any competition here, right?"

Hareld gave Tifinity a wary glance before shrugging. "Not really."

"Well, as Confucius said, 'It's only in the winter that you can see the special nature of the cypress tree.' And *I* don't think *they* are cypress trees.

The Deepest Cut

Time to bring a little snow."

What the **hell** *does* **that** *mean?* Tifinity could only watch as Joshua proceeded to the center circle for the reset, taking over the point guard position against Marcus. She looked at Hareld, whose face mirrored her confusion.

"Snow? In Cypress Grove? He *does* know there aren't really cypress trees here, right? And who is Confucius?"

"How should I soppin' know? And who cares what some Japanese guy said a hundred years ago?" Tifinity scowled as the buzzer warned she had 10 seconds to get into the right forward reset circle. *Okay, Boy, let's see what you got.*

With the penalty shot made by Marcus, the Blues were on offense. Joshua did not even pretend to set up a play, but dashed ahead to go one-on-one with Marcus. After head faking to the right, he snapped a two-point bouncer out of the upper right corner, perfectly anticipated its path in his sprint between Marcus and Rynk, retrieved the ball, and snapped it though the circular inner target of the goal. They were not playing in advanced mode, so it did not earn a double, but it made the boy's intentions very clear. Tifinity nodded with a mixture of admiration and annoyance at the ease with which Joshua took control of their offense. She detected a glimmer of the meaning behind his earlier cryptic reference when he caught her eye with a small smile and raised an eyebrow at Marcus and Rynk arguing over who had failed to stop his scoring move.

Joshua's strong post up of Marcus as he crossed midcourt forced an early pass to Clydel on the left wing. Tifinity was astonished at the transformation in Hareld. His aggressive defense had become a wall and she followed Rynk cross court as he sought to break Clydel free. *No doing!* Hareld slipped the attempted pick and Tifinity's anticipation put her in a position to prevent the quick pass off the roll. This failure prompted Clydel to throw a harried cross court return pass to Marcus. Joshua, who had backed off from Marcus, totally committed to the steal, even though a miss would have left a wide-open goal and resulted in a three-point lead for the Greens. However, the timing of his jump proved perfect and Marcus was not even close when Joshua crossed half-court and over handed a bullet through the circle in the center of their goal. *Down the throat!*

"I know, I know, it was risky. But they always throw it back for Marcus to take the shot, so…," he smiled and shrugged.

Hareld beat Tifinity to the punch, "Yeah, and he *never* turns down a chance to shoot." Tifinity saw the look exchanged between Clydel and Rynk, aware that she would have completely missed it if she had been playing against Marcus.

Tifinity almost felt pity for Marcus as he tried to "Tower" a shot over Joshua's defense, the ball bouncing off the shield out of bounds for a turn over. She realized he was totally unaware of how Joshua's comment had impacted his teammates. *I should really look for a chance to help the boy out.* Her opportunity came after Joshua caused the defense to collapse onto him with another hard break toward the goal and then tossed the ball to a wide-open Hareld for the easy score. Rewarded in her expectation that Marcus would again try to reestablish his dominance, her nemesis took the ball down court and quickly missed a forced shot. She commented to Clydel just loud enough for Marcus to hear, "Maybe you should just go to the water fountain for a drink next time you're on offense."

"Yeah, maybe so."

At first stunned by the dissension, Marcus then became angry, "Well, if you'd make a break towards the goal, I'd have a reason to pass." *Oh, this is good.*

The Blues took a 5 to 4 lead following a second turnover on an unforced out of bounds pass. Tifinity grinned with Joshua as Hareld guffawed, "I think I'm beginning to like the snow."

"Yeah, me too," she chuckled in response to Hareld's unrestrained glee. Her euphoria was not just a product of seeing the dominion of Marcus in the process of being systematically dismantled. Tifinity still did not know anything about Confucius, but watching Joshua's "snow" transform a once mighty cypress into a leafless aspen tree had sparked a transforming epiphany. She now *knew* that her anger had always been the barrier to her mastering stickball. She looked at Marcus, his face twisted in frustrated rage, and he appeared to actually be physically smaller. Her fear of him evaporated with her own long held wrath. She determined to never again let anger cloud her vision of the game.

A glowing blue 10 dwarfed the green 5 before Marcus finally got the message. He began feeding the ball to his teammates and focused more effectively on implementing the Phoenix defense. Tifinity noticed that while Joshua remained silent whenever Marcus slipped past his defense and scored, he provided a congratulatory comment when either Clydel or Rynk made a good play. But despite his urging to "make 'em earn every point," the divide and conquer strategy had lost its impact, and improved team play helped the Greens regain some ground to an 11 behind the Blues' 14. However, their rally was too late. Game point came when Joshua made a look away pass to Tifinity, who immediately flipped the ball to Hareld, who pounded in the goal.

Even though a third game had been forced, the enhanced Green teamwork had at least partially repaired the rift between Marcus and his teammates. And the big leader had been frowning more and more frequently at the new boy. He lifted a chin at Joshua. "I recognize you from somewhere. Where are you from anyway?"

The boy shrugged. "Up North."

Marcus, of course, jumped on that, "Ooh wEEE! You're a putroid? I *thought* I smelled Swamp on you!"

For the first time, Tifinity saw a crack in the stranger's calm demeanor. He stood a bit taller and looked hard at her nemesis. "You sure talk a lot for someone who just lost."

"OH? You don't like me talkin'? Well, I'll say whatever I *want* on my own court, stinkbait."

"Yeah, you do that. But you know what they say. Talk is cheap."

Marcus stepped closer with a challenging smile. "How 'bout *you* put your money where your mouth is and we make this last game a little more interesting?"

To Tifinity's ear, his cocky demeanor had taken on a hollow tone. Even so, *raising the stakes will stretch everyone's nerves.* She stepped in, "Come on, Marcus, you know all games have table stakes. You already raised the ante to a quarter to keep us out, you can't buy us out of the match."

Driven to the Hilt

"Okay, Tiff-in-it-ee, calm down. Don't get your pink panties in a wad."

Although the girls in the stand obligingly twittered a laugh, the taunt fell flat in the face of Tifinity's newfound serenity. Somewhat nonplussed, Marcus turned to Joshua. "How about a personal wager?"

Before Tifinity could interject, Joshua replied, "Sure." He then looked with envy at the McKinsey 301 Marcus held in his hands. "I know my Orson 150 is pretty old, but it's worth at least a buck and I can sweeten the pot with some cash."

"How much?"

Joshua pulled his hand out of his pocket to reveal a shiny Universal Dollar. This represented almost three home cooked meals for the average adult and he appeared hopeful it would be enough to set the wager, especially in this neighborhood. It was not.

"Ya know how much this thing cost?" Marcus sneered, holding up his McKinsey. "Six UDs."

Tifinity could see Joshua knew that was a lie, but he simply responded, "Okay, but it *is* used. So, at most, it's worth three dollars."

"What? Listen slag brain, this is worth at least four UDs and I could probably get five if I posted it on the Net. Hell, I..."

Joshua forestalled him with a raised hand, dug into his pocket, and pulling it all the way inside out, lifted his fist and opened it to reveal an extra $2.31 in change. "This is all I have." He dropped the UD coin among the other cash. "So it's this and my Orson against your McKinsey, right?" Joshua lifted his brow and waited.

Tifinity stared; that was a lot of money in their neighborhood. Apparently Marcus agreed.

"Deal."

The Deepest Cut

The green 13 glowed in triumph next to the blue 12.

"MAN!" Joshua reset their defense. Despite the bloom of confidence in Tifinity and Hareld after their win, the three of them were not yet a smoothly integrated team. In contrast, Marcus, Clydel, and Rynk had been playing together a long time and Joshua could see their instinctual play, where they reacted without thinking to complement each other's' moves. And even if their faith in each other had recently been shaken, they were still skilled athletes. The difference showed on the scoreboard.

A tiny voice of anxiety whispered in Joshua's inner ear, lamenting his risking all of his cash reserves. It was money that he and his mother desperately needed. He tried to quell his mounting uncertainty. *I'll be able to make a lot more money in the long run if I get that McKinsey 301.* The tiny voice countered, *Yeah, and if you lose, not only is the cash gone, but you won't have any lance at all. How you gonna play and hustle money then?*

Stop it! It's too late now. Joshua clamped down on his doubts and focused on the approaching Green point guard. Although Marcus now passed the ball much more consistently, Joshua was confident he could not resist taking the next shot to extend the Greens' lead to game point. He had been burned twice in this game when Marcus had switched hands to hold his lance behind him just before making a cut, using his body as a barrier to maximize the distance from the ball. So he did not bite on either of Marcus' fake passes and worked his defensive stance, occasionally wavering on maintaining the left side of his shield. *Will he take the bait?*

There! Marcus made his quick hand switch and cut for the goal.

Everything hinged on whether slowtime kicked in on this play. Joshua had found that sometimes, if he focused on how critical a particular play was, it increased the likelihood that time would slow down. But Marcus was already nearly past him. Joshua pictured his mother's face as he told her about the lost money. And at that second, everything   *slowed.*

Joshua guided the tip of his lance just behind Marcus' back

as it drifted by, aiming at the ball while also avoiding contact during his step around. As Marcus inched by, Joshua made minor corrections to account for the receding ball until the tip of his lance intersected the ball. He pressed his trigger and continued his body rotation to complete a full 360, stretched his first long step away from Marcus, and snapped back into real-time.

Just past half-court, Joshua made the shot and then slowed to watch the ball streak toward the throat of the goal. He smiled as the blue 12 transformed into a 13 with a ding, totally unprepared for the jarring impact from behind. The world blurred and he rocketed forward to land hard on his left shoulder. Three repeated pings followed the time out buzzer, signaling a major infraction. Joshua eased up into a sitting position with a grimace.

Marcus held out his hands and proclaimed with innocent sincerity, "Gosh, I'm *so* sorry about that. I was trying to catch up after that great move of yours and I just couldn't stop."

Joshua looked up in shock, hand automatically reaching over to rub his throbbing left shoulder. Through his amazement, he could see Marcus' sly smile, and realized that he hoped either the pain from the injury or the psychological intimidation would be sufficient to overcome the disadvantage of turning over the ball on a major foul. While his eyes watered from the pain in his shoulder, Joshua saw Marcus' eyes widen in triumph.

"HOLD it!! *Now* I know who you are!" His finger stabbed forward, "*Your* Pop was the muckin' guard that betrayed that cargo ship to the space pirates a few years back. You were cryin' back then too, on *all* the news shows. Bawlin' like a baby! Shamed of having a Pop what was a traitor!"

It was true. A videographer had caught him holding his mother's hand as the police accused her of being an accessory, tears streaming down his face. He had been terrified his mother was going to be taken from him and then she would be gone, just like his father. Such a dramatic image of "human interest" had guaranteed the clip ran every night for the three weeks the police were investigating his mother. It all ended abruptly when they failed to find any extra money in their house or bank account and after the ship security tapes had mysteriously disappeared. Even then, the Police Chief had described his mother as "a person of ongoing interest," leaving the hanging implication that she was involved, but they just could not quite prove it. And, of course, Marcus was not the first opponent to revive such accusations towards his parents. And even though it had been a while, it still hurt. Joshua tried to ignore a rising burn at the base of his neck.

"Look at him. LOOK at him! Can you *see* it?   I can see it! It's true! That was *his* dad!"

Joshua kept his eyes on the ground and shuddered as the first wave of rage swept through him. He knew if he looked up, the hate in his face would prompt a reaction from Marcus, one that would lead to blood on the court. The first time that sequence of events had occurred, most of the blood had come from someone else, and it had turned out to be his last day in public school. The second time, he had only survived because an unknown adult had stepped in and forced the mob of kids to stop kicking him. The man had been guiding him to the hospital, but Joshua knew they could not afford that, so when he had recovered enough strength, he had broken free into the crowded street and somehow made his way back home. The look on his mother's face when she had arrived home that day came to his mind now, and instead of another shudder, there was an inner *buzz* of determination. With that odd sensation came a well-worn word *resolute*. Joshua looked up through misty but calm eyes.

"We going to finish this or not?"

Marcus whooped, "Oh *hell* yes. At least   *I* am. *You* now, I'm not so sure. I mean, *can* you even see the goal through your blurry little eyes? Course, you can always just shovel over the money and call 'er quits. You'll have to go cry in the bleachers though. We wouldn't want someone to run into you and have you get hurt all over again. Right?"

Joshua grimaced as he pushed himself up off the court. As usual, the blush that had begun on his neck had risen to his cheeks, intensifying his embarrassment and submerging him in a flood of helplessness. It was infuriating that whatever the cause of his embarrassment, he became even more embarrassed by the blush, which in turn fed the blush even more until his entire face was red. He could feel the fatalism in his burning face as he

Driven to the Hilt

gave a laughing Marcus a final dull glance. Then, turning away from a spreading triumphant sneer, he heard another of his mother's well-worn sayings, *Adversity is just an opportunity to shine brighter.* An idea formed. *This is perfect!*

Allowing a slight tremble in his lower lip, Joshua staggered a bit, then shuffled back to the blue side of the court, his head down and lance loose in his hand. Someone *probably Tifinity* signaled their lance for an injury timeout. As the computer waited for confirmatory input from the opposing team, an angry female voice yelled, "Come on Marcus, after the mugging you just gave him, you can at least confirm the injury." *Definitely Tifinity.* Joshua thought of something his father had told him, a quote by a basketball coach named John Wooden, something about how sports didn't build character, but instead revealed it.

Joshua shambled back toward their goal and stopped in front of Tifinity and Hareld. Joshua maintained his forlorn expression and then sank onto both knees. Tifinity and Hareld each dropped to a knee before sharing an uncomfortable glance. They became even more concerned, *and* slightly embarrassed, when Joshua wiped the tears from his eyes with the back of his hand.

Tifinity was uncharacteristically tentative. "Was your   I mean   uh   did he   Is it true?"

Joshua lifted hard eyes and asked softly, "Do you still want to win?"

She blinked in surprise, but then set her face in a determined scowl and hissed back, *"Yes!"*

"Then it doesn't matter if it was my Dad or not." Their expressions shifted to confusion when he whispered, "But you want to *act* as if it was, OK? So, good job with the concerned looks, but try to get back that 'how embarrassing' attitude. Yeah, that's it. Now not only do we have this extra injury timeout to set our plan, but we also have the ball."

Tifinity glanced upcourt, gave a very brief, tiny smile, then snapped to her feet and exclaimed with an undertone of disgust, "Come on, kid, shake it off."

Hareld interrupted his look of dawning comprehension by also standing. He looked down on Joshua and shook his head. "At least give it a try, man." With a heavy sigh, he reached down to help Joshua get to his feet.

His back still to the Green team, Joshua whispered, "We need to really piss off Marcus on this next play, to set him up for the long fall at match point, so…"

He had just finished explaining his plan when the buzzer sounded and they resumed their start positions. At the chime, Joshua sluggishly jogged forward from the point guard position with the ball. When Marcus came up to challenge him, he immediately passed off to Tifinity and drifted to the left wing. This displaced Hareld, who looked at Joshua with an exasperated frown before going over to help Tifinity get an outlet pass. She appeared totally stymied by Clydel and gratefully threw the ball to Hareld. Sensing they were both almost as rattled as Joshua, Rynk began a full press defense. Hareld quickly tossed the ball back to Tifinity, who made another halfhearted attempt to get around Clydel before throwing it back to Hareld. During this entire exchange, Joshua had eased farther toward the left edge of the court. Marcus had allowed the greater separation, obviously contemplating whether to join the press against Tifinity and Hareld.

As soon as Hareld hauled in the next sloppy pass from Tifinity, Joshua exploded across the middle toward the goal. In his excitement at seeing Joshua make his move, Hareld lofted the ball high and wide. Joshua leapt high to catch the ball, but the off-target toss had allowed Marcus to recover. Only a bit off balance, Joshua might have regained control if Marcus had not thrown himself forward to once again slam him in the back. A long step kept Joshua from going down immediately and with another lunge, he pulled himself upright, but the out of bounds sidewall rushed toward him. Three pings sounded in sync with his next three small rapid steps, which slowed him, but Joshua knew he would not be able to stop in time. He took another short step, desperately hoping for slowtime to kick in. It did not. Only two steps from the wall *I'm going out!*

In the middle of his last step, the world did slow down. Joshua discarded his sense of relief to begin moving the tip of his lance toward the adjacent wall, frantically twisting his head, trying to see the goal. His weight shifted off his left foot and finally, the goal came into view. He made slight adjustments to the trajectory of his cross body swing before pressing the release trigger on his lance handle. He held on until the ball was three inches into its journey and he knew his team had match point. With this realization, the world shifted back into regular time and he hurtled forward through the tightly woven white wall of light.

Knowing he was going down, Joshua tossed his lance and tucked into a forward somersault as he flew forward. He rolled and came upright on his feet in front of the stands, right before the three Green team "cheerleaders." They were all leaning back with the same wide-eyed look of astonishment, lips formed into round Os, sucking air in preparation to release a shriek of shock and displeasure. *This wasn't part of the plan, but* Joshua gave a quick wink to the middle girl and grinned when she blinked, her scream silenced by confusion. In fact, all three girls were immobilized by his gesture. Joshua then turned, retrieved his lance, and jogged back to the far side of the blue quarter line, avoiding eye contact with Marcus.

Before taking up his position, he high-fived first Tifinity and then Hareld, making it clear that they had all worked together to fool Marcus. In preparation for the penalty ball, Joshua took a deep cleansing breath and some calm returned along with a small satisfaction at the quiet emanating from the Green cheerleading section. This time when he advanced the ball, he moved with confidence and precision. Marcus was only too happy to race forward to block his progress. Joshua cut to his right, pulling Marcus with him and providing a screen for Tifinity, who slid behind him toward the goal. Without transitioning into slowtime, Joshua swept his arm behind him, making a behind the back pass that led Tifinity perfectly. However, Clydel made an excellent adjustment and placed himself in position to block. Tifinity lunged to her right and sprang up for a look at the goal, both hands whipping her lance backward for a kill shot. Clydel rose up to defend, good stick discipline maximizing his shield size. As her back swing slowed in preparation to whip forward, Tifinity instead flicked the ball to her left and then continued her fall to the right, pulling Rynk even farther out of position. Hareld gave a lazy lift of the tip of his lance to catch

The Deepest Cut

the ball and stood for a second, completely uncovered at the Green team's quarter line. He looked Marcus in the eye, then turned and whipped his lance forward to drive the ball into the throat of the goal.

Marcus and his teammates stood slack-jawed as the "Happy Chimes" rang out in rhythm to the blue 15 flashing on the scoreboard over the goals. All heads swiveled simultaneously to lock onto Tifinity, who stood shaking both fists to the sky, her head tilted all the way back.

"YYYYYEEEEEEEEEeeeeeeeessssssss!!!!"

Joshua clamped down *hard* on his animosity for Marcus and instead put out his hand to the Green point guard and said, "Wow, we were pretty lucky on that homestretch." After all, a lance transaction still needed to be completed.

He could see Marcus struggling with himself, but eventually, even he could not ignore the cultural imperative of displaying sportsmanship at the end of a match. However, the look of determination on Marcus' face as he reached for his outstretched hand provided enough warning for Joshua. He shifted his hand forward just in time to keep Marcus from grasping his fingers instead of his palm, preventing the Green team leader from grinding his knuckles together. Before Marcus could apply the full pressure of his grip, Joshua nodded and turned toward Hareld. Marcus let go with a scowl, knowing that if he pulled Joshua up short, it would be clear that he was a loser AND a poor sport.

Joshua went to shake hands with Clydel and Rynk before running up to Hareld, arms held wide, and exclaimed, "Look who scored match point!" After a long hug, he turned toward Tifinity, still at center court, hands on her knees, looking down at her feet. Once close enough for only her to hear, Joshua said, "Now THAT was a major league assist!"

She straightened up with a shrug and met his eyes, her smile almost demure. "Thanks."

Before she could say something else, out of the corner of his eye, Joshua saw Marcus exiting the court. He told Tifinity to "Hold on" and ran over calling his name, but Marcus ignored him. Joshua closed the distance and then yelled out so loudly that everybody turned to look, forcing Marcus to stop. With a quick flip, the lancetip of his Orson 150 slapped into his palm and he extended the handle to Marcus.

"I really have to get going, so I need to settle up right now."

Marcus looked around and saw the other tenement residents watching with interest. Joshua could see the struggle on his face, wanting to vent his hatred for the stranger who had humiliated him on his home court, but knowing he could never wager again if he welched on a bet. Finally, self-preservation won. Marcus reversed the grip on his McKinsey 301 and they exchanged lances.

Into that quiet moment Tifinity's voice called out with a lilt of excessive innocence, "Marcus, you can keep the court in case you guys want to practice or something."

Marcus glared for a moment before he let the air out, shrugged with a forced nonchalant smile, and answered, "Naw, I'm good." However, he shifted his gaze to Joshua and his eyes burned with rage.

Joshua nodded once *Don't think I'll be coming back here again* before turning to jog toward the access tunnel. No longer able to see Tifinity, he gave one last wave to Hareld and headed for the exit. Just inside the tunnel that led to the exterior of Sunny Day, he heard a small "hey." He turned and was surprised to find Tifinity coming up to him. He was astonished when she jumped up against him and wrapped her arms around his neck. As he returned the hug, she pressed her lips against his left ear and whispered.

"You were right. It feels better when you *win.   A LOT* better!"

With a final wave, Joshua turned toward the exit, but his grin slid down to a frown when he remembered his destination. With a start, he checked his sheet. *2:12!! Mom's due back at*

He began running.

The Deepest Cut

◀6▶

Rounding the corner in his loping run, Joshua looked down at his sheet *2:42* and eased into a fast walk. *There's plenty of time before she gets home.* But then the pungent stink of decay forced him to a dejected stop.

He stared at the arched gateway that announced the entrance to NorthPoint. The rust streaked bare metal letters stood out against the approaching dark cloud bank that held the promise of heavy rain. The inky clouds blended with the gloomy, drab buildings behind the gate. A leaden gray, against an ashen gray, all surrounded by a dreary gray. The intensity of his reluctance to step through the gateway surprised him.

Most structures in New Cincinnati were made of Greystone, since that was where it had been invented. At first the mining refinement slag was simply pushed farther and farther out over the vegetation at the foot of the mountain. Over time, this pile was compressed into an impromptu plateau, which then became the footing for larger refining facilities as M3I expanded operations. The process had been repeated until the compacted slag pile eventually became the 35 foot high foundation on which all of New Cincinnati now rested.

It was a M3I biochemical engineer named Oliver Greyson who had discovered how to process the slag into Greystone. The construction panels were both remarkably durable and relatively light weight. It had become a popular building material throughout the Sector, with export revenues rivaling the valuable trace minerals and precious gemstones that had originally enticed M3I to establish the commercial colony on Cypress Grove. Pigments could be added during the refining process to change its normal light grey tone into virtually any color. Joshua realized how much he missed the vibrant hues that typified the middle class neighborhood they had lived in only four years ago. Of course, such decoration came at a premium, and M3I was not interested in aesthetics, only the creation of cheap housing for its miners. In fact, the lowest bidding contractors for the early miner's quarters had often skipped some of the manufacturing processes, resulting in building sheets with streaks and swirls of impure elements, which often cracked or flaked off over time. Ironically, so much slag was now converted to Greystone that there was not enough to extend the city's foundation, forcing the expanding population of New Cincinnati to reoccupy previously abandoned housing complexes. *Just like Mom and Lucky Me.*

Joshua sighed and stepped through the gateway. He hefted the plastic bag of insurance in one hand and looked at his "new" stickball lance in the other. He pushed down the rising shame at having to lie again to his mother and told himself she would not even notice he had a different lance. Besides, when he eventually made it to the semi-pros, there would then be plenty of money to help his mother with the Homehearth Café. *Those ends would justify the means!* He pictured her reaction at that future event and could almost hear her musical laugh. His entire body flushed at the thought. Whenever he felt down, she always found a way to make him laugh, and when she joined in, it came without restraint or pretense. A grin creased his face. *Besides, there's more than one thing to talk about.* Eager to share about the Sunshine Event, he leaned in against the coming darkness and set a pace that would hopefully keep him from being pelted by the big raindrops that he could tell were soon to come.

Joshua stepped under the second story walkway just before the watery onslaught. His sigh of relief was lost in the sounds of the runoff splashing out of a corner drainpipe, broken off a foot above the sidewalk. Joshua leapt over the gush of foaming water, turned the corner, and came up short at the sight of a slender man leaning against the wall of the first unit of the complex. The smell of sickly sweet cologne assaulted his nose. Mr. Donald straightened from the wall, adjusted his suit, and ran a hand over hair that was slicked back even before it had met the rain.

"Hey ya there, Josh."

After that morning, Joshua should not have been surprised to see the man.

"Hey, Mr. Donald."

He flashed a smile and tried to slide past to their apartment at the far end of the building. Joshua could not repress a cringe when spindly fingers gripped his shoulder. He spun out of the man's grasp and took two backwards steps.

"Hold on there a sec, Josh old boy. No need for that. I just want to be a friend to you and your mom. I thought maybe you could, you know, put in a good word for me, that's all. You know I've been comin' by extra ta take care of things. Might be I kin get ya both ina better livin' situation." The property manager leaned closer, a short laugh filled with promise, "You 'n Rachel'd like that, wouldn't ya Josh?"

Joshua blinked up at the man, not sure why he so resented the man's use of his mother's first name. And something about the man's laugh bothered Joshua. Not just that it came too frequently and did not fit with what was being said, but also that it carried a different meaning he did not quite understand. His mother insisted he not worry about it, saying, "Your Dad taught me a thing or two about how to handle unpleasant people." The combination of cloying cologne and swamp smell pressed in on him. He did not want to lie, but he was desperate to escape. The flash of Mr. Donald's bluish dentures tipped the scales.

"Sure thing, Mr. Donald. I'll uh tell my Mom all about you." He took a step back. "But, ah, I'm kind of late for dinner so, I'd better get going. Uh, thanks."

"Hey, now, speakin' of dinner, I just was knocking at yer door a bit back and there was no answer. Thing is, I could smell something mighty good a comin' outta there, so it was a bit surprisin' that yer Mom didn't answer the door, ya know?"

Joshua stood frozen in shock. *Mom's already home?*

"Well, now, I didn't want ta use my pass key on account of yer Mom gettin' annoyed when I done that before. But I kin see yer worried too. Maybe I oughta go check on things with ya, Josh, just ta make sure everything's alright."

"NO! No, that's OK." Joshua pushed aside his panic and frantically searched for a reason that might keep Mr. Donald at bay. "I'm sure she's all right, Mr. Donald. She just gets really focused on cooking and hates to be interrupted. And ah, actually," he tried to give a conspiratorial smile, "I think it's just that she'd be really embarrassed if you came in and there wasn't enough food to invite you for dinner." Doubly grateful he had taken the time to stop during his run home, Joshua lifted the bag of meal replacement rations originally developed to minimize the miners' meal breaks. "See? I just now had to go out to get these All-Day bars to get me through the next few days. So ah I'll hmm tell her to get some extra food in the next couple of days and let you know, OK?"

He turned before Mr. Donald could respond and took extra-long strides toward the far end of the building, uncertain in the heavy downpour whether or not the man followed him. Approaching the last unit door, he glanced back, and shuddered in relief when he saw that the manager had stayed put. He returned the man's wave of encouragement and waited with a fixed smile until the slick haired man finally turned and disappeared around the corner. Joshua's shoulders sagged in relief.

Then he turned toward the door, and with a sinking stomach, noticed the aroma of cooking. *I guess she really is here.* He steeled himself to trade a smaller reprimand for going out to stock up instead of the real reason he had been gone for the afternoon. He felt a flash of panic *What if she asks me how long I've been gone? I don't know when she got here.* He decided he would feign ignorance of when he left and estimate the time by checking the progress of the meal, figuring she would have started cooking as soon as she got home. Joshua took a deep breath and punched in the security code on the number box, amazed, as usual, that the mechanical lock still worked and allowed the handle to turn.

Stepping inside, Joshua immediately identified the smell as potato soup before he rounded the door toward the kitchen section of their tiny efficiency cubicle. His mental review of the steps for making potato soup was interrupted by the sight of his mother's head on the kitchen floor just past the front room partition. Confused, Joshua wondered why she was laying on the floor, realized she was staring blankly past him, and then both he and the world came to a stop. He stood, stock still, hand still gripping the handle of the front door.

A shift in focus brought awareness of many things, all at the same time: rhythmic wet noises in synch with the irregular slight shaking movements of his mother's head and shoulders; sounds of skittering echoing around the corner of the kitchenette partition; and his nostrils filled

The Deepest Cut

with a strong musky smell mixed with a more intense odor of The Swamp. Most of all, Joshua saw his mother's dead eyes, the green and gray irises thinned around dilated pupils. He knew he should feel something, *anything,* but nothing came. Instead, a separate part of him peeled away inside, looked on and wondered why the rest of him felt so numb.

A small flame of... something... flickered inside. It beckoned from far away, a plaintive question. *Something.* Something he, *I, something I should do.* What? The light from the flame grew such a tiny bit, giving the voice a shade more strength. *Can you be sure?* About? A sparkle of annoyance burned in the flame now, the sense of heat expanding. *How do you know?* About what? WHAT? What do you **WANT**?

His own voice appeared an inch from his right ear *Is Mom really dead?*

The observing Joshua focused outward on the woman lying on the floor, striving to answer the question. Then a new, incredibly small voice whispered in a tentative squeak.

"Mom?"

The sucking noise stopped abruptly. The air became charged with expectancy. Click, click. Click. Click. Something black shimmered halfway up the edge of the room partition. Click click. The end of a sharp black spindly appendage came into view and then a second extended past the partition, both quivering in expectation. Joshua immediately knew it belonged to a spiderviper. Everyone in New Cincinnati recognized the profile of spiderviper forelegs, raised and ready to snatch forward, sinking in those vicious backward angling hooks to hold onto its prey, while the long sinuous tongue snapped out its fang to inject its incredibly fast acting neurovenom.

But, how can that be? The last spiderviper sighting had been so many years ago, when George of the Jungle had been killed on live TV. *How how can there be a spiderviper in our apartment?* The hooked forearms stretched forward along with a fluttering sound that converted into a high-pitched whistle. With a clank, everything went black.

◄7►

Joshua blinked. He stood outside, back pressed against the front door. He had no recollection of how he got there. Then a distant roaring in his ears swelled, and with it emotion began surging up, his entire body flushed with a single violent tremor before his legs turned rubbery and he slid down to the ground. Joshua whispered into the rain rattling down in front of him, "She's dead."

The heavy raindrops exploded up from the barren hard packed dirt of the NorthPoint courtyard. As always, everyone had retreated from the assaultive downpour, leaving a feeling of abandonment that stretched out of the neighborhood and into the streets of New Cincinnati. Joshua could feel the certainty of it, the absolute conviction that he was completely alone in the world. First his father, *and now Mom. I'm all alone.*

His thought had pulled an irrational certainty from the deep swirls of his subconscious, the conviction that if he had been home, he would have saved his mother. *She would be alive right now.* Quivering hands covered his face at the horror of the realization and it finally came out, in huge body racking sobs. Time seemed suspended as Joshua released the agony from his core.

An indeterminable time later, the sound of a click brought Joshua back to the present. His first thought caused a welling sob to shudder to a halt in his throat *the spiderviper!* But he immediately knew that was not right; the click had been deeper and more metallic, and had come from the left. His head turned to look down the row of doors and a moment later, his brain placed the sound; it had been the click of a door being pushed closed.

Someone had looked out, seen him in his tortured misery, and had then stepped back inside and closed their door. *Nobody cares. There's nobody to help me. Why should they, after what I did to Mom.* And then, Joshua was floating up above, looking down at a little boy collapsed against a scratched and dented tenement door. *How will he survive?* Floating Joshua heard the words from a distance, from a familiar yet now different voice.

The Deepest Cut

"I don't *want* to survive."

But   that's   **me**   *talking.* Confusion wavered and then the cold metal of the door pressed against his back. Joshua felt the hot wet streaks on his cheeks, saw a crumpled Squarewich wrapper glistening in the courtyard, and heard it rattle each time it was struck by the less frequent raindrops of the now spitting storm. Bleak reality struck like a hammer on an anvil, and with the stark reverberations, Joshua made the decision: to go back in and be with his mother. Without her, he could not even form the idea of a tomorrow.

Joshua numbly rolled to his knees, pushed himself off the ground, turned, and pulled on the door. When it did not open, he stood for a minute, confused. At last, through his vast internal emptiness, he remembered   he had to reenter the security code. He pressed the buttons in sequence, pushed the door inward, eased himself around the edge, looked to the left, and stopped at the sight of his mother's face.

The sound of the door clicking shut behind him startled Joshua into taking a single step forward. Somehow,   now   she seemed to see him, seemed to be looking into his eyes. Her face transformed, came from a different time, leaned very close to his, taking up his entire field of vision, looking into his eyes with an almost savage intensity. Her hands pressed the sides of his face as she asked, "What was your father's unit motto?"

He knew it. "Resolute."

"And that means?"

"Never quit."

"And you know that *for you,* I will *never* quit."

"I know."

It had been their first night in what he had considered at the time to be a seedy two bedroom apartment, after his mother had finally abandoned the idea of maintaining their lower middle class home. Part of him marveled at how little he had understood back then, when he had asked his mother if she was going to leave him there alone, "Like Dad did." Ever since that night, whenever she saw him discouraged, she had reminded him, "Resolute."

Joshua snapped back into the dank efficiency cubicle, his mother's face coming back into view, eyes once again dull and unfocused. A deep resolve coalesced inside, hardening into a dense internal buzz, vibrating an unyielding decision *I will not give up.* Then he knew. He was going to kill the thing that took his mother from him. He looked down with surprise at the new lance, somehow still in his hand. He took two cleansing breaths in preparation. The total silence within the cubicle announced that those breaths had been heard. Joshua pointed the lance forward and stretched his other hand over toward one of the colorful pillows his mother had bought to brighten the faded décor, trying to make it feel more "homey."

Joshua waited until he heard the chittering again and saw his mother's body being jerked on. He then began edging toward the partition, holding the pillow as a shield. Before he could see the forelegs again, the connection between the sucking noises and jerking of his mother's head bloomed in his mind. With the understanding that she was being eaten, his rage flared to such intensity that his hands began to shake. Joshua forced another slow and silent cleansing breath, knowing he had no chance of killing the spiderviper if he could not control his emotions. The final play of the stickball game flashed into his mind with a feeling of unreality, as if it were a movie filmed earlier in the day, but that he had seen long ago. But he knew, *This isn't a game. This is* death.

Time began to slow down as he edged around the partition in a crouch, taking in more and more of the spiderviper's hairy legs until he could see its mouth pressed against his mother's leg. He was jolted out of slowtime by the white of her exposed bone. The spiderviper stopped feeding and rose up, lifting both forearms in response to his presence, pulling Joshua's gaze away from his mother's leg.

Time slowed almost to a stop. This had never happened before. The aura of an altered reality strengthened. Details shifted into clean focus: the musky odor mixed with a metallic smell of blood; the rolling sheen on the small segments of chitin that covered the main body of the spiderviper; the slow snicking sounds as they compressed together to form a locked shell; the inverted V shape of the two hind legs on each side of the animal, articulated and proportioned like a spider's, but covered in skin with tiny tufts of hair increasing in density down to tiny paws that

The Deepest Cut

were covered in fur; the clicks as the two large thick claws that protruded from the furry feet struck the linoleum floor; a large rubbery lip pulled back above a dripping circular mouth filled with teeth, revealing a black fang tipped tongue where a nose should be, the long proboscis engorging from its base above the mouth and filling forward, forcing the tube out toward Joshua, but then coiling back like a snake ready to strike; three black marbles looking forward over the retracted lip, their glistening dulled by a slow slide of membrane moving into protective position; a series of funnel holes arrayed across the front and sides of the solid shell of the face; the forward extension of the head on a bumpy dark grey leather neck. A swelling of urgency in the air warned Joshua that the stop in time was about to end.

Time accelerated, but not to normal speed. He threw the pillow at the face of the spiderviper as he sprang for the top of the narrow kitchen island, intending to stab down at the killer from above. His left foot only midway to the island, Joshua saw the spiderviper's forearms reaching for him at twice the speed of everything else. *So fast! I'm not going to make it.* Clamping down his revulsion, Joshua redirected and jammed his foot into the side of the island to propel him toward the spiderviper while he angled the lance to deflect the spiderviper's approaching forearm. *Not enough!* Twisting inside the claw, he pushed it away with the lance. Something hard scraped along his other shoulder as he completed his turn to fly backwards over the spiderviper. Straining his eyes to find the source of his spreading pain, Joshua saw his shirt being stretched off his shoulder, snagged by the hooked foreclaw. The material ripped away as he flew farther backwards. Joshua grasped the lance handle with both hands and began driving the tip at the spiderviper's head, which stood motionless, having reached the limits of its backward extension.

Driven to the Hilt

I'm going to do it! I'm going to kill the damn thing! He put all of his power behind the stroke, forcing the tip faster toward the head. **Oomph!!** Joshua's breath exploded out as his back slammed into the cabinetry behind the spiderviper. In realtime, he rebounded, hands knocked loose on the lance, and began to fall down toward the beast.

With a supreme effort, Joshua *commanded* time to slow down again. He re-gripped the lance and forced the tip down once more. A horrible sinking doom overtook him. *I'm not going to hit the head.* Instead, the tip was going to intersect the dark segment connecting the head and main body. It pushed into the leathery skin, but did not puncture it. As the lance rebounded, Joshua knew he had failed. *I'm sorry, Mom.* Slowtime receded and the clock resumed its normal pace.

Joshua's descending sternum hit the lifting handle of the lance and his fall stopped for an instant, until the weight of his body rammed the tip past the spiderviper's thick skin, through its narrow connecting abdomen, and onto to the floor. Joshua's chest stopped on the end of the lance handle and the little bit of air that remained in his lungs was driven out. Already falling toward the far side of the island, Joshua lunged off his right leg in the direction of the cabinetry. He bounced once on his right hip, and twisted around in flight so he could see the creature that was about to kill him.

The spiderviper finished its pain filled squeal before it turned to face Joshua, his lance handle wobbling as its tip scrapped against the floor. The monster let out a sharp whistle, lifted higher on its legs, and completed its turn toward Joshua. It widened its maw to give clearance for the fang tipped proboscis and began its approach.

Strangely, the death only a moment away concerned his body less than its more immediate need for survival. It craved oxygen – NOW! Short-lived and painful, he sucked in a very shallow breath, but it was enough to get the rhythm started again. A second, better intake, then Joshua pushed out the air with an extended grunting sound, AAAaaauuhhhhh, that finally released his locked lungs. With the next deep breath of air, he noticed the spiderviper had hesitated at the sound of his grunt, backed up a step, and flicked its forearms out as if trying to ward off a threat.

A few more quick breaths and Joshua pushed himself back against the corner of the cabinets, sliding up into a standing position. His terror was colored by exasperation at having come so close to avenging his mother, only to wound the spiderviper. *I FAILED!!!* Joshua again detached, mildly surprised as the creature continued to back away. It sunk down and compressed itself into the lower cabinet that stood open just behind his mother's feet. Floating above, Joshua now saw the scattering of square cans, boxes of noodles, and cubes of freeze dried vegetables around the spiderviper, and watched himself slide sideways, using the island as a shield. As he peeked around the corner, he surged downward and back into his body, seeing firsthand that the spiderviper was halfway into the cabinet. Daylight shimmered around the edges of the retreating creature, bringing the puzzle together: it was exiting through a hole in the back wall of the cabinet. *That's how it got in!*

Joshua jerked in response to the screeching whistle that issued from the spiderviper's abdomen as the hilt of the stickball lance caught on the edge of a cabinet door and slowly pulled free as the creature continued backing away. The lance clattered to the floor and the darkness dropped away to reveal distant trees through drifting sheets of mist that marked the edge of The Swamp. Joshua watched a piece of the imitation Greystone dangle from the top edge of the hole, then drop and rattle on the bottom of the now empty cabinet. A stillness descended upon the tiny apartment, so complete that he could hear the twittering whistles of the spiderviper fade as it scrambled back down the slag foundation of the city to The Swamp.

A part of Joshua found it hard to understand his sense of urgency as he made multiple trips to snatch up all of the colorful throw pillows, repeatedly stepping over his mother's still form to stuff the pillows into the cabinet. He closed the cabinet doors on the happy jumble of colors and stepped back over the wet black smears on the floor. He spoke to his mother without looking at her. *It's all homey again, Mom.* His mouth still smiling from his accomplishment, his gaze was pulled to her mutilated leg. The absurd juxtaposition struck him as humorous. A hysterical sob of laughter escaped. Joshua staggered to the living room and sat down with a

Driven to the Hilt

thump, this time his back against the inside of the front door. The burning tears rolled down his cheeks as his anguish turned to gasping sobs and he mourned for his mother   and for himself.

Time stretched until finally Joshua pulled in a large, more controlled breath. Out came a long, shuddering sigh, and then he again looked down again from above, amazed that the little boy had actually survived. A plaintive voice interrupted the quiet.

"What do I do now, Mom?"

The sound of a stronger, very composed voice sucked Joshua back into his body.

"It's okay, honey, I'll help you through this. You *know* I'll never quit on you."

◀8▶

"First, Son, you need to get me to a place where I can rest."

Joshua bent down, took hold of his mother's wrists, and pulled, trying not to look at her partially consumed leg. She was a relatively petite woman, having always said that his height had come from his father. Nonetheless, it took considerable effort to drag her to the other side of the cubicle.

"Just tuck me in with a sheet, Joshua. You'll need to take both blankets."

Joshua did as she instructed, pushing the sheet under her legs while careful to look away from the wound, pulling it up to his mother's chin. With her legs covered, she appeared to be just lying there and resting. He turned away so he could hear her talk again.

"Go ahead and get our travel duffels from the bottom of the closet, Joshua. Start by packing all of your clothes and the rest of the bedding into your bag."

"I'm taking all of our stuff?"

"Joshua, you know that once people around here find out that I'm gone, they're going to come and take everything anyway. Mr. Donald will probably leave the door unlocked when he's done scrounging for what he wants."

Joshua moved throughout the small apartment, gathering items at his mother's direction. He ignored a whispering inner voice that wondered whether he was going crazy. He *needed* his mother with him right now. In addition to his clothes, his large cloth school satchel, the bedding, and his mother's two slickers, he also squeezed his sheet and first aid kit into his own travel bag. He then began loading his mother's larger duffel. All of the electronic items fit in, including the adjustable lantern and collapsible cooler. Like his sheet, they were all powered by shielded miniature cold fission units (CFUs) that were virtually indestructible and would last for years of almost continuous use. He stopped, looking back at the kitchen.

"You need to eat, Son. You're going to need your strength."

Tears began to flow again. "I can't, Mom, I just *can't*."

"Just get the pot and bring it in here. We can talk while you eat."

Joshua dutifully went over to the pot, removing it from the heating pad, which he made sure to turn off. The smell of the scorched potato soup mixed with the odor of the spiderviper and caused his throat to seize shut. His entire body then locked up, unable to comply with his mother's request, but desperately needing her to stay with him. He thought maybe he should just sit down and shut the entire world out, but his inability to move prevented it. Joshua began to slide nearer to a dark place where he had no control, when he heard, "It's okay, Joshua, just dump it out. I couldn't get the seasoning right anyway." With that, he found he could move again. He stepped back to the sink, and turned on the water and then the disposal, before dumping the contents of the pot. When the ruined potatoes were gone, he filled the pot with water to minimize the smell.

"Go ahead and eat a day ration bar. You really do need to keep your energy up."

Leaving the pot to soak, Joshua went to the cabinet and his hand automatically closed in on the blue wrapper of a vanilla pudding All-Day bar. He walked over, sat down on the Vertabed next to his Mom to eat, then startled to find himself just looking at the empty wrapper, the All-Day bar gone. He had no idea what had been said, but felt certain he had just shared a normal dinner conversation with his mother, in the same reassuring way they always reviewed their day during the evening meal.

After scrubbing out the pot, Joshua dried it and placed it in his mother's larger duffel, along with the frying pans and cooking utensils, including all of the knives he could find. The two burner pad had cooled down, so he rolled it up and put it in an outside pocket.

Both duffel bags now packed, Joshua sat next to his mother's body. Not looking at her, he asked, "What now, Mom?" The silence stretched out and Joshua again slid toward the edge of the dark scary place inside of him. Relief flooded in when she finally spoke.

"I'm not sure, Son, but you know I don't want you to go to the Orphan Benefit Society. After all, that's such a hard knock life."

The Deepest Cut

Joshua froze. It was not only the tone of her voice, playful and light, but the fact that she had referenced their habit of singing along to old show tunes whenever they had cleaned the house or were cooking dinner together. To insist that he take on a cheery attitude in the face of such wretched circumstances was so *Mom.* His head swiveled to look at her face, half expecting her eyes to be crinkled and filled with laughter as she told him it had all been an elaborate prank. But he found the eyes empty, the mouth slack. A flood of despair was instantly displaced by desperate fear, and Joshua snapped his head back around, horrified that he had broken the spell. His breath released with a sense of reprieve when he heard his mother's voice again.

"Maybe you can find a back alley nobody is using, with a corner where you can set up the tarps."

Joshua had seen a few such places while exploring between warehouses on the motor level at the edge of the city. It seemed as good a plan as any.

"You can't get access to the Café Fund at the bank, but there is some cash left. Go to the writing desk and pull open the drawer."

Joshua approached the small desk his father had made for his mother before he was born. David Vernon had already decided to become a Space Merchant Marine by then and had wanted to leave a part of himself with his new wife while on deployments. It was small, but finely crafted, with intricate carvings on the face of the single drawer.

"Turn the knob until it clicks.   That's it. Now reach in on the right side   can you feel the lever up behind the facing? Pull on that, toward you." A false bottom pivoted down and forward. Money was scattered inside. Joshua gathered it up and counted it.

"There's $37.62."

"I'm sorry it's so little. But it was really important to get you your birthday shoes."

"But what about you, Mom? What do I do about   You?"

"First, you need to take the duffel bags and hide them in a place near where you are going to stay. Do *that,* and come back. Then it'll be time to figure out what to do next."

Driven to the Hilt

It made it easier to leave knowing that she would be there to help him again when he came back. Joshua froze outside the door. What if she was not "there" when he returned? *NO! She **will** be!* He locked down the thought, putting it in the same mental box where he had jammed his other doubts. Having a destination in mind, he stepped outside into the early evening and sprinted toward the possible refuge.

At least at first. He staggered to stop after half a block. The duffels thudded to the pavement, especially his mother's, being bigger and having been stuffed with the heavier kitchen items. Joshua thought briefly about repacking his loads, but he was driven by the urgency to get back to speak with his mother. Hanging the smaller bag over one shoulder, he heaved up the big duffel and shambled forward. His arms began burning again after a few steps. He kept moving, but could not hold the big bag out any longer and it began bumping his knees with every step. Then the small duffel came off his shoulder, yanked his arm down, and pulled his hand off the large duffel handle. Joshua collapsed into a pile. He was not winded because stickball kept him in relatively good shape. Unfortunately, stickball did not require much upper body muscle endurance. He clenched his jaw, gathered up the duffels, and struggled on.

With three more stops to rest, he finally arrived at the rusted open access gate. After needing yet another infuriating pause to spell his arms and shoulders, Joshua descended 10 feet via the spiral staircase into the darkness of the motor transport level. *It's not here!* The small stone he had used to prop open the exit gate when he had finished exploring just under a week ago was missing. Joshua took out the small frying pan from the big duffel and exiting the stair cage, wedged the door open with the pan. Vehicle lights were moving in the distance to his left, but the immediate motorways were surrounded by dilapidated industrial buildings, devoid of light or sound. *Not much reason for anyone to come this far North anymore.* With his grunt echoing off the walls, he hoisted the bags again and shuffled down the dead end motorway toward The Swamp.

He could almost picture black bogs billowing out dense puffs of steam, smelling of putrid rot. The smell mingled with the odor of oil and rusting metal to assault his nose as he shuffled under the burden of his possessions, seeking some dark shadow to cache his gear. At the end of the alleyway stood an empty void, ever widening before him as he stumbled deeper into the murk toward a dirty yellow rectangle that spilled out a distorted reflection of itself on the wet pavement. Joshua approached the doorway of the old storage warehouse on the right; an industrial bulb surrounded by a wire cage created an odd pattern of grey lines on the shining yellow walls around the entryway. *Too shallow.* However, the rusty chain and lock on the door suggested infrequent use, so Joshua decided it was safe to explore further.

Just around the corner, the contrast created by the dingy light from the entryway resulted in an inky narrow alcove. Joshua's eyes traversed along the windowless back wall of the warehouse *nobody wants to see or smell The Swamp* to where the building jutted out eight feet to meet a tall chain link fence *I might be able to set up a tarp in that far corner.* His gaze followed the fence back 20 feet and stopped where the pavement ended on his left. The alcove brightened as heavier clouds moved out of the way of the rising Big Moon. He could almost picture himself lounging under cover, dry in the corner, food cooking on the heating pad while he read from his sheet. *Not so bad.* Staying close to the building, he shuffled into the alcove about four feet before he allowed the bags to thump with a heavy squish next to the wall. Relishing the release in his burning shoulders and arms, Joshua edged nearer the fence until he could look over the ragged edge of pavement two to three feet beyond the fence, down the 35-foot drop to the beginning of The Swamp buffer zone below. He looked back at his duffels. *Should be safe here.*

He made sure to wedge the fry pan into place before he climbed back up to the pedestrian level and retraced his steps to their living cubicle. Sitting down next to his mother's body, Joshua waited, but he could feel a change in the atmosphere. The tiny rooms were colder,   vacant. Despair spread from a tight knot of reproach as he berated himself *I took too long! I wasn't here when I should have been. Again.*

Joshua clenched his fists and fought back the sobs. Once he had regained control, he took his sheet out of its pouch in his slicker and held it in trembling hands. He wondered if he would ever hear his mother's voice again. Tears once again blurred his view, but his finger tapped the correct numbers and his voice came out strong as he spoke,

"I have a death to report."

Officer Estanod's dark eyebrows bunched down toward the top of his nose, then one arched higher than the other. "So. *You* fought off a spiderviper, stabbed it while only getting a scratch on your shoulder, and *forced* it to go back into The Swamp?"

Joshua sat on the end of his Vertabed, his unfocused stare on the front door. Without looking up at the medium sized detective with a 6:00 shadow on his chin, he held up the lance with dried blood still on it. "Got lucky, I guess."

"Yeah, that's one way to put it. You *know* nobody in New Cincinnati has even seen a live spiderviper in 27 years, right? Since George of the Jungle?"

Joshua shrugged.

Estanod hesitated; he knew the boy was hiding something, but did not believe he had anything to do with his mother's death. He took the lance out of an unresisting hand. "All right. Just stay here for a minute, ok?"

Estanod walked over to Sergeant Sisryn, who stood in the kitchen with hands on hips, surveying the dark smears leading to the open cabinet. The short barrel of a man bent over to look out through the hole in the back of the wall, revealed now that all the pillows had been pulled out. He straightened up at Estanod's approach, face twisted with fascinated repulsion. "Un-be-leev-able! So, what's the kid's name?"

"Joshua."

"How do you spell it?"

"The old-fashioned way."

"Really?"

"Yep."

They always had to ask. Although people have often altered names when they immigrate to try and assimilate into a disparate culture, with humankind spreading out into space, the sense of increasing population and distances had trended toward individualization. Hence, there were a lot of unique spellings of traditional names.

"Were they Traditionalists?"

Driven to the Hilt

Estanod shrugged.

"Last name?"

"Vernon."

"Vernon?   What's the father's name?"

"Donno, Sarge, let me look." Estanod handed the lance to the Sergeant and pulled his minisheet from its holster, entering the boy's name into the secured police database. "Here it is   Oh.   His father was David Vernon."

"You're kidding me!"

"Nope.   But wasn't that name in the news a few years back? Let me pull up the file.   Here we go. Merchant Space Marine. Third deployment and already a Corporal. Serving on the Merchant Vessel Ultan, KIA in the Kasseron Sector four years ago. Tried in abstentia and found guilty of aiding and abetting an illegal spaceborne seizure activity. Yeah, he supposedly let the pirates on board somehow, but I wondered at the time wh-"

Silence pulled Estanod's attention up from the sheet to find the burly Sergeant with his eyes on the blood smeared floor, but clearly seeing something else. His words were soft, heavy with sadness, pity, and a touch of remorse, "It was a shame what the Mayor did to that guy..."

"The Mayor, Sarge?"

Sisryn looked up sharply, his face clouding as he realized he had spoken aloud. Stepping closer, his voice growled low, menace in every syllable, "If that comment ever gets back to me, I'll break you like a dry stick."

"Hey! I don't want her muscle dropping a load on my head! I'm not saying *any*thing to *any*body!"

"Yeah, well, you just make sure you don't, cause if that split tongued harpy gets on my trail, you'll be coming along for the blastoff."

Sgt. Sisryn reflexively made a quick scan of the kitchen and Estanod blinked in amazement. *What? He thinks there are listening devices in this dump?* Then he thought of the Mayor's reputation for ruthlessness and he found himself looking over his shoulder to make sure the kid was out of earshot. When he looked back, Sisryn was examining the lance, but he whispered out of the side of his mouth.

"So a friend of mine in IPF said the security tapes showed this Vernon guy, alone, in a five hour standoff with the pirates, countering their every move to breach the cargo hold. My buddy counted him dropping 17 pirates during the running gun battle. Said he made some incredible snap shots while under fire. Then the poor guy ran out of ammo." The Sergeant made a minute shake of his head. "With no way to fight, he depressurized half of the loot out into space and even then, they only just popped him before he jettisoned the other half." Sisryn's eyes became hard. "Then guess what? Those security tapes disappeared out of the IPF evidence locker. You know what kind of juice you'd need to pull that off? I heard the Mayor later laughed that it was lucky Vernon had been found out in space with the personal merchandize she had shipped on the Ultan, 'cause with the proof that he had sabotaged the cargo, the shipping company had to pay her a fortune. Two plus..."

"...two."

They looked at each other, the motive for future silence very clear. They then both looked at Joshua, still sitting, hands palm up in his lap, staring at the front door. His torn shirt revealed the large adhesive sterile bandage covering the wound on his shoulder, applied by the EMS personnel before they had left with his mother's body.

Sisryn shook his head. "First his dad and then his mom? That's tough. But all of this? By a spiderviper?" His gesture took in the mess of dried fluids in front of the broken wall. "Come on!"

Joshua roused from his stupor enough to glance over at the two police officers, who were looking at him and talking low *About me.* He could see the suspicion in the Sergeant's demeanor. *Does he really think I killed my Mom?* Joshua had no energy to give life to his offense at the idea. Listless eyes turned back to the door, which no longer served just as a surface to occupy his visual field. It now beckoned, calling through the morass of apathy with a louder and more insistent voice – *escape.*

Sgt. Sisryn regarded the crusty goo on the stickball lance. "Look, I may not know what happened here, but there is no way that kid scared off a spiderviper with this!"

"He's still sticking with his story, Sarge."

"How the *hell* could a 11-year-old boy survive against one of those, with one of these?"

"Yeah, I know. Hard to believe, but you don't think he killed his own mother, do you? She was definitely already dead, CSI said for at least 10 hours now, and with her leg," Estanod looked like he wanted to spit something putrid from his mouth, "something was obviously feeding on her, so..."

"OK, ok. Still, it just doesn't add up.   Anyway, it doesn't matter for the kid. We still gotta send him to OBS." Sgt. Sisryn's eyes twisted into a hard glare. "No! Don't even   *say it*, Estanod. He has no other family, right? And what with the Captain's wife pushing the Society **and** all of this *maybe*, **maybe** involving the first spiderviper attack in over 20 years, you know there's *no way* this won't splash the news vids, bigtime. And *that* means it's gonna get reviewed by the brass.   The **big** Brass."

Officer Estanod held his gaze for a moment before he sighed and mumbled, "Over 27 years."

"Huh?" Sgt. Sisryn looked up from the stickball lance, then his frown hardened his acne scarred face. "Yeah, I know, Smart Ass,   you got education. OK, 27 years.   *Whatever.*   Just make it happen. I really don't care about your personal preferences on this one."

Estanod fought his rising anger and bit back a retort. He turned, lifted a hand to his eyewear, and reluctantly walked back to Joshua. "So you're *sure* you don't have an Aunt or Uncle to stay with? Maybe a good family friend?" At the boy's negative head shake, Estanod informed him of the only other alternative. "OK, well, someone is coming pretty soon to take you somewhere to stay."

Joshua looked up, a touch of alarm in his voice, "The Orphan Benefit Society?" For the first time he noticed the small blinking red light on the police officer's large slightly tinted goggles. *He's recording all of this.* The observation tickled an elusive idea.

"Yeah, well, there is really nowhere else for you to go." Estanod seemed surprised at the harshness in his own voice. He stopped, took a deep breath, turned off the recording and tried again.

"Look, kid," he said softly, "I know OBS isn't the best place to live. But it's better than trying to survive on the streets. There are some pure mean gangs of kids roaming the motorways that you *don't* want to run into.   Believe me, I *know*.   So as bad as OBS can be, at least you won't get slagged for a moldy slice of bread. Thing is, once you're there, you just need to find someone bigger to hook-up with and then   well,   just stay tough!" He finished with intensity, frowned, then leaned back with a sigh. He glanced at his watch. "The social worker should be here any minute."

Joshua finally made the connection. "You can record this, right?"

The sudden animation alerted Estanod. "Yeah, that's right."

"OK, well, I want you to take my Mom's writing desk." Joshua pointed it out by the door. "My Dad made it for her when they got married, to write letters while he was deployed." A pleading tone crept into his request, "Could you please take it for me?   Please? I don't want Mr. Donald   uh the property manager to steal it."

Estanod looked from Joshua to the desk and back before he resumed recording. "So   you are requesting that I take *that...*," he aimed his goggles at the desk, "item of furniture into my personal possession until such time that you come to me and reclaim it?"

"Yes. I want-" Picking up on the formal tone, Joshua continued, "I am requesting for you to take that desk."

"Video log 17 regarding minor citizen's request for a security confiscation of item of furniture – one handcrafted writing desk."

Handcrafted...   that's   a nice way to say it.

"I need to go to the bath room."

Joshua got up and went over to the toilet closet next to the front door without waiting for permission. With the door closed, he dropped his face into his hands, feeling panic began to stir in his gut. However, Joshua had been in too many tight stickball games not to be able to clamp down on his emotions when necessary. *Mom didn't want me to go to OBS, so I am **not** going to go.* He heard a female voice outside the door and knew that the social worker had arrived. *The best defense...*

Joshua emerged from the bathroom to find Estanod speaking with a tall thin woman who would have been pretty if not for the long sharp nose. They stopped talking and she turned to face Joshua.

"Hello. My name is Ms. Tarree. I'm going to take you somewhere where you will be safe."

She held out a bony hand in greeting. Joshua reached forward as if to take her hand, but then lunged and shoved both fists into her midsection, forcing her to stumble back into Estanod with a shocked grunt. For just an instant, Joshua's eyes met Estanod's before the officer turned to direct Ms. Tarree's fall to the floor. Joshua almost sensed Estanod's approval, but wasted no time snatching open the front door and dashing out into the night.

As he rounded the first corner, Joshua heard Officer Estanod yelling, "Hey, wait up kid. Wait UP! I just want to talk to you."

The voice faded as he pounded through the puddles and drizzling rain, heading for the dark corner of the alleyway that held all that he had left in the world. He desperately hoped he could outpace the rhythmic splash of footsteps following him.

◄10►

Joshua slumped against the wet wall and slid down to sit across the two
duffel bags, blowing out and sucking in air with a primal urgency. He had
sprinted almost the entire way in order to finally escape the pursuing
officer. The rain had become a drifting mist and he pulled in the fetid rot of
The Swamp each time he filled his lungs. The taste reminded him of what
now loomed only 100 yards in front of him, a hulking black mass of danger
that seemed to be waiting in anticipation. He looked through the fence
down to the 100 yard buffer zone that separated the edge of the city from
The Swamp. Only The Small Moon was up, but with the added glow of
reflected city light, Joshua could make out general shapes in the gravel
filled zone. He searched for movement among the indigenous vegetation
that had already reclaimed much of the safeguard in the three years since
the last burn-back. *Nothing.*

His eyes then traversed his more immediate surroundings, from the
trash strewn corner of the building on his far right to the end of the old
motorway on his left. It stopped at a sunken five foot section of asphalt that
stretched under the barrier fence for a foot before coming to an abrupt end.
An oppressive gloom pressed down on Joshua and darkened an already
black world. *So   this is it?   This is my new   Home, Sweet Home?* His
face sunk down into his hands, blocking out his surroundings.

His breathing had almost returned to normal when a creak and shuffle
came from the pedway above his left shoulder. Joshua became statue still,
desperately hoping the security light from the warehouse door created a
dark enough shadow to conceal him. Officer Estanod's voice was quiet,
almost intimate, pleading, "Come on, kid. Don't make this so hard."

With painstaking care, Joshua rotated and tilted his head up until he
could see the dark mass through the weave of the pedway, standing still,
waiting. *Is he looking down at me? Can he see me?* Seconds ticked by
until the dark presence turned and the fading footsteps signaled that
Estanod had redirected his search.

Joshua eased his compressed lips and let a breath of relief escape, but his heart seized when the rhythmic thump of footsteps on metal stairs echoed down the motorway. *He's coming down!* The alcove to his right now felt tight and constricted. *I'm trapped!* Joshua's gaze skipped from shadow to shadow, seeking a place to hide. The sunken pavement by the fence drew his eye, the intense blackness of its shadow suddenly appealing. Joshua gritted his teeth to hold back a grunt as he hoisted up the large duffel. Then, stepping around puddles to avoid making even a tiny splash, he moved toward the depression. *Hurry, hurry, hurry!* He eased the heavy bag into the darkness, wincing at the scrape of the canvas as it slid into place. He ran back, grabbed the smaller duffel, and turned again toward the depression of pavement, all while trying to move both with speed and without making any noise.

A loud clank echoed off the walls, followed by a circular rolling sound of a round object wobbling with a rhythmic warble of slowly increasing tempo. The image of a cartoon character smashed flat like a coin came to Joshua's mind, forcing him to clamp down on the hysterical giggle trying to rise in his throat. He was almost to the depression when the scrape of the frying pan being retrieved from the pavement floated down the wet alleyway. Stepping on the large duffel, Joshua put the smaller duffel down next to it and eased himself down as flat as he could possibly lie.

Footsteps approached squish squish squish stopping only a few feet away from where Joshua pressed his face against a broken section of wet pavement, striving to keep his shallow breaths as slow and silent as possible. Time stretched on, and on. Joshua became aware of the tar smell of the pavement, the almost musical sound of dripping water all around, even a slight vibration from the gurgling under his cheek. With a sense of detachment, Joshua pictured a scene from a pVid war movie, when the sentry approached a commando who crouched in the dark. The hero's blackened face stared at the shiny boots of the guard, waiting to be discovered. Not in the movie, of course. *The hero* never *gets caught.* The thought made the current juxtaposition surreal, the idea of watching a movie showing the reflection of shiny black shoes versus hearing the steps and actually feeling the real mist coalesce on his face.

A loud sigh snapped Joshua back to the present. He listened

and   waited.   Finally, footsteps faded back up the motorway before stopping.

"Look, kid, I know you're around here somewhere. Listen,   I really don't want to send you to the Society.   I spent five years there myself.   But I *survived* and   I'm doing ok for myself.   Come on,   it'll be better than living on the street.   How are you gonna eat?   Where are you gonna sleep?   You *don't want to be alone.*   Come on out, kid."

With the once cozy feeling alcove transformed into a wet jail cell, a deepening despair descended upon Joshua. *He's right. I don't want to be alone.* He let a final breath ease through his lips and then gathered himself in preparation to stand and give up. Just before he pushed off of the bag beneath him, he heard Officer Estanod turn and walk away, freezing the words about to form in his mouth. The fading rhythmic squishes tore at Joshua. *I have to decide. Now!* He heard the softest of whispers *Resolute.* He hesitated…

Then the footsteps were gone.

Alone with the murmur of thousands of raindrops gathering into tiny rivulets all around him, Joshua pushed up to his hands and knees and peered into the empty darkness of the dead motorway. In the distance, the lights from a single vehicle slipped across the motorway, leaving only a few far away dull islands of yellow from security lamps and the soft murmur of a city at night. He lifted himself up and thumped down into a sitting position on the duffels, trying to get more comfortable and decide what to do next. The screeching moan of bending metal mixed with the low rasp of stones grinding together and then   a metallic snap! Joshua had only enough time to tighten his grip on the big duffel before the broken section of asphalt shifted beneath him, and with a deep and growing rumble, both he and the duffels slid under the fence

off the edge of New Cincinnati,

down

into The Swamp.

Driven to the Hilt

The Swamp

◄1►

Joshua hit hard.

The smaller of the duffel bags, mostly filled with his clothes, provided enough cushion to keep his ribs from breaking. He bounced back up into the air, where he   hung   just long enough   to reflexively roll into a ball before helplessly dropping to another confrontation with the punishing rocks below.

Ummph!

He struck on his right hip with a sharp crunch of gravel and lifted again as the world spun faster.

Uunnnh!

Another impact on his right shoulder in the midst of irregular streaks of reflection and then whirling shades of blackness as he spun down among the cracking of stones against rock. When the rotations began to slow, he put out an arm to stop the world from revolving. This cost him a sharp rap on the elbow and a ricochet off of a larger stone. He had just slid to a stop when something heavy slammed into his left shoulder, ramming the right side of his face deeper into the gravel. The large duffel bag continued its journey over him, rolling a few more feet before grinding to a stop with a final scattering of pebbles. Joshua braced himself to be struck again, keeping his eyes closed tight and his face pressed against the pebbles. There were the cracks of several smaller stones bouncing past him, and then   silence.

Finally, when it seemed nothing else was going to assault him, Joshua opened his eyes, but only saw a dark jumble of dirt and stone. He dared not move, the pain in his torso forcing him to take shallow gulps of air. He lay for several minutes, smelling a mixture of tar and wet soil, until at last, he could breathe somewhat normally. With great care, Joshua levered himself up into a sitting position. He winced at the burning tenderness from the scrapes and abrasions on the side of his face, palms of his hands, and up his right forearm. A deeper throbbing came from both legs, his right side, and right shoulder. *Well, everything seems to move.* He climbed to his feet and stood on wobbly legs, just to be sure he could. His initial sense of relief was slammed aside by the realization   *I am* **in** *The Swamp!*

Despite the pain, Joshua turned and scrambled up the slope of loose wet stones until the face of a sheer wall barred his return to safety. Terrified, he scratched for a handhold on the slick earthen barrier. A stickball sized stone gave way to his frantic scrabbling and bounded down with sharp cracks on larger boulders below. A high-pitched screech stabbed out from the jungle behind him.

Joshua stood transfixed as the scream transformed into a series of low hoots. He crouched and turned with the utmost care to peer out between the sheer walls on either side of him toward the looming black wall that was the face of The Swamp. The darkness was so intense, he had difficulty gauging the distance to the watching mass of trees, but he did sense some intervening shadowy shapes that did not move and then remembered the earlier view from above *the burn zone.* He stood for several moments listening with focused intent, searching for any sound of movement. As his eyes adjusted to the deeper gloom, the increased visibility produced enough calm for him to check his more immediate surroundings.

Joshua sucked in his breath from the stabbing pain in his neck as he looked back for a way to climb up to New Cincinnati. His stomach sank. He looked up at a sheer 10 foot stone wall that glistened with rain, standing just out of reach above a compressed wall of rocks, soil, and mineral dust. He blinked against the falling droplets and watched as a clump of dirt transformed to mud and completed a lazy slide off the rock face, plopping into the wet earth in front of Joshua. For the second time that day, Joshua found himself looking down from above, this time taking in a pathetic little wet bundle of boy facing an insurmountable barrier to safety. Even the detached, observing Joshua sensed a portion of the depth of despair rising in response to the accumulation of the day's events. *There is no way out.*

Another screech from the jungle snapped Joshua back into his body. He shuddered while turning back to face The Swamp. A reinvigorated drive to survive forced his risen anguish into the background. His night adjusted eyes traced a path from the not distant enough edge of The Swamp to the silhouette of spiked plant leaves that covered most of the opening to the alcove in which he found himself. *Maybe nothing can get through.* With a small ember of hope, he eased his way down the gully etched into the foundation of the city by the constant draining of water. This took time because he would stop and wait every time a dislodged stone announced his presence by cracking down the slope of rock debris through the gloomy fissure. Eventually, he was back to the duffels.

With great care, Joshua moved his smaller duffel behind a huge boulder jutting out from the sidewall of the small gulch. He then retrieved the large duffel, and while sitting on the softer small duffel, searched in the big bag. A moment later, he sat with the large butcher knife held in both hands, at the ready, pointing out between his knees. He settled down to wait for the dawn.

With the abrupt lack of activity, nothing prevented the despondency and hopelessness from welling up, matching the sounds of water, dripping, sliding, gurgling down to The Swamp. The terror of possibly drawing attention to his location stifled his weeping, but even the sneaking, lurking monster shadows of his imagination could not stop the tears from brimming in his eyes, sliding in hot paths down his cheeks. Visual images from the day's events forced their way to the surface. Joshua instinctually knew this would lead to the very dark place that he had glimpsed earlier, a deep pit of internal despair even more confining than his current surrounding rock prison. With great effort, he pushed away the image of his mother's blank stare and instead focused on re-creating the framed photo on the writing desk. Although he held himself there, looking at the family portrait from a better place and time, a sense of apprehension began to mingle with the foreboding gloom pressing in all around him. *How had all that happened? How could Mom have been talking to me?* The lurking trepidation found its voice in a hoarse whisper, "Am I crazy?"

Joshua recalled a news story from several years ago about a miner who had jumped from the M3I corporate tower after his family had died from a fire in their tenement apartment. *I'd wanted to die too, after finding Mom.* Then Joshua remembered the secret compartment in the writing desk. *She'd never told me about that before.* Although he did not quite understand how it could be true, Joshua clung to the belief that his mother had somehow been there with him when he had so desperately needed her. That comforting thought forced his misery to retreat a step or two, allowing him to take a deep breath and lean back into the rock. He could almost picture his mother saying, "Hope comes with the beginning of every new day." Joshua could not quite produce a smile, but he did feel his mother standing near him at that moment, even if she was not speaking out loud anymore. A more distant low moaning howl emanated from in The Swamp. *Mom?*   But no answer came   and the silence became deeper against the patter of the swelling rainfall. At that moment, as he sat listening to the water moving all around him, Joshua was certain he would never hear her speak again.

The raindrops became heavier, thumping down on the hood of his slicker. Joshua waited for the despair to reassert itself. Instead, he could almost feel the warmth of her arm across his shoulders as they looked down at his father's unit shoulder patch on the second anniversary of his death. "Resolute. That's you, Josh. Just like your Dad. That   that's what *we* need to be from now on." She squeezed him closer. A warm drop penetrated the buzz cut on the top of his head. She whispered, "Thank you for being so strong."

Again, her presence encompassed him. While he grieved the loss of the sound of her voice, Joshua now understood, with a strong conviction, she expected him to face his fears as his father would have done. Besides *this way doesn't feel so crazy.* His voice croaked out, "Thanks for staying with me, Mom." The downpour slackened as her presence faded away. *Now, I just have to make it to "the new day."* Joshua settled down, knowing he had a long wait before the arrival of dawn.

◀2▶

The buzzing annoyed Joshua more than the pain in his neck. *What is that sound?* When he turned his head to better locate the noise, a stab of agony forced his eyes wide, revealing a rock wall 12 feet in front of him, glossy from a falling mist. Joshua blinked in confusion and then looked down at his empty hands with a growing swirl of panic spreading through his gut. *This is not right!* With a snap, it all flooded back in the early morning light. The engulfing realization of his mother's death halted at the sight of the butcher knife handle in the stones between his feet.

I'm in The Swamp!

The heavy hum now took on meaning. Joshua snatched up his meager protection and pressed his back into the boulder behind him, eyes flicking wildly, trying to take in everything in his immediate vicinity and then the buzzing stopped. His eyes fixed upon the edge of the huge boulder on his right that blocked The Swamp from view.   He waited.   The knife tip began to tremble in the silence, before   the deep thrumming returned. He gripped the handle in preparation and then it stopped.   Then started again,   and then   it stopped.   Joshua reached out with his ears, striving to locate the buzzing each time it resumed. After a few moments of intent listening, he became convinced that each time the buzzing started again, it was not coming closer to him, but remained on the far side of the big boulder and farther down the slope. It seemed to be coming from the spiky plant he had seen the night before. The one that he had thought   and urgently hoped   *still* blocked access into his crevice.

Looking back up at the edge of New Cincinnati, Joshua confirmed in the growing daylight what he had determined the night before. *No climbing back up that.* With great care he rose up and stepped forward on protesting legs to lean against the massive slick boulder that provided his sole, tenuous refuge. Checking his footing before each step, Joshua began creeping around the curve of the stone, leading with his left eye. He kept circling forward until he saw the tips of the spiky leafed plant. Another slow step and it all came into view: the mass of outward pointed spikes, a number of central stalks with blue blooms, and the source of the buzzing noise.

The deep burgundy creature was about the size of a small rabbit and the buzzing came from the blurred yellow wings on its back. Like the spiderviper, it had segmented chitin that covered the body, flexing open and closed rhythmically, but with deep reds of alternating intensity to create a mottled effect. It hovered above one of the huge blue blossoms clustered on the upper two-thirds of the five to seven foot tall stocks that extended up from the middle of the plant. Two small paws reached out to hook onto the petal of the blossom. The buzzing stopped, revealing yellow leathery wings that reminded Joshua of a bat, but moving separately in two separate segments like a butterfly. Upper and lower appendages stretched out and independently flicked the attached wings several times before folding them down against the back. A long snout unrolled and sniffed with caution before the creature started to work its head up inside the blossom.

Oh, pollination. I know about that! Recalling something he had previously learned felt familiar, calming. Several years prior, as they had moved closer and closer to The Swamp in search of cheaper rent, Joshua had begun having nightmares about becoming lost in the jungle. Joshua's mother had suggested he start researching jungle and swamp ecosystems on his sheet during his late morning hour of "educational exploration." Resources such as e-encyclopedias and public library databanks were considered to be part of general public works, like upkeep of roads and sewers, so the free limited domain wifi allowed Joshua to use the GlobalNet to access numerous resources on any topic. Already a voracious reader, he had learned a great deal about common plant and animal interdependencies within jungles and swamps, including the process of pollination and various defense mechanisms utilized by plants and animals in such environments. Joshua had tried to research material specific to the swamps of Cypress Grove, but virtually nothing came up. Spidervipers discouraged field studies, it seemed. Nor had there been much information about spidervipers, but what little there was always came accompanied by the famous picture of the spiderviper in its pre-strike pose. It had been taken by the sole survivor of the second search and rescue team that had set out to locate the missing original Biodiversity Expedition.

It was standard practice for new colonies to catalogue local biological resources for possible commercial exploitation. After losing 17 biologists and security personnel on the two failed forays into the jungle around the mining operations, M3I decided the more economical solution was to simply burn the dense vegetation to create a barrier around the living quarters and refining operations. The road that led to the initial mining site was eventually replaced by the current electromag monorail. Aside from the slightly blurred picture of the spiderviper and warnings about the toxicity of their poison, he had found nothing more about any indigenous life on Cypress Grove.

Watching the burgundy and yellow creature back out of the blossom, Joshua named it a *Bumblebat.* Assigning labels to things somehow made the vast unknown of The Swamp just a bit smaller. Joshua noted movement beyond the large aloe-like leaves of the *hmmm, Bluebell* that extended all of the way across the entrance of the narrow alcove. In fact, no longer fixated on the Bumblebat, the variety of different sounds coming from beyond the Bluebell was almost overwhelming. Joshua calmed himself by recalling a video from his swamp research that had shown a funny looking monkey that screamed like a woman being tortured. He knew that scary sounds may not represent a threat at all, since predators were likely to be quiet when they were the most dangerous. He just needed to figure out which sound went with which animal.

A moment later the Bumblebat buzzed away in search of more nectar and Joshua decided to learn more about the Bluebell. He rounded the huge boulder and descended the last of the rocky slope to level ground, which was a small gravel covered by large swaths of silvery sage green spongy lichen, interspersed with smaller patches of light scarlet clover like plants. An aroma swelled in his nostrils as Joshua approached the Bluebell. It smelled sweet, but with a note of cinnamon and *cayenne pepper? That's weird.* He crept forward to examine the large leaves at the bottom of the Bluebell, which rose from the base of the plant in a high arc that eventually bent and brought the spear tips to the ground. Once close enough, he saw

The Deepest Cut

small needlelike protrusions along the edge of the blade shaped leaves and resolved not to brush up against any new plants before a close examination. There were also clear little droplets covering the surface of the leaves that might have been nectar or simply dew from the prior night. Joshua reached out a finger, but jerked his hand to a stop. Looking around, he found a small twig and touched it to a drop near the tip of the closest leaf. He was unprepared for what happened next.

The Bluebell shuddered and the twig was pulled from his hand as all of the long leaves rose in unison. Joshua sat with a thump and then his feet began scrambling at the gravel, sliding him back on his butt until he rammed into the earthen embankment of the gulch. By then, all of the Bluebell leaves had lifted up against the stocks, exposing the immediate area of the burn beyond the massive plant. Joshua sat transfixed by what he saw.

A large spiderviper was ambling by in the dim morning light, less than fifteen yards in front of Joshua. He watched, terrified, as the spindly legged killer stopped, crouched,   and   slowly   turned   to face him. Remembering how sensitive the spiderviper's hearing had been in their living cubicle, Joshua opened his mouth and forced himself to breathe in long   slow   breaths.   His heart pounded out the seconds   until   the Bluebell's leaves began a gentle descent back toward the ground, eventually blocking the staring spiderviper from view. Joshua carefully crawled forward and anxiously peered between the leaves, to see   the monster moving away. His arms and legs shuddered as he watched the apex predator disappear into the foliage. The thought of doing some research on basic survival skills was suddenly very appealing.

Thirty minutes later, Joshua sat on his duffel behind the boulder with his sheet on his lap, extremely annoyed. *That's the fifth time I've tried to load this stupid video!* He snapped open the bottom edge of the casing, slid out the quarter inch thin sheet of clear polymer, and turned it over to examine the intricate circuitry painted on the back. He could not find any scratches on either side of the sheet. Next he inspected the almost indestructible sheet case. *Ummm, power leads look OK.* The sheet could run for several hours on its own internal battery, but the miniature CFU in the case could produce constant power for years. The case also provided shielding from the cancer causing microcomm waves.

Joshua's first seventh grade research paper had reviewed the height of the personal communication revolution on Earth, when almost everyone had implanted devices that ran off the body heat of the host. This had become feasible because of the enormous bandwidth provided by the use of ever larger transmitters and signal boosters found all over Earth. Once the cancer connection was irrefutable, the de-evolution of pCom devices began, and now the strategy was to deploy many more less powerful transmitters, along with increased shielding on all communication devices. *Mom gave me an A- for*

The flood of anguish was immediate and devastating. Joshua could not stop the body wrenching sobs for almost 30 minutes. When at last the crying subsided and he had wiped away the tear streaks, a pang of hunger came, followed by an immediate stab of guilt. *How can you think about food when she's **dead**?* The tears welled again, but were halted by the image of the empty All-Day bar wrapper in his hands. He stood in the living cubicle with his mother lying under the sheet on the floor next to him. He was enveloped by the mingled odors of scorched potato and musky spiderviper. The confluence of odors and locations caused a convulsing of his throat that pulled him back to the present.

Knees watery, Joshua looked at the sheet in his hands. He pulled in a shaky breath and tried to focus on something other than the word "crazy." *OK, maybe it'll have better reception without the case.* He held up the sheet high over his head and tapped the download button again. Just when he thought his arms were going to give out, the last of the three videos on jungle survival finished downloading and he collapsed back onto the duffel. *Finally!!*

At the end of the third "how to" download, Joshua slumped back in disgust. The basic message of all of the survival tutorials had been the same: become knowledgeable about the environment. He was advised to learn which plants could be eaten, which ones had healing properties, which animals were simply dangerous, and which were to be avoided at all costs. *Well, I guess I have a leg up on the last one.*

The Deepest Cut

The rumbles in his stomach returned and Joshua recalled the collapsible cooler bag. The available space in the larger duffel had been very limited, but *Here it is.* He extracted the shiny silver bag and looked inside. There was almost a pound of chicken block, even more of the beef and pork blocks, three partial cheese cubes, and four apple squares *Always better when they're cold. Better eat some of this stuff before it goes bad.*

With his belly full and his disposition improved, Joshua rigged one of his two tarps to cover the duffel bags, which were still in their original position behind the Big Boulder. They served both as cushions and barriers to the wet ground. Now out of the rain, he held up the sheet and searched "The Swamp" on the GlobalNet. Topping the list was a link to the famous George of the Jungle video. It was blocked. *Well, Mom, I really think I need to watch this now.* There was almost an air of acquiescence as he bypassed the parental controls. He had known the password for several years, but *I would never go against Mom's rules.* He froze, his words replaying in his mind. For the second time that day, Joshua rode out a flood of intense emotion; this time shame and regret rolled over him as much as grief. He could no longer avoid asking the question *Would she be alive if I hadn't disobeyed her? If I'd been there to hear it, or to help her fight it off, or to have just done* some*thing?*

It took 20 minutes of misery before the futility of his self-flagellation finally exhausted him. He sat under the tarp, staring out at The Big Trees that towered up on the far side of the burn, until at last, he was overcome by the urge to be productive. Squeezing out a wash cloth left out in the light rain, he wiped the tears from his face. Then Joshua picked up his sheet and returned to his research.

First, he read a news blog covering the 20th anniversary of George of the Jungle's Epic Expedition. It traced the origins of the name to a 1967 television cartoon. *Pre-Internet! How could they live like that?* Then the blog described Richard Huusein's legal change of name to George of the Jungle and his blending of the stage name with the Great White Hunter trope. "George" then spent a year seeking every possible opportunity for publicity. It was clear from his pre-event posters that George knew the first rule of advertising: sex sells. His khaki short shorts revealed muscular legs braced with feet apart, an elephant gun at the ready in both hands, but held low to keep from obstructing the view of his tanned pecs and rolling abs through an open hunting vest. A bandolier of gleaming bullets hung from one shoulder and a safari hat buttoned up on one side completed the presentation.

The blogger noted that Richard had actually completed a degree in biology and provided excerpts from several of his college papers that espoused the right of human colonies to exploit native resources. George's Epic Expedition was exactly 10 years after the second biodiversity expedition had been lost in The Swamp, its single survivor having taken the famous partial picture of a spiderviper's reaching foreclaws. Not that the creature was identified as a spiderviper at that time. That moniker would not emerge until after New Cincinnati saw what happened during George's event. The blogger concluded that although George knew how to promote a business, "he obviously little understood why The Swamp so thoroughly deserved its reputation for lethality."

Joshua settled in to watch the entire 11:42 video…

The Deepest Cut

◄3►

It begins with two male commentators introducing the *LIVE!!* coverage of the Epic Expedition. After a few moments of commentary about both the bravery and foolhardiness of George, the scene switches to the face of The Swamp, pulling back and sliding sideways along a completely barren strip of land until a waving figure comes into view at the bottom right of the screen. A rapid zoom down from on high reveals George in his poster outfit, flashing a wide white smile. He then becomes serious and taps on an earpiece that sports a thin wire microphone wrapped around to the left corner of his mouth. After a second series of taps, his voice stutters in with some break-up, "...lo, ar... ..ou picki... ...up?" He looks directly into the camera, asking in a deep and sincere tone, "Martyn? Ernast? Do you read me?"

The commentators' confirming replies bring back the sparkling teeth. A few more moments of conversation follows, with George allowing the commentators to describe the history of the prior failed excursions and their associated fear for his safety before he steadfastly asserts, "Ernast... Martyn... All The Swamp needs is a strong hand and the right tools," he pauses to hold up his large caliber rifle, "to be tamed for the benefit of *all* who live on Cypress Grove!" The scene dissolves into a live video feed looking forward from George's hat. His deep voice rumbles, "Time to *do* this!"

At first, George frequently pauses and allows his hat camera to linger on different plants *There's a Bluebell!* while he wonders aloud what medical breakthroughs might be contained in each. Such speculation comes less often as the density of vegetation increases, forcing George onto a "game trail." Soon after, the uplink connection to the commentators becomes unreliable and they try to fill in the dead air between George's increasingly sporadic comments.

The next six minutes were more and more difficult for Joshua to watch, not only because of the deteriorating connectivity that caused the picture to break and jump, but because of the sudden shifts of scene as George began to look around himself more and more quickly. His once confident voice, when the audio did come through, now emanated with a higher tone and at greater speed. Knowing the outcome, Joshua's tension rose as the video timer ran over the 10- minute mark. *This is real. He's really about to die.*

The barrel of the gun extends into the bottom of the screen as the surrounding trees pull back and George emerges into a small 25-foot gap in the jungle. The audio connection is restored and the relief in his voice is palpable, "Aaahh, a bit of room to maneuver!"

There is a rapid scan of the clearing from right to left, revealing a dimly lit space with only a few dapples of light seeping through the high canopy from the overcast sky. Then a few more steps in and a reverse look reveals where the trail exits the undergrowth. Turning back forward, George begins with renewed confidence, "So... you can see we have progressed quite a ways into The Swamp, with no diffi–"

A sharp whistle pierces his word and the camera snaps to the right, pausing for an instant on a dark blurred shape with upside down V legs. A sinuous white streak of a tube extends forward, *like a striking snake!!* A yell chops short with a grunt, a flash, and a startling BOOM. The world spins in a disorienting whirl that jars to a stop with the ground upside down and tilted somewhat to the left.

Joshua quickly rotated the sheet to reorient the scene, listening in horror to the hisses of labored breathing, before he realized the tan color that almost filled the screen was George's forearm. It begins jerking to the right, a slight grunt accompanying each jerk. A stronger pull brings George's hand into view, the fingers' slight twitching of feeble grasps at the air making it clear he is still alive. A dark furry articulated foot with claws obstructs the view before stepping back out. George's hand is yanked out of view. The sounds of something heavy being dragged away is interrupted when the video feed is cut and the scene ends.

Joshua exhaled his tension and allowed the sheet to drop into his lap. He had expected another re-experiencing of his mother's death, but his memory had only skittered over the events, without actually seeing the details. *No wonder everybody is so scared of The Swamp! I can't imagine watching that live.* He knew he needed to learn a great deal more about the inhabitants of The Swamp before hazarding an excursion beyond the Bluebell.

By the end of his first day on the edge of The Swamp, Joshua had named six different plants he had observed from his hiding place as well as a larger number of different swamp animals. It was not until the third animal that he thought of recording videos of the wildlife on his sheet. Most plentiful were the SlugBunnies, frequently sitting up on large hind legs, four smaller forelegs pulled in tight to the chest, surveying for threats with big eyes and rotating long ears, hence the Bunny designation. The Slug half of the name derived from the smooth hairless skin covering their bodies. When wet, which was most of the time, it looked slimy. He also observed the locking chitin on a number of the animals and decided a temperature regulation mechanism that could also form a shield made evolutionary sense.

As evening gathered, Joshua looked at the cooler. He was unsure how long the perishables would last. *They're still plenty cold, so they should stay good for a while at least.* Based on the amount he had eaten for lunch, he estimated another three-days of fresh food. Of course, to make the most of what he had, he should avoid eating until he was full. *So, it'll be a balance between making them last as long as possible without letting any of it spoil.* He decided to go to half rations on the perishables, which would stretch them to almost a week.

He peered into the duffel, surveying all of the spices and flavorings his mother had accumulated. She had been gaining a reputation as someone who could work magic in creating delicious dishes by transforming the bland over processed food products shipped trans-space to Cypress Grove. They had been so close to making the Homehearth Café a reality. Through watery eyes, he refocused on counting out of the All-Day bars   *20, 21. OK, do the math.* By eating no more than two per day, he could survive an additional 10 days on the concentrated protein and essential nutritional elements in the bars. *Just over two weeks of food. Great. Then what?*

The futility of his situation settled heavily on Joshua's shoulders and immersed him in a wave of self-pity. *I'm just a kid! How am I supposed to stay alive in The Swamp?* The tears began to flow yet again. *First Dad and now Mom. Why* **why** *is this happening to me?   Why me?*

A strengthening awareness began to crowd in on Joshua's misery. His survival instincts surged in response to the feeling that someone was nearby in the deepening darkness of the oncoming evening, someone watching,   waiting. His sobbing stopped and he stepped out from under that tarp, standing ready with the chef's knife clutched in both hands, searching for the threat in the gathering shadows.

As seconds ticked into minutes, the initial alarm evaporated and the atmosphere became one of expectation. Joshua's shoulders sagged in relief and he tilted his head up, allowing the rain to wash away his tears. For once, instead of avoiding the falling drops, he embraced them, realizing that the ability to feel *anything* meant   he was *alive*. He became aware of the surrounding space with an incredible intensity of all of his senses. It was a turning point that Joshua would often recall later, whenever he found himself in desperate circumstances. He looked forward at the dark mass of The Swamp and whispered, "Resolute." Still concerned about what cooking smells might attract, Joshua settled back under the tarp for a dinner of "fudge" flavored day ration bar. *Thanks, Mom.*

Her close comforting warmth only lasted through the meal. He settled down for another long and hopefully sleepless night, trying to quell the apprehension that swirled in his stomach. The image of George's arm being pulled away came unbidden, and with it, the bleak question

What's going to happen to me tomorrow?

The Deepest Cut

◄4►

The clear bulge shook twice, hesitated,   then slid into another transparent bump. Together they created a larger bulge, which moved just a bit faster, barely pausing as it ate up another clear upside down hump *It's going now!* and began to accelerate lower down the edge of the slicker hood, gathering into a single large drop that broke free   wobbling in its fall toward   Joshua's cup. The kerplunk of its impact into the almost full cup produced another drop that surged free into the air, before gravity returned it to its compatriots below. *No escape for you*   As he raised the cup to his lips, Joshua wondered *How can I feel thirsty with all this water around ALL the time?* Still, despite the slight plastic flavor, the gulp felt good going down.

As it had turned out, his worry about what was going to happen next had been answered with *not much, not much at all.* And with not much to focus upon, he struggled to keep his mind off his empty stomach. He knew that other than air, water was the number one survival need for the body. He stared at the pot full of rain water. *No worries there. Food on the other hand...*

During the past three days, he had thought many times of how he had just expected a hot delicious meal to be ready at the beginning and end of the day, for food to be waiting in the refrigerator so he could fix lunch while his mother was at work, how it had been such a big deal when the budget had forced him to give up his favorite afternoon snack. Now, food was *always* on his mind – when could he allow himself to eat next, trying to decide how much he should eat, and even after deciding, always struggling not to keep eating when his stomach *screamed* to be filled.

In addition to the constant gnawing stomach pains, his hunger prompted fantasies about eating a favorite meal, but since all of his best food memories reminded him of his mother, they slammed home the realization that she was gone. But after three days of this, he now rarely broke down when he again saw her dead staring eyes, and sometimes, he even felt a flash of warmth with the recollection of a special meal they had shared. And then, for those brief periods after eating when he did not feel *quite* so hungry, the unrelenting dampness insisted upon stepping into the spotlight.

I am SO tired of being wet. As a rule, Joshua no longer noticed the rain unless it was a heavy downpour. Even though the slicker was made of a breathable fabric, the humidity insured his clothes underneath never really dried out. And Joshua was increasingly concerned that the smell from the makeshift toilet he had established across from the huge boulder would eventually attract the interest of one of the nasties from The Swamp. With each infrequent meal, his thoughts returned to his limited food supplies, only adding emphasis to the obvious conclusion *I'm going to have to leave Hidey Hole sooner or later.*

The single thing that pushed the misery of being wet and hungry to the edge of his consciousness was learning more about The Swamp. Joshua had cataloged several more creatures after reprogramming a night image video app on his sheet to function as a proximity alarm. At night, he placed it in just forward of the Bluebell to take in the area immediately in front of the Hole. It would chirp in response to any change in the overall image pixel strength within a three-second time period. Joshua had also set it to record the scene throughout the night. He then fast-forwarded through the video until he saw movement and saved any new creature or behaviors.

Joshua set down the empty cup. He had saved the previous night's video to provide a diversion as the long afternoon marched toward evening. Nearing the end of the recording, his finger stabbed out to stop and then rewind the video. He digitally zoomed in on a Monster Millipede that had worked its way halfway up a thick stalk of the Nutblossom bush that stood a few feet to the right of Hidey Hole. He knew millipede was a misnomer (there were only one pair of appendages for each of the nine shell covered segments), but Joshua liked simple descriptive labels ***and*** *it's good alliteration.* The Millipede's long body undulated as it vigorously shook one of the fronds, causing a large hanging cluster of approximately 20 yellow "nuts" to fall and bounce around in all different directions. With surprising dexterity, given its long and low body, the Millipede launched from the stalk to land amongst the released nuts. It turned toward the camera and Joshua's mouth twisted in disgust.

What he had previously thought to be a mustache, the sheet's maximized resolution revealed to be a wriggling mass of little smooth serpentine *Arms? Tongues?* that reached forward to grasp the balls and push them back to an unseen mouth. *That's just gross!* The Monster Millipede approached the Bluebell in search of errant seeds, but was careful to avoid the glue covered leaves. After it disappeared off screen, Joshua rewound the video to replay the scene of bouncing seeds. As he had thought, several had rolled out of screen view in the direction of Hidey Hole. Joshua stopped the video to crouch and look under his Bluebell.

Well looky there! Three wrinkled pale yellow orbs lay under the needle edged leaves. *You missed some, Mr. Millipede!* Carefully checking to ensure there were no predators in sight, Joshua tickled the Bluebell to allow access to the *Nuteggs*. He scurried to gather them up before the Bluebell leaves descended again, and was soon back sitting on his duffel bags, examining the pale yellow globes that were a little larger than a golf ball. He sliced through the thick convoluted leathery skin to reveal a substance with the consistency of a set, heavy custard and the hue of egg yolk. *That fits.* A single black kernel resided in the middle of the yolk. Joshua cut a small piece from the outside skin and smelled it, taking in an aroma similar to rosemary and cinnamon. Recalling advice from one of survival videos, he rubbed it on the back of his hand and set back to wait for 15 minutes. Seeing and feeling no reaction on his skin, he cut another small piece of the exterior and put it in his mouth. Along with the rosemary-cinnamon flavor, it had a slight peppery taste and reminded him of the consistency of a slice of chicken cube.

Again, after 15 minutes produced no gastrointestinal reaction to the chewy outer covering of the Nutegg, Joshua turned his attention to the custard like interior. However, the past half hour had produced a film of a sickly brown color and he decided to cut open a second Nutegg. Joshua smeared some of the custard over the back of his hand and waited the prescribed 15 minutes without any reaction. Not wanting to waste a possible edible resource, he scraped the oxidized layer from the surface of the custard and dipped a spoon into the deep yellow substance below. It had a sweet, slightly citrusy taste, with an even more pronounced peppery finish, and surprisingly, no hint of rosemary or cinnamon. Having once again waited without experiencing any nasty consequences, Joshua examined the small dark kernel. A swelling impatience prompted him to forgo the skin test and he just popped it into his mouth.

Crushing the gel-like capsule between his front teeth released a much sweeter fluid onto his tongue, with a barely detectable peppery aftertaste. He chewed and swallowed. *Strange combo, but not bad.* A moment later, Joshua felt a slight euphoria. Everything around him appeared sharper, sounded crisper, and odors were more clearly defined. He also felt as if he could run faster and shivered with a desire to dash out into the open, just to experience the thrill of moving with speed. *Wow, that's a little creepy.* He got up and walked around the Big Boulder to look out through the late afternoon drizzle into the burn zone, bouncing lightly on the balls of his feet.

Well, I have to start exploring some time. Joshua had no intention of leaving the safety of his refuge at night, but *Maybe it would be okay to move around at dusk.* The open areas seemed less exposed than during the full light of day, and besides, *I just feel more confident.* It did not occur to Joshua that such conditions would make most predators feel more confident as well. Joshua rolled the final Nutegg in the palm of his hand, then popped the entire thing in his mouth. The combination of the skin and custard interior was surprisingly good, especially when the sweetness from the "Speed Seed" entered the mix.

Joshua tickled the Bluebell to make his exit, butcher knife in hand, and eased out into the open, swiveling his head, alert for any movement. A BumbleBat buzzed a full 60 yards in front of him at the edge of the dense wall of The Swamp. A family of SlugBunnies were squeaking and cavorting to his far right, which was reassuring, since he knew they would vanish at the slightest hint of danger. Continuing his scan, Joshua experienced a strong desire to move, a jitteriness that could only be contained by action. He did not like the feeling of being on the edge of out of control, but his thoughts were disrupted when something wide, but low to the ground, scurried under a distant bush to his right. He had not seen

The Deepest Cut

any details, but the sighting reinforced his decision to head in the other direction. He locked his eyes on the triangular top of an Ice Spike Tree standing just over 20 yards in front of the Hidey Hole. *I'll at least explore up to that.*

A few minutes of careful advancement brought him to his goal, a small tree almost eight feet tall with the namesake long thin pastel blue pods only drooping from the bottom branches. Closer, Joshua now saw that they were actually very slender blossoms that emanated a rosy aroma with a hint of smokiness. *No food here then. Speaking of food* Joshua's stomach gave a slight twist and a sourness filled his mouth as he scanned his surroundings. He liked *needed* the extra alertness the Speed Seed provided while away from Hidey Hole, but the jitteriness also meant he should limit his intake of Nuteggs. *I have to find some different foods.*

He then spotted the remains of a dead Bluebell an additional 20 or so yards farther to The Swamp proper. It lay overturned with its roots exposed, its wilted blossom stalks horizontal to the ground. After a quick 360 scan revealed nothing alarming, Joshua gave in to the continuing urge to move and decided to extend his search. Once at the dead plant, Joshua took in the deep claw marks and heavy stones that had been thrown back from the excavation site as well as the skull and remnants of several other broken bones in the bottom of the hole. He crouched, knife thrust forward, and turned in a slow circle, looking for movement. *I don't want to meet whatever did that.* Seeing nothing, his breathing slowed, and he moved around to the dried out stalks. *Perfect!* Selecting the one closest to his height, Joshua began to cut at the inch thick base of the limb. Following several minutes of sawing while simultaneously checking for threats, the shaft came free.

His scanning had revealed a new plant even farther to the left of Hidey Hole. The persistent urge for action overrode his alarm at the descending gloom of evening. Joshua ran across the open expanse of gravel and lichen to the low bush with mahogany colored vines radiating out from underneath a golden mass of small round leaves. When a touch of the nearest vine with his newly acquired pole elicited no reaction, Joshua stepped up and sliced off approximately three feet of the vine. The foliage at the base of the bush rustled and his heart almost stopped at the piercing shriek that followed.

Jumping out from the bush's interior, a bird like creature hopped forward, its elongated neck stretched upward, sharp beak vibrating, head turning back and forth to allow golden eyes on each side to track Joshua's position. The creature came to an abrupt halt as it extended fingers of bone connected by a light blue membrane, exposing a brilliant red breast and orange inner wings that fluttered with rhythmic flaps of aggression in concert with the undulation of its cry. Joshua stopped its resumed advance with a panicky yell and jab of his pole. This did not, however, stop the Siren Swan from continuing its angry warble. Another frantic check for threats revealed Joshua's greatest fear.

A spiderviper had scampered from behind a nearby Nutblossom to investigate the disturbance. It skittered to a stop 10 yards away and flattened its belly against the ground, making it look more like a cockroach than a spider. The screeching came to an abrupt stop. Out of the corner of his eye, Joshua saw red disappear into blue and heard a rustle of leaves. He held himself completely still as the monster pivoted toward him with small rapid steps of its four feet, its hooked forelegs reaching forward with tentative grasps at the air, searching. *Oh please, oh please...*

Joshua stood riveted as the spiderviper stopped, facing toward him, and raised its belly from the ground. When its maw opened and the proboscis seemed to fill with fluid and extend directly at him, he knew it had locked onto him. He spun for Hidey Hole and heard a screeching whistle become lower in tone as time slowed. Joshua willed his muscles into action and the distinct clatter of scattering pebbles told him the spiderviper was giving chase. He flowed across the ground, every movement maximized to increase the speed of his stride. Halfway to safety, the sounds of pursuit changed and he turned his head back, almost stumbling at what he saw - the pursuing spiderviper had risen up high on his legs and was galloping like a horse. Turning forward, Joshua cut hard around the Ice Spike Tree, and his Bluebell came into view. He heard the spiderviper overshoot and slide by in a clatter of pebbles. Another glance showed the predator low to the ground, but scrabbling back up into a run. Turning forward and accelerating his stride for the final stretch to safety, Joshua was shocked for second time. *The Bluebell leaves are down! I can't get in!* He shifted the pole, butcher knife, and dangling vine to his left hand and slowed to lean down, snatch up a small stick, and lunge back to full speed in two long steps. As the stick spun toward the Bluebell, the louder clicking behind him signaled the spiderviper was gaining. *The leaves are up!! Faster!!!* Air roared in and out of his lungs, but he needed more. His muscles were becoming less responsive. At 10 feet out, the leaves began to redeploy downward. *NO!!!* Joshua forced every ounce of speed into the next four strides, launched himself feet first to slide under the descending needle-edged foliage, head tilting back to look behind, seeing the spiderviper's feet skid to a stop before *Uuummmph!!!!* His slide had ended in the nearby rock wall. Lungs still heaving, he scrambled to his knees and extended the pole in front of him, oblivious to the inadequacy of this defense.

Through the Bluebell leaves, Joshua watched the spiderviper bob and skitter back and forth, short whistles sounding its frustration. However, it did not try to break through the Bluebell barrier. Again breathing as quietly as possible through his wide open mouth, Joshua crouched lower as the creature backed away 10 feet and rose again to the full extent of its gangly legs. Its whistles stopped and it began a slow rotation, interrupted by pauses accompanied by long intakes of air, which were exhaled with a harder and shorter whoosh. On the second rotation, the spiderviper dropped back into a crouch and slunk off in a different direction. Joshua collapsed to the ground.

Darkness completed its descent as Joshua lay recovering, listening with mounting relief as the toots of the spiderviper became more distant in its search for less well defended prey. Joshua limped back behind Big Boulder, settled onto the folded blanket that covered the two duffel bags, eased his back to the wall, and looked out from underneath the hanging tarp through an easy early summer evening shower. He put aside the hard earned shaft and binding cord, knowing he had no energy to fashion a spear until the next day. He wondered if he would wake up in the middle of night throwing up from a delayed reaction to the Nuteggs or to find some as yet uncatalogued creature creeping up his leg. Such thoughts kept him awake a long while, listening to the different sounds of the nighttime jungle. Finally his exhaustion pulled him into a restless slumber despite the mysterious calls from the depths of The Swamp. Then…

Joshua's eyes snapped open in terror. Just as on previous nights, he had been frantically searching for his mother, smashing through the dense foliage among the inky shadows that were The Swamp at night. Out in the dark, alone, among the spidervipers. He searched the alcove *nothing* and then listened intently, but no sharper sounds broke through the monotonous slow wave of deep trilling that was The Swamp's normal undercurrent of sound. Joshua's breathing slowed. He tried to reason out the steps needed to fashion a spear, but fatigue relentlessly pulled his eyelids lower and his fading thoughts soon dissipated completely under the weight of his exhaustion.

The Deepest Cut

◄5►

The stench of death filled his sinuses. Joshua stood stock still, 30 feet into the first major water erosion gap in the city's foundation that he had discovered in his exploration to the south of Hidey Hole. He could not recall having ever smelled the aroma before, but he *knew* something around the hulking boulder before him was dead and decaying. The question remained *Is the thing that killed it still here too?*

Joshua adjusted his grip on the heavy spear he had crafted that morning. His ears strained to pick up any sound that deviated from what should normally be heard during a cool autumn mid-day rain. *Nothing. So* He stepped around the stone wall and was frozen by a surge of terror when he saw a spiderviper facing him!

Seconds later, Joshua exhaled with relief as he registered the grey sickly color of the skin on the legs and the deflated abdomen. A step closer intensified the smell of putrefaction, but he still needed to convince himself that spidervipers were vulnerable, that they too could die. His visual scan of the body halted at a darker scab partially covering a hole in the right side of the leathery connecting section behind the head. He looked up the ravine to the dilapidated buildings at the edge of New Cincinnati and calculated the distances. *I went north from the apartment to stash* Joshua's gaze returned to the round wound in the dead spiderviper. A sob escaped. *I got it, Mom. I killed the damned thing!* He sat with a thump on a nearby rock, laughing and crying, no longer aware of the stink of the rotting carcass.

When he finally wiped his face free of tears, Joshua noticed something black glistening in the slack lips around the mouth. He leaned forward through the renewed stench for a closer examination. *That's it. The fang. That's what killed my mother.* He knew what he wanted to do, but the thought of touching the rotting tongue brought a surge of acid to his throat. He swallowed, reached out to grasp the black fang, and pulled *For Mom.*

His scream echoed off the stone walls as he leapt back from a blanket of small red dots that swarmed out over the ashen skin of the proboscis. By the time his heart had slowed, most of the tiny ladybug like creatures had returned to the interior of the spiderviper. *No wonder it looks deflated.* Proceeding with extreme care, Joshua held the fang steady while he cut into the grey-green flesh just behind the slick black tooth, occasionally stopping and stepping back with a shiver to wait until any reappearing Rot Eaters had disappeared back into the mouth.

He deposited the fang into his slicker pocket as he eased away from the carcass. Joshua took a final last look at the creature that had killed his mother. Satisfied that it was truly dead and that he had killed it, he turned and headed back to Hidey Hole. He had set out that morning just before noon, intent on finding a path back into the city. While he had only made it one gulch away from his current refuge, it had led to a momentous discovery. *That's enough exploring for today.*

Joshua spent the rest of the day working on the fang. Scraping off the flesh around the base of the fang revealed the tooth underneath to be a bright white enamel instead of the iridescent onyx black surface on the exposed tapering part of the fang. Luckily, the white enamel section was more yielding than the exposed black part, and using the sharp tip of a paring knife, he drilled a hole through the base. Using the laces from his single pair of dress shoes *Why did I even bring these anyway?* he hung the fang around his neck. Because the fang only had a slight downward curve, the tip did not poke his chest. The feel of it against his skin bolstered his confidence, renewing his determination to venture away from Hidey Hole to find an escape from The Swamp.

Over the next week, Joshua continued exploring his immediate surroundings. He found several other edible plants. Orange Taters were round onion sized tubers found under what turned out to be *very bitter* violet blooms. They had a crisp radish consistency and oozed a sweet, bright orange syrup when cut. He also discovered large pods that contained hundreds of tiny black seeds that expanded ten times in volume when boiled, They had an earthy taste with undertones of coconut and ginger, and were *very* filling. Joshua was particularly pleased with his name for these - Night Puffs. However, having already eaten all he could find in the immediate area, the aching void in his stomach was a reminder of the limits of these successes.

The Deepest Cut

Joshua had not even considered trying to kill any of the swamp animals. First, the nearby looming Big Trees of The Swamp proper still imposed a pervasive atmosphere of menace. Even in the full light of day, the shadows constantly shifted under their canopies and seemed to be alive, waiting, warning that even the SlugBunnies might possess some unseen poisonous stinger, or claw, or *Who knows?* Second, even if he proved successful in bagging one of the creatures, Joshua was not certain he could actually eat real meat. After all, he had grown up on the homogenized lab creations that passed for food in New Cincinnati.

He had no problem in eating the Nuteggs, though. In fact, he always ate one before setting out to explore and took an extra with him on longer excursions. Their enhancement of his alertness and speed of thinking made him feel much safer while he explored in the openness of the burn zone over the four hours of midday.

While the supplement of native foodstuffs had extended his window of survivability, Joshua used the original two-week deadline as an impetus to take the first step in his plan of escape. He intended to proceed in short relocating hops to other water eroded recesses in the cliffs of New Cincinnati's foundation.

That day, he found a defensible alcove about a quarter mile to the north of Hidey Hole. The entrance did not have a protective Bluebell, but there were several other large plants and Joshua figured he could stretch one of his tarps across the entrance as an additional barrier. By putting his arms through the handles of the big duffel and carrying it like a pack, he made it in one trip, holding the smaller duffel in front of him. He kept his homemade spear resting on top of the small duffel for ready access and made frequent stops when his strength gave out. Finally, his weary arms dropped the heavy bags for the last time of the journey. *OK. Here we are at our new home, Hidey Hole #2.*

After setting up camp, his eyes fell on the erected tarp across the opening and his plan suddenly seemed foolish. *A spiderviper could just knock that down without even trying. Then I'd be trapped in here!* Fully aware of the gathering night, he struggled to slow his breathing, *Well, it's better than being out in the open, and I can't just live the rest of my life in*

the first Hidey Hole. There is *no other choice.*
 Still, it was a long night with very little sleep.

The Deepest Cut

◀6▶

Joshua squatted with his back to the northern edge of New Cincinnati, facing the rising slope of Mount Lipsig. Out on a scouting trip to find Hidey Hole #4, he was watching a dark elongated opening about seven feet under the edge of the Permacrete foundation for the ore train monorails. Water emerged from the right side of the opening and split into two streams, one cascading down in a brief series of drops and the other, farther to the right, dropping in a single long stream to rumble into a large pool of water at the foot of the mountain. The pond rested on a somewhat elevated plateau that was free of large vegetation, extending to the east away from New Cincinnati. It fed a stream that worked its way down a lichen covered slope before angling into The Swamp. The cave was just under where the monorail transitioned from the ground onto elevated Permacrete pillars, beginning its way up into the mists, from the refinery at the foot of the mountain to the mining operations high above.

Joshua observed all of this through bleary eyes from within a loose cluster of Rosebushes, which had no blossoms, but he had so named because of the deep rose color of the bark. He looked out across a deep depression of quasi-open bush land and contemplated the dark opening underneath the monorail about 200 yards away. "Security" for the last two Hidey Holes had simply been a combination of one of the tarps set up across the entrance and his best efforts to be silent, especially once night had fallen. This meant even less sleep than usual. *I can't remember what it's like to actually feel good when I wake up in the morning.* Thus far, his assumption that spidervipers located prey primarily by sound rather than sight had not been disproven, but *Maybe I've just been lucky.*

Joshua allowed his gritty eyelids to close for a moment of rest and then, from his vantage point 40 feet above the bottom of the narrow valley, he tried to pick out a possible path down the sharp slope and through the tall bushes. He had just decided upon his course when he discovered the source of a noise he had been hearing since Hidey Hole #3. It had come at infrequent but somewhat regular times throughout the day and the night.

Although he had earlier recognized the sound as mechanical, he could now specifically attach it to the banging of the couplings from the long line of ore cars rattling down the elevated track. He also sensed a low frequency humming from the activated electromagnetic rail. *Never been close enough to hear that before.*

Joshua puffed out a frustrated sigh of indecision. He had just passed a break in the city foundation that had ended in an extended scree pile. It had not offered a place to set up camp, but the long slope of boulders and stones might provide access to the city. The waning afternoon had prevented him from climbing it to find out. Now he needed to decide whether to continue forward, looking for a new crease in the city foundation, or head back and stay another night at Hole #4. He eyed the dark spot under the monorail. *Sure would be nice to have a safer place to set up camp*, but Joshua also realized such a highly visible hole might look appealing as a den to any number of creatures in The Swamp. *OK, so it's back to Hole #4. But that means I still have some daylight to burn.* He settled down to watch for a bit.

Less than twenty minutes later, a Swamp Fox emerged from the bushes and seemed to contemplate the opening. The moderately sized animal looked like a cross between a toad and a turtle without a shell, except for its two pointed leathery ears and elongated snout. Having never seen it feeding, Joshua had no idea whether it was a herbivore or a carnivore. The large brown beak at the end of its long snout looked to be equally effective in shredding vegetation or flesh. It had started up the hillside when an empty ore train arrived to begin its climb back to the mines. Turning to face the approaching train, The Swamp Fox squatted down, ears flattened back against its head, mouth open with an extended long red tongue mottled on top with black dots, and released a loud guttural hiss. *Ahh, another sound identified!* The humming from the electromag rail swelled in intensity and the Swamp Fox began bobbing up and down off the ground while taking a series of backwards steps. Finally, as the train accelerated past the cave, the Swamp Fox broke and turned to scurry back into the underbrush with a quick agility that surprised Joshua. He decided it would not be wise to antagonize a Swamp Fox, especially with that beak.

The Deepest Cut

So it appeared the Swamp Fox found something aversive about the sound or vibration produced by the ore train. If that happened to be true for the other swamp creatures, the cave might be uninhabited. Joshua took in the gathering gloom and decided *Time to go. But I'll check it tomorrow.*

As dawn broke the following morning, Joshua left Hidey Hole #4 to retrace his path to the Rosebushes. He carried his adjustable lantern configured for a directional beam. Once he had arrived, he stood looking out over *Bushland,* and selected a path to the cave that took full advantage of all available cover.

A careful descent into the valley revealed that "Bushland" was inaccurate. What had originally looked like "Bushes" from a distance turned out to be small trees two to three times his height. The narrow bore of the trunks was smooth except for an almost geometric diamond pattern of dimples. The source of the indentations was obvious from the placement of the branches farther up the tree, each extending straight out with no bifurcations, ending in a small globe of triple tipped leaves. He glanced at the ground around the *Stick Tree* to find it strewn with straight sticks of different lengths and thicknesses.

Continuing toward the bottom of the valley, Joshua was relieved to see a nearby Nutblossom bush, but confused as well, since it lacked its typical bushy foliage and seemed to be growing out of one of the Stick Trees. Deviating his path slightly for a better look, it became clear that the blossoms and Nutegg clusters were actually part of a vine, this one climbing up the tree. He realized he had never looked close enough at the bushes before, only assuming it had all been one plant. He grasped a Nutegg, pulling gently while pressing the stem sideways with his thumb. It released and Joshua popped the golden orb into his mouth before resuming his journey.

Reaching the foot of the mountain, he climbed a series of ledges to a plot of soil extending out five feet in front of the cave opening. Sinking to one knee near the waterfall, Joshua peered into the opening, but could detect nothing in the shadows. He leaned to the side and looked down at the large murky green pond 25 feet below, unsure whether there were sinuous dark shapes moving beneath the foam that spread out from where the dropping water pounded into the pool. He slipped over to the left of where the cave opened and strained to hear any noise above the muted roar of waterfall. Joshua directed the beam of light to a small area right inside the mouth of the cave and eased into its shadow, still listening intently. About seven feet back and to his right, water flowed out of a black opening a foot high and four feet across, sliding down over a short slope of stone into a long shallow pool, swirls of current rippling the surface before plunging over the edge. The rumble of the waterfall lessened as he took another step into the darkness, spear held before him, his moving circle of light chasing away the shadows. Allowing another moment for his eyes to adjust, he made out the sides of the outer cave and *Whoa! Low bridge!* Ducking a few inches under a ridge of stone glistening with condensation, he entered a larger cavern.

Joshua almost panicked. Shadows jumped and pounced as he tried to shine his light over the entire interior of the cave at the same time. *Stop! Just slow down and listen.* But he could only hear his own breathing, so he forced himself to systematically survey the area. First he directed the light to the deepest and darkest section of the cave, finding a solid rock wall standing 15 feet away across an open flat area. To his left, a flat shelf area rose up more than two feet off the cavern floor, extending back to create a six foot square elevated alcove. To his right, a stream of gurgling water flowed out of the back of the cave, sliding down in a gradual three foot drop to a deep pool of eddying clear water that stretched five feet across to the far side of the cave. Only when he had assured himself that no spiderviper lurked in the shadows did he take in a deep breath and was struck by the relative coolness of the air.

Joshua moved deeper for a closer examination. There were no droppings anywhere on the cave floor or any organic materials to suggest a nest, reinforcing his observation that none of the swamp denizens cared for the periodic passing of the ore trains. Finally, he approached the pool. The light beam easily illuminated the shimmering rock below the streaming crystalline water. He knelt and pulled up a handful of the cool water to his mouth- *AAack!* He spit out the water that tasted as bad as he knew he must smell. Scrubbing his hands together under water, Joshua was gratified to see the resulting haze of grime being quickly pulled across the pool. His eyes followed the cloud of dirt that had accumulated over the past weeks as it crested the lip of the retaining rock, slid out the slot in the wall into another smaller outer basin, and then accelerated out over the edge of the falls. The next gulp of water glided down his throat and settled in a cool pool in his stomach, leaving a lingering sweet sensation on his tongue. *THAT is good!*

Stomach sloshing, he went and sat on the edge of the elevated alcove, contemplating the gentle gleams that marked the eddies flowing under the surface of the clear pool before him. His primary goal for the past *almost four!* weeks had been to get back into New Cincinnati. *I haven't found a way in, but now, at least, I have a safe place to stay.* Joshua looked back out through the opening of the cave at the distant Swamp.

I have a new home.

"I don't know."

Joshua tried to look innocent, but he was not practiced in the ways of deception. As the shopkeeper's eyebrow rose, so did his sense of frustration. *I spent 15 minutes agonizing over whether I should spend $8 on this and now she doesn't want to sell it to me?* He put his hand back over the $20 UD note.

"OK. I'll just tell my Mom you said you had to have a note." His eyes became wet at the thought of his Mom. "I   I don't care. I don't really like my cousin that much anyway."

Like the stickball game so long ago, he did nothing to hide the tears. Her eyes were skeptical when she looked up from the money, but they then took on a quizzical expression. "He's a bully," Joshua elaborated. He eased the note back,   farther,   farther,   a tear dropped and rolled off his chin to splash next to the retreating bill.

"Wait!   All right.   But I want your *word* that your mother approves of this purchase." The heavy set woman leaned forward in earnest.

The warm glow formed just behind his shoulder. Joshua looked the merchant in the eye and said with conviction, "Yes. She approves."

He stepped out of the shop with the inflatable mattress in his duffel, along with the matching sheet set she had thrown in for an extra quarter, somewhat amazed that *Misty eyes paid off again.* The duffel also held a large box of biodegradable laundry soap, a sewing kit, some dress shoe laces, and a variety of green and red die packets. He also had a full assortment of meat cubes in his collapsible cooler. The real prize, however, was the two bottles of non-fragrant body wash. It had taken most of the trip to find those. *Everyone wants to smell froo-froo!* Joshua knew sound was a major attractant in The Swamp, but was still uncertain about smell. He *had* liked the smell of some of the soaps, but *I'm not taking any chances when it comes to spidervipers. Maybe some of those holes in the face are for smelling instead of hearing.* The duffel also contained a bundle of some of the cleaner clothes he had scavenged from impromptu dumping areas he had found in the dark motorways. He would add them to his growing collection back at Sweetwater Sanctuary. *Keep getting better at this naming thing.* He had even broken the $20 bill with the purchase of the mattress. The smaller denominations would attract less notice. The only bad news for the outing was that his bankroll now stood at $25.36.

He stood and looked down the scree pile with the loaded bag on his back. It had taken so long to find *that stupid soap* that dusk had almost advanced to the end of its relentless march toward night. So, it was either hurry and break a leg when he slipped on a wet stone or get eaten by a swamp nasty as he tried to cross Bushland in the dark. However, as Joshua picked his way down the scree pile of different sized boulders, he noticed that even when rocks shifted under his weight without warning or his shoes occasionally lost their grip on a rain smoothed slick surface, he adjusted without even coming close to losing his balance. *All that stickball practice paying off.* His descent accelerated along with his confidence.

Made it! He squished onto the lichen covered earth with relief and quickly retrieved his spear from beside a large boulder. Choosing a path nearer to the monorail track, Joshua was rewarded when an ore train passed by on its way to the refinery. He splashed his way through the Stick Trees, confident that the train had scared away all of the swamp life in the vicinity. Moments later, he ducked under Headbanger, welcomed home by his lantern's warm glow. After discovering that the scree pile provided access to New Cincinnati, it had taken a week to work through the abandoned motorways, marking the best dumps for rummaging and where the buildings with security cameras began to show up. Only then had he found the courage to dress up in his nicest outfit and go shopping.

Turning up the lamp, he organized his newly acquired possessions. Then he sorted through the pile of scavenged rags he had been sleeping on and folded the thicker pieces of cloth to fit into the depressions in the alcove, creating a relatively level surface. He unrolled the mattress and flipped the internal air pump's switch. As the mattress filled, he returned the cooler to its place next to the cooking station before turning to the large pile of discarded clothing in the far corner of the cave. He had just finished sorting out the rags made of the lightest fabric when a chime sounded from the mattress. He climbed on. *Ahhh. Nice and level... but too soft.* Rolling off, he checked a small flexible clear panel next to the switch. The illuminated blue 50 went up as his finger slid up the green vertical bar on the right side of the panel. After some experimentation, he left it at 72 and put on the sheets. *THIS was worth the money!*

Joshua put his Clingers in their place next to his polished dress shoes. The sight of the shiny black shoes brought forth an echo of his father's hearty laugh, a reaction to his son's look of horror at the suggestion that he spit on his Dad's shoes. With his father's urging, he finally spit, and then they had laughed, and spit, and laughed until Joshua had run out of saliva. He smiled at the memory and stepped into the warmer water in the last pool before the waterfall, soap bottle in hand, and sat down to splash water over himself. Joshua stopped at the image of his Dad's stern face, a smile still in his eyes, as he explained that spitting was only allowed when they were polishing his shoes. *I almost forgot about that. I was ready to spit on everything!* He first washed his hair, then took off all of his clothes and vigorously rubbed them together with some laundry soap. When they were a sodden heap on the stone shore, he attacked the rest of his body. Joshua had intended to savor the feel of his clean body on cool sheets, but he was asleep before he had fully stretched out.

It was a gentle awakening. The morning light had suffused through the entrance and whispered a soft call to his subconscious. For the first time since falling into The Swamp, Joshua awoke feeling as if he had truly rested. It felt as if he had not moved the entire night. Even his joints were loose, needing a satisfying full body stretch to snug them back into place. He luxuriated in the feel of the mattress beneath the sheets. Finally, he rose and made breakfast before setting about his next big project.

At an assortment of containers stacked in a corner of the cave, he selected a medium sized cube made of thick, but still slightly flexible, opaque white plastic. Since all of the containers had come to Cypress Grove as space cargo, they were all either cubes or rectangular boxes that could be assembled into a larger cube. This was a consequence of the Leviathan Disaster of 2126, when ship designers decided that the capacity of the Faster Than Light transfer process was unlimited and made a mammoth increase in the scope of ship design. They discovered their miscalculation when less than a third of the remnants of the super-sized cargo vessel, Leviathan, were found at the intended destination. Over the course of decades, ship builders had gradually increased the size of FTL space ships until they found the optimum size that balanced maximum cargo capacity within allowable structural stress. To squeeze every possible bit of merchandise into the ships and thereby maximize profits, all FTL merchant vessel cargo holds were either cubes or rectangles, which were also cheaper to design and build than ships with curves. The American government had agreed to adopt the metric sizing of containers in order to encourage Intersector trade with the European territories, but stubborn American Cargomasters insisted on referring to the major subdivisions of the standard meter cube in fractions. Hence, 333 centimeter cubes were a "one third" and the 667 centimeter square meat containers were "two thirds" cubes.

In any case, Joshua found the two thirds cubes to be the most plentiful and the most versatile. One of these he had repurposed as a drinking water basin. Placed just under one of the larger rivulets emanating from the far wall of the cavern, a v carved into the lip permitted overflow into the pool while the container was constantly being replenished with the sweetwater. For his current project, though, he picked up a "one third" cube, dipped it into the pool, filling it a quarter full, and added the brightest of green die packets. Selecting one of the pieces of light fabric he had separated earlier, he pressed it down into the emerald liquid with a stick and left it to saturate. He repeated this process until the die was used up, spreading the green fabric scraps onto various rock surfaces to dry. *That'll take a while. OK, I'm going to need the whole week to get all of the colors. Better find something else to do in the meantime.*

In preparation for an exploring excursion, he walked out to the Porch, as he now thought of the entrance area outside of Headbanger, and retrieved one of the remaining Nuteggs from a prior harvesting trip. It stopped halfway to his mouth, Joshua noticing a spot of green. The orb also felt smaller and harder than usual. Closer examination revealed a small green sprout had pushed out of the end of the Nutegg. Joshua looked at the ground in front of the entrance to Sanctuary *I wonder.* He dug a hole in the soil and planted the Nutegg. *Let's see what happens.*

Over the next two weeks, Joshua came to know every foot of Bushland and had even penetrated a few strides into The Swamp proper. But then Joshua now knew The Swamp was not really a swamp. Based upon his GlobalNet research, it should actually be called The Lowland Evergreen Broadleaf Rain Forest. *But that doesn't have the same snap, somehow.* The GlobalNet page referenced the Pacific Northwest of the United States as an example, but there were differences. First, temperatures did not fluctuate as much in this area of Cypress Grove, with highs in the summer rarely exceeding 90 degrees and only dropping into the low-60s during the winter months. Also, temperatures only differed by about 15 degrees between day and night. Another difference was that the omnipresent cloud cover produced rain virtually every day, sometimes quite hard, but rarely for very long. Joshua had no idea where all of the water went, but the loam drained the water with great efficiency and the ground just did not become waterlogged. Not that the massive trees that formed the face of The Swamp needed a real swamp to be intimidating. They were eight feet wide at their base and soared 75 feet into the air, their canopies melding together to cast the forest into a permanent ominous shadow. Worse, the stronger breezes at canopy level kept shifting the beams of light that broke through the leafy ceiling, causing shadows to come alive in the underbrush. *There's plenty of good stuff to find in Bushland anyway.*

And there was. Although he had seen an occasional Ice Spike tree, almost all of the Bushland forest consisted of Stick Trees. Joshua had been startled by the weight of the first stick he had retrieved from the layer of sticks surrounding a tree and he sported a bar shaped bruise above his knee several days after his failed attempt to break it in two. *I hereby and forevermore dub you the Ironwood Tree.* Not exactly sure how he might put the Ironwood to use, he had nonetheless formed piles of assorted sizes of the sticks in the back corner of Sanctuary.

While Nutblossom vines were scattered throughout Bushland, Droopers were the predominate vine, weaving up approximately one quarter of the Ironwood forest. The vine spiraled out along the Ironwood branches until it took a final turn and "drooped" six to 12 inches, with a large green bulb dangling from its tip. The wrapping leaves peeled back at the bottom of the bulb to allow a group of hanging shoots to descend almost to the ground, where small red buds formed, the lowest of which opened into crimson flowers with butter colored interiors. Joshua had to lay flat to see the small beetle-like creatures with iridescent purple shells going in and out of the blooms. *OOow!* The back of his hand had burned and a quick glance revealed one of the purple beetles to be the source of his pain. Joshua virtually levitated from the ground, knocking the attacker from his hand and then frantically brushing away the rest of the Fire Beetles off his clothes as he backed away.

After regaining his composure, Joshua had circled back in, constantly checking the ground at his feet for moving purple dots. He eventually discovered a single hole in the debris pile of Ironwood branches and Drooper pods with a heavy traffic of entering and exiting Fire Beetles. *Definitely need to avoid that!* Going to the opposite side of the tree, he found what he had been looking for – a Drooper pod that had fallen along with an outgrown Ironwood branch, devoid of blooms to attract Fire Beetles, but with still pliable shoots. Pulling it away and repeatedly giving it an energetic shake to dislodge any possible Fire Beetles, he harvested the shoots. A loose idea came together and he set about gathering more willow-like Drooper shoots from other trees, as well as some very thin branches from seedling Ironwood trees.

Having deposited his bounty on the Porch, he grabbed his sheet and climbed up above the waterfall to Lookout Perch, where the wireless reception proved sufficient to allow him to download video files off GlobalNet without taking the sheet out of the case. He soon had a tutorial on how to weave a wicker basket using the Stake and Strand method. The project ended up taking several days since he had to wait for some of the shoots to dry sufficiently to create cords of stiff pliability. The depth of his satisfaction surprised Joshua as he went out with his new wicker basket to gather Nuteggs. *It's not a writing desk, but   it gets the job done.*

Placing the basket on the Porch with a week's supply of 14 Nuteggs, Joshua turned to gaze out over Bushland through a cool light rain. He had to look past a lattice of lashed Ironwood sticks that had a thin Nutblossom vine weaving its way up at the bottom. It was late morning and a war of competing emotions welled up as he pushed back the wet hood of his slicker. There were still times when he could feel her standing just out of reach, observing, radiating concern or approval, or satisfaction with his accomplishments, but no longer speaking to him. *It's safe here, but it's lonely. I miss talking with Mom. I miss her laugh.* Tears now came without the desperate, forlorn bouts of sobbing.

Joshua finally let himself think about the trip into the city almost three weeks ago. Getting back into New Cincinnati had been his primary goal since his fall into The Swamp. *And yet* when it had at last taken place, when he had pulled himself back up onto the asphalt motorway for the first time, there had been no elation, no sense of coming home. He had been just as alert for danger in the dank motorways as when he walked a path through the place that every other human on Cypress Grove would consider a death sentence. In fact, the first humans he had seen were other children, scrounging through the numerous impromptu refuse dumps on the motorways under the northern part of New Cincinnati. Luckily, the caution that had become habitual while in The Swamp asserted itself and squashed his desire to make contact. While still observing from the shadows, Joshua watched two teens brutally beat a boy his age for trying to hide half a bag of peanuts. The larger of the teens distributed some of the booty to his enforcer, but ignored the smaller children who occupied the edges of the group. When they moved to the next pile of trash, the victim whimpered, but then limped after the gang of feral children. The lesson was clear to Joshua: avoid contact.

He recalled how his gut had clinched while he stood in the gloom, imagining himself sitting under a tarp or in a motorway corner, constantly vigilant, frequently moving to avoid the police and the roving gangs of children. With a shiver, he was back in Sanctuary, astonished to realize he now felt more anxiety about being in the city than in The Swamp. *I'm alone. Either place, I am alone.* Joshua struggled to force back the same scary, crazy darkness that had almost taken over when he had found his mother. *The Gilley suit. I gotta make a mannequin for the Gilley suit.*

The Deepest Cut

He went out to gather longer Ironwood sticks and more green Drooper vines. It took the rest of the day to weave together sticks to form a wicker barrel with attached tubes for arms and several looped rods at eye level for the hood to go over. He did not finish until well into the night and when he lay down on his firm mattress, he immediately fell into a deep sleep.

The next morning he organized all of the dyed cloth. Starting with a greyish green, Joshua draped each shoulder and then placed a large dark red swath to create a hood. He used a slip stitch to join the fabric and did not care about the unevenness of his stitches or how the cloth gathered. *The rougher it looks, the better.* He did not want to augment the Gilley suit with natural foliage, as snipers traditionally did, too fearful of running into another Siren Swan when trying to collect leaves and branches. Selecting the darker neutral greens and reds he had created by double dying, he then cut out oblong pieces with uneven edges and sewed them end to end until they reached the stone floor. These strands were tacked together with overlying rectangles of the brighter greens until reaching waist level, where the elements hung free, as they did over the arms, bringing to mind his next mission. *I'll need to keep those free.* And to get what he needed for *that*, he would have to go much deeper into The Swamp.

In among

the Big Trees.

◄8►

Joshua found it almost impossible not to make gagging noises in reaction to the odor radiating from the yellow Stink Blossoms beside him. He did it, though, desperate not to further agitate the largest spiderviper he had ever seen, skittering back and forth just 20 feet in front of him. The putrid smell seemed to be the only thing holding the spiderviper at bay. *All the more reason to stay close to the flowers.* He pulled his eyes from the prancing spiderviper to again regard the swirls in the murky water on both sides of him, black fins occasionally breaking the surface and causing splashes, which in turn further antagonized the spiderviper. He could not clearly see to what the fins were attached, but glimpses of malevolent red eyes that flashed when sinuous heads broke the surface dispelled all thoughts of stepping into the lake. *Ever.*

Joshua was unsure how long he had been on the small peninsula at the edge of the dark lake. It had taken several hours of careful creeping through the damp underbrush to reach the glade in front of him. Oddly, a surge of caution had swelled when he had gained the opportunity to see beyond one foot in front of his face. Having begun the foray afraid to be in the underbrush beneath the big trees, he had come to feel most safe while hidden there. When he had eased his head out from cover, Joshua's eye had been drawn to the edge of the open body of water and the splash of orange attached to rods of green. *Straight Reeds!* They were just like the much smaller bunch he had found at the edge of The Pond outside Sanctuary, only taller. This batch had been the length and thickness of Reeds he needed.

Despite his excitement, Joshua had thoroughly checked the open area between his position and the Reeds before pushing the foliage aside and easing out in a crouch. Even then he reached out with his ears, seeking any sound that did not fit. Hearing the constant drips of water making their separate ways down from the gently swaying top knots of foliage at the tops of the Big Trees, Joshua again scanned the glade. About ten yards to his right stood a very large bush with thick round drooping leaves and a thick single stalk rising out of the middle, adorned from the midpoint down with small purple buds. *That's a new one.* The extended effort to find the Reeds overrode Joshua's immediate curiosity and he had decided to examine the new bush on the way back out.

Delighted to find Reeds of a variety of lengths and diameters, Joshua had thought about several new uses to which he could put the flexible rods. Difficult to cut, the Reeds possessed the needed strength to be suitable for his purposes, but they also took more time to harvest. Once he had tied the bundle to his satchel and secured the prize over his shoulder, he looked up to discover a massive spiderviper had wandered into the glade. *It hasn't noticed me yet.* Backing away onto the peninsula, he had approached some star shaped flowers at the edge of the water. The yellow blooms had opened as he neared and the smell had hit him like a physical blow.

Joshua had staggered away, stopping with hands on knees, gagging, struggling to keep down the late lunch eaten less than an hour before. He looked up through his eyebrows to see the huge spiderviper headed toward him in response to the sound of his retching. He froze, drool still dripping from his open mouth, forcing his breaths to be slow and steady, silent, waiting. *Still coming...right toward me* He had lifted his spear, on the verge of throwing it and making a break for the jungle, when the spiderviper had stopped, huffing repeatedly through air slits at the front of its large abdomen. It then began skittering back and forth, unable to penetrate the defensive barrier of the Stink Blossoms. *Standoff.*

So here he was, struggling not to vomit, facing an agitated spiderviper, with at least two *Water Dragons* blocking his only other escape route. *At least I answered the question of whether they can smell. Not that it'll do me any good if I don't get out of here.* He glanced behind at the sky over the lake, seeing the darkness gathering. It had already been late in the day when he had found the opening. *But no, I had to be Capt. Jungle Ninja. Well, pride comes before the fall, as Dad used to say.* Joshua had learned a great deal of patience in the last few weeks, usually taking his time to wait and watch before proceeding. He believed such precautions had saved his life on a number of occasions. *And the one time I forget, I get sopped.*

He could not wait until nightfall. Having rarely seen spidervipers except at dawn and dusk, he believed they were nocturnal predators, but the gloom of the forest must have extended its hunting time to late afternoon. Also, Joshua was not sure, but it seemed that the intensity of the repulsive odor was lessening. A quick check confirmed his fear – the huge spiderviper was inching closer. *I have to do something **now**.* Joshua tried to relocate where he had emerged from the underbrush, deciding he had come out just to the right of the large plant with round leaves and purple buds *It wasn't that close, though, was it? No time for that, stupid!*

Afraid he would lose his nerve, Joshua did not allow himself to think further about his choice, and looked down to locate a round, palm sized stone. The spiderviper's huffing slowed even more as it edged closer. Chosing a bush to the left of the plant with purple buds as being close enough to draw away the spiderviper, but not too far for it to ignore, he heaved the stone. It smacked into a large Fantail leaf. The spiderviper spun around and as soon as its back was completely turned, Joshua began sprinting for the edge of the clearing.

Time did not slow until the spiderviper pivoted away from the distraction and began galloping toward Joshua. When its maw spread and the fang zipped out toward him, Joshua brought his spear around to intercept the uncoiling snake-like appendage while willing his stride to lengthen. *I'm not going to make it.* The blade was not going to get in front of the proboscis *God! I'm so close* a flash of green in concert with an AAUuuggghh sound shocked him out of slowtime so suddenly, he fell to the ground, rolling once before sliding to a stop.

Joshua stared back in awe at the large green spike that had slammed into the spiderviper from above, pinning it to the ground. He could not quite comprehend what he was seeing until the spiderviper was lifted up, impaled on the stalk, legs wiggling feebly, to be brought down to the quivering eager green "leaves" of the purple bud plant. *So it HAD moved!*

Not wanting to test the extent of his savior's appetite, Joshua gathered his possessions with care and slipped into the nearby bushes. *So, you're not the King of the Jungle after all.* Joshua's exhilaration at having escaped the spiderviper was short lived. He shuddered with the realization that had the new "plant" been just a few feet closer, he might have gone to examine it before harvesting the Reeds. He knew he would forever be vigilant for the color purple and vowed never to get within ten feet of an Imposter Plant.

Now, if he could just pull off what he intended to do with the hard won Straight Reeds.

◀9▶

Joshua examined the sizzling SlugBunny meat. His simple descriptive names usually stuck, but he decided he really needed to change this one if he wanted to use it as a food source. And he had done it with the Ironwood trees. *OK, let's see   SwampBunny   no, still too cute.   Ahh, SwampRabbit should work.* He considered delaying the moment of truth by cooking it some more, but he had already scorched one side of the hind quarter. Bringing it closer to slice off the blackened edge, Joshua realized his mouth was watering at the smell. *JUST DO IT!* The bite filled his mouth with juices; the sage and salt and pepper mingled with an intense meat flavor as he chewed. It was… *SOooo Good! Dad! You were right!*

Joshua sat back in his wicker chair in front of the fire at the back of Sanctuary. He savored the flavors of the meat and spices, the warmth of food in his mouth, the feel of the swallow delivering sustenance to an eager, waiting stomach. He opened his mouth wider for an even bigger bite, chomping down with vigor   OOOWW!! His teeth had hit something hard! Joshua examined the bite marks before trying a smaller bite and pulling away a hunk of meat. He stopped mid-chew at the sight of the exposed bone. The image of his mother's leg flashed into his mind, but before he could hurl the roasted SwampRabbit into the fire, a warm presence formed behind him. The image of her leg faded with the warmth behind him, leaving the smells of the roasted meat and the lingering tastes in his mouth. Joshua found he could take another bite. He began working around the bones. *It's weird, but*   he no longer felt any revulsion.

While he devoured the remaining meat, Joshua tried to recall his father's stories of having grown up on a frontier planet. David Vernon had been proud of his shooting skill, something he had learned from hunting on Teton. His family had been among the original settlers to sign on with the mining company from Wyoming that had sponsored the colony. He and his older brothers had supplemented the larder through hunting, one of the more enjoyable tasks among the many chores they had to do. They became so successful at selling native meat and furs that his oldest brother quit mining and the family flourished at their Trading Post. Joshua recalled his father's wistful tone of regret that they had not made that decision sooner, since it might have saved his grandfather from dying in the mines. The business proved self-sustaining, but Teton was still in its Generation One phase. The limited population constrained business expansion. There were already two married brothers with young mouths to feed by the time David turned 18. His excellent shooting on the qualifying range helped him land a coveted slot at the Space Merchant Marine Academy.

While most of these stories had been retold by his mother, Joshua could remember his father's baritone voice saying, "Son, even though your Mom can make old shoe leather taste like heaven, there is nothing quite like biting into a choice cut of meat slow roasted over a campfire." *Well, Dad, the only problem was I didn't know how to transform a dead carcass into meat. You never talked about **that***. Joshua had watched three different pVids on how to dress out game before he had taken a shot at cleaning the SwampRabbit. The Gilley suit had allowed him to stalk close enough to successfully use the bow and arrows he had created from the hard earned Reeds. *And only on my fifth try no less!*

Placing another leg bone on the growing pile, Joshua attacked the main body of the carcass. As he sunk his teeth into a thick part of the back, he had a sudden insight about his father's phrase "choice cut of meat." This bite was less chewy and juicier, with a milder flavor. The idea that different parts of the animal could taste differently was a revelation. He took his time eating the rest of the meat, exploring the varying textures and flavors with relish.

His meal finished, his fingers licked clean, and his belly actually satisfied, Joshua leaned back and watched the smoke gather and eventually exit Sanctuary above the waterfall. The low white ceiling of smoke eddied and flowed sideways before it moved up and out, mirroring the clear liquid currents pouring forth down below. *I'd be coughing if I stood up.* There were some swirls in the smoke up where the water entered at the top of the cave. *Maybe those holes not only let water in, but also let air out.* Gauging the distances, he remembered that one of the dumping spots had included several lengths of discarded drainage pipe. *I know exactly where to find the perfect piece.*

The following morning, Joshua continued his exploration around the northern edge of the city foundation, hoping to find other viable access points. *Having more options is always better.* He came upon a narrow crevice, and after a climb two thirds up the foundation, found a wider spot where a massive horizontal slab created a dead end. His gaze followed a stream of falling water up to the source of the erosion, a rusty drain pipe four feet over his head. *If I could reach that, it's only another seven or so feet to the motorway.* He could find no workable sequence of hand holds on either side of the rock chute. To the left, he saw a ledge five feet up deep enough to stand on. *From there I could easily jump the gap up to the pipe.* An idea formed as he spotted a six-inch outcropping about two and a half feet up from the slab. After a few practice leaps, Joshua felt confident the outcropping would hold as a launch pad. He retreated several feet, shook out his hands, and then sprinted at the outcropping. His foot hit perfectly and he turned to launch to the ledge, but he overshot, his hands slapping the wall before he slid painfully back down the big slab.

Joshua stepped back, rubbing an abrasion on his left elbow, and reconsidered. *I have to commit to the whole thing.* He mentally rehearsed the sequence, seeing himself push off and up from the outcropping, place his toes on the ledge of the far wall, and then launch up and back across to grab the drain pipe. Finally, he felt prepared and exploded toward the wall.

Joshua was somewhat surprised to find himself hanging onto the pipe with his feet splayed on either side. Only then did he realize that slowtime had not kicked in. Despite its rusty appearance, the drainpipe was solidly attached to the wall and he had no trouble pulling himself up the rest of the way to the motorway level. However, despite there being no fence to protect the end of the road, the motorway still ended over four feet from where he hung on the pipe.

Joshua considered the distance and then looked down between his legs to the stream of water splashing on the stone floor 15 feet below. *Not so good.* The only other choice was to go up another 20 feet to the warehouse roof top. Two minutes later Joshua could *feel* the open space behind his back and his brain automatically did the math. *35 feet down.* He mentally clamped down on that thought and instead focused on getting over the roof wall above him. He grabbed the expanded opening at the top of the drain pipe where water gushed through a rectangular hole at roof level, but quickly let go when the metal began to bend. The muscles in his shoulders started to burn and his breath became more labored as he considered his options. As far as he could determine, the only alternative to sliding back down would be an all or none proposition. Joshua's weakening fingers made it clear he needed to act on one choice or the other... *NOW!* He threw his left hand into the opening, grasped the top edge, switched his left foot to the side of the pipe and pushed off, throwing himself up sideways, grabbed with his right hand and hooked his leg over the roof wall edge. The view down was shocking and fear surged with enough strength to heave his body over the wall. He splashed onto his back into the streaming water and rolled twice up the slanted roof to rest with his right cheek against the cool slick surface, grateful he could feel the large raindrops slapping the side of his face. When he had recovered, he went to the edge to look down over the wall. *I'm going to do **that** every time? Don't think so!*

He turned to discover that the warehouse roof formed something of a low pyramid, shedding water in four directions from the peak in the middle. A short jog to the apex provided an unimpeded view of the surrounding roofs, most belonging to larger structures of other warehouses and abandoned refining operations. Almost universally, the larger structures had the pyramid design, with smaller extensions and secondary wings using a single slant to divert rainfall. There were a variety of materials covering the different roofs in the immediate vicinity. Some were created by seamed sheets of plastic, like the one he stood on. Others appeared to be a solid coating, usually darker, occasionally with the sparkle of some other water shedding additive.

Joshua lifted his eyes from the roofs themselves and felt a flood of exhilaration. Fading into the rain, ridge upon ridge of building tops stretched into the distance. They were mostly of the same height, with occasional structures lifting another 10 feet in elevation. Bands of golden glow stretched out in a golden lattice, the lines becoming a brighter whitish blue in the distance, marking the more frequent and expensive halogen streetlights used in the newer suburbs. Joshua blinked when a large section of the light maze to the far right disappeared, replaced by the rhythmic flashing of a multitude of colors. *The laser light show at Sky Creek Mall!* He could make out diffuse glows even farther away, but the rain obscured the details. He made another 360 scan of his immediate surroundings. No one was in sight. His personal kingdom lay spread out before him.

Joshua spent the day exploring his new domain, beginning in the industrial northern section of New Cincinnati. Since most of the buildings in NorthPoint had been built in the early days of the colony, the lack of forethought often resulted in an odd arrangement of buildings. There were many crevices between closely constructed buildings, narrow passageways that typically exited the other side, but sometimes came to an abrupt dead end. The three foot gaps were easy for Joshua to leap across. Even with the wider alleyways, he almost always found connecting covered walkways that allowed access to the next block of structures. If not, buildings were also connected via "drain trees," large central pipes fed by clusters of roof drains from nearby buildings. These central drains ran down through both the pedway and motorway, with cylindrical gratings protecting the openings. Joshua discovered these gratings all had doors, most of which were not locked, at least in the northern section of the city.

Joshua's elation in roaming the empty rooftop expanse did not fade as the day wore on and he was astonished at how much "ground" he could cover when not having to contend with traffic. Farther to the south, among the more affluent communities, there were fewer industrial "drain trees," but more rain arches to facilitate street crossings. After all, rich people did not like getting caught in the open during intermittent downpours. In the course of his explorations, he also learned that tarpaper surfaces were only a touch less slick than the melted together plastic sheets, while the painted on solid black sealant with sparkles, more common in the affluent south, provided the best footing. Evening had crept close when Joshua remembered his original mission from that morning. He headed back north and descended into the motorways.

The Deepest Cut

Dawn arrived the following day and revealed several lengths of scavenged drain pipe leaning against the back wall. Joshua worked the rest of the day hauling stones and filling three cube containers with a powdery substance scraped from a vein in the city foundation. Taking numerous stops to catch his breath, Joshua manhandled two large base rocks into place. Their flat tops were almost the same height and they formed shelves with a gap that allowed his pans to be placed directly over the fire. His GlobalNet research had provided schematics of fireplaces, hearths, and wood fired pizza ovens. Using the body of his mannequin as a temporary support, he created a keystone arch in the front of the dome of reeds he had lashed together over the flat heating stones. Joshua covered the reed dome with pieces of screening cut from a broken door. Mixing the stone powder with ashes and water created a mud to mortar small flat rocks onto the dome. The two lengths of the drain pipe acted as a chimney, with the curved sections inserted into the holes above where the water entered the cave.

It was late at night when Joshua finally sat back in his chair, exhausted. His sense of satisfaction intensified when the warm presence coalesced right beside him. Together, they watched tongues of flame cast out flickers of light onto the cavern floor through the arched opening of the oven.

It's the Homehearth. For you, Mom.

◀10▶

His eyes opened   blinked twice   closed   then opened again   before
finally focusing on a dancing light jumping along a ribbon of folded
movement, racing up and out of his field of vision. As a low rumble
stepped forward into his awareness, Joshua realized it had been there all
along, but had just now been kind enough to answer his unarticulated
question *Where is it going?* To the waterfall, of course. He blinked once
more   stretching open his eyes much wider   and extending his depth of
vision to the far wall of the cave, where light from behind carved a jagged
diagonal line down to the rushing water. *I'm   in   Sanctuary. But   it
it   is   so hard   to think.*

He lay with a deadness throughout his body, but particularly on the
right side of his face. He did not feel any pain; his cheek was too dead for
that,   it was more   a heavy pressure. He wanted to move, but   *I   don't
think   I   can*   Focusing only on his left hand, which was extended out
behind him, he became aware of the press of cool stone against his
knuckles. With monumental effort, Joshua WILLED his arm to contract
and pull his left hand forward across smooth stone to flop in front of his
face. Seeing the part he wanted to move made it easier   and he rotated his
palm onto the cavern floor. He pushed against a ridge of rock, forcing his
shoulder off the floor   before collapsing back down. NO! *I can   DO
this!!*   The next push, along with a meager twist of torso, lifted him over
to flop onto his back. Even though his legs were still crossed, the release of
pressure off his face was at first blissful and then torturous as pins prickled
deeply and without mercy. He let loose a yell of frustration and release. As
the intense prickling receded and feeling returned to his face, he tried to
think. Then   he remembered.

The Chapple! He had found the large, apple sized, bright red orbs
yesterday, hanging in clusters of two or three from a small, sparsely leaved
tree. *Well, mostly red.* Wherever the skin of the fruit was not yet red and
dry, it was shaded orange and covered with a wet sheen. Joshua had been
deep in the Big Trees at the time, surprised to find ripening fruit in the

middle of winter. Having successfully tested the red peel and underlying sweet juicy pink translucent flesh on his forearm, he had eaten several Chapples before discovering the third orb still had a small section of orange skin. Holding it by the long oval pit, he had thought, *"Oh well!"* before biting off the remaining fruit. It took two chews before the bitterness forced him to spit the wet mash out. Joshua spat as much as he could to clear the taste and then harvested all of the completely red Chapples before heading home.

The lightheadedness began before he had reached the half way point and soon after, stomach cramps literally staggered him. The basket of Chapples still lay somewhere out in Bushland, abandoned when pain had forced him to totally focus on making the climb to refuge. He made it into the cave before the acid lifted into his esophagus, but he did not make it past Headbanger before it all came up. Joshua vaguely recalled trying to wipe the vomit off the stone between heaving spells, hoping to wash away the smell to curb the wrenching of his stomach. It did not help. And the contractions would not stop. Soon he laid exhausted, trying to catch his breath before the next series of spasms. Finally the vomiting stopped and he could breathe. However, before he could drag himself to his bed, an intense pain formed at the base of his skull and Joshua could feel it spread down his spine and up around his brain. It had been incapacitating. He had tried to think of ways to kill himself, but the agony had not only been immobilizing, it had also prevented any coherent plan of action.

Seconds crept by as he laid in his fetal position at the edge of the passing stream. *I thought it would not end. That I **was** in Hell.* Then the presence came. In contrast to the blur of misery he had endured most of the night, Joshua recalled with startling clarity the warm pressing of a soothing and gentle hand on his back. He had held on to this sensation with a magnificent desperation, *anything* to hold the intense agony at bay.

Knowing what had happened brought orientation and some sense of normalcy, as well as renewed strength. Joshua rolled back to the exiting flow and slurped a handful of water. At first his stomach contracted, but before he could vomit again, the coolness spread, and with it, his stomach unclenched and expanded. With increasing energy, Joshua scooped up handfuls of water and slaked his thirst. It took several attempts to push himself into a sitting position against the wall. After weathering a wave of dizziness, he decided he could not walk to his bed. *Gotta crawl then.* The water slopped in his belly as he waddled forward on hands and knees, only to stop and look up at the mountain that was the sleeping ledge.

I know. Resolute! Right, Mom?

Joshua dropped his head and began laughing. Even the slightest of guffaws hurt, but he could not stop. He flopped down to his side and laughed through the torment until the tears squeezed out of the corners of his eyes. *Resolute! RESOLUTE! To climb less than three feet just so I can lay down again.* He rode out another laughing spell. Once he regained his wind, Joshua gathered himself, trying not to think of the word Resolute. Still snickering, he pulled his chest up halfway onto the mattress, where the fear of falling back to the cold stone floor in a heap helped suppress his giggles. He then fought and heaved and yelled until, *at last,* he rolled onto his bed. His last thought before losing awareness was *RestorAde.*

When he awoke late in the afternoon, Joshua had a brief moment of disorientation before lucidity flooded back into his mind, along with his last thought of – *RestorAde. Yep, Blue Raspberry.* Although she did not normally allow sodas or sweet drinks in the house, his mother had brought him a quart of RestorAde whenever he had been sick, acknowledging that the drink helped to restore his electrolyte balance. The more he thought about the sweet tart blue liquid, the greater the craving became. He sat up. When no hint of vertigo visited, he risked standing next to his bed. *So far, so good. But first things first.*

Fighting through several waves of nausea, Joshua finally completed a bath and put on his City Outfit. He sat on the bed for quite some time, taking tiny bites from his next to last energy bar. *Need to get some more of these.* He estimated one UD note would cover the energy bars and RestorAde, as well as the baking mix needed to put his oven to the test. *Oh, and black thread!* recalling that the Gilley suit had taken most of his sewing kit supply. Another UD in change jingled into his pocket.

Dinner finished and still in his stomach, Joshua headed for the scree access way.

The Deepest Cut

◀11▶

Wanting to avoid having to forge a note from his mother, Joshua eased into an all-purpose store in the industrial section on the far side of The Avenue. Three steps inside the door of Mom's Vital Supplies, a raspy male voice barked out.

"HEY! You!   Kid! Show ur money 'r beat it!"

The owner of the ultimatum was a lanky unshaven middle aged man with a drooping untrimmed mustache, loose wisps of hair waving from the mostly bald front half of his head, the rest pulled back into a short pony tail. Wanting to avoid confrontation, Joshua turned toward the door, but then spotted the blue containers through the glass doors of a bank of coolers in the back. He *really* wanted that RestorAde and the journey in had already sapped his stamina. Pulling the UD coin from his pocket, he went over to set it on the counter. At the sight of the money, the proprietor's glare was replaced by amazement, followed by a grunt. He leaned back in his chair and flipped a hand toward the aisles, granting permission to proceed.

Joshua went immediately to the coolers, grabbed three blue bottles of RestorAde, and returned to the counter, putting two bottles next to his dollar. He then opened the third and placed the cap beside the coin. Breaking eye contact, he quaffed down half of the bottle in one   long and   glorious   pull. *As good as I remembered!*

His resentment faded as he walked the aisles with a hand basket, recalling his demeanor when he came in: edging around the doorway, head down, eyes averted, quiet feet slipping along. *Ha. I **was** trying to duck in unseen. Not for the reason he thought, but*   He ended up glad he had stayed, having found everything on his list   and   at reasonable prices. On the way up the last row to pay at the counter, he spotted a spice wheel in a bargain bin at the end of the aisle. He spent the next several minutes digging through the bin, coming up with three wheels. Although two were identical and all three had the basic salt and pepper compliment, there were also a number of spices and herbs he had never used before. *Mom* *would've loved these!* He made a quick calculation, added all of them to the basket, and went to the counter.

After paying, Joshua stood at the door and debated whether he should open another RestorAde. *Well I am recovering from a serious illness!* He smiled at his excuse for self-indulgence and stepped outside while pulling a bottle from his bag. His amusement disappeared in the harsh flood light over the front door that illuminated the entrance to Mom's. He felt naked under the hard white light, his already wet slicker launching flares of white with his every movement. Joshua let the blue bottle drop back into the bag, and took a swift sideways step into the safety of the darkness, except that the comfort of concealment did not come with his transition out of the shimmering circle of light. Instead, the reflected light from the wet surface at his feet exposed him, marked him for intent eyes he could *feel* were staring out from the inky corners and alleys. Joshua's shoulders hunched forward and he walked rapidly along the outside wall of Mom's, trying to be smaller and less noticeable on the edge of the pedway. His *need* to escape spiked when he realized *I still have to cross The Avenue before I can get on the roofs.* Head down, he strode around a corner into a dark intersection and

Uummph!

He bounced off a hard body, bag flying away from his loosened grip, butt bouncing twice on the pedway, the hood of his slicker knocked back, allowing small cold raindrops to assault his face. Before he could blink into focus and see what he had struck, there was a swirl of darkness and then a cool hard wetness under his chin, lifting him off the pedway. Joshua pulled on the arm that encircled his neck, straining on the tips of his toes so he could continue breathing, but he became very still when the edge of something cold and *sharp* pressed against his stretched throat. The warmth of the expelled words that caressed his right ear was oddly intimate and in stark contrast to the squeaky voice that produced the casual question, "Do you wish for me to dispose of this, Sir?"

Joshua's wide eyes took in the man who was deciding whether he would live or die. He was of medium height, but a tight fitting shirt revealed the V shape of a muscular man standing under a wide clear

The Deepest Cut

umbrella. Mom's security floodlight from down the block illuminated half of the face and Joshua blinked away water to look again. Staring down at him with flat eyes were the features of the classic benevolent father from a pVid sitcom. He was clean shaven with regular features that seemed smaller and pressed down toward the chin by a bald forehead that stretched up to a gleaming dome. Short cropped hair darkened the sides of the head just above the ears and extended around behind a contemplative face. The voice that pronounced Joshua's fate was deep and carried a low gravel.

"No, Fenster, not tonight. We're late and I'm not going to arrive at *this* meeting with blood splattered on me. Just *move* him."

Joshua had no time to wince from the sharpness that slid into the skin of his throat before the world whirled, his feet flung outwards, and he spun in weightlessness. Everything stopped with an abrupt hardness on his left side, followed by a brief falling sensation, and then wet wire mesh pressed against the side of his face once twice and the night paused.

Joshua could not move. With a terrified urgency, he reached out with his ears while he tried to regain his orientation. A gravelly and a squeaky voice took turns exchanging unknown words, but the critical thing to Joshua was that they were fading away. He let out his breath and lifted his bruised cheek from the cool unyielding weave of the pedway, feeling the finely defined pain from the cut on his throat, a blooming ache along his entire left side, and an immense relief that he was still alive. He pushed himself up, legs splayed apart, savoring the fact that he could feel the raindrops pelting his face. However, it only took a moment before his sense of reprieve turned into a sense of exposure and he gingerly levered himself onto his feet. Locating a dark lump near the corner of his almost fatal encounter, he limped over to his bag. Once the spilled contents were reinserted, he stepped to the edge of the thin alleyway, and checked the far side of the intersection where the voices had gone before he twisted and cautiously peeked around the corner. *Nothing.* His limp became less pronounced as his muscles loosened from the walk toward the bright lights of The Avenue.

Joshua stood well back from the opening of the alley and peered out from under his replaced hood, searching the shadows of several gaps in the buildings on the far side of The Avenue. He had crossed farther down The Avenue when he had come in, where it was darker and less populated. But after his brush with death, he was eager to get to the roofs. A tight gap between two buildings opposite him beckoned with the promise of being the shortest path across the well-lit barrier to home.

A confident male pronouncement brought a tittering female giggle. The voices were approaching from the right and Joshua waited until a well-dressed couple came into view. The woman hung onto the rotund man's arm, and although Joshua knew nothing about high fashion, he knew their clothes had cost a great deal of money. Wealth was also bespoke by the fact that two large men were walking just behind the pair, each holding out a wide umbrella to protect their charges from the night's rain. At first confused to see both men wearing dark glasses, when the closest guard's face swung to look directly at him, Joshua realized they had infrared lenses, just like he had once seen in a spy thriller vid. He stood very still as the group processed down The Avenue, the finely attired couple chatting and laughing, oblivious to the tense locking of gazes between two pairs of eyes. Halfway across the opening, apparently satisfied that Joshua was not a threat, the guard looked toward the bark of a merchant hawking a fabulous buy from farther along The Avenue.

Giving plenty of time for the procession to walk a safe distance UpAve, Joshua sidled up to the edge of the infamous pedway until he could check in both directions. No one was nearby on the right, and the couple was 30 feet to his left, haggling with the merchant. The same guard tracked Joshua's rapid crossing, but otherwise took no action. He entered the black gap with a sigh and relaxed as the comforting darkness once again closed around him. *Just like when I'm in the Big Trees.* He checked for drainpipes along the narrow passageway, but the search proved fruitless.

Emerging into a wider gap between buildings, his eyes were pulled to the windows on either side of the lane. The people inside were difficult to make out because the only illumination came from low red lights. Looking more closely, Joshua noticed they were wearing unusual clothes, and not many of those at that. He was not sure what it all meant, but when the figures in the windows began pointing at him and howling out jeering laughs, Joshua felt an intense flush of vulnerability for the second time that night. He dropped his gaze and hurried down the middle of the pedway.

A brighter rectangle swung open ahead on the pedway to his right, then mostly disappeared beneath the stretched silhouette of a man. Joshua veered left and lengthened his stride. A quick thump, Thump, THUMP and his way was blocked by a tall man in fancy clothes. Joshua's sudden stop forced his slicker hood half way back on his head.

"Oh my, my, Boy-yo, aren't you a pretty one!"

The light from the doorway illuminated a suit of velvet, purplish black, ivory lace protruding out the collar and sleeves. A wide matching velvet choker made the pale face seem to float disembodied above the outfit.

Joshua heard his voice creak out, "Just leave me alone, please."

"Leave you alone?"

The ghostly face swelled as the man bent at the waist, his looming closeness revealing multiple earrings, a small tuft of hair under the lower lip, and make up to create an Asian slant to the eyes.

"You look like you're *already* alone, Boy-yo!"

A darkening of the doorway pulled a brief furtive glance from Joshua, the after image showing a girl in a short, low cut dress leaning against the door jam in a provocative pose. She had been smiling, but the grin was neither friendly nor helpful.

"Now why don't ya come with ol' Uncle William and I'll gets ya something to eat?"

Thin lips slid apart to uncover the gleam of two gold capped front teeth. The man leaned even closer, hands on his knees, and the greater proximity exposed greater details: yellowing teeth, a body odor mixed with sweet flowery perfume, loose threads in the lace cuffs on the arms that were now reaching out -

Clutching his bag, Joshua stepped to the left and then lunged to the right as he ducked under a grasping hand. He was accelerating away when a pale leg emerged from the gloom to tangle his feet. He made one corrective step, but his foot slid out and the woven wire of the pedway came up Glang! This time the right side of his head rebounded off the surface and his bag flew away yet again. Stars were still in his eyes as he tried to scramble to his feet to follow his possessions. In sync with his grasping of his bag, a larger hand squeezed deep into his shoulder. He was wrenched around and a fist drove into his stomach. With the whoosh of air out his mouth, Joshua dropped to his hands and knees.

"Don't want to hurt that sweet money face, now do we, Boy-yo?"

Joshua struggled to pull in a breath, vaguely surprised he was not vomiting up his RestorAde. The bag was ripped from his grasp and his arm twisted behind his back, then used to lift him to his feet. If he had possessed enough air in his lungs he would have gasped from the pain. His body had to settle for a very brief, hoarse grunt.

"Lucky I took a little longer to get my makeup on right or I wouldn't of been in the right spot to trip him up."

The girl from the doorway attempted to look coy and petulant at the same time. Both expressions dissolved into one of subservience beneath the pressure of Uncle William's stare. Joshua's bag slammed hard below her chest, forcing her to step back as she clasped it to her belly.

"Well, Kandee, ya keep that 'tude up and ya ain't gonna be my #1 girl fer much longer." Then he smiled and pointed his chin at the bag. "But since ya did help nab the little bugger, I'll let ya look through that for what you want." The smile vanished. "*After* yur finished with the 'or-ee-in-taa-shun' for my little pretty boy here."

Joshua's arm elevated to the man's laughter at his own wittiness, and the pain both forced him onto his toes and propelled him toward the open doorway. The intensity of the smell as they passed the door frame almost pushed aside the agony of his twisted elbow and contorted shoulder *almost*. The sour odor of human sweat, and some other organic smell he could not identify, mingled with several different cloyingly sweet perfumes to obscure Uncle William's words and make them drift above Joshua's head, something about *pirates* and *a happy crew*. Everything seemed surreal as he was marched down a bare concretaform hallway, forced farther and *farther* away from the street and freedom. In a snap, he was turned and his face was pressed into a slab in the wall he had not even noticed, a door handle rammed into his stomach. Breath harsh with the smell of alcohol and decay washed over his face.

The Deepest Cut

"If my sweet Kandee has to call for me, yur gonna hurt in places you don't even know ya got."

The looming heat from the fetid breath retreated to the sound of a click and Joshua was pulled back to allow the door to swing open, revealing an inky black rectangle. For the second time that night, a forearm wrapped around Joshua's neck, which along with increased pressure on his contorted arm, lifted him off his feet. He grasped the forearm with his left hand and hung on, struggling for air, only seeing the grey ceiling at first, but it became a line of black as they entered the doorway. Darkness closed in, but the rhythmic yanks of his dangling body and the scraping of leather on concretaform told Joshua he was being carried down a flight of stairs. Suddenly he was flung forward into the air. His head snapped down to see the rising floor, which was a surprise, showing he was farther down than he thought. Able to partially roll on impact, his back came up hard against the wall at the bottom of the stairs. Scuffing noises oriented his eyes upward and Joshua made out Uncle William's back lit figure, already returned to the top of the staircase.

"You just stay down there and think 'bout how lucky you are to have yur 'ol Uncle William to provide you with a roof over yur head and maybe, *if* you git the proper attitude, Pretty Boy-yo, you might git something to eat, too. Soz you can think, without any distractions, we'll just keep the lights out fer now." The door slammed with a note of finality, shutting out the light from the hallway. Joshua heard the scrape of first one, then another, latch being slid into place.

His eyes were drawn to the slit of light that glowed along the bottom of the door. It was cut in half with a muffled clunk at what Joshua assumed was his bag being thrown against the door. His guess was confirmed by Uncle William's voice as steps retreated back down the hallway, "You can look through that AFTER yur done with your regular work. This is prime time, Sugar! Now get your skinny ass out there and be in-vii-tin'." After a moment, a second door thumped shut in the distance.

Joshua worked his way up the stairs to confirm what he already knew; the door would not budge. Despair began to envelop him as he sagged down, but he stopped at a sound from the bottom of the stairs. Pressing his back into the door, he strained to detect something climbing up from the inky blackness below. Nothing   then a whisper of movement as he sucked in his breath. Waiting   waiting   *There!* Another wisp of sound at the foot of the stairs when he adjusted his position.

Then, a warmth formed next to him on the stairs and his panic subsided. *Oh, Mom!* A sob escaped and with it came another noise from below. *Hold it*   Joshua slapped his knee and heard the retort roll back up from the hard floor at the bottom of the stairs. He clapped his hands to reassure himself with a sharper echo that sailed back up from below. *There is nothing to fear but fear itself.* The warmth was gone.

Joshua curled as best he could at the top of the stairs where the light was strongest, but found himself to be relatively calm. This surprised him, because he had no idea how he was going to get out of this predicament. Already exhausted from the previous night's ordeal with the Chapple poisoning and the near death encounter outside of Mom's, the humid fetid air of the cellar pulled him into oblivion.

The Deepest Cut

◄12►

A distant, jauntily whistled tune awoke Joshua several hours later. He immediately knew exactly where he was and the nature of his situation. The whistling stopped and he listened to two long scrapes that had metallic snaps at the end. The door was wrenched open, almost blinding him, but he could tell by the silhouette that it was not William. She spoke from the open doorway.

"What's your name?"

He responded automatically to her unexpectedly conversational tone, "Joshua." *Maybe she **will** help me...*

Kandee continued reasonably, "So this is how its gonna work, Joshua. You *are* gonna do whatever you're told or William will make you hurt in ways you can't even think of. Now he won't touch yer face or yer *workin' parts*, understand?   Cause that would damage the merchindice. But he WILL make you do whatever he wants, so you might as well skip the pain and just get on with the program."

She waited   until a moment later, she chuckled without humor, "...but I guess that aint gonna happen, now is it? You gonna keep yer Pur-it-tee, right? OK, dumb ass, do it the hard way. You may now 'fficially consider yer orientation to of bin delivered."

Kandee knelt down to her left, "Now,   let's see what you got here, J-Boy.   What is this crap, anyway? Well at least there's-" she cursed. "Blue? You like BLUE? Damn! Why couldn't ya be like any *normal* person and have orange?" His bag landed farther down the hallway with a muffled thud. She looked him in the eye. "Don't it just figure? Why'd I think YOU'd have any haulin' thing worth me keepin'?" Joshua started to move for the bag, but stopped at her upheld finger. "That don't mean you get it back just yet, Mr. Josh-Boy." She stood and pointed down the stairs. "Back 'er down, Josshheee!"

At his hesitation, her eyebrows dropped together and her lip curled. "Don't make me call Uncle William, BOY!   Not that I can't handle you myself." She took a step toward him. He eased down two steps. "Aalll the way down!" Kandee stood feet apart in the door frame. "*Now!!*"

Joshua turned to move down the staircase. He saw his shadow on the wall at the bottom of the stairs contort, and two quick scuffs gave him a second's warning before Kandee's palm smacked between his shoulder blades. He jumped with some coordination, but made the mistake of grabbing for the railing, which caused him to twist as he fell. One backward step allowed him to sit on the concretaform floor without too much of a jar, but he slid back into the wall with an "uummmph!" *Again!*

"Oops! Forgot to tell ya   'watch your step.' "

Kandee matched Uncle William's earlier mocking tone and wide stance at the top of the stairs. "Sorry 'bout that.   Well,   no,   I'm not. After all, yer the muck brain that wants to do this the hard way. Now you git to wait until Uncle William comes to **explain** things to you." She looked across her bare shoulder toward the street and her voice softened, "Then you'll have something to cry about   " Her head swiveled back to stare down the steps and her tone became rock hard, "And I aint joshin you 'bout *that*, Joshee-Boy!" In a flash, Kandee emitted a genuine laugh at her cleverness. "Be sure to make friends with all the little critters down there."

Joshua involuntarily surveyed the cellar, taking in tarps that covered jumbled forms in the corners, some opened wooden crates, a large dented metal tank, piles of empty cube containers…

"I think… Yeah, I'm   *pretty sure*   Uncle William said he saw a spiderviper down there once." Joshua's eyes snapped back up to Kandee.

"Ooohh, does that worry you some? Well it oughta. You just be **reall** quiet and think **reeaall** hard and maybe, just *maybe*, it'll leave you alone." The door slammed, the bolts struck home, and Kandee's laugh faded with the clicking of her high heels.

Well, she's right about being quiet to avoid spidervipers. With the realization that he knew vastly more about spidervipers than Kandee,   or anyone else for that matter,   her comment shrunk into a petty, ill-informed threat. Joshua almost laughed in relief. With a slight start, he realized *she's also right about needing to think.* Something about what he had seen stored in the basement was important. He sat and thought   bringing the visual images to mind. *The wooden crates!* In his mind's eye, he could still make out a thin bent line standing up from one of the lids. *Now, where was that?* Joshua fixed on a point as close as he could estimate, stood, and shuffled over to the far wall until his foot stopped with a hollow thump. *Wood!* His hands explored and soon found the protruding nail. It took a few moments to work the loose nail out. *Ok, now what?* Joshua could not come up with an answer, but he felt better having something sharp in his hand.

He was no longer afraid of the dark, but the nail provided adequate warning against trying to explore further by feel alone. The thought of perching on the stairs again as he waited was unappealing. However, that is what they would expect and he did not want to do anything to raise their guard.

It seemed he had only just found a comfortable position when the faraway slam of an outer door brought his eyes open with a jerk. By the time the second bolt was thrown back, he had huddled forward in a ball. He did not move when the door whipped open, but did curl tighter when it slammed into the hallway wall.

"Ah, there ya are my little chick-a-dee. Time fer us ta come to a understandin'."

Joshua gagged as he was hauled up and out by the back collar of his slicker and swung into the wall on the far side of the hallway. Uncle William transferred a hand from the collar to Joshua's chest, pressing him into the wall. The shift in grip had allowed Joshua to spot his bag against the wall a few feet down the hall toward the street door. A smooth warm hand took a firm grip on his chin and forcing his face up, then a quick shake of his face commanded him to focus on the bleary eyed man in front of him.

"Ya best be paying attenshun to what I'm about to be saying, boy-yo. Now the sooner y–"

Joshua's right hand flashed over the restraining arm, turning Uncle William's face to the side as the nail slashed a dark line against soft white. Both of the man's hands let go from the shock of the unexpected pain. He staggered back into the wall, one hand against his left cheek, eyes wide. He looked down at Joshua as blood began to seep out from under the edge of his palm. A manic rage contorted his features.

"You *cut* my FACE!!"

Joshua clamped down on the urgent desire to escape and instead stepped forward and kicked upwards with all the speed and strength he could muster, his foot slamming into *the workin parts* before he leapt back out of the reach of a hand that suddenly redirected to between the owner's legs with an escaping, high pitched wheeze. Knees buckled and with a gasping groan, Uncle William twisted down to all fours in front of the cellar door. He was helpless to avoid Joshua's lunge with both hands as they struck the seat of his pants and propelled him head first into the black maw of Joshua's former prison. The rhythmic grunts told the tale of Uncle William's journey down the stairs on his stomach, stopping only when one foot snagged the side of the doorway.

Joshua was halfway down the hall and slinging his bag across his shoulder when an enraged inarticulate roar issued from the basement. He stretched a hand for the handle of the door at the end of the hall, but it swung open and Kandee pushed through with an expression of concern and fear dominating her face. She clearly was not expecting to see Joshua so close, allowing him to drop a shoulder and ram it into her gut, forcing her back out and aside with a blast of oommph and then she was gone with a squeal and a thump and he was sprinting down the street toward The Swamp through the breaking light of a new day. Emerging into a cold January rain from under the local ion shield, he heard Uncle William's vow chase after him over the splashes of his retreat...

"I will find you, Boy-yo! I will *hunt you* **DOWN!!!**"

The Deepest Cut

◀13▶

Joshua had almost reached the top of the scree pile access way. It was late at night, and since his main entry point to the city was several blocks away from The Bordello Section, he thought it was probably safe. After almost four weeks of being alone in The Swamp, Joshua had convinced himself that Uncle William had forgotten him. Almost.

A predatory feel permeated the air, but *that's just my imagination.* Still, Joshua paused just below the top of the pavement. He had grown accustomed to frequently stopping and listening in The Swamp. Several minutes passed *nothing.* He inched his head up until his eyes lifted over the lip of the asphalt. He scanned the area, back and forth, back and forth. *Nothing.* About to rise and step onto the street, Joshua froze. There had been a faint scuffing noise from the darkness to the left, as if someone had shifted their weight. Joshua's eyes zeroed in on a bulge of shadow on the wall. Something about the shape seemed unfamiliar. *Has that lump been there before?* He eased back down, searching for sounds coming from between the raindrops hitting the hard surface of the pavement. His internal clock ticked off several more minutes. And then a light cough drifted out from the suspect shadow. It sounded *young. Why would a kid be out here at this time of night? Come on. This can't be for me! Can it?*

It just seemed so unlikely that Uncle William would have someone watching for him at the end of a motorway that faced The Swamp. *Just because this was the way I had run to get away from him? That doesn't make sense.* Still, regardless of who the sentry was looking for, Joshua did not want to reveal his main access point into the city. *Maybe I can scare him off.* He worked his way to the right until he came to the rim of pavement jutting out from the warehouse wall. Making quick short scrapes with a small stone against a flat rock, he mimicked the skittering sounds of spiderviper claws on a hard surface. Then he let out a lifting whistle imitation of the spiderviper alert signal. *Slops, that wasn't even close.* Even so, he was rewarded with the small yelp of a startled child. Hoping he might actually get the kid scared enough to leave, Joshua upped the ante and lifted his arms with fingers curled and pointed like grasping claws, reaching tentatively, the way he had seen spidervipers do when trying to locate prey. He hoped they would be just barely visible against the grey wall, but not show too much detail in the dim shadows of the alleyway.

"Holy space crap!" A boy's whisper sailed out from the shadow. *Well, it was close enough, I gues-*

The shot boomed out and the wall beside Joshua's face exploded. A stab of pain sliced into his right cheek as a whine dwindled away into The Swamp. Ignoring the burn along his cheekbone, Joshua ducked down and scrambled toward the other side of the opening, instinctively vacating the spot where he had last been seen. On his second step, a large rock shifted under his foot and he stepped off to one, then another stone, before he reached a perch under the lip of the pavement, hoping the noise of the rocks careening down into The Swamp had covered his movement. He crouched, slowing his breaths into long, but deep pulls of air in and out of his mouth. Just as his legs began to cramp, he heard the slap of approaching steps, then an older boy's angry voice, "What the *hell* are you thinking?"

"I   I saw a spiderviper and I ain't getting' snicked full of poison for nobody! You *know* they been sayin' one killed some lady up at NorthPoint."

"Listen, Tylir, there's nothin' on the news about any spiderviper in the city. Besides, all you had to do was watch for the kid. The gun was just to scare the little punk into coming with you if he showed up."

"Yeah, well, I hears jus' fine and it's what everybody's been talkin' 'bout and all the talk on da Ave *is* that it was a spiderviper! I ain't stupid! I'm a Shadow Boy. You *said* I was!"

"That's right, Tylir, you're a Shadow Boy. But that means being quiet like a shadow.   Look, I'm the Top Shadow Boy, right?   So, I *know* that's what's floatin' on Ave. But it's just not likely that one of them was coming up here to snatch you. It's been, like,   30 *years* since someone was killed by a spiderviper, and that was that guy that went out looking for them in The Swamp."

"Yeah   well   how'd you know they ain't got too crowded in The Swamp an   an are comin' into the city now?   I'm tellin' ya, Glin, I *heard* sumptin   it made like a   a whistlin' sound! And then I *saw* it!   Those claws they was   like   tryin' ta find me!"

A frustrated sigh slid out of the darkness. "All right, Tylir, I believe you. You saw something move. But that's no reason to pop off a shot. You don't hear the other Shadow Boys shooting at everything they hear, do you?"

"Aw, come *on* Glin, I was *scared.* 'Sides, we've been watching fer that kid for a haulin' month, an there ain't been no sign of him."

"Oh,   O K.   Tell you what, Tylir. Let's just go tell Bossman to give Uncle William his money back, all because *you're* tired of lookin' for the turd butt that slashed the creep's face.   Let's just see how he takes to *that!'*

"Well, they all's older 'n me, an   an they ain't right up against The Swamp like I am here, Glin.   'Sides, it was just one shot."

"Yeah? And guess who's gonna pay for that bullet?" There was the long blow of another exasperated sigh. "OK, come on, Tylir. We gotta move. Cops may not come UpAve very often, but they'll be coming after triangulating on that shot. Besides, if he's still alive, there's no way he's going to come back 'round soon, not after you blew out half a wall. Maybe, just *maybe*   I can keep The Bossman from killing you."

Their voices faded as they moved back up the alleyway. Joshua peeked up over the edge of the wet crumbling asphalt, watching the figures outlined against a harsh security light, one almost twice the size of the other. As the larger boy put his arm around the long-haired shooter and turned his head to say something, Joshua realized he was not much older than him. They turned a corner, leaving small clouds of condensed breath shimmering in the cold winter air.

Joshua decided he needed to find other ways, *safer ways,* to get in and out of the city. He considered continuing with his reconnaissance, now that the boys were gone. But the older boy had sounded like he knew his business and Joshua definitely wanted to avoid the police.

Besides…

He reached up to his cheek, winced, and pulled his hand away. In the gloom on the edge of the unused motorway, Joshua watched the raindrops strike and eventually erase the dark slick of blood across his fingertips. He blew out his own exasperated sigh.

Driven to the Hilt

...I need to take care of this. Then *maybe I can figure out how I'm going to get back into the city without getting shot.*

The Deepest Cut

◄14►

It took several nights of searching to locate additional access into the rain drenched city. Fortunately, the older low-rent structures in the north end used the cheapest choice for water control, external drainpipes. Joshua sometimes pictured himself as a monkey as he scrambled up the drainpipes, but preferred the image of a leaping panther whenever he jumped across the gaps created by the narrower internal alleyways.

It was his third night on the same roof top looking down upon the Bordello section near The Swamp end of The Avenue. Joshua had surveyed the backstreet brothel from every angle, seeking a pattern. He thought he had found it. Uncle William took his meal breaks on the edge of a nearby alleyway, sitting on a cushion atop a metal crate. Just outside the ion shield, he sat under an eave that kept him out of the rain, but still allowed him to keep an eye on his "merchandise." Occasionally, he would invite one of his "children" to eat with him, usually Kandee. So far, he had always sent them away at the end to enjoy his post-meal smoke in peace.

And so it had gone this time. Joshua crouched in the darkest corner of the alley, wanting one more practice run to ensure the feasibility of his tentative plan. The back of the narrow alleyway was dark enough for Joshua to get down and back up the drainage pipe without being seen. There was a loose section at the bottom that made a loud creak when pulled, but a jump either way solved that.

Uncle William leaned back, eyes closed, filaments of the pungent smoke escaping from the corners of his mouth. A small puff rolled out and lifted to briefly obscure the long pink line across the man's left cheek. Joshua wondered whether Uncle William would call it even if he saw the developing scar caused by Tylir's ricocheting bullet. He flinched when the man's eyes snapped open. A second later, Joshua heard someone approach.

"Ah, me boy-yo, coming with good news, I hope?"

A tall boy came into view. He was lean, but moved fluidly, suggesting he was in good physical condition despite the ragged state of his clothes. The medium brown tone of his skin sparkled with small drops of rain he had not bothered to wipe away. He walked up with the confidence of someone who knows he has the protection of a person with power.

"Sorry, Mr. William. No sign of him anywhere. Bossman figures he's spiderviper meat somewhere in The Swamp. He wanted me to ask if you still wanted us to cover all three of the motorways at the end of The Avenue every night." Joshua sat up straighter *I know that voice!* It was the boy who had corralled the shooter several nights ago. *So you're Glin.*

"Hell, yes I do! I'm gonna make that little skank bait pay!"

"Ok, Mr. William. Sure thing. You'll just need to come up with another 20 UDs for next month."

"Now, now, my friend, you can call me *Uncle* William." Uncle William's teeth flashed in a friendly smile. He reached into his pocket to pull out a $20 note. He hesitated, eyed Glin, and then retrieved another bill. "Tell you what." He held out the second note. "Here's a fiver for you."

Glin did not move. "What do I have to do for that?" His eyes flicked to a nearby doorway where Uncle William's workers took their customers.

"No, no, my boy-o, although you could make some awful' good money if you let me fix you up right. After all, *everybody* loves chocolate!" The impact of Uncle William's charming smile was diminished by the jagged scar on his cheek.

Although his eyes remained hard, the corners of Glin's mouth lifted as he took a step back. "I'll just tell Bossman that you're good for now."

"Ok, *Okay*, just relax, sonnyboy. Here! Take both of these. All you've got to do is spread the word that I'm offering 100 UDs to anybody what can find me that little snot maggot alive. You just spread the word."

"You got it, Mr. William," Glin replied as he stepped forward and snatched the two notes from the outstretched hand. The swiftness of his retreat revealed his eagerness to be someplace anyplace else.

"Yep, I could make a pretty penny off of you, boy-o, yes indeed," Uncle William muttered to himself as he watched Glin go. He looked down and cursed, annoyed to find his smoke had gone out. His face became a flickering yellow skull with sunken eyes as he relit. Pulling in a deep drag, he closed his eyes, let his lighter flame extinguish, adjusted his slicker hood forward, and then leaned back into the wall.

The Deepest Cut

Joshua watched tendrils of smoke escape from the black hole that hid Uncle William's face. His vague plan of approaching the man and trying to make some sort of deal dissipated like the smoke drifting up to meet the falling rain. *100 credits? For me?* He could not escape the bare boned truth: Uncle William would *never* let go.

On the way back out over the roofs, another option came to mind, but made his gut twist and brought forth the image of his mother's face, filled with disapproval and disappointment. Joshua tried to put the idea out of his mind. But after several days of trying, he could not produce a better option. He decided he would go ahead and make preparations, and *maybe I'll think of something else before it's ready.*

◀15▶

If they both keep coming, I'm dead.

Despite the approaching threat, Joshua kept tapping on the baited reed, hoping the trailing spiderviper baby would lose interest in the unusual sound while the lead baby did not. He was near where a stream from The Pond entered the edge of the Big Trees, making its way to Dark Lake. He hoped he survived his attempt to test out his risky new plan.

He had been returning from a Reed harvest, about to cross a small clearing, when his way had been blocked by a Swamp Fox. It had almost passed through when a spiderviper had burst from the nearby leaves and struck. It did not keep its foreclaws latched onto the target as Joshua had expected, but instead disengaged and skittered away as the Swamp Fox tried to stagger back the way it had come. Before it had gone five feet, it paused, and managed one loud hiss before it collapsed, quivered, and became still. The spiderviper reemerged from cover and emitted a loud fluttering sound before hooking the dead Swamp Fox and pulling it onto its side. The hair on the back of Joshua's neck stood stiff when almost 20 baby spidervipers had scampered out from under an adjacent bush and began latching onto the exposed underbelly of their mother's prey. He shuddered at the sight of the small spider shapes swarming over each other to get at their dinner. The mother advanced into the clearing, on alert while her offspring fed. His exit still blocked, Joshua had eased down to one knee. *Looks like this is going to take a while.*

He had hoped the brood would move on when it was done. However, after they had finished feeding, the babies begin roaming the area while their mother proceeded with her own meal. Hoping she was sufficiently preoccupied, Joshua had decided this would be his best chance to escape and he began to circumvent the clearing with as much stealth as he could muster. At the far end of the opening, he used his spear to support his weight so he could lean far out to the side of an intervening bush and check on the mother's status. *Still eating. Good.*

Joshua had pivoted to exit, but before he could take a step, a little whistle had sounded at his feet. With exaggerated slowness, he tilted his head to look down. Less than a foot from his leg was a baby spiderviper, rising up into strike position. He barely stopped himself from taking a step back. Instead, he shifted his balance so he could pull the butt of his spear an inch across the ground. The slight scuffing noise prompted the baby to let out a loud chirp and turn toward the spear. It scuttled back a few steps, its protruding obsidian fang tipped tongue extended and quivering. Joshua then had become aware of the complete silence. With immense effort, he looked up from the menacing baby to locate the mother. The hairs on the back of his neck stood out again at the sight of her creeping over the Swamp Fox carcass in a predatory crouch, open mouth dripping with the gore of her feast, her own venomous proboscis pulsating as it shifted from side to side, almost as if the tongue itself was seeking him out. Joshua tore his eyes away from approaching death to the more immediate threat and found that the baby was the mirror of its mother, creeping forward with raised hooked foreclaws.

He shifted his weight to lift the butt of his spear, then swung it at the baby, striking it under its belly, lifting it up and out to fly above the clearing. The stillness was pierced by a high-pitched trilling as the baby tumbled through the air toward its mother. A questioning whistle blew from the mother and she turned in sync with the trajectory of the baby's squeal. It hit with a short loud squeak, rolled on the ground, and got up with a stagger, but based on the volume of its angry whistle, was not seriously injured. The mother took a few steps in the direction of the baby before it issued a fluttery, rhythmic flapping sound. It spun back around toward Joshua, who then realized he had been watching when he should have been running.

It took three steps to clear the brush and emerge onto a game trail, where the greater visibility allowed Joshua to maximize his speed. He glanced back when sounds of crashing underbrush stopped and saw the mother standing, watching his retreat. Time resumed its normal pace, but Joshua did not. Only after another 50 feet of sprinting did he slow and look back over his shoulder.

Driven to the Hilt

Joshua could still picture her, high on extended legs, fang stretched forward on rigid tongue, promising to find satisfaction at their next encounter. He had slowed to a quick jog and his final glance revealed the mother's back, her maternal instinct having prompted her return to her brood.

That had been two days ago. On this morning, he had gone out in search of Chapples, and not the ripe ones. Once located, he had painstakingly collected the clear beads of liquid that dotted the unripe greyish orange skin and deposited them into an old small condiment jar. Just moments ago, he had poured the contents of that jar into a slit he had just cut into a SwampRabbit thigh. He had then affixed the bait to the end of a sharpened Reed and pushed it out from under the leaves of his concealing bush. Afraid of coming into contact with even the smallest amount of the Chapple Dew, Joshua had rolled the jar under the bush he was now crouching behind. He had then begun making the soft taps to attract his intended prey. He had come knowing that without the distraction of feeding on a fresh kill, his odds of again escaping the mother were much, *much* slimmer. Those odds had plunged even father now that more than one baby spiderviper was taking an interest in the unusual noise.

His intended target came closer to his hiding place in a slow and steady advance, hooked forelegs lifted and wavering like questing antenna. tap   tap   tap   A quick 360 check ensured that the trailing baby was the only extra spiderviper in the vicinity and Joshua mentally anchored the location of the Bluebell to his rear, just in case he had to sprint for refuge under its leaves. tap   tap   Unfortunately, it continued its approach from behind its more adventurous sibling.   tap   tap   tap tap   tap *Just a little closer.*   The lead baby spiderviper paused six inches from the bait, prompting its twin to stop as well. *A little bit more...*   tap   tap   His target lifted up high on its legs, then dropped its belly to the ground. Joshua placed his tap stick on the ground, gathered a nearby small pebble, and waited. When the lead baby scampered forward and struck, he flicked the pebble at a stone behind the second baby spiderviper. The resulting tiny click caused both babies to spin toward the sound. Joshua gave the tiniest tug to the bait laden Reed. The soft rustle prompted the closest baby to hop back around and lunge, latching onto the bloody meat with its foreclaws. It then began eating in earnest.

Another pebble flew into a more distant bush and the second baby disappeared in pursuit of its ghostly prey. *Now it all depends on whether the Chapple Dew has the same effect on spidervipers as it did on me. And if so how long that takes.* As it turned out, within a minute, the feasting baby stopped, lifted up on wobbly legs, and turned to leave. Joshua saw a small dark shape moving in the far brush. The second baby was coming back his way. *It's now or never.*

He stepped out from behind the bush and snatched down, making sure his hand covered the air slits on either side of the sluggish baby's abdomen. He plunged his knife down through the leathery mid-section and the furry legs struggling against his hand became still. Joshua looked up to find that the other baby had emerged and stood in a prestrike pose, four feet away. Leaving the knife pinned through his victim, he grasped the baited Reed, and tossed it at the second baby. It jumped with an alarmed chirp after the meat splatted onto the ground inches from its side. When it turned to examine the unexpected gift, Joshua gathered his prize and eased back around the bush. As soon as he was out of earshot, he put his prize into his shoulder satchel and made a quick retreat from the area.

Sitting on Sanctuary's floor, knife once again in hand, Joshua spent the next hour cutting down through the head of the baby spiderviper, discarding membranes, pieces of chitin, and anything else that did not look to be associated with the small striking proboscis. As he prepared to cut into the fang tipped appendage, Joshua was surprised to discover he no longer noticed the stench. Heartened, he leaned closer and began stripping away more membranes, eventually exposing two tubes attached to the ivory base of the fang. Working his way back to the base of the proboscis, he discovered two sacks bulging with fluid, one about twice as large as the other. Joshua sliced the proboscis so that the two tubes were separated and then cut off the black fang. He milked the fluids into two salvaged glass containers, one clear and the other with a blue tint, being extremely careful not to allow either fluid to touch his skin. The larger sack had contained a greenish liquid, which he had deposited in the blue jar. The other sack had yielded a substance the color of black ink with the consistency of motor oil.

Per GlobalNet instructions, he had already worked on the previously acquired Reeds to create a hollow Reed tube just under three feet long. His shoulders still ached from having spent most of the prior evening ramming a narrower Reed in and out with sand to produce a smooth interior to the bore of the blowgun. It had actually been his discovery of the Parachute Seeds that had led Joshua to the idea of a blowgun. The hard brown seed looked like an elongated tear drop, with the tapered end of its one and a half inch length festooned with a spreading array of tiny feather shaped leaves. The Swamp was filled with flora that had evolved sharp defenses, so it had not taken much time for Joshua to find a thorn with a hollow tip. Using contact glue from a general repair kit, he had affixed the thorns on to the end of the Seeds to make some practice darts. A stained shirt on his manikin was soon filled with holes.

It only took the sight of two SwampRabbits bounding into the distance for Joshua to learn the necessity of taking in a slow deep breath instead of inhaling sharply. Once he had mastered that skill, he tested the two spiderviper fluids. Not surprisingly, it was the black oily substance that immediately brought down his target. He said a prayer as he walked away from the sacrificial Bunny, unwilling to eat something that had been killed by spiderviper venom.

At the end of that long day, Joshua sat on The Porch in his wicker chair. He stared out at a heavy, cold rain falling from fast moving black storm clouds. The blowgun lay across his knees. Two darts were inside, thorns filled with venom, tips sealed with a tiny ball of Bluebell sap. It had been 13 days since he had pulled the chip of stone from his right cheek. His fingertips idly traced the length of the three plus inch scar. During those two weeks, he had immersed himself in the mechanics of the project in order to avoid thinking about its purpose. Now the weather prevented further action and forced Joshua to face the implications of what he was contemplating. He tried to think of some other   *any* other   alternative, but   without success.

He had no friends or family to assist him, he could not go to the police, and he did not have sufficient money to buy off Uncle William or hire someone else to carry out the last option left available to him. Although he had not thought of it since his encounter with the OBS social worker, only one strategy seemed to offer a possible solution, one that he had often heard from his father as they had watched stickball matches. He stared at the sheets of falling water and decided

The best defense is a good offense.

◄16►

Joshua accessed the city via Rusty Pipe, the second of his five primary entry points. All but the scree pile took him directly to the roof tops. He had developed the habit of always using different routes going in and coming back out. This night, the cloud cover shifted between offering up a light rainfall and producing a fine mist. Joshua climbed, ran, and leapt his way to the Bordello district.

After peeking over the edge of the roof to ensure the narrow alleyway was empty, he slid down and took up his former observational position. Joshua estimated he would have to advance another 10 feet to get within a range where he had confidence in his accuracy. Soon Uncle William arrived with Kandee in tow. He sat on his crate and pulled out a cheese and sausage stick. He almost seemed human as he sliced off pieces of the stick and handed every other one to Kandee.

"How do you like your new outfit? Is it fitting ok?"

Striking a pose, Kandee retorted, "Well, what do *you* think?"

"Ah, you look ravishing, my dear." He handed her another slice of the swirled cheese and sausage. The tone of the conversation sounded so normal that Joshua's hard-earned resolve from the night before began to dissolve. *Maybe he really does care about her.*

Kandee leaned forward to expose some more skin and looked up through her brow with coy eyes. "Maybe now you can let me take a little break to run some of the girls and,   you know, save myself for special customers. And *you*, of course."

His mouth full, Uncle William nodded and chewed in consideration before he finally swallowed. His smile seemed sincere up until the instant before he dropped the processed food stick and snatched Kandee by the hair, pulling her ear in close to his face.

"Don't even **begin** to think about takin' my place."

"I wa-" the flat blade of his knife pressed against her lips, demanding immediate silence.

"Didn't I just buy you that new outfit you have on?" He removed the knife and waited.

"Yes, bu-" the blade resumed its negotiating position.

"Then I suggest you get back to work so I kin get a return on my investment." His left hand propelled her back several steps, causing her to stumble in her high heels. "NOW!"

Kandee scuttled back up the street with a slight limp, a tiny sob escaping just before she stepped out of Joshua's field of view.

Uncle William pulled his hood up against the return of a light rain and retrieved the food stick. As he finished his meal, Joshua painstakingly placed one foot in front of the other until he had gained the additional 10 feet needed for an accurate shot. Then he knelt back down and waited. Finally, Uncle William slid the remnant of food stick into an inside pocket of his slicker and leaned back to relax.

Joshua's rising anxiety subsided when he realized Uncle William was going to keep his slicker hood up due to the medium rainfall. He relaxed, not having an unimpeded shot at his current distance and unwilling to risk getting closer. As if on cue, the rain transformed into a drizzle and then a drifting mist, prompting Uncle William to throw back his slicker hood.

Joshua knew he would not have the courage to come back if he had the time to think about his plan over the next day. *I have to do this now.* He pulled the sap ball off the end of a dart tip, loaded it into the blowgun, and sighted along the tube just as he had practiced. This time, however, the end of the blowgun would not remain steady.

His sudden lack of control was unnerving. Over the end of the wavering blowgun, he saw Uncle William light his smoke and lean back to exhale upward, mingling the waste from his lungs into the drifting water vapor. Joshua lowered his hand and took a deep, but very quiet, breath. *The poison probably isn't enough to even kill him, maybe just stun him and scare him so he'll leave me alone.* Joshua did not allow himself to examine the illogic of this thought, but lifted the tube, and puffed hard.

As soon as the dart left the end of the blowgun, Joshua felt the irreversibility of his action and was overwhelmed with an intense desire to somehow pull it back. Time slowed and the dart drifted away in a slight arch toward Uncle William's eye. The white puff lost elevation as it continued on its inexorable journey toward the man leaning back against the damp alley wall. *It's dropping too far. It's going to miss!* There was a small thwacking sound as it hit the exposed expanse of throat.

Uncle William's eyes snapped open impossibly wide and his jaw dropped in shock, releasing a puff of smoke that turned into an escaping white translucent snake, moving up past his nose. His right hand made it halfway up to his neck before it stopped with a tiny tremor. His mouth twitched instead of obeying his command to yell out. Both arms slid down to hang along the sides of his body and his head turned in Joshua's direction, lower jaw jerking up and down, spreading into a spasm through the entire neck, and a second later, the upper torso.

Joshua knelt rooted in place, blowgun lowered just below his mouth, taking in every detail. Uncle William's entire body jerked once, twice, his legs stretched rigid, then a final jerk dislodged him from his cushioned perch and he fell onto his side with a wet thud. With agonizing slowness, as if an invisible hand pulled on his shoulder, Uncle William rolled onto his back, but with his face still turned to the side, facing Joshua.

The lighting shifted and Joshua saw his mother's face in place of Uncle William's. The alley gave way to their living cubicle at NorthPoint and he again stood just inside the door, looking down at his mother. *This isn't real. It can't be real.* Rain drops made expanding circles in the puddle behind his mother's body. *Rain? Inside?* Joshua was back in the black shadows of the alley, Uncle William's frozen expression accusing him.

He slapped his hand over his mouth to hold in the scream. Tears filled his eyes as he fought for control. He rocketed to his feet and slammed against the wall beside him. An inner voice urged action, *to do what?*

You have to get the dart. Don't leave it behind. Do it. NOW!

Joshua staggered from the wall, but shuddered to a stop, unable to move forward.

Someone's going to notice him. GO!!

Joshua's eyes locked onto Uncle William's large, glistening black boots. *He's NOTHING like Mom.* Sliding toward the body with as much stealth as he could, he snatched a look up the street. *No one's coming.*

The Deepest Cut

You MUST do it!!

Forcing his head to turn back toward Uncle William's face, Joshua braced himself, knowing he could not stop himself from running if he saw his mother again.   It was still   Uncle William.   He was close enough to see wrinkles not quite concealed by makeup and the large blood vessels in the bulging eyes, looking at him accusingly, almost as if he were about to speak. Joshua focused away from the face to the neck, but   could only stare at the dart   hand extended, but frozen   until   something made him glance up the pedway. Sensing more than seeing an approaching figure, he snapped back around, snatched the dart out of Uncle William's neck, and sprinted back toward the drain pipe, letting the dart fall into a large outer pocket of his slicker as he ran. He was almost to the back wall when he remembered   *the pipe!*   and leapt up high to avoid the noisy loose section at the bottom.

He gained the roof and then

found himself walking past the entrance screen of hanging Nutblossoms at Sanctuary, with no recollection of having traversed the rooftops or Bushland to get there. Joshua mechanically took off and hung his slicker, walked to his bed and stiffly laid down, staring up at the rock ceiling.   He floated,   unaware of the passage of time,   waiting   for something   before the answer coalesced in his numb mind.   *She's not there.*   His mother's warmth had not come to comfort him.   *Will I ever feel her again?*   He could not muster up an answer.

Joshua's single sob echoed in the cold and empty cavern. Despite being under both blankets, Joshua's entire body shivered. *I am   alone.* A warm wet trail traced down one cheek. *Maybe that's the way it should be.*   His grief was silent, but tears flowed until all energy had been squeezed out of his wrenched guts and exhaustion began to pull him closer to an uneasy slumber. Eyes clamped tight against the emptiness, Joshua heard his raspy voice croak out words, as if spoken by someone else.

"You killed someone today.   Nothing will *ever* be the same."

Overwatch

◀1▶

Joshua wakes up. He is lying on a stiff mat looking up at a slot of light cutting down from behind and above, slicing through the black murk that presses in upon him, a heavy, musty, *old* smell in the air. He *feels* someone is in the cellar with him, *behind* him. *This is wrong! No one else is supposed to be down here.* A hand from behind grasps and squeezes down on his shoulder! Joshua's eyes fly open!

He is back in Sanctuary, but   he can *still* feel the fingers digging into his flesh! He   can   not   *move*, not even   *breathe*. Desperate to make a sound, he pushes against the paralysis, but cannot force any air out of his constricted chest. The fingers   dig   deeper. Finally, a guttural stutter issues from deep in his throat *Aa…aaa… auuhh!!*

Sleep's spell released its grip. Joshua scrambled off of the sleeping ledge and hit the stone floor, hard. The top sheet tangled in his legs, he twisted around to slide away on his butt, looking back, *knowing* he would see Uncle William's wide gold toothed smile, but   there was nothing. Air rasped in and out of his contracted throat as he took in the familiar shadows of his home. He sat and allowed the pounding in his chest to become   slower,   the heavy thumping   eventually   fading away. It had been yet another nightmare.

Joshua unwrapped the bedding from his legs and pushed himself off of the stone floor. He sank down onto his mattress and looked over at his sheet, which leaned against the wall at the head of the sleeping ledge in nightlight mode, numbers glowing red. It was slightly disorienting to discover it was not yet 9:00 at night. *That was faster than usual.*

Now wide awake, Joshua considered his options. With Spring having paused to gather steam for the heavier storms of Summer, most of the shops would be open well past midnight to take advantage of the lack of heavy rain at night. Joshua rose and went to the wall adjacent to the waterfall, pulled out a rock from a crevice at shoulder height, and removed his treasure box wrapped in cloth. He returned to the sleeping ledge, pushed aside the rumpled bedding, and sat on his bed with the box in his lap.

With one exception, he had spent just over a month alone in Sanctuary. *If I stick to the middle section of the Avenue, maybe no one will connect me with what happened to   him.* Opening the wooden box, he picked up his father's unit shoulder patch. *Resolute. Is that what I was? Or*   He put the patch aside and focused on counting his money *$12.38.*

Joshua surveyed the crumbs strewn next to his wicker chair and around the oven. After several tries, the baking experiments had turned out fairly well. The smoked SwampRabbit pizza with BBQ sauce had been excellent, and once he had added vegetable shortening, the round Orangecakes made a delicious dessert. The natural sweetness of the Nutegg custard along with grated Orange Tater had only required a little additional sugar in the baking mix. The ripe Chapples would have been a great natural sweetener, but Joshua could not even think of that fruit without becoming nauseous. In retrospect, the price he had paid in terror during the entire trip to acquire his baking supplies had been worth it *Just barely.*

He had entered via the scree pile at the end of The Avenue so he could use the roof tops the rest of the way in. From a spot on the roof across the street, he had observed the entrance to Mom's Vital Supplies. For an hour. Finally, he had worked up the courage to poke his head in the door, ready to flee in an instant, only to have "Mom" give him a croaky "hey" from under his mustache. Confirming the store to be otherwise empty, he had hurried to fill his list: flour, sugar, baking mix, yeast, BBQ sauce, shortening, and three boxes of tissues to deal with his allergy flare-up. Sniffling as he paid, Joshua had realized that the bulkiness of his purchases would require him to exit the city at pedway level. Furtively working his way UpAve toward The Swamp, he had been certain at every crevice and alley opening that the police were going to leap out and grab him.

Three days of blowing his nose had almost filled a two thirds cube with used tissues. The second tissue box was half empty, but whatever set off his sinuses at the beginning of every spring only pollenated for four to five days, meaning he had almost made it through the intensely unpleasant annual honking tradition. And he *did* honk when he blew his nose. His mother always called it Goosetime. With a smile, he filled another paper victim and arched the damp wad toward his make shift trash can. It fell short and bounced to a rest alongside a previous errant shot. *I'll get those later.* The used tissues stood out next to the only orderly things in Sanctuary – his two pairs of shoes lined up against the back wall. Guilt stirred at the sight and Joshua recalled the way his father had always kept his shoes and clothes neatly arranged in the closet. He looked at the dishes submerged in a water filled cube and the pile of clothes awaiting a wash by the exiting stream. The laundry reminded him of his underwear, most of which were now in varying states of holiness. *I'll have to tell M...*

The unexpectedness of the massive surge of despondency made it even more overwhelming. Joshua did not cry as he floated submerged under the wave of melancholy, but the awareness that he was so utterly alone crushed in on him. There was no one to get him new underwear, no one to help with the dishes, the cooking, the washing   no one to pick up the tissues. He looked at the white wads as if from a great distance. *Only me.*   If those tissues were going to be picked up, *he* would be the one to do it. *Whether it's now, 10 minutes from now, tomorrow   it will be me.*

The depression ebbed away while Joshua stared at the accumulated clutter. He was almost embarrassed by the clarity of his sudden insight, it was so obvious. *I can either live like **this**, or I can take care of it right away and live in a clean home.* He knew what his mother would have said, but *Now, I have to decide...*

He got up to retrieve the tissues, and stopped   a warm glow expanded into the space behind him. *Now* the tears flowed with the release of his long held subconscious weight of dread. It was the first time since he had used the blowgun that the presence had appeared. Joshua soaked in the sense of comfort that came from having the warmth hovering over his shoulder again. The warmth faded but somehow was not gone and he set about cleaning and straightening up his home. His tears of relief soon dried and his resolve hardened into a conviction that he would never again let his chores pile up. With that decision came a feeling of self-sufficiency that lightened the burden of being alone. *It makes things simple – it's me or it's nobody.*

Once Sanctuary was nice and tidy, Joshua looked at the time on his sheet and considered. He still had time to get in and out before midnight, when danger waxed as the sobriety of potential patrons waned. He scanned the just completed laundry hanging on the tall wicker screen he had created as a door to hold in some of the heat during the winter. He sorted through the less worn underwear until he could read the faint manufacturer screen printed label and determine the size. *Getting a bit snug, better go up a size.*

He had never seen clothes on his trips to Mom's, so *I have to go somewhere new.* Joshua mentally reviewed the three blocks of The Avenue nearest The Swamp, which he considered to be the safest section, and Aberly's Curio Shop came to mind. Among other odds and ends, it had featured a leather jacket in its single large display window. It was also the only completely enclosed shop on that block, which to Joshua suggested the potential of greater resources.

Aberly's it is.

◀2▶

I can't believe this.

Joshua was waiting for some rain, but for once, the clouds were not cooperating. *No one* in New Cincinnati missed an opportunity to walk with their heads uncovered. To do otherwise when it was not raining would draw immediate attention.

Finally, he slid down a pipe in an alleyway near the Curio Shop. As he had anticipated, the night was too early for much traffic, especially so far UpAve. Trying not to walk too fast, he crossed the dim street with slicker hood down and his face exposed, feeling as if a spotlight illuminated him on every step. He quickly slipped into the shop, but pulled up short once he closed the door. It did not feel cooler, exactly, but it was somehow much more comfortable than outside. His curiosity about the strange quality of the air vanished when he focused down the aisle before him and saw the shop owner.

Mr. Aberly's bald head gleamed, and his neatly trimmed goatee had a few grey streaks, but his face had no eyebrows. His tall, lean figure stood hunched over the back counter, a long, high collared tunic unbuttoned to reveal a clean white wicking undershirt. He was looking up from an open ledger, tapping it with a pen, staring at Joshua. But it was not the fact that the man was using an actual book and writing instrument. *It is a curio shop after all.* It was the scar. The thick red line ran from his sharply defined left cheekbone, across a narrow nose to intersect with the ridge of his hairless right eyebrow, lifting it in an arch that gave him a permanently quizzical expression. It continued up and around his shiny scalp to just above his ear, which sported a dangling, sparkling earring.

Aberly looked to the door, back down at his ledger, hesitated, and then looked up again to scrutinize Joshua. "You're alone?"

"Yessir."

Another pause   then   a decision. Mr. Aberly stood erect *He's Tall!* "I hope you will forgive my casual presentation," he made no move to button his outer garment, " and what might I do for you this fine evening,

The Deepest Cut

young sir?"

Joshua could not tell whether or not he was being mocked. "I... umm, I need some underwear."

"Well, I don't have much call for children's clothes, but I occasionally make some bulk acquisitions. I *do vaguely* recall an underwear purchase. Let me see, it would be... back under the human skulls to your left. You'll have to dig. If they are there, they'll be buried deep." In contrast to the menacing scar, he possessed an expansive smile that revealed straight bright teeth. "And when you are done there... Please, feel free to browse at your leisure." His arms swept wide in a grand gesture of inclusion, ending in a slight bow. *He **is** making fun of me.* Strangely, Joshua did not feel offended despite this conclusion. It in some way seemed Aberly was as much poking fun at himself.

Sure enough, he found a box of children's garments under the counter displaying three skulls, which actually did look real. The clothes were outdated in style, with bold patterns of garish colors. Luckily, all of the underwear were black and, of course, made of soft and stretchy HyperWick. Aberly had also been accurate about them being far down in the box. Nonetheless, Joshua eventually found one three-pack of the correct size. After reloading almost the entire box and sliding it back under the combined gaze of three dead people, he headed for the back counter with his prize, but stopped short when his eyes fell on an even more versatile treasure, Shark Tape. It was an extra sticky, super strong, and extra water proofed variant of the ever useful duct tape. He grabbed two rolls. As with every merchant Joshua had met thus far, Aberly appeared surprised when he actually produced the money to pay for the underwear and tape.

Completing the transaction, the tall bald man smiled at Joshua's repeated covert glances at his scar. He chuckled and confirmed, "Yes, it's real." Aberly's deep resonant voice invited Joshua's curious stare. "This," indicating his embroidered tunic, "is just window dressing. There's nothing like a good costume to get you in character." Seeing Joshua's befuddlement, he grinned and continued, "Used to be, I wouldn't have had to put on a show up here at the end of The Avenue. It was truly the Wild West when I arrived. I was fortunate to obtain employment with Mr. Aberly, sweeping out the water when it rained. *That* kept me occupied much of the time, obviously, and then there were the *desperate* attempts to repair leaks in the roof between storms. Got most of them,   eventually." His laugh rumbled low in response to Joshua's look of confusion. "No, my real name isn't Aberly. I just didn't have the money to buy a new sign when I inherited this place. Besides, it is   a *good* name."

"What *is* your real name?"

Aberly's eyes sharpened. "That   is simply *not*   a question you ask people here on The Avenue, boy. Even now. Not if you wish to retain your health."

Startled by the swift change in demeanor, Joshua stepped back, "I   I'm sorry."

The merchant's face softened. "If you are to survive The Avenue, you need to know the Rules of The Avenue." He pierced Joshua with an appraising squint before his eyes flicked to the empty front door. When his gaze returned, his eyes were softly apologetic above a sympathetic smile, "Please,   forgive my   *abruptness*. I too have walked a path of   self-sufficiency.   Allow me to share a bit of my story."

Aberly's gaze became distant for a moment, then he refocused into story telling mode. "I earned this scar the *hard* way, defending this shop against those who wanted this space. Back then, you had to *fight* to keep your stall. I was quite the mess after that one," he traced his scar from the eyebrow back, "scalp wounds are always *extra* bloody. It wasn't the cut that almost got me, though,   it was the infection that set in afterwards. *That* made it touch and go. After I almost died protecting his territory, old man Aberly started to move me up, teaching me how to acquire merchandise, to make sales. Years later, he sold me the shop so he could retire offplanet. Things have calmed down a lot since old Paul left, ...oh, I know the reputation is fierce, but property lines are pretty well drawn on The Avenue now and no one makes a   *violent* move to expand anymore, hence   " gesturing at his clothes, "sometimes the need to add *a little drama* to the shopping experience. Not to say it is totally tame nowadays. Just last month, the top pimp over in the Bordello section died of mysterious causes."

Joshua could not keep his eyes from widening, but Aberly did not see the reaction. He was stroking his goatee while contemplating the front door. Then, with a puzzled frown, he resumed talking.

"The cops were strangely quiet about that. Usually they come in and at least make a show of asking questions, even for a lowlife scum like that William fellow. This time,   *nothing.* They obviously don't know that not saying something sometimes draws more attention than yelling it out with a bellow."

Joshua could still feel the flush on his neck even though he had removed the look of shock from his face. However, his luck held. Aberly now looked inward with a distant smile, gathering the threads of his past, preparing to weave a tale.

"It was a small part, of course. I was mostly just a stage hand, working props and set changes, although   I became a pretty good set designer by the end. We were on Waverly's Outpost in the Carthineon District, mounting a revival of *The Bridgeman's Detour.* I tell you, provincials absolutely *love* melodrama. And I *love* that play, but   it was such a *God Awful* place – they had a *real* stockade, *literally* constructed out of logs! Needed it to keep out the Marauding Bull Weevils, whatever *they* were. Fortunately, we never found out.   *Anyway,*   my grand entrance was at the end of Act 1.   My role?   *Traveler #2,* a poor wretch who had stumbled into the deserted mansion located deep in the forest and, *of course*, he was seeking shelter from the storm. After slapping the lightning switch a couple of times, I would walk on stage and call out plaintively," Aberly paused with trembling hand to mouth, furtive eyes dancing about, then leaned forward and stretched out a loud, but tentative, "Hellllooo?"

He laughed and looked down at Joshua. "That was it.   *That*   was my line. But I tell you, I put *work* into that single word! I thought about it constantly   between   rehearsals,   how   Traveler   #2   was   driven   by circumstances beyond his control into a situation where he literally did not know what was behind the next door. How the dark external forces conspiring against him tested his courage to the utmost! And how with his choice to press forward, intrepid Traveler #2 was revealing the very Nobility of Humankind!" Aberly looked sideways at Joshua and gave a little shrug. "A bit over the top, I know, but such is the enthusiasm of youth."

He smiled and reengaged the story, "Now, according to the script, I was supposed to just walk up and open the door, but   *this* was my time on stage,   *alone!*   I could *feel* every eye on me, wondering   *what*   was I going to do next! So I   hesitated, turning first in one direction and then   in the other, s t r e t c h i n g out the tension. Aaannnnd," his eyes twinkled in amusement, "it just so happened that while frantically motioning for me to get on with the scene, the director dropped her clipboard. I'll tell you, with the screeches that came from me **and** the audience, well, *that* was **true** method acting! To her credit, when Miss Ross saw the crowd's reaction, she milked it for all it was worth throughout the rest of the run. She kept adding creaks and scuffs and knocks to the scene until it took me a full three minutes to reach the bedroom door."

Aberly crouched down and stretched forth a quivering hand about to grasp an imaginary door handle. "And **then,** just before I touched the knob, the lights went out! I'd let out a horrible shriek and fall to the floor with a thump. When the audience screams at last faded, cue the back light to shine through the now open door, splashing a bright rectangle across my fresh corpse to reveal the knife, driven to the hilt, only its handle protruding from my chest!" He finished with both hands grasped in front of his chest.

Aberly shook his head as his hands dropped from his chest, "And many other challenges have driven me to the hilt since then." His laugh from the belly made a hearty rumble, "Oh, Ho! Goodness, I haven't thought about that in years! Now what made me think of that? Oh, yes, silence speaking more loudly than shouts." He shook his head. "Well, no telling why the police do what they do. Really don't see them down here that much anyway, which is odd in itself, given our reputation."

Seeking to keep the merchant from returning to unwanted topics, Joshua blurted out, "Do you need someone to sweep the shop for you?"

Aberly smiled, sighed, and shook his head again. "Why do you think I enclosed this place anyway, if not to avoid *ever* having to squeegee out a floor again? Well, *and* to add the dehumidifier. How *do* you people live in this constant humidity? It's been 20 years and I *still* can't stand it. I lived on travel rations for an entire year paying that thing off. And I'm here to tell you, it was worth every haulin' non-bite!"

Aberly responded to Joshua's silent question, "Born and raised on New Phoenix." He shook his head. "All of the new colonies clung to memories of Earth back then," he stopped and smiled ruefully, "but then, I guess things haven't changed so much, seeing as we're having this little conversation in New Cincinnati. I have just always thought they could come up with some names that possess a little verve and excitement!   I mean, instead of New Phoenix, which I always considered to be redundant, why not name it Inferno?   or   The Oven?   or even,   Dry Heat!" Joshua's blank look startled him out of his brief rant. "But, I'm sorry, you were asking for a job." He looked down and tapped the ledger with his pen. "I am *truly* sad to report that business has been very slow of late. Mostly a consequence of being this far UpAve. That's the Dark Side of our nasty reputation as far as profits go, in that most customers seem afraid to venture all the way to this end of The Avenue. Sorry, son, I'd like to help you out, but I'm just barely keeping afloat."

Joshua sighed, then gave a sly smile. "Well, that's ok, 'cause   the sun will come out   to-morrow."

"Ho, HO! *Annie!*   Don't tell me you are an aficionado of musical theatre?"

"Afec what?"

"A connoisseur. Someone who is very fond of and knowledgeable about a topic."

Joshua shrugged. "I don't know about that, but my Mom and I always listened to show tunes when we cooked or cleaned."

Aberly's eyes narrowed at Joshua's use of past tense, but then he smiled expansively. "Well, there you have it then. You are an aficionado of musical theatre!"

Joshua returned the smile. "Did you do music theatre?"

The bald man's face contorted in horror. "OH good heavens, NO! *My* singing would bring tears to a cat's eyes. The very *essence* of caterwauling!" His face softened, his voice imbued with sincere concern, "I regret I cannot offer you employment." Aberly's head cocked in hesitation. "You might try farther up The Avenue, but if you decide to take a shot with those   'merchants,'   be sure they pay you after every shift, or you might find you have put in a week's worth of work without recompense,   er,   a paycheck."

Joshua nodded. "OK." A grin stole across his face. "Because I'm not throwin' away my shot!"

Aberly's finger jabbed out at Joshua. "Hamilton! Now *that's* a musical theatre role I *could* play," jazz hands spread wide as he intoned, "no singin', just faaaast talkin'."

Driven to the Hilt

Joshua's smile was bittersweet. The fond memories of his mother came with a hollow ache of loneliness. For just a moment, he had found someone who shared the same enthusiasm for exchanging lyrics he and his mother had enjoyed, someone who offered the possibility of bringing his mother back to life in a small way. But then,   Aberly had neither the need nor the money to hire him it seemed.

He closed the front door behind him, making sure to pull it tight into its frame, and turned about in the shallow inset of the doorway, feeling the moist air envelop him. Unlike during his trip in, Joshua did not peer into the surrounding shadows, seeking out possible threats. He had been reassured by what Aberly had told him about Uncle William, the lack of a police presence, and the less violent nature of The Avenue in general. He checked the density of raindrops against the nearest streetlamp. *Oh sure! Now it comes.* Joshua pulled up his hood against the drifting sheets of rain and walked away from the shop with a lighter step, despite the melancholy of his remembrances and his lack of income.

A pair of eyes locked onto the boy as he moved through the medium rain, the broken reflections of the colored neon from the Curio Shop sliding across the back of his wet slicker. Shiny black shoes fell into step behind the receding figure of the boy as he walked UpAve toward The Swamp.

◄3►

That's odd. Why's he turning into that dead end? The man picked up his pace and rounded the corner to see the boy facing a blank wall, finishing an adjustment to the strap of his shoulder satchel so his bag rested against his lower back.

"Hey kid!"

The boy's head snapped around, black opening of his hood taking a fraction of a second to assess, and then the little body erupted into motion toward the dumpster on the right. But instead of jumping on top of the dumpster, as the man expected, the boy ricocheted off its side back to the left and elevated with hands outstretched for a previously unnoticed exterior drainpipe. As the hands grasped the tube halfway up, the hood of the slicker fell back to reveal a thin boy's face looking back at him. In that brief moment of eye contact, Estanod was struck by the appraising quality of the boy's expression. *No fear.* He then noted a familiarity to the lines of the boy's features. Before he could place the face, the figure moved with an unnaturally quick precision to streak up to the roof. Estanod activated his slack-jaw and heard the bouncing echo of his voice, "WAIT! KID!" He quickly added, "I just want to talk," but the form had already disappeared over the edge of the roof parapet.

Detective Estanod sensed that the boy was waiting just out of sight. He struggled to put a name to the face while he searched for the right words. Pulling back his cowl, he stepped forward, ignoring the rain and allowing his face to be revealed by a rare working security lamp over a nearby door. Then it came to him *The spiderviper kid! Holy Space Crap! He's still alive.* Estanod squatted down, holding his hands out to his sides, palms forward.

"Look, kid, I *knew* you didn't have anything to do with your mom dying. I *know* it is too late, what with you already running and all, but the labs *did* come back proving it wasn't human blood on that stickball lance. I kept checking at OBS to see if you'd been picked up, but " He waited. Nothing. "I guess you found someplace to stay.   So   I can give you back your Mom's desk if you want."

From five feet to the right of where he had vaulted the roof wall, a young voice drifted down, "No   Thank you."

Still polite after all this? When it became clear that the kid, *Joshua something,* had no intention of revealing himself, Estanod continued.

"Okay. Anyway,   well,   I need your help.   It could mean some money for you," he enticed softly.   Nothing.   *I need to find some common ground.*   "Listen, ah   Joshua," *Oh yeah, Vernon! How could I forget, with all that the Sarge had spilled about his Dad.* "I gotta be honest with you." He kept his tone casual, "Some guy got stuck by a spiderviper a couple of days ago, just like your mother. Now this guy was a real sputum bag, so it's not like anyone misses him, not even the whores that worked for him, but they found him two lengths into town. And I can tell you, **that** got City Hall all in a wad.   They'd be *real* interested in knowing about you, *but*   I'm not going to tell them anything."

The boy's question came three feet to the left of where he had last spoken, "If he was such a bad man, why didn't you arrest him?"

Pretty cagey, kid. He might just do the trick.

Estanod looked away in disgust as he spat, "That's a *great* question, kid. I'm not in Vice, so I can't really say. But I do know what he did to children," he was surprised to see the small dark head rise up several feet further to the left, then continued, "kids like you. I **know** he was a bad man and he *deserved* to die. Not like   your Mom." Estanod waited, feeling the eyes of the boy weighing him. A moment later, he was surprised yet again.

"How am I going to make money?"

Straight to business, huh? OK. "I need someone to keep an eye on everyone who goes in and out of a warehouse just to the west of The Avenue."

"Why not set up a camera?"

"My *budget*," he said derisively, "won't cover a video camera with enough electronic shielding to get past their sweepers. Besides, I'd have to find a place to set it up where it wouldn't be found overnight. I, ah   don't know where that would be, to tell you the truth.   So, bottom line?   I need some eyes on."

"Are they bad like Uncle William?"

"Well, they **are** bad, but for different reasons. Earl Bosemon is bad because he is getting people hooked on the drugs he's bringing here from off world."

"Has he just started doing that?"

Officer Estanod peered up at Joshua, but could not make out the boy's expression from where he now stood, looking down from behind the roof wall. Deciding the boy's tone was sincere, Estanod sighed before continuing, "OK,   well,   *certain people* don't mind about the drugs until they start causing problems with production,   at say,   the mines, for example." From the way the boy said "OK," Estanod did not believe he understood the implications. *Should I try to explain further?*

"How much?"

The interruption gave Estanod an excuse to focus away from his dilemma about explaining. And he *needed* greater emotional distance to justify involving the boy. Besides,   *Hell, if even **I** don't understand everything involved, how can I explain it to him?*

"So?" The boy pushed the issue.

Estanod brushed aside his sense of unease. *This kid's smart,   a survivor.   He'll be OK.* He began the negotiations. "Three credits per week."

"How many nights a week?"

"Well,   I need all seven covered."

"How long each night?"

"Prime time is between 8 and 2."

"Nothing *really* happens before 9."

This is getting out of hand. "Yeah, well,   all right. 9 to two. *Every* night. Deal?"

"Five."

"Huh?"

"Five UDs a week."

"No *way*, kid.   I *told* you, I'm on a limited budget." The head disappeared.

The thought of the time it would take to find another street urchin, compounded with his lingering guilt, forced Estanod into a quick decision.

"OK!   Ok.   Five a week. But you'll have to come down here so I can give you something you're going to need."

The head appeared above the drain pipe. *How does he* do *that without making any noise?* Again Estanod perceived the intense scrutiny of an appraising look. Then, in what seemed to be one motion, the boy leapt over the wall, slid down the pipe, landed on the ground, and turned to face Estanod. Following a moment of hesitation   the boy walked across to just within arm's reach, but he stood sideways, prepared for an instant break to the pipe.

With exaggerated caution, Estanod extended a metal rectangle that filled the palm of his hand. The boy made no move to take it.

"What's that?"

Estanod pulled open the top layer of the device, making it pivot back like a clam shell.

"It's called a flip phone, but it's really more of a flip walkie-talkie. And I can tell you, it wasn't easy to find. Turns out, they are used by warehouse workers to monitor inventory. For security reasons, owners don't want anyone to know exactly when workers are checking inventory during off hours, so they keep most of the warehouse lights out the entire night. This pCom device takes low frequency infrared photos of the merchandise in the low light, with the squarecode matrix automatically uploading to the data management system. The system is low wattage, so it shouldn't be detectable by Bosemon's counter measure sweepers from across the street, especially since you'll only be taking an occasional photo. The images can be converted from infrared to black and white, even full color. That's why this works so great for us. Wouldn't be good for you to take flash photos of everyone coming and going from Bosemon's headquarters."

His chuckle died in the face of the kid's flat stare. He snapped the flip phone closed and turned the face of the device toward Joshua. "So, you press and hold this button under the viewscreen like this," the screen that occupied most of the phone face popped to life, "line up the shot on the screen,   see? and when you let go-" There was a blinding flash.

"Crap!! I thought I had that disabled."

Estanod blinked furiously to ease the afterimage of the dumpster from his vision, only to discover that he stood in the alley, alone. He looked up. Joshua looked back down at him from the roof.

"Geez, kid, how do you *do* that?"

Not really anticipating an answer, an expectation that was duly rewarded, Estanod focused on blinking through the green ghost of the dumpster while reviewing the settings. He talked out loud as he worked through the screens, trying to reassure Joshua that he really had made a mistake. Finally, he took a picture of the dumpster without incapacitating himself and then held the flip phone up in the air. "There!"

Estanod looked up and gave a start when he discovered Joshua had again descended and stood several feet away. With a slight shake of his head he extended the phone.

"Check it all out on your own, just to be certain. I'm sure you can figure it out better than me."

The boy took a long step and made a smooth snatch of the pCom device extended forward in Estanod's fingertips. Immediately returning to his prior distance, the boy said, "I'm sure too."

Estanod voiced his amusement, "HO! Wall climbing **and** a sense of humor. Perfect!"

The boy shrugged and took another step back as he looked at the phone. *So different. So much more cautious – and in control. What changed this kid?*

"So I have programmed it to send the images to– *What?* Look, kid, I tested the transfers out and it works, OK? OK. So, I have it relaying through five public IP addresses before it gets to my personal computer. Now, I know, that's not enough to stop a really determined scorpion, but Bossman has no reason to look for our transmissions and even *he* doesn't have the resources to monitor **all** of the wireless traffic on The Avenue. Not yet, anyway."

"Who's Bossman?"

"Oh, well, that's what Mr. *Bosemon* makes all of the punks who work for him call him. I really don't know what's up with the names in this place – The Avenue, The Swamp, Bossman What? What's so funny, kid?"

"Nothing. Someone else said the same thing a bit ago, that's all.

Should I call you The Cop?"

"Ha, ha, you *are* the comedian, aren't you? No, Estanod is fine."

"But I guess I'm The Kid?"

Estanod looked at the boy for a moment, but saw no waver. "It's not as if we parted as the best of friends last time, but   fair enough, *Joshua*. And you still haven't *said* you are going to do this."

Joshua shrugged. "Yeah, well, you can call me The Kid if you want." Then he surprised Estanod by stepping forward and stretching out his hand. As they shook, The Kid said, "Deal."

"Good. So I'm gonna head over to Bossman's. You can follow me from up there, right?"

"Right."

"Great. So,   what I need is for you to take a picture of everyone who goes in or out of this warehouse. Once we've figured out the regulars, you'll just shoot anyone who's new."

"That's it?"

"That's it."

Estanod did not spot Joshua once during his trek over to the drug dealer's headquarters, even though he tried to sneak regular peeks without drawing attention from others on The Avenue. When he arrived, Estanod slouched against a wet wall, took out his minisheet, and dialed up the flip phone. Joshua answered on the first ring.

"You there?"

"Yep." The connection terminated.

Making his way away from the warehouse through a sudden heavy shower, Estanod continued to reassure himself that involving the young orphan did not violate his personal integrity. *That quick disconnect shows he already knows surveillance security. Besides, he probably really needs the money,   and Bossman isn't going to pay to check* a sudden blast of wind driven rain slapped his face and knocked his slicker hood back. Head down, Estanod's hand held onto his hood, pulling the edge down to block the driven raindrops. He held it there, covering his face, long after the winds from the passing squall line had moved on to pound down rain into The Swamp.

◄4►

This sucks.

The smell of wet tar seemed to assault his nose with the explosion of each raindrop in front of his face. Joshua lay belly down on a sloped rooftop, right ear already sore from pressing against the hard surface through the hood of his slicker. His head rested as far back in his hood as he could get it before the opening closed and cut off his view, but that kept it close enough that splatter off of the asphalt shingle roof still reached his face. His entire face had become wet within five minutes and every few seconds a tiny droplet would hit his eye to make him blink. Despite it being a relatively light rain, the upsplash from the drops obscured most of the field of vision for his right eye.

This REALLY sucks. And I'm just getting started.

It was his first night of surveillance. He lay on the roof of the building across from what seemed to be the main warehouse entrance, although he was not sure of that. It had just been the first feature he had come to after he had started working his way around the huge building, so he had settled down to observe for a while. He could see Glin leaning against one of the walls of the inset entryway, conversing with a stocky man whose burr cut accentuated the way his ears stuck out from the side of his head. *I wish I knew what they were saying.* They occasionally laughed at something one or the other said, but they would always look out at each passerby, heads turning slightly as they made their determination of the potential threat level. When the traffic became light, they would sometimes look out to check the rain status, which all residents of New Cincinnati did frequently, out of habit. Such checks became more frequent with stronger precipitation, as Joshua was appreciating at that moment, with larger raindrops now pounding down in earnest.

Joshua endured the water torture for almost 40 minutes before deciding to check for other entrances to Bossman's warehouse. He eased his left hand up to his face until he could wipe off the sheen of cold water. When he opened his eyes after the long swipe, his heart seized to a stop.

Big Ears had stepped to the front of the alcove and was looking right at him. The door guard seemed to be squinting. A moment later, his eyes began moving back and forth over the roof as he expanded his search, but they quickly came back to rest on Joshua. Another squint of concentration for three   four   five heartbeats before the thug's face relaxed and he turned away, apparently making a humorous comment, because Glin laughed. Joshua let out his breath in a quiet whoosh, irrationally not wanting to do anything that might draw attention. Once his breathing and heart rate had returned to normal, he recalled his close encounter with Glin's young compatriot, Tylir.

It must have been some vague memory of the way the shadows were supposed to have looked on the wall that had warned him. However, Joshua knew he had almost ignored that warning just as Tylir had made a noise. He had been lucky then, and he was lucky now, having stopped moving just before Big Ears had looked up and seen something that did not quite fit. But he had to find a way to lower his risk of being spotted.

He pivoted his head to look up the roof. The gradual slope continued another 20 feet up to where an uneven wall extended the height of the interior space. For some reason, a narrow cut back had been put in the second story wall that created 10 foot deep recess before coming back out and across for an additional 15 feet and ending. The peaked first story roof to the right of where the second story ended had been Joshua's path in to his current observation spot just under an hour ago.

Joshua started to turn his head back to check on the entrance, but he stopped, realizing that he had no way of knowing whether or not Big Ears or Glin was looking up at him at that very moment. Finally, he took a deep breath, spun his head back around, and heaved a sigh of relief to see they were occupied with another person in the alcove. He took the opportunity to scramble up sideways to the second story recess. Laying down with his feet flat against one wall, he stretched his left arm out and felt that two knuckles were past the corner of the far recess wall, all the while keeping an eye on the entranceway. Waiting until several people were walking by the warehouse entrance, he slithered across the extensively patched roof and made his escape over the crest of the first story roof.

Once far enough down the opposite slope, Joshua sat in the easy rain and caught his breath. Regaining his nerve, he worked his way completely around Bossman's warehouse. There was no other pedway access to the structure except for a second story fire escape with a ladder that was rotated into a horizontal position 12 feet above the pedway. It might provide an exit for people in the warehouse, but not an entry for business associates, which was the kind of visitor in which Estanod had expressed an interest. Leaving nothing to chance, Joshua descended to the motorway level, and on the back side of the warehouse, found three loading dock bays with a metal door to one side. Hood covering his face, he sauntered up as if on a scavenging run, and saw that the locks and chains were rusted. That confirmed it: the entrance guarded by Big Ears and Glin would be the only one where any important visitors would go.

Joshua stood in the shadows and struggled to decide. The thought of going back up and lying on the roof was intolerable, but he did not like the idea of failing to do his job. Finally, he rationalized that if he did not come up with a long-term solution, he would not be able to do the job at all. *Besides, if he gets mad, I'll just tell him not to pay me for tonight.*

Already at motorway level, Joshua worked his way back toward the oldest part of the city, where the good citizens of New Cincinnati dumped their unwanted possessions. It proved to be a banner night. Not only had someone made extensive changes to their window coverings, but he had the incredible good fortune of coming across a bundle of plain black children's ponchos. This was unexpected, since *no one* in New Cincinnati easily threw away something they needed every time they opened the front door. But the really big bonus was the discarded stereo system. True, there could be no actual "stereo" with only one speaker, but it was still better than nothing at all and a quick check showed the CFU was still functional.

Having slept much of the day in preparation for a full night of work, Joshua was not tired after depositing his loot on Sanctuary's stone floor. Although the music system appeared to have made the journey without getting too wet, he decided to let the single speaker completely air out overnight before turning it on again. *Show tunes 'll have to wait. Besides, Fun is always funner whenever your work is done-er!* He had made up the awkward rhyme when he was five. Joshua could still picture his parents doubled over laughing and recalled his puzzled reaction. *It did rhyme after all.* The memory brought a sad smile. Joshua sighed and then got to work.

Using an old serrated steak knife, he cut three long plastic curtain control rods into five foot lengths. Lying with his feet flat against a wall, he adjusted two more rods until they reached from the wall to just under the two knuckles on his stretched out left hand. He then taped these pieces together with Shark Tape to create a cross piece before taping on the prior cut rods as upright supports. After experimenting some with his mattress to imitate the sloped roof, he cut three more rods, which he attached to the cross piece and connected at the back ends to form the frames for the roof panels. Cutting up the ponchos, he had completed both roof panels and half of the front wall of his blind when he ran out of tape.

Sleeping until mid-morning, a quick trip to Aberly's gained him a silent rise of both brows in response to his need for two more rolls of Shark Tape, but the old thespian said nothing as he made change. It took until midafternoon to find three more opaque slickers and return to Sanctuary, where Joshua quickly finished the front drape and constructed the side walls. After an hour of putting his nose to the slicker walls and forcing his bleary eyes to search for leaks, he almost kicked himself for stupidity. He climbed into bed and slept until his alarm woke him in the late evening.

Turning on the lantern to full luminance, he placed it inside the blind, which he had set up on the back wall of Sanctuary. Once looking back from Headbanger, tiny creases and holes of light were visible in a variety of spots in the front walls and roof of the blind. It was not long before he had patched all of the light leaks. His satisfaction was short lived.

How am I going to see out?

Several hours later, Joshua stood at Headbanger with his sheet glowing red in nightlight mode. While watching pVid, he had asked his mother why the lights in the submarine were red during battle stations, prompting a pause of the movie and quick research to discover that a buildup of rhodopsin in the eyes was responsible for night vision and that it did not break down under red light. This time the memory of his mother brought a fond smile. Joshua turned off the nightlight and only had to wait a moment to see the tiny glow in the middle of the front blind panel where light leaked from the hole he had cut for the phone camera lens. He crawled inside the blind and added a piece of tape to the small pocket he had attached to the inside of the slicker wall. The inserted flip phone clamped on both sides of the pocket, the front screen on the outside of the pocket facing back, the lens on the back of the phone facing out through the hole. Another check at Headbanger and the flip phone was ready to take photos.

The next night, he had to wait almost three hours for a downpour loud enough to cover his erection of the blind. He anchored the back edge with Shark Tape and then affixed three small corners of a cube as cups for the ends of the upright poles. This way, when Joshua departed at two in the morning, he could rotate the poles up to allow the black blind to lay flat on the building roof, hopefully looking like another roof patch during the day.

With the blind up, he crawled in and faced the phone pocket. Despite having repeatedly tested for light leaks, Joshua's anxiety mounted as he activated the flip phone control screen. He had already put the screen on its lowest light setting, but still felt as if he sat in a glaring spotlight. He rushed to slip the phone into its pocket and became almost frantic as he manipulated the screen controls to zoom in.

Joshua sighed in relief. Even through the pummeling rain, he could see Glin and Big Ears lounging in the front alcove of the warehouse. They were not looking out much because no one was on the street. Everyone knew such summer squalls did not last long. *Speaking of which...*

Joshua took the opportunity to place an All-Day bar and old Restorade bottle filled with water next to him on the roof so that he could fold his now empty school satchel for use as a seat cushion. He sat so he could place a knee on the flap *just right* putting the lens on target, and waited for the real test. It came less than 10 minutes later.

The downpour had fizzled out into sporadic waves of light rain. Such stroll in the park conditions increased the flow of traffic, prompting Glin and Big Ears to look out and check on people Joshua could not see as they passed by. Although his nervousness had ebbed during the intervening 10 minutes, his gut seized when Big Ears stepped out, looked up, and scanned across the roof. But the turn of the man's head did not pause, and after a brief moment, he stepped back under cover.

Joshua's shoulders slumped and he wiped the accumulated sweat from his face. He still could not hear anything from the entranceway, but he could see and   he could stick out an entire shift under the blind. *That's all I need to do my work.*

Or so he thought.

This is going to kill me.

Joshua tried not to grunt as he went through his series of stretches, all while keeping the now hated flip phone screen in sight. Over the last fifteen days, he had become quite adept at detecting which movements on the screen involved the arrival of a visitor. Of course, *then*, he had to sit at the ready for anywhere between five and thirty minutes, since he had to wait until they exited the warehouse before their faces would be revealed. Joshua switched legs, shifting position while making sure to avoid knocking the curtain rod propped from the roof to the side of the phone pocket. He had rigged the rod system after just one night of being stuck constantly holding the front flap so the lens stayed on target. It sometimes slipped off when the wind gusted, but at least he could move around some.

Bouncing an ear at his other knee, Joshua appreciated the pain in his hamstring and lower back, since it also served to keep him awake. As had been the case for the last several days, nothing of interest was happening. He had already photographed several dozen mostly male visitors. Estanod had sent back texts that tagged the converted photos as low level street dealers, so Joshua now knew every regular gang member on sight, most just by their clothes, although he always confirmed their identity when they exited. While Estanod had verified their profession, their dilapidated clothing and haggard faces signaled they were also regular customers.

Joshua liked the ten UDs he had thus far collected, but he did not know how much longer he could stick with the excruciatingly boring duty. *I'm actually starting to miss spidervipers chasing m- Wait!* **this** *guy is new.*

The man approaching the entrance was of medium height and build, but it was the designer slicker that made Joshua scramble to the phone. His readiness paid off. While Big Ears coded open the door, the man gave a furtive glance back over his shoulder. *There!* Joshua caught a glimpse of a sharp nose on a narrow face snap before the man turned back around and entered the warehouse.

Joshua touched the flip phone screen to pull up the transmission menu, pressed in a code and settled to wait for the man's exit and a better shot. He was shocked when the phone immediately vibrated and "2 35" appeared on the screen. *He wants to meet? What the heck is going on? OK, I've still got 35 minutes.* He continued to watch. Strangely, Glin came out into the drifting heavy mist to lean against the wall next to the entrance. Then they both waited   and   waited   until, Hawkface stepped from the door. Joshua grimaced. The man had his head down as he emerged. But then he hesitated in pulling up his hood and lifted his face to look in both directions, giving just enough time for Joshua to see snap his face with much greater clarity. Hood up, Hawkface stepped from the warehouse and set off on a quick pace DownAve. A moment later, Glin followed the man.

Joshua felt torn. This was very unusual and he thought about following too, but it led in the opposite direction from the #2 rendezvous point. He pulled out the phone and checked the screen clock. *OK, there's some time.*

After an agonizingly slow exit from the blind to avoid drawing Big Ears' attention, Joshua was exhilarated to be sprinting across the roofs. Luckily, he soon picked up Glin's slicker and then caught a confirmatory glimpse of Hawkface 20 feet farther ahead. He settled into an easier pace, making periodic deviations to the edges of the roofs to ensure he did not lose them. Then he came to the edge of downtown and ran out of upper story roadway. Joshua looked across at the four square blocks of office towers and massive governmental buildings. *Can't run those roofs.* He squatted down and watched in frustration as his query entered the high rise district, turned a corner, and disappeared.

Joshua wondered if he could circle and pick them up on the other side, but with a lurch of his stomach, he pulled out the phone and saw *I should have been there 5 minutes ago! Time to scat.*

The words came as soon as his feet hit the ground in the isolated back alley. A gruff, "You're late," preceded Estanod as he emerged from the shadows.

"There was something I had to do." *That came out wrong,* Joshua realized as he heard himself. Before he could explain that he had stayed to follow up on a new visitor, Estanod retorted.

"Nobody likes a smart ass, kid."

Already off balance, Joshua's come back slipped out before he could stop it, "It's better than being a dumb ass."

Estanod contemplated him impassively. Joshua wanted to look away, but held the gaze until...

"That's what my dad always used to say." Relieved by Estanod's slight smile, he pressed on with business, "I waited for a better shot."

Joshua was confused when Estanod's amusement faded and his face became uncertain, his unfocused eyes looking pensive. The tension built as the patter of raindrops grew in intensity until the only thing Joshua could think to do was-

"I'm sorry. I don't remember a lot about my Dad anymore, but I do remember he liked to joke around with me."

Estanod tilted his head. "Huh?"

"I'm *sorry*. About the smart ass thing."

"Oh. Right." The cop seemed to shake himself back to the present and gestured toward the covered alcove that was Rendezvous #2. Once out of the rain, with slicker hoods pulled back, there was just enough light for Joshua to see the intensity in Estanod's frown. He steeled himself.

"Look, about your Dad there's ah something you should know about him."

Joshua's stomach twisted. His jaw clenched along with his fists.

"He didn't help the pirates."

"Huh?" The 180 degree turn completely threw Joshua. "What?"

"Listen. Joshua. This is one of those I heard it from someone who heard it from someone else kind of things, you know? So it's not like you could take this to court or anything. But I just thought you ought to know, you know, for *yourself*. What I heard was that there was a lot of evidence that he fought hard against the pirates *really* hard. Even after he was the last guy left, he didn't give up. He kept on fighting up until he well, to the end." Estanod gave a tiny shrug. "I just thought you should know."

Joshua blinked, pushing the tears out to drop and mix with the rain splatter he had not yet wiped from his face. He saw his mother, much younger, squatting down in front of him, her hands holding his shoulders tight, earnestly trying to convince him not to believe what people said. He had tried *really hard* but, buried so very deep inside, no matter what he had said to please his mother, there had always been unanswered questions of doubt. *I'm so sorry, Mom.* Wet eyes squeezed tight, he finally gave voice to those whispers.

"Why would all those people lie? They wouldn't *all* lie, would they?" He opened his eyes and fixed Estanod with a hard stare. "The *police* wouldn't lie, right?"

Estanod's voice was soft, "Not many people knew the truth when it first happened, Joshua. **I** sure didn't. It wasn't until *much* later that I heard what I just told you. And know this, the way that person said it, I *believe* what he told me about your Dad."

Joshua frowned, "But why would the people who *did* know, why would *they* lie about it?" His mouth twisted and the next word escaped with a sob, "WHY?"

Estanod knelt down and put a hand on Joshua's arm. "This is gonna sound obvious, Joshua, but outer space is *big*. Hugely *vastly* **big**. So the only way for one ship to find another out in space is for them to communicate with each other, *or* for one ship to know exactly where the other is going to go. In other words, someone *had* to betray your Dad's ship." He squeezed Joshua's arm in emphasis. "Now you and I *know* it wasn't your Dad, but whoever it was would want to blame it on someone else and people in power *always* want to blame things on *someone,* so that no one blames it on *them.* I guess your Dad was just the easiest to blame."

Joshua could feel his insides quiver, *buzz* with a desire, *a resolve* to someday make those people pay for what they had said about his Dad. He leaned in, face intent. "Thanks for telling me." Then, feeling goop on his upper lip, he looked away and wiped his nose with his free slicker sleeve.

Estanod let go of his arm and smiled. "You're welcome." He stood back up. "So. I couldn't tell much from the first picture. Bad angle and a bit blurred." A grimace of annoyance, and worry, slid across the man's face. "It looked sort of familiar. That's why I called the meeting. I'm hoping you got a better exit shot." When Joshua nodded and reached for the phone in his slicker pocket, Estanod tried to lighten the mood again, asking in a soft teasing tone, "Aanndd, you were *late* because you had something to do after sending the first shot?"

"Yeah. When Glin followed him, *that* was totally new, so I followed Glin to see where they went."

"And?"

Joshua shrugged. "I don't know. I ran out of roof when they went into the Downtown complex. So I headed back here. It took a little while." He handed over the flip phone.

Estanod worked through the screen menu to pull up the exit photo of the new visitor. He frowned and then pressed the screen several times to convert it. Estanod's vile curses shocked Joshua. When his displeasure finally ran out of steam, the policeman handed back the phone and pulled out his minisheet. With a few slides of the finger and some brief typing, he brought up a stock photo and turned the device to show Joshua.

"That's him."

Estanod cursed again. "Fabulous. That's just fab u lous." He lifted the sheet, "*That* is Owan Tiast, the Mayor's personal assistant."

"Why does that make you so mad?"

"Joshua, the slime *always* spreads when politicians stick their toes in the water."

"So, you don't like the Mayor?"

"No, I don't," Estanod admitted. "I'm pretty sure she's not using drugs, but if this means she's connected to the people bringing the drugs in, then this is a whole new ball game." Estanod shot Joshua an uncomfortable glance. "Mayor Greenwood has a *reputation*. She's a real Iron Maiden." Seeing Joshua's confused frown, he elaborated, "She has a rep for being a hard ass. She is *not* a person to cross. Of course, Mr. Tiast could be operating on his own, but anyway you cut it, things have just gotten a lot messier." Estanod dug into his pocket and extended a $5 credit note.

Joshua hesitated, "Ah, there's still most of the week…"

"Yeah, that's OK, I'm just paying you a little in advance, you know, while we're already meeting. Simpler that way."

Joshua reluctantly accepted the money. It was not in keeping with all of Estanod's grousing about his limited budget and there was something very unsettling about the way The Cop stole glances at him. Clearly something had changed, but Joshua did not quite understand what it was, other than "not good." That made it all the more surprising when Estanod's face suddenly brightened.

"Oh, that reminds me." The Cop's face assumed a sly eagerness. "I have something for you." He reached into a large outer slicker pocket, pulled out something wrapped in butcher paper, extending it to Joshua.

Joshua took it, squinted at a grinning Estanod, then began unwrapping. He held up a 10-inch long thick wire, with a bulb on one end and an equal length of cord coming from the other.

"A directional mic!"

"Yep. Had to finagle things a bit and call in some favors, but I thought you were right. It *would* help to know what's being said down there."

"Yes. This will *definitely* help. Thanks!"

Joshua's mood buoyed up. Not only would he be free to just listen, instead of having to watch the screen every moment, but eavesdropping on Glin and Big Ears might provide some clue about what was worrying Estanod. His dread at the thought of finishing his shift lessened considerably.

"Keep an eye, *and ear*, on things, but make sure you don't get spotted."

Joshua turned to leave, but Estanod reached out to grasp his shoulder, bringing him up short.

"I mean it, Kid!   Be *careful*."

Joshua looked at the hand in surprise, prompting the policeman to release his grip. He searched Estanod's face for a moment, nodded once, before scurrying up a drain pipe and vaulting over the roof wall.

Estanod let out a long breath and looked down to stare at Tiast's face on his sheet. Eventually, screen saving mode kicked in, prompting him to turn and head back to police headquarters. Returning his minisheet to its holster under his slicker, Estanod muttered, "This isn't going to end well."

◄6►

A distant metallic clunk pulled Joshua's eyes up in time to see the front door swing open. *Did I just hear the lock bolt?* Big Ears' feet appeared and then brought the rest of him out into the entryway, where he turned and fell back against the wall with a thump. "Ummph!" The grunt confirmed it *the mic does work!*

Joshua leaned forward eagerly, excited to finally have something else to occupy his attention during his long hours in the blind *this is so much better.* He also hoped to discover why the evening had started so differently, with only Glin standing watch for the first half hour. Bossman's top street eye obviously wanted to know the reason as well.

"So? What's the deal?"

A headless Big Ears grunted again, before asking his own question, "So, exactly what have you heard about the Lady in Red?

Only Glin's lower jaw was visible, but Joshua could see his shoulders shrug. "Hardly anything, you know, *specific.* But everyone's antsy about her being here. Seems she brought along some ultra serious muscle."

"Oh, yeah. She's pullin' some slick security, fer sure. Especially some blonde dude. Dropped three guys at Charlie's Bar before any of 'em could git a shot off. Sounded like he could give Fenster a run fer his money."

Glin grunted at the idea that anyone could challenge Fenster. Then the rain abruptly slacked and pedway traffic picked up as people hurried to their destinations, hoping to beat the next cloudburst. Once the flow slacked some, Big Ears shifted topics.

"How 'bout you? How much longer you on Door Duty?"

"Don't know. Bossman didn't say."

"He still pissed?"

"Not that much, really. But I had to report in front of *her.* And *she* went off."

"Whew! *That's* never a fun thing." Joshua could almost see Big Ears shaking his head in disgust. "So the BossBitch riled up the Bossman?"

"Oh, *yeah.* It was close, and Tylir's still riding choppy waters, but he'll be safe as long as he keeps his head down."

"In the meantime, you've got Door Duty. Not that I'm complainin'. Havin' company makes the time go a lot faster. But, it's gotta suck pullin' a shift here an' then runnin' the streets the rest of the night after that."

"Well, like you said, it's not so bad out here with you, cause we can joke around while we do our security checks. But, yeah, by the end of the night, I'm pretty much soggy toast."

"I'll bet. Welp, it ain't never good fer *nobody* when a mean spirited woman knows she has big time back-up. But then the way I reckon, she's 'bout ta hit her limit. It's been six months and Bossman's girlfriends rarely last longer 'n seven or eight. Gotta say, I'd rather it was sooner than later. She's a 'ticularly nasty one."

"That's for-"

Glin had stopped at the approach of a medium sized shrouded figure. Joshua immediately recognized Sniffler. The mousy man constantly rubbed his nose and now Joshua could hear the frequent snuffles in between the wipes. *Should've called him Snuffler.* Estanod had said it was because of his drug of choice and Joshua had wondered why anyone would keep taking a drug that made their nose so runny. The silence stretched over the seven minutes it took for Sniffler to come back out with his sales quota for the week. He gave Glin and Big Ears a quick salute between nose swipes before disappearing from view.

A grunt appeared to be Big Ears' way of announcing his intent to speak. "Ah-umm. So? You gonna take the deal? Once yer off Door Duty, that is."

Glin became very still. "You want to talk *here?*"

"I swept this place fer bugs before the shift. 'Sides, Bossman's up in his office waitin' on a 'Big Player' ta arrive. And it must be a 'Big Deal' 'cause he was extra touchy 'fore I came out here tonight. So, what ya figurin' to do?"

Glin checked the pedway before he replied, "*Everyone* gets an extra ration?"

"Hellfire, Sonny, I don't much care which of your rat pack gets the day bars. But *you* get 10 more every night you make a numbers run."

"It's not rat pack, man. We're The Shadow Boys. You know, you gotta establish your brand."

"Uuun!" The grunt was dismissive. "Whatever.   Not as if Bossman's gonna let ya sell yer services on The Avenue. Personally, I think ya need to incentivize your *Shadow Boys* a bit more. *Incentivize.* How's *that* fer marketing lingo?" Joshua could see Glin smile at Big Ears' self-amusement.

"You're good, man, real good. So.   It's one bar for each business I collect tickets from and deliver to the dead drop for your silent partner. I'm not sure I can make any more than 10 collections and still keep this operation under wraps from Bossman."

"What?   You think I'm brain bogged? I got no 'ntention of gettin' greedy. Been around long enough to know where *that* leads. Yer eyebrows under the water line 'stead of yer nose above it." Big Ears paused long enough to stick his head out and insure no one was loitering nearby. He leaned back against the wall and his words became hard. "Bossman finds out I'm running this side lotto using his drug profits as the bank and we're *all* walkin' dead. An' I guarantee ya Fenster would take his time turnin' us into zombies.   Look, we jus' gotta last a couple months until we have our own bank, *then* if the Bossman finds out, we offer him a cut.   S'long as he don't know we started off puttin' up his money, we're good."

"Well, none of the Shadow Boys even know about it and *I'm* not going to let it slip. Can you trust the business owners?"

"Speakin' of incentivize, self severation is a might powerful one. Bossman'd make an example outta them jus' like me 'n you 'n yer Boys. Bossman likes being the BOSSman. Soze they'll keep their yaps shut, trust me. Ken ya feel my drift?"

"I can feel it.   I'm in."

Big Ears nodded solemnly and then held out his hand. As they shook, he intoned, "Here's to the storm clouds scattin' soze the creek don't rise."

The rain slacked and pedway traffic picked up, leaving little opportunity for chit-chat over the next hour. Then a muted clank roused Joshua from his quasi-trance. He leaned forward to see the front door open and Bossman step out. It was the first time he had seen the drug lord since bumping into him in the alley near Mom's. The man walked past the other occupants of the entranceway without giving them a glance, stopped at the threshold and looked first in one snap then the other snap direction. Joshua's finger froze and his blood chilled when Bossman's face swung forward and up, seeming to look him right in the eye.

The visage had the same nonchalant detachment as when he had been deciding whether he would have an 11-year-old boy's throat cut. Joshua's intake of air slowed and his heart thumped to a less frenetic cadence. With these calming sensations, his mind cleared and he saw that Bossman's eyes were actually directed *over* his head- whooooof! With the release of his breath, time sped up to normal and Joshua's poised finger pressed snap as he realized *He's just checking the weather*.

Bossman turned toward Big Ears. **"Anything stirring out here?"**

"No sir, quiet as a bog mouse."

The back of Bossman's head nodded forward once, then his face swung toward Glin. **"Shouldn't you be out checking retail sales?"**

Glin pushed off of the wall. "Yessir."

"Then git!"

Clearly relieved that his guard duties were ending early, Glin threw out another "Yessir" and slipped out into the medium fall of small raindrops.

Bossman watched him go and kept his head turned in that direction for a moment before stepping over and occupying the spot on the wall vacated by Glin. **"How are the spot checks on him going?"**

"Good. He covers the entire territory every night and tipped us on both Fishbain and Bradlee. Course, Bradlee didn't respond to our 'rehab' efforts 'n we had ta 'pink slip' him, but Fishbain's eased off his use of product and is staying above quota."

Joshua heard how Big Ears' words were still deferential to Bossman, but more relaxed and confident in tone. He was surprised to learn the man was more than just a guard, realizing he had underestimated Big Ears because of his poor vocabulary and use of gutter speak. He then thought about how difficult it would be not only to set up a business under Bossman's nose, but to somehow get access to the boss's drug profits to finance the enterprise. His estimation of Big Ears rose even further by the way he set up Bossman with a casual observation.

"Does seem ta hit the tail end of the string a bit late, though. Ya know, with the last few salesmen sumtimes already too far gone ta git lagit sales data."

The Deepest Cut

"Oh?"

"Course it's up ta you, Boss. Jus' saying this Door Duty's gettin' him out on his rounds kinda late, that's all."

Bossman rolled his head and shoulders forward off the wall, his words coming out harder and more clipped, "As soon as I let up on one person, then *everyone* will think *they* deserve a break too. *That's not happening.* So bottom line? I have to keep those little sewer roaches in line, and to do *that*, it's best to start at the top."

Joshua had not expected Big Ears to laugh at that, and from what he could see of Bossman's expression, neither had he. The big guard hastily explained, "I was laughin' 'cause ol' Glin was sharin' his marketin' strategy with me earlier." He chuckled again, then became incredulous as he challenged with a stunned tone, "Don't ya know who they are? Why, they ain't no sewer roaches, Bossman. They are the *real* deal." Big Ears let the pause stretch, but not long enough to further annoy an already annoyed Bossman. "They're *The Shadow Boys*."

They both broke into laughter. Big Ears followed up with a dire warning, "If yer not careful, they'll be in charge 'fore ya know it!"

More laughter. This time, Bossman sobered up before his door guard. "And there you go. I give Glin some extra opportunities to advance, then he gets some big ideas. And what do we have? All of those gutter pukes strutting around thinking they're hot stuff. Now don't get me wrong, I want them to be confident. But only enough to get the job done. But as soon as one of them screws up, he has to *feel the heat*. That's why I have to put the hurt on. Everyone has to learn how it works. Just like *you* know, if *he* screws up, *you're* going to feel the heat."

"Got it, Bossman. That's why I was askin', jus' tryin' to figure whether I needed to throw in a couple extra spot checks is all. Ya know, dependin' on what sorta time frame you and Ms. Samanatha had for him to do Door Duty."

The patter of rain stretched as Bossman stared at Big Ears then he relaxed back into the wall. "Yeah, well, the costs associated with that particular asset are looking to outweigh the benefits." Bossman stepped back to the front of the entranceway and checked the pedway again. When he returned, his tone was more collegial, almost chummy, "Let me give you a clue on how to handle a woman like her. You have to be patient,   *enjoy* the benefits of what she brings to the table, let her assert herself on this little thing, make the decision on that little thing, feel more and more in control. You bide your time un*til* Bam!" His fist smacked into his palm. "You end it. After you have squeezed all you can out of the relationship, it's time to move on. *That's* how the game is played!"

Big Ears grinned. "You sure know how ta work 'em, Boss!"

"*Damn* right I do." Bossman's finger stabbed out to emphasize the point.

Big Ears' voice was casual, "Are you gonna end it?"

Bossman tilted his head sideways and considered the big man in front of him. When his words did come out, they were decisive, "Yes.   I'm going to end it." He stepped to the door with a final instruction, "Let the little sewer rat know what I decided," and then he went back inside.

Joshua spent the rest of his shift trying to figure how the new intel could be used against Bossman. He came up with nothing. He fumed as he sloshed up the hill toward Sanctuary. *I've got some really good dirt on Bossman, but I can't figure out how to use it!   Maybe Estanod'll have some ideas at our regular meeting tomorrow night.*

However, the next night, The Cop shook his head. "Not sure how this can help with the Mayor problem. It only gets the guard and boy into trouble with Bossman. It might reduce his operational efficiency a bit while he replaces them, but that won't hurt him much. There's always someone out there eager to step into empty shoes when it means more money in their pocket or food in their belly." Seeing the disappointment in Joshua's face, Estanod changed the subject. "Did I tell you I'm almost finished with my degree in General Exobiology?"

This out of the blue statement startled Joshua. "Huh?   What exactly is *exo* biology?"

"Well, way back when it started, it was the *search for* extraterrestrial life. You know, those missions to Mars looking for microorganisms in the soil, or some type of fossils or organic byproducts. Of course, with FTL drive, we soon *found* life outside of planet Earth. So now it is the *study of* extraterrestrial life forms."

"They have classes to study animals *here*? Like in The Swamp?" Joshua's mouth hung open in amazement.

"Oh no," Estanod laughed, "the only classroom topics here in New Cincinnati are related to mining operations. All of my studies are done over the GlobalNet, well *actually*, over the AstroNet, since the correspondence goes to the Exobiology Department at New Republic University on Faulken. It doesn't take as long as you might think, though, with our healthy mining operations insuring lots of Sector space traffic to and from Cypress Grove, and cybermail transfers automatically each time a ship enters the system. But no, not only is M3I *not* interested in local flora and fauna, they actively discourage any exploration. They don't want any alternatives to their monopoly on steady employment. Besides, there were some not so successful early attempts at exploiting the natural resources."

"You mean the two expeditions and George of the Jungle?"

Estanod's eyebrows rose in appreciation. "Wow, not that many people remember there were two expeditions."

"I guess I wanted to learn more after what happened to my Mom."

"Oh. Yeah, right. That makes sense. So, what else did you learn?"

"That it was the clip of video from the George stunt that led to the spiderviper name."

"Stunt? Hmm, I suppose that's an apt description. But what most people don't know is that George had created an entire business structure to be in on the ground floor of the market. He planned to build ExoFoods, Inc. into an exobiological empire. And *anybody* could still use his basic business plan to begin producing whatever can be found out there. Did you know that 90% of all successful exobiological companies are based in jungle or rainforest ecosystems? No? Well, most people don't. We are sitting on a gold mine here, Kid, and I don't mean what's coming out of that mountain up there! There *has* to be a bunch of food in The Swamp that could be sold for good money!"

Caught up by Estanod's fervor, Joshua exclaimed, "Yeah, like SwampRabbit jerky!" He froze, realizing what he had just said.

"Swamp *Rabbit*? Like from *The Swamp?*"

Joshua just sat with wide eyes, unable to form a response.

"Listen, Kid, *rabbits* don't live in The Swamp. Trust me."

His condescension angered Joshua and prompted a sharp reply, "Well you're *wrong*. There *are* SwampRabbits. From *The Swamp*. And I *know*, because I hunt them with a bow and arrow that *I* made!"

"Easy, buddy." Estanod held up both hands, palms out. "So you are trying to tell me that you *live* in The Swamp?"

"What?! You don't believe me? You think I'm *lying?"*

"Hey, hey, easy now, Kid. I know you wouldn't lie to me. It's just hard to get my head around, OK? So you *do* live in The Swamp? Ahh... alright. Well, I did wonder where you kept disappearing to. So, how did *that* happen? Did you go there on purpose?"

Joshua broke eye contact as his anger shifted inward. He had revealed too much, but he also *really* wanted to share what he had seen and lived through with someone. After a moment, he decided.

"No. It wasn't on purpose. It was in that alleyway near the edge of the city, the night I ran away. When you said I needed someone to take care of me. Remember?"

"I *thought* I'd seen something from ped level, but   "

"Yeah, well, I hid in a sunken area just in front of the barrier fence. After you left, the whole section gave way and I dropped into The Swamp. It took a few weeks, but I lucked out and found a safe place to live."

"You lived down there in the actual *Swamp* not the burn zone, but The Swamp for more than a week?" Estanod shook his head in wonder. "Wow! That really takes some balls, Kid. And you have really *eaten* some of these these SwampRabbits?"

"I wouldn't have made it without eating what's out there. Here, try it," he dug in his pocket, pulled out a strip of dark dried meat, and extended the jerky to Estanod. At the man's hesitation, Joshua took a bite off one end and then offered the rest as he chewed.

"This is *real* meat?"

Joshua laughed as he chewed. "Yeah, sorta weird to think about, uh? But my Dad's always said he *loved* eating game roasted over a fire. So, I tried it. Besides. I was **really** hungry by then."

The Deepest Cut

Joshua could see Estanod steel himself before taking a bite. He felt a glow of pride when The Cop's face immediately transformed.

"This is **good**!"

Then, as he chewed a second bite, "No, this is *excellent!*" Between slow chews to savor the flavors, Estanod listened intently as Joshua described what spices were in his rub and how he dried the jerky. When Joshua fell quiet, The Cop eagerly leaned forward. "So what other animals have you seen?"

Joshua eyed him. "You probably want to know more about the spidervipers."

That brought Estanod's chewing to a stop. He sat up straighter, then gave a small shrug. "Only if you want to talk about it."

Joshua nodded and told him about spidervipers hunting alone, preferring the darkness of night, stalking mostly by sound, and the way their chitin locked together when in dangerous situations. Estanod was a rapt listener, rarely interrupting to ask questions. He nodded at Joshua's theory about the possible cooling function of the segmented chitin.

"That's just like the Algorian Sand Tortoise, only their shells extend up in concentric circles. Same function, though. Or, at least that's the speculation. Pretty smart, Joshua."

The compliment reminded Joshua of his Mom. Whenever she had praised him, it had been sincere. They talked about more of his Swamp adventures before the conversation wound down.

About to pop the last of the SwampRabbit jerky into his mouth, Estanod snatched his hand shut and put the remnant in his pocket. "I'll just save this for later." He smiled. "Wow! I think I would have just stayed in that first 'Hidey Hole' forever after being chased by a spiderviper. But you obviously found your way out and back to the city."

Joshua's stomach clenched at The Cop's tone, which sounded as if he was trying to redirect his attention. Reviewing the last few minutes of conversation, there seemed to have been a series of leading questions. *Is it just the cop in him, or is he **trying** to get as much info as possible?* Estanod's expression held a hint of disappointment when Joshua simply responded, "Yeah, I got back in eventually."

Joshua no longer felt like sharing. He could not say why. Perhaps he had just worked too hard to earn the knowledge. Or maybe he did not completely trust Estanod, who seemed sincere, but also strangely indirect.

Estanod leaned back and the atmosphere of shared fascination deflated. Still, he smiled. "That is absolutely amazing, Joshua. Thanks for telling me your story. Maybe you'll share more some time."

They stared at the soft rain in silence, then Estanod sat upright and asserted, "Back to business. We need some *proof* that the Mayor is involved with Bossman. That way, even if she denies it, the whole thing would be too public for her to make a move on us."

The image of reporters shoving microphones in his mother's face came to Joshua's mind. "Ahh, what do you mean, like showing the proof to the news people?"

Estanod was momentarily taken aback, then he nodded with vigor. "Once we have the proof, it would be safe for you to come out into the open. I mean, I would I'd introduce you at the press conference and and," Estanod's eyes lost focus. He blinked several times, then he looked at Joshua with conviction and continued with determination, "I could take you in. You could live with me and go to school, get back to a normal life."

The thought of a "normal life" appealed to Joshua, but somehow, he could not completely warm to the idea. So he smiled and let The Cop keep talking until it was time to go. It would take some time before he understood the reason for his reserve.

◄7►

This is pretty good. Joshua examined the mixture of Night Puffs and diced SwampRabbit held together with peppery Nutegg custard while he chewed. *No it's* really *good!*

He eagerly dug his spoon for another bite. He had tried this combination before, but the addition of a new herb had transformed the flavors. He had found the golden lichen on the top of a big tree trunk laying on the forest floor deeper in The Swamp. He could not precisely identify the taste created by the dried and crumbled herb that had turned the custard into a deep ochre. However, the flavor was unmistakably savory.

As he chewed, he started the recording he had made during his previous shift, having already downloaded it from the flip phone to the sound system. Joshua's self-satisfaction bumped up another notch. The review would take a fraction of the normal time, since he had successfully run his Slack Delete program, which identified and deleted stretches of recording without voices. Hearing the clank of the front door, Joshua knew Bossman had arrived, and anticipating what came next, slowed his chewing and leaned forward to concentrate on the conversation.

Bossman's voice was impatient, **"Nothing?"**

"No sir, ain't seen no Big Player in no red coat yet. Been lookin' hard too."

Bossman snapped, **"It's not as if she's going to try and sneak up on you!"**

Joshua heard the sigh and recalled how the drug lord's shoulders had eased down. Bossman continued in a more patient tone.

"Just remember to let her right through without talking, *after* you code Fenster that is. Got it?"

"Yessir. Got it." Big Ears was treading softly this night. "You, ah, you sure this Big Player's comin' tonight?"

The drug lord growled, *"Hell* no, I'm not sure. Why do you think I keep checking with you?" Bossman did not wait for a response. "All I *know* is that there is some woman one of my main Sector sources said was," he had flashed air quotes, "a 'Big Player' who I *really* had to meet. Wouldn't tell me why, and with this guy, I wasn't going to press. Still, he made it clear that we needed to roll out the red carpet for this bimbo. Other than that? Absolutely no clues. I mean, he didn't even drop a *tiny* hint. **That's** what I don't like. This guy don't scare easy. All he said was that she'd arrive planetside in a few days. That was five days ago. Yesterday, we finally got word to expect some chick in red to come by."

"Got it covered, Mr. Bossman. Code Fenster first thing 'n don't talk to her."

Apparently satisfied, Bossman had tapped the security pad, causing the door to clank again and crack open. "**Don't forget to code Fenster.**"

"Right, Boss."

Joshua put aside his empty bowl, "Soundbox. Stop the playback." Something about what he had just heard had tickled a memory of another conversation, but it eluded him. Frustrated that he could not make the connection, he set about cleaning up after his meal.

Once done, Joshua decided to finish his housekeeping efforts. "Soundbox. Move current sound file into Archive folder, April subfolder."

Joshua watched the designated file name lift up and float over to an opening file folder next to the larger folder labeled Archive. Seeing the March folder above, Joshua's eyes flew wide *That's it!* At least, that was partially it. He now realized his prior association was related to the very first conversation he had recorded with the directional mic.

He opened the file with the earliest date and skipped forward to the conversation between Glin and Big Ears. It did not spark the association he knew was there. Joshua recued the recording and listened again. *Still nothing.* His head flew back in exasperation. *I know it has to do with this!* When almost through for the third time, he became confused about whether Bossman was talking about Samanatha or the Big Player. And then he had it. Joshua realized that both times Bossman had been talking about a woman. *If I can make it sound like he was talking about the Mayor, maybe that would work!*

"Soundbox. Dubbing function."

It took him two days to transcribe all of the statements from both clips into his sheet and then finish his splicing project. He almost danced with excitement after arriving at Rendezvous #1, waiting for Estanod to hear the two audio files he had created.

Estanod's eyebrows rose as he handed the flip phone back to Joshua. "Wow. How did you put those together?"

Joshua's enthusiasm ebbed at The Cop's tone. "I salvaged a sound system."

"I'm telling you, that's really good, Kid. But there are three problems. First, Bossman did not admit to anything illegal in the first file, just makes it clear that he wants to stay the Big Boss. Second, in the other file, there is no specific mention of the Mayor, so his talk about how he thinks he can handle 'her' doesn't tie the Mayor to what he says. Third, and this is the biggest problem, even though you and I can't tell, forensic experts will isolate the separate recording noises and prove that the rates of the background rainfall are consistently different between the different voices at different times. Sorry to tell you, Kid, but these files won't hold up in court."

Joshua deflated like a pierced balloon. "Uh, okay. I had just thought, well, well, since it was about a woman both times, and the Mayor   ah, OK. Shoot." He could see Estanod felt bad for him, so he shrugged with a smile, "Guess we'll have to wait for better proof."

"That's right, Joshua. And we'll get it. Sooner or later, they'll slip up."

Joshua climbed to the roof and headed off through drifting mists toward the blind. *Well, at least the weather's nice.* The positive thought could not dispel his disappointment in discovering all of his hard work on the recordings had been for naught. He also heard Estanod's voice again and the pessimistic tone that had flowed underneath the encouraging words.

Sure would be nice if things took a turn for the better...

◄8►

Estanod was on a box under the small porch overhang of the abandoned refining building, leaning back into the corner of the double doorway, legs extended straight out and crossed at the ankles. The #5 rendezvous spot was well away from Boseman's warehouse. Well away from pretty much anyone. The cheery tone in his voice made Joshua wary.

"Howdy! Have a seat."

"Uh, it's going to take me some time to get back-"

"Don't worry about it, we have *plenty* of time.   Sit.   Relax."

Joshua eased down on the edge of a smaller box in the opposite corner and wondered at Estanod's expansive mood. It was in such contrast to the silent apprehension that had oppressed all of their terse communications since he had seen Hawkface a week ago. Joshua was also on guard because there had been no new faces since Tiast either. He had begun to believe Estanod's sullen demeanor was a reflection on his own lack of productivity. He had come ready to be fired.

Joshua was not prepared for the detective to bring out a small cooler bag from beside his make shift seat and set it on a crate between them. The Cop extracted two large bottles of Fruit Tea, handing one to Joshua. *That's nice and cold!* Joshua pulled the sealing sleeve down along the neck of the bottle and took a swig of the sweet energy drink. He traced the cool swallow down to his stomach while he watched Estanod pull out a thick stick of expensive salami and a small cheese box. When the policeman cut down the front and side panels of the box after unzipping the lid, Joshua knew he intended to share the entire box. Sure enough, the detective looked up, smiled, and exclaimed, "Let's eat!"

Joshua had no idea why Estanod wanted to celebrate, but he was relieved at the change in outlook. He was also grateful for the delay in the start of his surveillance shift. He had come to hate the confines of the blind more and more. He followed the detective's example, leaning back into the corner and stretching out his legs.

This made the sinking feeling in his empty stomach all the more surprising when Estanod offered him the first slice of the meat stick. He almost did not take it, despite his hunger and desire to maintain the party atmosphere. Joshua forced his hand forward, grabbed the disc of meat, and focused past it to the rain outside the entrance to their alcove, struggling to control the flushed feeling that had encased his entire body.

"Don't like salami?"

"Uh, no, no." He took a bite. "It's good." And it was. *Why am I so freaked out?* Joshua stopped chewing as another image overlaid the night scene before him. He was in the Bordello District, watching Uncle William sharing a meat stick with Kandee. The blowgun weighed heavy in his hand as he lifted it up to his mouth. He wanted it to stop, but it continued its rise to his lips. *No, NO!* Uncle William stopped chewing, turned, and looked right at him.

"Joshua, are you alright?" *Why would he ask that? I'm about to kill him.*

A circle of meat with the crescent of a small bite mark trembled in front of his eyes. He was back. But the expected flood of relief did not materialize, instead the churning of insistent apprehension only lessened a little. His eyes shifted to Estanod's face. Joshua was touched by the man's expression of genuine concern. "Uhh, yeah. I'm fine."

He tried to smile before he popped the rest of the slice into his mouth and began chewing. He could tell that this episode was over, but could not quell the shaking inside. *Am I going crazy?* He swallowed and his hand only trembled a little as he took a drink and tried to calm himself.

Estanod's frown eased and he held out a combined slice of salami and cheese. Joshua was gratified that he could take the second offering without hesitation. His feeling of reprieve intensified as he watched Estanod settle in to discuss a topic about which he clearly held a great deal of interest. He hoped his smile was encouraging.

The Cop gestured toward the cheese box and meat stick. "I had meant all of this to be something of a celebration, actually. Surprisingly, after days of *nothing*, the Captain came to me and was all over this development with Tiast, providing extra resources, and Oh!" He pulled out a ten UD note. "Here. It's for the last week *and* something of a bonus." When Joshua looked at the proffered money with a frown,

Estanod insisted, "Really. *Take it*. It is just a part of what the Captain gave me and you deserve it."

"Ok, thanks." Joshua pocketed the folded bill, feeling guilty for his earlier mistrust. Feeling the need to reciprocate, he extracted his sheet from under his slicker and gestured to Estanod. "Let me see yours." Joshua prepped his sheet for an infrared transfer as Estanod pulled out his minisheet.

"What're you giving me?"

"Some video files you might find interesting."

When the transfer window shrank away, Joshua saw the time on the sheet face. He stood up in alarm. "It's *way* past 9:00! I have to–"

"Relax! I'm giving you the night off. Consider it a paid vacation. Besides, I want to check some of these out."

Estanod became completely engrossed in the video clips of the creatures of The Swamp. He asked numerous questions, and at the end of the last one, pressed for more, "What about the flora?"

Joshua shared descriptions of the Orange Taters and the Night Puffs. Estanod's enthusiastic questions were so contagious, he also transferred all of his still photos of The Swamp plants to the policeman's sheet.

Estanod was extremely interested in how he had determined he could eat the plants, repeatedly asking if Joshua had experienced any sick feelings, "Anything at all?" Then he really perked up. "Say, who knows, with all that you have learned, maybe we could figure out a way to grow some of those Swamp plants in the city. You know, pick up on what George of the Jungle was trying to do and commercialize some of these food plants!" The Cop seemed to catch himself and lowered his voice, "You know, after we get the goods on the Mayor and you move in with me." When Joshua did not react, he added, "That is, if you want to, whenever *that* happens."

Joshua nodded and smiled, but could not understand why he did not take Estanod up on the offer of a home. It just seemed too far away at this point. He returned to a former topic. "Thanks for my vacation day, er, ah, night."

"Yeah, no problem. In fact, not only do you have tonight off, but tomorrow night too. Yep, 'cause I want you to have a chance to

watch The Ultimate Night Beat tomorrow night. At 8:00.   On
Channel 362.   You know, on ARPV?"

"My Mom never really liked me watching PV too much. And my
reception isn't all that great right now ," Joshua shrugged.

"Oh. Right. Being out in The Swamp and everything... That is still
SO hard to get my head around!   Sorry, it's just   it amazes me,
that's all.   Anyway, just come on in to one of the GlobalNet cafés
for the show. That's the All Reality PV channel.   362.   I think it'll be
worth the trip."

◄9►

The opening montage of The Ultimate Night Beat featured a series of cut scenes of Mickey Spade, "Hardboiled Investigative Reporter," sticking a microphone into the faces of startled people. They were all flashed to the beat of low, bass driven music, which was flared to a crescendo by a brass horn section as the screen dissolved and reformed into a publicity head shot of Mickey himself, looking up through his eyebrows with a mixture of aggression and seduction. The trench coat collar was popped up and the fedora pulled down, but not low enough to cover those smoldering eyes.

Joshua sat back as he watched, hands on stomach, satisfied. *It was worth the $1.13.* He had just finished his first meal in a restaurant in *I really can't remember the last time. Years!* Saving money for the Café had meant very little eating out. Besides, his mother had produced far better fare that any of the restaurants they could have afforded. Joshua assuaged a tinge of guilt about the price by rationalizing that he really *had* to spend the money after it had been so very clear that Estanod wanted him to see the show. Besides, it was part of the unexpected bonus, so he was still $3.87 ahead.

"And we are **live**!!" There was a slight reverberation to the urgent, but softly spoken words, and the screen filled with Mr. Spade's face.

"I'm tellin' ya, folks, this one goes **all** the way up! To the **top**! That's right! This could implicate the Mayor herself! This is **so** big, well, I can't even **say** how big this is! But I can tell ya, the Chief of Police **himself** is here to serve the warrant!"

The handheld camera swung to take in the face and shoulders of a small intense man in full dark blue uniform, four stars on his collar and peaked cap, a thin strip of mustache emphasizing the severe set to his mouth and rendering his expression even more authoritarian. He nodded once to the camera. The light olive Greystone walls in the background indicated they were in an expensive condo complex.

"We are in final preparations for making the bust!"

Spade's voiceover came as the view panned back to include five uniformed officers behind the Police Chief on the steps of an enclosed stairwell. Joshua sat up straighter when he recognized Estanod as the third officer back. *Why's he back there? This should be **his** bust!* The Chief's head recoiled a fraction as Spade shoved the microphone under his chin. "What's the story, Chief Henry?"

"We have developed intel to suggest the perpetrator is a major link in a drug trafficking crime organization in our city. As you said, it was a shock when we discovered who it was." Chief Henry looked into the camera, reciting with stiffness, "Yes, the person involved is very, **very** high up."

The camera followed the mike back to Spade's face. "Coming up, you'll watch us take down this soon-to-be infamous public figure! And   as *always*, we **may** have to interrupt our commercial messages if the suspect makes a break for it, because   The Ultimate Night Beat   **always**   brings it to *you*   *live!!*"

Joshua sat dumbfounded, unable to understand why Estanod had been toward the back, without his surveillance work even being mentioned. But then, *maybe they're keeping it secret, so we can keep watching Bossman. Now* it all made sense to Joshua, *that* must be it! He refocused on his sheet. An ad for Fruit Tea was wrapping up with their promo jingle "Fruuuit Teeea, is Ab so luuuute   leeee, the–"

The back of Spade's fedora hat snapped into view. He looked back at the screen and whispered, "I *definitely* heard it that time!" The camera jiggled as it panned back to include Chief Henry, who looked at Spade. They stood in a hallway, in front of an apartment door. Spade gave him a nod, then turned to the camera, speaking with more force, "Let's do it, then!" The Chief stepped up to the door. He struck three sharp raps before his voice dropped an octave and commanded, "Open up!! NCPD!!"

He waited for a count of two, stepped aside, and pointed at two officers with a heavy metal battering ram.

"DO IT!!"

They smoothly swung back and did not stop the forward motion at the sound of a chain being slid aside inside the door. Wood cracked sharply as the ram made impact, instantly followed by a startled yell. The crashing door stopped a foot into its inward swing with a sharp grunt, followed by a thud. The rammers shuffled aside and, gun in hand, Estanod kicked the

Driven to the Hilt

door open the rest of the way. Spade and Chief Henry had moved back out of the line of potential fire, and not incidentally, the camera view, which now showed a tall slender man flat on his back, one hand on his forehead. Estanod entered, leveled his pistol, and yelled, "POLICE! WARRANT!! Do NOT move!"

The camera rushed forward into the room, images jumping and shaking with the advance, focused on Estanod as he rolled the prone man over, yanked a bloody hand from his forehead, pulled it behind his back, and cuffed it to his other wrist. The view lifted up to take in Spade just as he pulled down a restraining hand and allowed the Chief to enter the room. He followed immediately and the shot zoomed in on their faces.

"Chief. Who *is* this man?"

The camera swung down to Estanod helping the man into a sitting position, zoomed closer with the focus adjusting, taking in the large red welt across the forehead above his right eye, with a smaller smear of crimson producing a line of blood that ran down to his jaw. *Hawkface!* The man looked at the camera with a befuddled frown, then up sideways at Estanod, who remained out of view. Just as the man opened his mouth to speak, the scene swirled back to the Chief and Spade, the former's pronouncement rolled down his outstretched arm to flow off his accusing finger. "**That** is Owan Tiast, personal assistant to Mayor Greenwood!!"

"Mayor Greenwood!?! How is *she* involved in this, Chief?"

"Well, Mickey," Chief Henry looked into the camera with a severe frown, "I just don't know."

"Chief, everyone knows that we at The Ultimate Night Beat will **not** be intimidated by those in power! So we have called on Mayor Greenwood and **demanded** she speak to us about this! Just a moment   our other crew is at her residence   patch us in headquarters   here we are." The screen split to show a view approaching the solid walnut double doors of a private residence. A hand stretched forward into view and rang the doorbell. One door opened immediately to reveal a woman in her late 40s, whose curled blonde hair framed a tastefully made-up face that enhanced her features, but was not overdone. Fists went to slender hips encased in casual, but chic, jeans. "What is the meaning of this?!"

"Mayor Greenwood! This is Mickey Spade of The Ultimate Night Beat.

Police Chief Henry has just served a warrant on your personal assistant, Owan Tiast! Do you have any comment?"

Joshua lost track of the next several minutes of back and forth between the two sides of the screen, only partially absorbing the Mayor's denial and then shocked dismay at the possible fall of her friend and confidant, Owan. Instead, his focus was on the background, trying to read Estanod's face as he stood beside Mr. Tiast, who by then sat in one of his dining room chairs, still appearing dazed from the blow to the head. *Estanod looks angry and scared at the same time. This isn't what he expected.*

He heard the Mayor valiantly trying to defend her assistant. "Have you found any proof? Any evidence that Ow...Mr. Tiast is involved in drugs?"

Chief Henry stepped forward. "Our intelligence indicated he has some drugs on site. Do you know of any safe boxes Mr. Tiast might use to secure such items?"

"Well... Of *course*, when he became my assistant, we installed a safe in his credenza for official papers and so forth... *surely* you don't think..."

The camera zoomed past Tiast's bewildered face to the long low wooden chest along the wall behind him. The Chief slammed aside a middle wooden panel to expose the metal face of a large safe, with five glowing blue zeroes along the top of a keypad in the middle of the door. He waved a folded paper at Tiast. "This warrant says you *must* open this safe. Right *now!*" *Hawkface seems so out of it. He's not acting right.*

Tiast stood, wavered, then walked to the credenza. In route, he spoke for the first time, "This is all a mistake. There's nothing in there except projects for the Mayor. It is just updates on the Biodirectionality Project and some oth-"

"Just open the safe!" the Chief barked. "We'll *see* what we see."

Tiast had enough presence of mind to position himself between the keypad and the camera. After five beeps came a soft clank and the Chief yanked Tiast back by the shoulder, forcing him to sit down hard on the carpet. The camera zoomed in on the cracked safe door and the Chief's hand pulled it open all of the way to reveal a clear bag of black balls resting on top of a stack of papers and folders.

"Well looky here. That is more, **way** more, than a felony amount of Black Betties."

Driven to the Hilt

"Those   *those* are **not** mine! Mayor Greenwood, tell them what I was doing! Tell them I was investigating connections to The Unseen Planet *for you!*   WAIT! That's **it!** *They* found out! The Black Daggers! *They* put those drugs in there to discredit me!!"

On the right side of the screen, the Mayor looked puzzled. "Black Betties?   The Unseen Planet?   The Black Daggers? This is   heart breaking, Owan.   I promise you,   I'll do whatever I can to get you the *best* psychological treatment."

Joshua watched the close up of Tiast's face transform from animated hope, to shock, to realization, and finally, resignation. He deflated right before the eyes of New Cincinnati. Probably few in the audience besides Joshua noticed the same progression of emotions subtly mirrored in Estanod's face as he stood in the background of the shot. Two of the other officers grabbed Tiast by the arms and walked him out of the condo. Giving one last look into the camera, Estanod followed behind with lifeless steps. His back dissolved into black and a bright red diagonal AFTERMATH clanged onto the screen like the closing of a cell door. The split screen came back with the two live shots.

"This must have been quite the shock for you Mayor. Are you going to be all right?" Spade's question dripped with concern.

"Yes, I   I *think* so. But I *do* need some privacy right now, if you don't mind."

"Of course, Mayor, of course." The Mayor's wooden door clicked shut and the screen returned to a full shot of Mickey Spade. He turned and the camera widened out to include Chief Henry. "So Chief, what do you think about Tiast's Unseen Planet allegation?" An overtone of derision rode atop Spade's question.

Police Chief Henry laughed, "Wow. How long since *that* pVid show was on air? It's not even on rerun channels anymore, is it?" They both laughed together. "No. We always check every possible *viable* lead, but NCPD will not expend valuable resources trying to chase down the   *Black Daggers.* That's   *absurd.* They are a myth. A *fantasy* dreamed up for PV."

Joshua deactivated the PV app as Spade began promoting his show for the following week. He stood to leave, his meal now heavy on his stomach. He hesitated, knowing from his mother how much servers relied on tips, then placed a dime next to the plate, but still feeling guilty, dug out two more pennies. *An even buck and a quarter. It's really all I can spare.* Stepping out of the café, he took two quick steps to cross in front of two pretty young girls, heading for the alleyway on the far side of the street.

"HEY!"

Joshua glanced back at the girls and froze when he saw that they were addressing him. Completing his step off the sidewalk to the mesh of the pedway, he turned and offered a confused, "Yes?"

"Don't you remember? It's me! Tifinity! You played that game with Hareld and me a while ago..."

Stickball? He had not thought of stickball for months – it was *a lifetime* ago. Joshua looked closer and then could not stop his mouth from dropping open, stunned when he recognized Tifinity under the makeup and in the bright sun dress shining through her transparent slicker. She looked so much older, so much more *mature*, somehow.

"Hey Tifinity, you you look great!" And she *did*. Not that Joshua really thought about girls that way. He had not had contact with a girl since playing with Tifinity and it had *definitely* not crossed his mind during their stickball game, when she had been all business and angry elbows.

Her friend giggled as Tifinity spun a quick twirl. "Really? Do you think so?"

Panic began to stir in Joshua's stomach. He recognized the flirting tone in her response, but had absolutely no idea how to respond to it. Then he looked again at Tifinity's companion and it came back to him *Marcus' girlfriend!* "Aren't you didn't you weren't you cheering for Marcus during the game?" He looked back and forth between the girls as they laughed and exchanged knowing glances.

"Well, after Yira came to *understand* Marcus better...," another shared secret look, "we got to talking and-"

"-started doing things together. *I* provided some fashion advice," Yira paused, allowing Tifinity to strike a pose, then continued, "and helped Tiff to appreciate her elegant bone structure." Tifinity sucked in her cheeks and they both broke out in laughter.

Joshua smiled at their easy laughter and felt *utterly* alone. They reminded him of how he used to be,   and could *never* be again. Melancholy threatened to envelope him, only held back by a surreal sense of disconnect, as if he was surrounded by a glass bubble.   He had found his mother dead, he had struggled all alone to survive in The Swamp, he had lived for months without speaking out loud to another person,   he had *killed* someone. How could he ever be normal again?

The girls finally composed themselves, but when Tifinity looked up, her face instantly transformed with concern.

"Hey are you OK?"

"What?" Joshua pulled himself back to the moment, trying to find something *relevant* to say. "Umm ah What are you doing out here?" He could see her confusion, but had no way of explaining. His cheeks flushed at the awkwardness.

"We're heading to the SpiderViper game! Hey! Do you want to come? They're playing the Shirleen Strikers. Could mean another berth in the regional playoffs!" Tifinity paused, placed a light hand on Joshua's forearm, and then glanced at her friend.

"We're meeting Hareld there he and Yira are *seeing* each other now and..."

The pause stretched and Joshua gave a start when Tifinity removed her hand. His blush burned even hotter when he realized that he had been transfixed on it the whole time. It had been so long since someone had touched him with affection.

"I I'm sorry. I was just I..."

"You sure you're OK?"

"Yeah Yes. Just ah a lot on my mind, I guess."

"Well, all right. I guess I was thinking we could make it a foursome!"

Now the bottom dropped out of his stomach. *Foursome? Like a date?* The concept was so foreign, so beyond anything he had ever done or even considered, Joshua could not even visualize how it could unfold. All he knew was he had no idea of how he should act and he was *certain* he would do or say something wrong.

"I ah My Mom, she's not feeling " he stopped, not wanting to lie. In a flash, he realized that in a strictly literal sense, he had not lied *yet.* Still, his mind remained totally blank. So he just shrugged an apology, looked down to his feet, but glanced back up in time to see Tifinity's disappointment and embarrassment. Yira radiated a disappointed glower as Tifinity turned to go, speaking over her shoulder.

"Oh, OK. Well   we've gotta get going. Don't want to be late. See ya."

"Yeah   ah   OK. Bye!" He stood, face blazing, and watched their backs recede until they turned the corner and disappeared from sight.

Joshua sloshed through the rain to the alley, feeling supremely foolish. He quickly ascended to the roofs, and once up top, he began to run. He was halfway to the edge of the city before his pace slowed under the weight of his despondency. He attempted to push aside his social ineptness. *I'll probably never see her again anyway.* That thought was at first rather comforting, but sadness swelled in the undertow,   tasting of   a missed opportunity. He forced a jog across the rooftops, but the prospect of returning to the blank stone walls of Sanctuary slowed him to a walk. He had a fleeting image of Tifinity's face, twisted in disgust after he told her the truth – that he was an orphan who lived in The Swamp, a boy with no job and little money, a *murderer.*

His gloominess would have become total darkness if he had known that his relationship with Estanod was also about to turn sideways.

10

Joshua pressed the flip phone screen and was again rewarded with *nothing*. He settled back down to wait. Within minutes, Joshua had fallen back into his typical surveillance quasi-trance, where he only roused to sound or major movement on the flip phone screen. He could not have said how much time had passed when…

A slight figure boldly strode into the entryway. Joshua could not tell if the long slicker was red because the infrared mode rendered everything green. But Big Ears' quick turn to the security pad without his usual question as to the person's business suggested the Big Player had arrived, except *not so big.* Standing next to Big Ears, the new arrival's slight build was even more evident. After shaking off, retracting, and leaning the umbrella into the corner of the alcove, petite gloved hands pushed back the slicker hood to reveal what Joshua could tell was long glossy black hair, even with the low light setting. Following a beep and click, Big Ears pushed open the door. She flowed through and the door clanked shut.

Given all the buildup about the visitor, Joshua decided to risk resetting the phone screen to full color, but at the lowest luminance possible. His tension eased after Big Ears checked the weather twice during the 30 minute wait without looking in his direction at all. With the setting changes, he had an excellent view of the slender woman as she emerged, a long red leather overcoat draped over one arm. Her head was down, surveying the state of her iridescent purple blouse and tight black skirt. After a few brushes to smooth the fabric, she stepped forward to glance at the sky, the Asian features on her porcelain face twisting in annoyance. *snap* She retreated a step, held out her coat to Big Ears without giving him a glance, and pulled a silver scarf off her neck. This time her step forward was to check the pedway. First she looked left, then to the right, revealing a red tattoo *snap* on her neck above the collarbone.

Joshua was surprised when slowtime kicked in, slowing her hands as she shook out the silk square. The slow tick of seconds allowed him to see details of the tattoo: a stylized sun with seven hollow sharp points, the bottom point extending straight down three times farther than the rest, the second point on the right side filled in with a black triangle. Then slowtime released as the woman retied the scarf around her neck. She flipped back her long silky hair and allowed Big Ears to help slip on her coat. In preparation for stepping out into the light rain, she gave a final shrug to settle everything, pulled up her hood, snapped open the umbrella, and pushed it forward and above her head before striding out and up the street.

The look on Big Ears' face mirrored how Joshua felt. Something momentous had just blown in on a blast of arctic air, swirled around everyone's heads, and then exited with a promise of a return visit. *Soon.*

The electricity on the air ratcheted even higher when Bossman stepped through the door. He walked right past Big Ears to stand just under the lip of the opening. His eyes followed the people walking by, but they lacked intensity, just an automatic scanning while Bossman was deep in thought. A moment later, he turned with decisiveness and went to lean on the wall opposite Big Ears. The burly guard responded to the non-verbal cue to talk.

"How'd it go, Boss?"

Bossman's words came out flat, "They're moving in. We can be with them   or   we can just   not *be*."

Big Ears' whistle turned into a deflated sigh. "Well, *that's* a splash in yer eye. What cha gonna do?"

"I'm not going to just lie down, I can tell you that!" Bossman folded his arms across his chest. "Fenster says one of her people is strutting around all alone. Some blonde guy. Maybe him getting broken up develops a bit of leverage and I can negotiate some better terms. So, I think Ralff and Lynyrd are going to go out tonight and demonstrate just how dangerous it can be on The Avenue." Suddenly impatient, he gestured for Big Ears to press in the entry code. Pushing open the door, he speared Big Ears with sharp eyes. "That Dragon Lady comes back, you do just like before. Any of her slant-eyed goons show up without her, just start shooting."

"You got it, Boss!"

The door clanged shut and Big Ears unzipped his slicker and reached in to loosen the gun in its shoulder holster. He left the slicker open and stepped forward to more actively survey the pedway from both directions.

Joshua gave himself a mental shake and then got down to business. Sending the new images reminded Joshua of Estanod, which made him think of the pVid show, increasing his vague sense of uneasiness. He had realized before that something was wrong with Estanod's situation, but now things had also become extremely dangerous at Bossman's. He had no idea why or quite in what way everything had turned so sour, but he knew that he was up to his nose in two bad *REALLY bad* situations.

And that   *is REALLY bad for me.*

11

The cloudburst came down so heavy that Joshua almost did not hear the flip phone signal. Hunkered down next to an overflowing trash bin, he had been watching the main entrance to the warehouse for almost four hours. He had heard from Estanod just once since sending the Big Player's pictures, a terse text message that invited no reply - "will call when i can." So, Joshua had returned to maintain surveillance of Bossman's operation. It was his job, after all, and his mother had taught him to take his responsibilities very seriously.

But tension had been building over the past three nights. It was ominous that Estanod had not sent back a converted picture of the beautiful Oriental woman as he had with all the others. Although Estanod had established a clear protocol against him initiating a call except under dire circumstances, Joshua no longer cared. Months in The Swamp had sharpened his instinct for survival and it screamed like the screech of a Siren Swan, hitting a crescendo when he had arrived on station this night. He had already decided he would quit if he did not hear from Estanod before the end of the shift. Having nothing to lose, he had made two direct calls earlier in the night. There had been no response. *Until now.   Finally.*

After a quick check of his surroundings, he eased up to stand, and then waited for the blood to flow back into his legs. Once the wateriness in his legs had dissipated, he slid farther back from the mouth of the alley. With a sudden step around the corner of a nearby crevice, he strode back deep enough to prevent the light of the phone from revealing his presence. Joshua pulled out the pCom device to find the small screen glowing with red numbers   *3 10*. Normally he could have easily made it to the #3 rendezvous within five minutes, but he did not want to use the rooftops near the drug warehouse. It had been the beginning of the Siren Swan's warning, a strong sense of being observed as he had approached the blind that night. So strong that he had decided to watch from the street. *And I can **still** feel it.*

He put away the flip phone, moved to the crevice opening, and surveyed all of the dark doorways nearby. Satisfied, he exited, turned away from The Avenue, and soon emerged onto a less traveled pedway. As he put more of the new downpour between himself and the warehouse, Joshua felt the cascading water begin to wash the crosshairs off of his back.

Once well away from the warehouse, Joshua had regained the rooftops, and by the time he arrived at Rendezvous #3, the rain had eased up. He descended the drainpipe in the darkest corner of the long, but dead ended alley. Once his feet touched ground, he glanced over and then struggled to control his breathing when he did not see Estanod on the stoop of the boarded up pVid repair shop, where he had always been during previous visits. With his heart beginning to accelerate, Joshua tried to penetrate the many shadows of the extended box alleyway systematically, while at the same time mentally mapping out multiple escape routes. *Nothing.*

After several minutes of building tension, Joshua was convinced a different police officer was going to step out and arrest him. He decided to act. He reached into his slicker pocket to grasp the flip phone. He walked along the end wall away from the repair shop toward a pile of refuse in a shallow doorway. The little folding phone made a small wet sound as it disappeared into the folds of a crumpled plastic bag. Joshua rotated toward the drain pipe farther up the other side of the alley and was about to sprint for a high grab, when he heard a nonrandom tapping. *The all clear code!*

He stopped and looked back. The signal had come from an uneven joining of two buildings near the alley's sole opening, which glowed with the garish lights of The Avenue. A small security light sliced a stream of pale yellow back into half of the alcove, casting the other half into an even deeper shadow. Joshua did not move. Estanod's ghostly face appeared suspended in the dark half, his activated sheet held under his chin. The screen snapped dark and the face vanished.

First ensuring The Avenue entrance remained empty, Joshua headed for the recess. Rounding the corner, he stopped abruptly, taking in the limited space in the alcove. Reminding himself that Estanod could have grabbed him many times in the past two months, Joshua eased down onto an overturned shipping cube across from the cop, and feeling exposed in the yellow light. He shifted sideways to put his eyes into shadow.

The Deepest Cut

Estanod spoke from the gloom with uncharacteristic bluntness, "It's over, Kid. I've been reassigned."

Joshua's heart sank. *I really need this money.* "OK. So you need me to watch someone else or-"

"NO!"

Startled, Joshua jumped to his feet.

"Sorry!" Estanod said it quickly enough to forestall an abrupt end to their meeting. A deep breath blew out from the inky opening of Estanod's hood. "I'm sorry. But it's just that   none of it matters anymore, and the last few days have been   *difficult.*"

Joshua slowly lowered back onto the cube. "Are you sad because the police chief took all the credit?"

"What?   Oh, you're talking about the Ultimate Night Beat." Estanod's hand came into the light and waved with impatience. "No, I *expected* that. Actually, I was ok with it too, because I thought it was a legit bust,   that we were taking down someone who was truly bad, who-," disgust filled his voice, "I was an *idiot!* Everyone was slapping me on the back, 'Great job, Estanod!' And I thought   *now* we'll get to the source! We'll actually *do* some GOOD!" Water droplets sparkled as they flew off his shaken fist. Then his fingers loosened and dropped into the dark, along with the volume of his voice. "But," Joshua could now see him shifting in the gloom, "it's just that   I *believe* him. Tiast wasn't faking his surprise. That stuff was planted."

"By   The Black Daggers?"

Estanod grunted a short laugh of disgust. "Yeah, The Black Daggers. Well   it *could* be, I suppose. Ever see the pVid show?"

"Mom didn't let me watch many vids."

"Oh, yeah,   right.   Well,   good for her. It was probably before your time anyway. But the show was based on some fairly convincing stories that have floated around for years, about a covert group of vigilantes that sneak around and expose evil doing, or some such. Not that anyone has ever proven the existence of The Black Daggers and their hidden base of operations, the Unseen Planet. Even so, those rumors have persisted." The Cop shrugged and then shook his head. "No. Even if The Black Daggers did plant those drugs, someone much closer to home paid them to do it. And I'm about as likely to prove *that* as I am the existence of The Black Daggers."

"So, who do you think paid them?"

"Good question, Kid. Word is that ever since the new Sector Bureau of Investigations facility was completed on Eytan, the Mayor has been on edge. Insistent that everyone stay up on all their paperwork, paranoid about a snap inspection, that sorta thing. If she is worried about the SBI getting on her back, maybe she gave up her assistant to throw the heat off of her and her cronies."

"How do you know she did that?"

"I *don't* know for sure. But while the Chief was dealing with the press at headquarters, I was escorting Tiast back to the Interrogation Chair and I figured I'd soften him up a bit with some indirect questioning. Besides, I was actually curious about what he had called the Biodirectionality Project. I mean that *had* to be something to do with The Swamp, right?"

"Right."

"Right. And it *did*. Tiast told me the Mayor had funded a research project to see if Cypress Grove wildlife could be influenced to move in a desired direction. Then he got this funny look on his face and said, 'I had assumed that was to help repel them further from the city, but the data seemed to' *That* was when the Chief burst in and told him to shut up. Now that was a bit confusing, but I figured he was just setting up a Good Cop, Bad Cop scenario, right?"

"Right."

"Wrong. He kicked me out and I wasn't allowed anywhere *near* the Interview Room for the next few hours. *That* was my first clue. I had thought at the very least, I'd be allowed to sit in the observation room and watch the psychophysio readings, even if I wasn't the one asking the questions."

Joshua's eyes had adjusted enough that he could see Estanod's dour expression twist even further.

"But *no*. Nada. After a bit, the Chief appears in the squad room, all smiles. He comes over to me, slaps me on the shoulder, and announces to everyone that Tiast had made a full confession! 'Case closed! Records sealed, of course, what with all the Mayor's confidential projects to protect. Yep! He pleaded guilty so he wouldn't serve at Crystal Cove Corrections.' Now I don't blame him

220

Overwatch

for that, of course.   What a hellhole.   So, everybody's all congratulating me on helping make the big bust and then acting as if everything is wrapped up. You know, 'Whew, glad that problem's all taken care of.' But *then* the Chief went on to announce that since the drug problem was 'over' now, the Mayor had decided to terminate my 'special assignment.' Of course, he dangled the hologram of a carrot in my face, 'Why in three years   wink wink   an officer with your record could put in *early* for detective.' "

"You got   *demoted?*   From Detective?   After solving the case?"

Estanod's laugh was bitter. "Apparently it was a '*temporary*' rank. No, that's not it, Kid. I mean, yeah, I 'solved' their problem, all right. I found someone to take the blame so they can keep doin' what they're doin'." The self-loathing in his voice welled up again, "Course, *that* was only because they led me by the nose right to where they had tied him up for the slaughter."

The policeman sat silent for a long moment before giving himself a shake and continuing, "But like I said, even *that* doesn't matter anymore. I mean, they knew *I* couldn't take down the Mayor and the Police Chief single-handed. No, what *does* matter is your picture of the Oriental woman. When they saw **that**,   *everything* changed."

"The woman with the red star tattoo on her neck?"

"**Blood** Star, Kid,   *Blood Star*.   And unlike The Black Daggers, Blood Star is *very* real! *Deadly real!*" Estanod turned his head and spat, "Yeah, I knew I was in deep when the Chief looked me in the eye and told me it was a birth mark distorted by the low level lighting. When *that* bucket dropped on my head, I tried to play along, tried to keep the shock off my face. But   they knew." He shook his head and blew out into the shadows. "Then,   two days later   I found the bugs in my apartment." Another bitter laugh grunted into the dark. "I had to work my ass off just to shake the tail to make it here tonight."

Joshua stood, took a long slow step to the side, and edged one eye just beyond the corner, keeping the other closed. He half expected to see dark forms against the bright lights of The Avenue, blocking their escape.

Estanod half lifted off his box seat. "Still clear?"

His night vision ruined in one eye, Joshua nodded and stepped back into his corner, but did not sit down again. Estanod slid the rest of the way

Driven to the Hilt

to his feet in response, but continued to prop up the wet wall behind him. "Kid, don't let **anyone** know you were involved in that drug bust, in *any way*, ***ever!***" He extended a clenched fist, palm down. "Here," he prompted Joshua with a shake of his fist. "This is all I can afford."

Joshua became emotionally numb as the weight of the heavy 20 credit coin dropped into his palm. "Thanks." He automatically pocketed the money.

"Listen, Kid, these people don't play around. A few years back, one of the miners tried to get the company to provide some treatment for drug addiction, some sort of employee assistance program. For trying to get some help for his fellow miners, they killed his entire family! Wife *and* kids." He looked off, his voice softer, "It was my second week on patrol. I was first on scene." His voice dropped even lower, as if speaking to himself, "Now I'm not so sure whether he offed himself like they said or if he had a little help."

Estanod bent forward with a jerk so his face emerged from the shadow of his slicker hood and Joshua repressed an urge to lean back from the intensity in his eyes. "They will *erase* you too, Kid, if there is even a *sniff* that you were involved. And they would squeeze every last drop of information out of you before doing it."

Joshua held his gaze. Through the thumping of his heart, he heard his reply, "And then they'd get you, I guess."

Estanod's face flashed with surprise that melted to remorse and then reformed into determination before it disappeared back into the darkness of his hood. The pounding rain rattled off their slickers as the pause stretched on. Joshua was about to head for the roofs when Estanod broke the silence.

"Okay Ki-, *Joshua*. I'm telling you all of this because I pulled you into it and I don't want you dead on my account. I know that's not much, but at least you know the score now. And, believe me, Blood Star is ten a *hundred* times worse than the Mayor's thugs. They aren't held back by the possibility of bad publicity. In fact, the Lieutenant says they sometimes leave evidence at the scene so investigators know it was them, to help spread their reputation." Estanod's back made a wet slap against the wall and his head tilted toward his shiny black shoes. "And I uh, need to tell you you should also know that I'm quitting the force. So what little protection I might have once been able to give to you   that's *gone.*"

Joshua tried to keep his voice matter of fact, but it still sounded forlorn, even to him. "Where are you going?"

The policeman stood quietly before finally looking up from his feet. "I've saved up just enough money to go full time for my last year of school."

This time Estanod's hand was open when he stretched it forward. As Joshua shook it, the cop provided a final warning, "I don't know if they'll buy me dropping out of all this, but maybe it'll take some heat off of you. In any case, you should probably stay low in The Swamp for at least a few weeks. Even Blood Star will think twice about going in there.   Probably." He gripped Joshua's hand harder in emphasis, words hissing out hard, "And stay away from that warehouse. *Permanently.*"

Again the silence extended as they stood in the rain, hands clasped. Joshua had no idea what to say. Estanod finally let go of his hand and stood for a moment, the dark hole of his hood inscrutable. A screen of fine mist drifted down in the soft yellow light between them. Joshua could feel Estanod about to say something, but only a long sigh came out, creating slight swirls in the shining sheet of tiny droplets, the eddies distorting as they fell away, and then the wall of vapor reformed. Estanod turned and exited the alcove.

Joshua edged out from the corner of the niche to watch Estanod's silhouette recede toward the bright lights of The Avenue. His steady footsteps broke the colored reflections on the pools of water that had gathered along the solid uneven surface at the mouth of the alleyway. The scene transformed and Joshua watched his father's back as he strode up the covered gangway into the merchant ship. It was the last time he and his mother would see him off. A moist blink brought him back to the alley. Unlike his father, there was no turn and final wave from Estanod before he disappeared into the UpAve foot traffic without a backward glance.

A low rumble brought Joshua back to the present, unsure how long he had been standing in the alley. He watched the march of fat raindrops exploding the shimmering reflections of the Avenue lights until   the sheet of water attacked the hood of his slicker with a deafening rattle. The assault was a physical manifestation of the emotional blows he had just been dealt by Estanod's departure. Staring out into the dark downpour from under his hood, the pain drained away, leaving only a hollow core.

Joshua woodenly turned for the drainpipe and ascended into the black rain.

Into the Belly

Dark eyes flicked underneath a wide rimmed black hat, then locked onto a figure emerging from the alley opening. They picked up the ever so slight hesitation that signaled the man's last second decision to turn in a different direction. The owner of the dark eyes turned back to the merchant standing nearby, a silent flat stare disengaging him from their bartering session so he could move in pursuit of his quarry. As he flowed to a stop in the spot on the pedway just vacated by his target, one hand flipped down a pair of lenses and he looked into the alley. The other hand lifted up a few inches and stopped, palm forward, while he took in the heat signature of a mid-sized child, *male*, standing *two-fifths* back into the dead end alley. *Decision time.* He glanced back toward the initial target and saw his back disappear into a crevice. *Not sanctioned on the cop yet, but the proper disposal of his CI could make him more* pliable *when that time comes.* Two fingers on the palm forward hand flicked toward where the policeman's infrared image had vanished. He sensed rather than saw his pair of associates move by in pursuit. When he turned back to the mouth of the alley, he experienced a rare surprise- the heat signature was *gone*.

He readied his hands as he entered the alley, preparing for when the multicolored image of the boy appeared out of a crease between buildings or deep doorway, making his break for the exit. The man was supremely confident that his prey would not escape. His fluid progression into the recess was almost sinuous and he cleared each doorway and alcove as he went deeper. His curiosity mounted into annoyance the farther he proceeded. Soon, he had finished with the entire alley. *And no boy.*

Fenster considered checking each and every door in the alleyway, even though he knew he was close enough to have heard the closing of any door in the small enclosure. Besides, any well prepped Alice chute would also be well fortified against entry, and thus, not worth the extra effort. It was highly unlikely that the pair had taken the time to prepare such an elaborate escape route ahead of time, but *when all other options have been eliminated, the remaining possibility, no matter how improbable, must be true.* He turned and left the gloom of the dead end alley.

Once back on the Avenue, he placed two calls simultaneously from his earpiece by tapping the codes on the fob in his pocket. He knew there was going to be a problem after the second ring. The third ring was interrupted and he experienced a paltry measure of gratification to hear the straight forward acknowledgement of failure.

"We lost him."

"Location?" As soon as he had the necessary information, Fenster disconnected. Making his way to where the cop had last been seen, he mentally marked the man who had answered *what was his name? Something quite pedestrian except, of course, for the spelling Ralff. That's it* for only minimal pain during their next sparing match. The goon who had not answered at all would not fare as well during those hand-to-hand combat exercises. Fenster almost sighed. *My training responsibilities are simply endless.*

He strolled into a long passageway between buildings. Halfway to the next pedway, he stopped in front of two large, but timid figures. "Report."

The same voice that had answered the phone gave the explanation. "We was followin' from a distance, 'bout 25 feet, one on each side o' The Avenue, just like you tell us, and we tailed him in here and *he was gone.* I tell Lynyrd ta run all the way to the end n' check the next pedway, on 'count he's a better runner 'n me, and I waits until he gives me the all clear. Then we pro-ceeded from both ends at a slower pace ta make sure he don't slip by either way. We count five doors, all locked up real good, and there's that one lil' bump in the side there," an arm lifted to indicate the designated "bump," "and we checked it and there just ain't no way outta there. He couldn't a run all the way to the end before we got off The Ave to where he done came in, Mr. Fenster. We woulda seen him fer sure. All I's kin figu-" He stopped the instant Fenster's hand lifted.

"I will do any necessary *figuring,* thank you."

"Yessir."

"So, while I recheck the doors, you two will go into the 'bump' and stomp on every square foot of the ground."

"Yessir."

Fenster liked the man's eagerness to please, but "Do you know *why* you will be stomping on every square foot of ground in the 'bump'?"

Fenster could almost hear the gears grinding, but his expectations were surpassed when Ralff finally simply said, "Nossir."

"Very good Ralff. Although we both know very well that honesty is virtually never the best policy, I am delighted to see that you understand I am the exception to that rule." Fenster did not wait for the gears to resume their slow grind and immediately explained, "You and your mute compatriot here, *Lynyrd*, will be listening for a hollow sound, Ralff. As in the sound you might expect if you stomped on a trap door. *As in*, some type of access to the motorway below. Do you understand?"

"Yessir."

"Excellent. You may begin." Although reluctant to issue a two-step command, Fenster took a chance. "Oh, and Ralff? When you are finished with the ground, assuming your search is unsuccessful, use the hilts of your knives to tap along the walls of the 'bump.' And you will be listening for?"

"Hollow sounds, Mr. Fenster."

He understood. How refreshing.

The process took over 30 minutes, with Fenster using first his infrared lenses and then his sheet light to examine every inch of all five doors, before doing some tapping of his own. In the end, the three resumed their huddle outside the "bump" without having produced any hollow sounds or an explanation for the target's disappearance. Fenster decided he was going to take a gradual approach to prepping his target for full intel extraction. *He is going to explain, in exquisite detail, exactly how he eluded us, and he is going to tell me tonight. I will dispose of his street urchin CI at my leisure.* He lifted his voice to be heard over the thumping deluge of a passing squall, "Set up observation posts at both entrances to the policeman's apartment building. Contact me immediately if he leaves."

"Yessir."

Bossman's strong hand watched his two charges fade into the rumbling rainfall. He gave a final glance at the "bump" before heading for the nearest access stairs to the motorway below. *I know I'm missing something.* But he was confident it would come to him later. In the meantime, he set off for the target's residential structure, where he would make easy entry via its roots. After all, he was well practiced at bypassing much more extensive security measures. Once he had incapacitated the policeman, he would just have to improvise on his repertoire of interrogation techniques. *And I **like** improvisation.*

~~~~~~~

This is getting scary.

Protected by the overhang of a storefront portico, Joshua watched the tall cloaked man stroll by in the downpour. Although the cloaked head did not turn as he passed and Joshua could not penetrate the black shadow created by the cowl, he could *feel* the man's eyes on him as he passed. And then   the dark green cloak was swallowed by the wash of water released from the Spring storm cell above.

Joshua's entire body shivered. It was yet another thing to keep the Siren Swan singing. It had started with the intense feeling of exposure as he had approached his blind, had continued while he traveled the rooftops, and after *that*, had been extended by the spooky guy with the hat who had stopped in the middle of The Ave and turned his head to look right at him.

The almost overwhelming wave of sinister intent that rolled off Hat Man had spurred Joshua to scramble up the corner drainpipe as never before. Once crouched on the other side of the roof wall, his instincts had stopped him from lifting his head for a quick check on Hat Man. Instead, he had crawled away from the dead end alley and not risen to his feet until he was a full block removed. *Then*, as he had made his way toward the Rusty Pipe, it had hit him again – the intense feeling of vulnerability. Even though he was only a few blocks from his exit to The Swamp, Joshua had again descended to the pedway to mix with the crowds on The Ave. It had been surreal to feel safer in the light among the shoppers on The Avenue than on the rooftops above. And *now…*

Mr. Green Cloak shows up,   again. Joshua didn't really know anything about the man other than that he was seeing him more and more frequently; on The Ave, the surrounding pedways, even around the warehouse. And each time, he had the feeling that the tall man had known his *exact* location. Which Joshua knew could not be true, since he usually spotted Mr. Green Cloak from above, but still-

Ummph! The shove to the middle of his back propelled Joshua into the slacking rainfall.

"Shelter's for payin' customers only!"

Joshua did not bother to look back at the merchant, just happy that he had not been expelled while Mr. Green Cloak had walked by earlier. He plodded his way UpAve toward The Swamp, weaving through the growing collection of daring customers, now that the squall had almost passed by. His sense of impending doom receded with the rain, but the implications of Estanod's departure loomed in his mind. He could feel the weight of the 20 UD coin in his pocket, but instead of reassurance, its rhythmic slap against his hip called forth the image of an empty space on the rock shelf in Sanctuary where he stored his foodstuffs. The barren pantry echoed the emptiness in his life now that he had lost his purpose. Although he had been hesitant about moving in with Estanod, knowing that the possibility of normalcy was now gone brought on an aching depression.

Competing thoughts made brief appearances on the surface of his melancholy, each sinking back into the morass of despondency before he could actively think them through. What was he going to do for money now? Was he really in as much danger as Estanod thought? Should he hole up in Sanctuary again, just to be safe? An image of Sanctuary elevated above his jumbled thoughts, along with a sense of foreboding at the prospect of being stuck there again for weeks on end. His feet automatically turned toward an alleyway that possessed a drainpipe to exit from the city. *I'm tired of being alone.*

"Look who's all alone."

Joshua came up short, momentarily confused by the voice's echo of his thought. His focus shifted outward and in the direction of the comment. A figure in a full length slicker stepped into the still heavy rain from the deeper shadows of a doorway. His mind accelerated out of the turbid waters of his depression, but did not quite shift into slowtime. *That voice as tall as me   Glin!* A dark hand lifted and a glint rolled over a curved surface. *A gun barrel!* Joshua's vision zoomed in on the hole at the end of the revolver Glin had stretched forward in the rain.

Just as when he had first seen the spiderviper that had killed his mother, time slowed almost to a stop. Joshua could see raindrops exploding off the top of the revolver and Glin's outstretched arm and hand, fractured bits of water moving away in lazy, rotating, uneven twinkles. Round spots of less intense shadow marked the tips of the bullets awaiting escape from their resting places in the gun's cylinder. Joshua could even make out the serrations of the rifling on the interior edge of the medium length barrel. The freeze frame broke under the impact of Glin's words…

"You shouldn't of got into Bossman's business."

With supreme effort, Joshua pulled his eyes away from the gun barrel and looked into the dark of the hood where he could just make out Glin's eyes. "Are you going to kill me?"

Something flashed in Glin's face before he responded, "I do what I have to do   for people that are *important* to me." His jaw muscles flexed, "…and I don't even *know* you." The gun lifted higher, again commanding Joshua's complete attention. A thought flitted across as the end of the barrel grew even larger. *No slowtime because even **that** won't save me from this…*

A corner of Joshua's brain registered a whisper of a squish   not the first   advancing   from behind! He whipped his head around and slowtime finally kicked in   a   fleshy   block   was   expanding   near his   face   *A fist!*   He   pulled   *hard*   on   his   head   to   escape, but the muscle of his cheek began to press in and pain began to penetrate and radiate across

...the world tumbled and rolled until Joshua knew he was not moving anymore, but *Wha...?* a rough surface pressed cool water against one side of his face worn shoes were turned sideways and peeking out from under a slicker *Who...?* a cloth smashed against his nose and mouth. *Smells like Mom cleanin-* He could not finish the thoug...

go....

GO!

can't m.. move...

Go! NOW!!!

something... holding
my hands won't go.

ESCAPE!!

Must see why hands

blink blink blink

A blurred shape appeared. Joshua thought *should* be his right hand. *I am looking at it, right?* He willed his fingers to lift and saw the corresponding movement. His attempt to lift his arm was stopped by a black bar across his wrist. *Uh?* Joshua blinked, dimly aware of how slow his thoughts were moving, and then came a reverberation from the inner voice that had yelled at him before, containing an emphatic tone of urgency, *CONCENTRATE!* but Annoyance flared when a deep baritone interrupted his efforts to think.

"He's coming around. Go get Bossman."

"Okay."

That voice! It was important somehow...

Glin! With a gun! The image of the cannon-sized opening to the revolver barrel hooked the entire memory and in a flash, Joshua understood his current circumstance with a blooming dread. The clarity of his vision cleared with his thoughts and he surveyed his surroundings.

The glare of a flood light forced his eyes downward, where it illuminated his torso, revealed that he was sitting in a hard plastic chair, wrists held down to the arm rests by buckled leather straps. Joshua's eyes were drawn to the front of his wet shirt and the large red stains on his stomach *slicker's gone.   Red?* He became aware of a blockage in the left side of his nose as well as a raw tenderness to his left upper lip. With that awareness came a deep aching pain across the entire left side of his face. He tried to open his eyes wider for a clearer view, but the flesh around his left eye was pressing in all around. There were also a series of sharper pains on the surface of his right cheek *scrapes.* Joshua tried to take his mind off the pain by examining the room, but the spotlight effectively made his surroundings an impenetrable blackness. He again looked at the chair that restrained him. He saw that the straps were built into the chair *a part of the chair* and a memory tickled just out of reach. Something Estanod had said once –

In front of him came the sound of scraping   a chair being pulled across a hard surface. A frighteningly normal voice spoke out from behind the glare in a conversational tone, **"So, you're the one who's been spying on me."** Something about its nonchalance seemed familiar.

"Spying? I haven't bee-"

Joshua's head rocked forward from a slap out of the darkness.

The relaxed tone vanished, the voice now angry and harsh, **"Don't lie to me, turd brain! I'll *know* when you lie to me! Do you understand?"**

Joshua blinked away stars from the blow to the back of his head. "Yes! Yes, I understand."

"Who's the cop you are working for?"

"I don't kn–"

This sharp slap landed on the side of his head.

"I TOLD you to   QUIT   LYING!!"

Joshua began sobbing. *Why is all of this happening to me? I just want to be back in Sanctuary right now, by myself! Why can't I be there?* He heard the answer in his head clearly, unaffected by the uncontrollable heaving of his shoulders. But you are not there, are you? So, you must think! THINK!

Joshua detached and rose up over his left shoulder, where he looked down upon himself. He could now see that it was Bossman who sat to the side of the spotlight with a large sheet in his hands, face reflecting light from its display. And it was Big Ears who stood behind the chair, slapping his head. Just being able to see his tormentors helped calm Joshua. *That's why they set up the room this way!* With his detachment and increased calm, his brain began to unfreeze *Interrogation Chair! That's the display Bossman is watching, my what had Estanod said? My "psychophysio" responses to the questions. He* can *tell when I lie.*

Bossman looked up from the display and nodded to Big Ears. Now that he could see it coming, Joshua minimized the next blow by rolling with it. His confidence increased.

"Who is the cop?"

"Look, he called me Kid all the time, you know, like with caps? And so I asked if I should call him The Cop. It was a joke between us."

Bossman scrutinized the feedback and appeared satisfied. "So, how long were you watching my place?"

"Uh, just over four weeks." *Why isn't he asking more about Estanod?*

"How'd you get the pictures?"

Joshua decided he had no reason not to tell. "The Cop? He gave me a low frequency flip phone that's used in warehouses. Has infrared to take pictures of codesquares to track inventory." Bossman's eyebrows rose in appreciation and he leaned back with a nod of satisfaction. *That's what he was after!*

"So The Cop has the picture of the Chinese woman?"

The casual tone was betrayed by Bossman's shift forward in his chair and his intense inspection of the sheet as he awaited his answer. *Just tell the truth...*

"I'm not sure, but I think he turned it all over to the Police Chief." When Bossman looked up at Big Ears, Joshua quickly added, "I *know* he gave the picture to the Chief because he said the Chief told him the red thing on her neck was a birth mark." Bossman held up a hand and stopped

The Deepest Cut

his lackey from providing additional motivation.

"So he may still have a copy?"

"I don't think so. They took away his, ah Detectiveship after the big bust on PV. So he quit. They would have taken all of his equipment when he left, right?"

"He left the force?"

"Yeah, he was pretty pissed about it all. He said he was going to finish his college. He was doing long-distance classes with a university on, where was it, hmm Asterton! That's it." Joshua pictured Estanod walking up a gangplank to a waiting ship, hoping to skip over his mislabeling of the planet by making his next statement more real, *because I really don't know if he went.* "Maybe he went there to finish his school."

Bossman narrowed his eyes and then shifted them from the display to peer at Joshua. "So." His eyes squinted again. "Do *you* think it was a birthmark?"

"Huh?" The observing Joshua was as caught off guard as much as the Joshua strapped to the chair. Their simultaneous intake of breath was so sudden at the springing of the trap that it sparked a coughing fit. At the exhalation of the second cough, the two Joshuas merged back together and time slowed...

I cannot fake past the Blood Star tattoo. I have to tell the truth, but not about that. Normal time resumed and his coughing fit finished with a wad of partially congealed blood flying out to plop somewhere on the floor in front of him. He squeezed his eyes tight and struggled to regain control of his breathing. He let the fear and despair that had overwhelmed him earlier come to the fore. He kept his eyes closed and focused on his words, *knowing* the truth behind each one of them...

"Listen, Mr. Bossman. Sir. I'm just an 11-year-old kid. Both of my parents are dead." Tears squeezed out through his clamped eyelids at the last word. "I just wanted to make some money to try and get by. I don't know about what's happening at City Hall, what a Dragon Lady with red marks is doing here I don't know!! I just want to be left ALONE!" He opened his eyes to look at Bossman. "How's a little kid like me going to cause trouble for a man like you?"

Joshua waited to see if his efforts would pull him through.

"You know, kid, I believe you." *It worked!* "But this one isn't my call. That *Dragon Lady* that *you* don't know about? Well, *she* knows all about *you*. And she considers you a 'roose end.'" A cold sinking flush rolled through Joshua's body as Bossman snorted at his mispronunciation. "Hooo, hoo, ah yeah. Oohh, anyway. I'm not happy about the shift in power here either, *believe* me, but... we have to make a good impression on " his mouth twisted on the bitterness of the next words, "the *new* Boss." His gaze shifted to Big Ears in an unspoken command.

Joshua pressed the words out as rapidly as he could, "Big Ears is running a numbers scheme on you!"

A hairy arm encircled his neck, cutting off his air, but eased up at Bossman's lifted hand.

The drug lord squinted in confusion. "Big Ears?" He looked over Joshua's shoulder for assistance and then his face lit up. "Big Ears! You mean my able assistant here, Mr. Grimes?" Bossman threw back his head and began laughing. He managed to get out words in between guffaws, "Oh GOD! ha, ha Big Ears! Hoo, ho ha Good one, Kid. First Dragon Lady and then *Ha* Big Ears. Sheeesh, Kid, I'm telling you. Whew!" He wiped his eyes and again looked above Joshua's shoulder. "I think you have a new nickname, Grimes."

The arm tightened around Joshua's throat.

"So, ah, Kid, I'm gonna let you in on a secret here. Umm, *Big Ears* has already come clean with me about his little side lotto business. Course, one of his 'partners' had already given him up, but you see, I *like* initiative, just so long as I get my cut."

"But he used y-aaacck-"

A large rough hand reached over to unbuckle first the right and then left wrist straps. Joshua was pulled by the neck out of the chair and his arm was twisted up until his hand was jammed between his shoulder blades. The hairy arm slipped away from his throat and a hand squeezed down a warning deep into his shoulder. Bossman's dark figure silhouetted against an opening door as Joshua strained to take in enough air to speak.

The Deepest Cut

"Wa WAIT!" Joshua furiously sought another angle, and despite the pain of his further elevated arm, he sputtered out, "I s-still have my f-flip phone!"

Bossman stopped and turned. "You find a phone on him?"

Before Big Ears could reply, Joshua blurted out, "I hid it on the way to my last meeting with E- eh, The Cop."

"Yeah, so?"

"It has all of the pictures still on it!"

"And?"

And   and what?

"*And* you hid it real good where no one will ever find it *and*, hmmm how does *that* concern me, exactly?"

"I uh, gave copies to a, uh, a friendly merchant." Joshua pictured Aberly as he filled his voice with conviction. "He'll turn it over to the SBI if anything happens to me!"

Bossman crossed the floor in three long strides, wadded Joshua's shirt in both fists, and yanked him up, nose-to-nose.

"Are you threatening me?" His question rasped out in a gravely rumble.

Joshua met his glare. "Yes."

Two pairs of eyes stared, unblinking, while the moment held until "Whoo!"

Bossman let Joshua fall back into Grimes' grasp. "I gotta hand it to you, little boy, you've sure got some moxy! But, you see, the only problem with your little daytime PV soap plot twist *is* the pictures don't *mean* anything. Unless, of course, you're saying that you have evidence of any of us *doing* something *illegal*? Something that, you know, would hold up in court?"

Joshua stammered, "Yeah, well, no, but..." he reached for the last straw, "but the Chinese lady won't like it!"

The drug dealer eased down on one knee, placed a hand on Joshua's shoulder, and again looked him in the eye.

"Now, see, you just went too far there. I believe I mentioned I was unhappy with the new management. Didn't I?"

Joshua just nodded. He was out of ideas.

"And then you went and *threw it in MY FACE!*"

Spittle sprayed onto Joshua's cheek and chin. Bossman wiped his mouth with the back of his hand before continuing in a calmer voice, "So, I'm just going to have my associate here, you know, Big Ears? make you dis a *peer.*" Bossman rose and walked to the door, stopping to look over his shoulder with a shrug.

"You shouldn't have stepped over the line, boy."

The faded cover from a very old book flashed into Joshua's mind, and with it, the germ of an idea from one of the ancient folk stories his mother used to read from that collection. *One last chance.* To sell it, he brought up the image of the sinuous eel-like creatures he had seen in the lake next to the Stink Blossoms. He could hear real terror vibrate in his next words.

"D- disappear? Y-you don't m-mean, you'd drop me in into The Swamp *Alone?*"

His eyes widened in horror as he pictured wading out into the murky waters of the lake, with those dark, red eyed creatures sliding closer in excitement, just under the surface.

Bossman paused with the door half open and frowned quizzically. "Sooo, you thought I meant drop you into The Swamp?"

"You *didn't* mean that?"

"Actually, kid, no, I didn't mean that." He stepped back up to Joshua with the smile of a proud father. "But upon reflection, I must admit, your idea has some merit. After all, you practically ran me over on the pedway, then you go and spy on my private business dealings, and *then* you injure my employee's knuckles with your face!" Bossman lifted both hands in helplessness. "What's a poor drug dealer to do?" His face beamed with a sudden revelation. "BUT! If we just drop you into The Swamp, as *you* suggested, *then* POOF!" His joined fingertips snapped open wide. "No more evidence, no more spying, no more *pesky* boy. Because as we all know, *nothing ever* comes back out of The Swamp. Alive, anyway. Now *that's* what I call a win win. *Not only that* but this gives me a chance to show Dragon Lady how I take care of business. Thanks, kid." He reached out and gave Joshua's shoulder a fond pat. "In the meantime, your 'Friendly Merchant' will just be sitting there wondering and *wondering*   'where *ever* did that   nosy   muck brained *annoying*   boy GO?!' "

Joshua gasped at the pronouncement of his death sentence. "Please, sir, PLEEES- ugk." His plea was cut off by Big Ears' arm again wrapping around his throat.

Bossman was back at the door. "Aww, now you're making me lose all respect for you, Kid. Be a man. Don't go out at the end like a sniveling little snot gobbler." He looked flatly at Grimes. "Drop him off the Seneca Street dead end. No one will be watching there." Then Bossman peered into a dark corner as his hand grasped the door knob. "*You* go along too, Mother Hen. Be sure to share with your *Shadow Boys* just what happens to people who push Bossman too far."

◄3►

Big Ears' arm lifted Joshua's chin until he stood on his tiptoes and then it propelled him into the blackness beyond the floodlight. Unable to see, he staggered each time they shifted directions in the gloomy hallways, only to be lifted up by his twisted arm and forced forward again. They left the warehouse through a door that opened directly onto a dark deserted motorway.

They made most of the trip under the pedways to the edge of New Cincinnati in silence. Glin walked a step behind, the squishes of their shoes punctuated by occasional sharp flashes of lightning, followed by the low angry rumble of thunder. As they turned onto Seneca Street, Joshua suddenly realized the serious flaw in his plan. If he allowed himself to be thrown off the edge by Big Ears, he would likely be seriously injured or killed by the fall.

As they continued his death march, Joshua began searching for an opportunity to test Big Ears' attentiveness. It came in the boom of a closer lightning strike. He cringed in fright at the peal of thunder and allowed himself to stumble, happy to note a delay in Big Ears' reaction of re-gripping his arm and snatching him back upright. *Now I have to get him to think about something else.* He looked over to Glin. "Y-you   you're going to let him throw me into   into *The Swamp?*"

Glin kept his eyes forward and took several more steps before replying, "I *told* you, I do what I gotta do for those *that matter.*" He looked over in resentment. "*You're* the one that was spying on Bossman.   So now   *we all* have to do this." He slowed down, forcing Joshua to look forward again and preventing further conversation. Something in Glin's response made Joshua uneasy and in the renewed rhythm of their wet steps it came to him. *He's doing this to save his Shadow Boys. I killed Uncle William because*   Joshua did not complete the thought. Their final destination had just come into view.

Oh man! NO Way!

Joshua could not believe his luck. They were approaching Rusty Pipe.

Now he just needed to get loose.

While he had been docile enough for most of the trip, Joshua knew Big Ears would be on guard for an escape attempt as they came near the end. So when they were within ten feet of the edge, instead of trying to pull away, he simply collapsed, letting his sudden body weight pull himself out of Big Ears' grasp. He landed in a heap, more on his left shoulder, head angled back to look behind and see an annoyed Big Ears widen his stance and reach down with both hands. Hands that began to slow; Joshua extended his right leg straight toward the groin, making adjustments to counter Big Ears' desperate twist to avoid the blow. That he hit at least some of the target was confirmed by the WHOOSH of air from Big Ears' pursed lips. Joshua scrambled on all fours toward the edge of the pavement and then leapt to his feet with his back to the empty air. His hand thrust out as he screamed.

"DON'T!! Or I *swear* I'll take you with me!"

The threat stopped both of his escorts from advancing farther, although Big Ears was still trying to catch his breath and Glin had not been eager in the first place. The storm had intensified, with the flashes of lighting increasing in frequency and the thunder coming quicker. Joshua waited for a boom to echo away before yelling through the lashing curtains of rain.

"OK! I know I have to go down there, but I am going to do it *myself!*"

He looked back again to place his heels at the very edge of the pavement, checking to his right for the pipe. Another flash of lightning gave enough illumination for at least an educated guess on how he would need to jump to *hopefully* grab the drain pipe. *Time for Br'er Rabbit to make an exit.*

His finger stabbed out at Big Ears. "*You* tell Mr. Bossman," his finger shifted and he locked eyes with Glin, "and *you* tell all of the 'Shadow Boys,' *this* is how a man goes out!"

Joshua's hair lifted just prior to the violent crack that split the air, almost simultaneous with the massive burst of light that exploded just behind him. He leapt, and while he hung in the air, an immediate after strike illuminated the tableau in front of him with another explosion of sound that hammered him like a physical blow.

Despite being stunned by the extremely close lightning strike, his hand still stretched out as he fell through space   reaching   and touching pipe. He gripped the tube hard, twisted to grab with his other hand, his plummet slowed, his feet rose and pressed against the rock wall   and he had almost stopped before he let go to drop the remaining four feet. Joshua immediately crouched into a ball under the drain, the stream of water pounding into his back, willing himself to look like a rock   to *be* a rock. His brain shifted gears, isolating the splashing of water rushing over and around him, reaching beyond the background clatter of rain striking the nearby rocks, to the buildings above, seeking the hollow sound of raindrops on slickers as Glin and Big Ears ran to the edge of the precipice.

"Can you see him?"

The next lightning flash came from deeper in the city, casting the groove in the foundation into deeper shadow.

"No. I can't make out anything. Do you have a flashlight?"

"Do YOU?   This is soppin' ridiculous!   There's no *way* he could've survived that.   Besides, Bossman doesn't even *want* him dead, *yet*, and there's *definitely* no way he's getting back up here! Come on, let's go."

Amazingly, Joshua thought he could hear the rattle of rain off just one of the slickers diminish as it retreated. The water hammering into his back really began to hurt, but Joshua did not move. From a greater distance he heard Big Ears' impatient yell.

"Come ON! We are *done* here."

Above the roar of the storm, Joshua could just make out, "Yeah,   I know."

The second slicker held yet another moment,   and then moved away. Still terrified of discovery, Joshua waited another moment before he dared to roll away from the punishing torrent.

The route out was very familiar, and it did not take much time to exit the alcove and begin jogging through the downpour. Although now less frequent, Joshua hoped the rolls of thunder would still be enough to keep all of the beasties tucked away just a bit longer. Even so, he maintained a constant swivel of vigilance as he ran toward Sanctuary; soaked, bruised, without his slicker, sheet, or parting money from Estabon. Despite the risk of being heard by the hunters of the night, Joshua could not hold down the chortles that kept rising from his gut every time he recalled the scene that would forever be frozen in his mind by that flash of lightning: The look of utter, dumbfounded astonishment on the faces of Big Ears and Glin when he had leapt out into space and plummeted down into *The Swamp.*

One down, four to go.

Joshua surveyed his efforts. The creation on the wicker mannequin was a patchwork of four different slickers he had salvaged from trash heaps in the motorways farther south in the city. He had decided against totally covering the slicker with the water proofing paint still remaining in the spray can in his hand. The glossy finish charcoal color covered the seams that were held together with Shark Tape, making an uneven pattern of dark and light greens and greys, interwoven with the irregular lines of almost black paint. *Nice! A camo slicker!*

After storing the remaining materials against future repairs, Joshua went to bed, even though it was only 9:00. He wanted an early start to the next morning, having figured Bossman and his underlings would be still tucked tight into bed at that time. Of course, he still would not go anywhere near the warehouse or The Avenue.

He put in a full morning's worth of surveillance on the NorthPoint apartments that had been the last stop for him and his mother. It was almost midday before he saw what he had been waiting for – two women moving away from the units, arms filled with bags or pulling battered suitcases. Noting the number of the unit they had exited from, Joshua retreated to The Swamp. Although it was unlikely Glin and the Shadow Boys were up and about at that hour and in that neighborhood, he took no chances.

The following morning, he stood waiting by the door when the branch librarian approached up the pedway. This earned him a series of puzzled but friendly glances as she thumbed the lockpad, made her way into the small structure, and came to a stop behind the even smaller counter.

"My, my, I don't often have such early risers. What brings you here at such an hour?"

Joshua squenched his mouth into a dour twist. "Mom said I *have* to get Jisse her account today before I do *anything* else!" He frowned in determination. "So I'm not going to waste **any** more time than I have to."

"Ahhh,   and Jisse is?"

"My stoooopid sister!"

The librarian frowned. "Now, that's no way to talk about your own sister."

Joshua looked down. "I guess not." *Don't overdo it.* "So could I please fill out an application for a GlobalNet account for Jisse Iverson? At JisS2pid@NCinn.gov.citnet?"

The librarian smiled as she swiveled up a large sheet attached to a folding arm. She had typed halfway through the address when she looked up sharply at Joshua. He looked down again and shrugged. "OK. It's JisSunnySideUp@NCinn.gov.citnet."

"Now *that* is sweet. And not taken. All right, let's get the rest of this application done."

Joshua provided the information as she asked, but his nerves stretched when he gave the address of the recently vacated unit at NorthPoint. Had Mr. Donald been lazy as usual and not marked it as unoccupied? Did the people leaving make sure to swipe out of their occupancy, eager to avoid charges for time they were not there? If so, the librarian should see "verification of occupancy without current identifying information" on her screen. *At least according to the GlobalNet, but you never know...*

"Hmmm, this data is not matching "

Joshua's sigh was more in relief than exasperation, so he rolled his eyes and let out a whine, "Aaawwwuu, I just *knew* it! Mr. Donald didn't put in our information. Mom *made sure* he had all the info before we moved in, but he is so *slow*. I **knew** it! I *knew* this would take me **all day!**" He could not quite work up actual tears, but he tried to look forlorn nonetheless.

"Now, now, let's stay calm." She pressed through several other screens, "Well, I see that a Roree Donald is the property manager, so I can verify based upon what I have here, but maybe you can take *just a bit more time* out of your day to remind Mr. Donald to update the renter information, OK?"

"Okay."

"OK then. Off you go. You don't want to waste any of the rest of your day!"

The woman's cheerfulness brought an upsurge of guilt as Joshua turned for the door. But his discomfort from having deceived her was washed away by a swell of relief. He was sure that by now, Bossman's scorpion had bypassed his meager resident security apps, scanned his sheet, and put a tripwire on his account. Joshua had no intention of ever using his prior account again and now he had a new one. He almost skipped out of the library.

And that's Number Two.

Since the morning had just begun and The Ave merchants catered to their clientele long into the night, Joshua decided it would be safe to run the rooftops and return to Rendezvous #3. He found the box alley deserted and slid down the corner pipe, but he stopped when he unexpectedly saw two doorways filled with trash. *I thought there was only one.* With the need to constantly check the opening to the alley behind him, the search was slow. His anxiety mounted when he gave up on the first pile of trash and shifted to the second doorway. Halfway through the mound, he looked back and froze. A cloaked figure stood at one side of the mouth of the alley, watching him.

Joshua forced himself to look away and continue his search, using both hands. *After all, there's nothing to see here, just a street urchin rummaging around, looking for something to eat.* His left hand struck something hard and he snuck another look over his shoulder.

The tall man stood ten feet closer, allowing Joshua to make out that the cloak that hung almost to the man's feet was a very dark green. Not turning his head away, his fingers explored the hard object. *That's it!* Firmly grasping the flip phone, Joshua slowly rose to his feet, but kept sideways so he could slip the pCom device into his side slicker pocket unseen.

With both hands free, he risked a quick look to his left, taking in the back corner of the alley and where a wall jutted out several feet forward. In that joint of buildings stood *A drainpipe!* Movement pulled Joshua's eyes back to the still figure. All still,   except for the slight sway of the bottom of his cloak. Joshua was not sure that the pipe was deep enough to cover the mode of his escape, but Mr. Green Cloak would probably figure it out anyway when he found the alcove was empty. Besides, the man's current behavior was just *too creepy.* Joshua exploded toward the pipe.

He was not sure he had ever made an ascent so quickly and he did not look back down, but moved across the roof with as much speed and stealth as possible. Soon he was running and leaping from one roof top to another, seeking the seclusion of the abandoned tenements' roofs to the northeast of town. Sitting in the shadows of an upper level alcove, he caught his breath while scrutinizing the empty expanse of patched pyramids behind him for any movement. Finally, Joshua decided he was safe.

That's Number Three – over halfway now!

Despite the freaky encounter with Mr. Green Cloak, Joshua was determined to try to find a replacement for his sheet. From his exploration right after he and his Mom had moved to NorthPoint, he knew there were several pawn shops in the vicinity of the library branch. They were not near The Ave, so he set off to try and complete Objective #4. What he found in the second pawn shop crammed his just regained sunny mood back into the mud.

Having found no one to greet him when he walked in, Joshua had made his way to the display counters in the back, where the more expensive items were usually held. On the way, he had spotted multiple security cameras covering every aspect of the pawn shop. *OK, but still you'd think they'd want to greet customers anyway.* He stopped, stunned, looking down through the security glass of a back case.

I   can   not   believe   this!

At first he had not been sure, but the small chip out of the upper left corner confirmed it. He was looking down through the display case at his own sheet. It had a sticker affixed, listing the price at $15.

"Ya interested in that one?"

Joshua had a hard time pulling his eyes from his sheet, and then when he did look up, was knocked off balance by the shop keeper's eyes – one blue and one green. The otherwise nondescript man had obviously become used to this reaction. He leaned forward, widening his eyes slightly. "Ya want to look at it?"

"Uh, alright."

It was the cheapest alternative in the case, but it just galled Joshua to think of having to pay for his own stolen property. He went through the motion of checking the OS specs and resident apps. It had been totally reformatted. Knowing he could not download anything from his old cloud account finally hit home. His papers and homework assignments – *gone*. All of the emails with his Mom - *gone*. The- Joshua sucked in a sharp breath– *The Swamp videos and pictures!* He had buried them in a folder deep in his files, putting them in a local cache instead of the cloud. *But did the scorpion do that thorough of a search?* He could only hope Bossman's IT expert had been satisfied at finding the surveillance photos and then had just wiped the drive without searching further. *Well, there's nothing I can do about it either way.* He sighed and looked up to find the shopkeeper, eyeing him with a puzzled frown.

"Ya want it or not?" The man blinked his eyes several times in an exaggerated fashion.

"Fifteen is pretty high for a used sheet – it doesn't even have a full terabyte of memory."

"Yeah, well that's what the cloud is for." The merchant reached out his hand for Joshua's sheet, leaning forward and again opening his eyes wide. *What's up with this guy?*

"This is all I have." Joshua pulled from his pocket the $12 he had allotted for a replacement sheet. He was unlikely to find anything cheaper unless he went to The Avenue, which he was not going to do. *Not unless I have to, at least.*

Now the man leaned back and peered through half closed lids. "Come on, kid, *really*?"

Then Joshua understood. *He's trying to rattle me with his weird eyes!* He decided to focus on the green eye, clamped down on his desire to fidget, and waited for the verdict. After a moment, the man shrugged and slid the money off the case into his hand. Joshua leaned over to examine the sheet cases. *Yep, there's mine. The one in the worst shape. Maybe...*

"You wouldn't throw in that beat up case, would you?"

After a moment of silence, Joshua looked up to find Evil Eye staring at his chest. He followed the gaze down to discover his black spiderviper fang was hanging out of his shirt, exposed.

The Deepest Cut

"What's that?"

Taken off balance, Joshua answered without thinking, "It's a spiderviper fang."

The man cocked his head down and looked up through his eyebrows, his flat stare giving full expression to his incredulity. "Yeah,   *right*. Where'd ya get the fake spiderviper fang?"

Joshua flared with indignation, because *he* knew the fang was real. He then realized that no one would believe the truth about how he lived in The Swamp and killed a spiderviper. Also, he had no intention of telling the truth for fear of somehow being linked to the death of Uncle William.

"I uh, found it. Dead. Ah, stuck on a fence next to The Swamp."

Evil Eye leaned over the counter squinting his blue eye. "Well I don't know where you got it, but it looks sort of real,   ya might get some cash for it." He straightened up. "How much?"

Joshua put the fang back inside his shirt. He made a show of considering a price, but he had no intention of letting go of Mom's fang, as he had come to think of it. Then he remembered the fang from the baby spiderviper that had supplied the venom for.... *Maybe I could sell –*

"I ain't gonna give much for a fake fang, kid, no matter how good it looks." The eyes once again widened with intensity. "I'll give you 2 bucks."

Joshua did not want to make a deal with this man, but he did want to keep him on the hook. "Wow, that's a *lot*, but   I don't know. I'll think about it and come back later, OK?"

Evil Eye looked at him for a moment before his gaze dropped to the bulge under Joshua's shirt. He frowned and returned his disconcerting eyes to again lock with Joshua's. *They really* are *creepy.*

Finally, the clerk shrugged. "OK."

"What about the case?"

Another delay in responding   before another display of Evil Eye's primary expression of emotion, a shrug. Apparently satisfied he had cheated Joshua enough, he handed over the case. "Don't forget to let me know about that fake tooth."

Joshua hurried through the late morning drizzle to get off the streets of New Cincinnati. As he made his way, some of his sunny disposition returned. He knew he would never sell the fang he wore, but *Maybe I can find a way to maximize what I can get for the baby fang. Which would be at least a temporary solution to Item #5 - getting some of my money back.*

By the time he reached Sanctuary, he was confident the plan he had developed would work without a hitch.

◄5►

It was amazing how much difference a block on The Avenue made. The shops where Joshua was currently walking had lighted signs, some in neon. Not as impressive as the laser advertisements used just a block DownAve, but still a step above the merchants just one block up. Joshua smiled when he saw a deep purple neon sign that advertised "Exotica." *That's a place that should be interested in a spiderviper fang.*

Alternating blue and gold lights flashed around the border of the doorway, making the shop appear more prosperous to Joshua. The proprietor was a fat man. *A very fat man.* He sat in a large leather swivel chair behind a half door counter, fat laden cheeks quivering with each grind of his jaws, working hard on something chewy. The summer humidity forced him to dab his face with a purple handkerchief that matched the silk lining of his lilac cloak, flung back off one shoulder of an ash gray satin tunic. The masticating jowls stopped at Joshua's approach, annoyance mounting until he jammed out two sausage fingers, "Don't bother with your spiel, Sonnie. I don't give handouts." His voice thrummed deeper than expected, each word clipped with disdain.

Joshua stopped, frowned, and took one step closer. "I've got something," he glanced at the neon sign, "*exotic* to sell."

"Oh, do you now?" Piggy black eyes flicked up and then down The Avenue before the silken mass shrugged. "Too early for any paying customers, so might as well have a little entertainment. Let's see what you got." The pudgy hand now beckoned him forward.

Joshua's hand dug in his pocket as he stepped up to the counter. He placed the baby spiderviper fang on the black velvet square resting on the counter in front of the merchant.

"No, no, don't tell me! That's supposed to be a spiderviper fang, right?"

"It **is** a spiderviper fang!"

"And I suppose you went out into The Swamp and just wandered around until you saw a, *very small,* spiderviper, killed it, and took its fang, hhhmmmmm?"

"It's real! Look at it!"

A resigned sigh issued between blubbery lips as the man put a jeweler's loupe to his eye, picked up the shining ebony fang, and held it under a nearby lamp. He grunted and leaned forward to look even closer before flipping a switch on the base of the lamp that made the ivory base of the fang glow. A moment later, he snapped off the light, returned the loupe to the velvet, and pinned Joshua with his eyes. "Where did you get this?"

Joshua's encounter with Evil Eyes had prepared him for this question. Trying to present a balance of uncertainty and honesty, he hesitated and then gathered a determined look on to his face. "I *found* it. UpAve. **All** the way up, right next to The Swamp."

"You found a spiderviper up in the city?"

"It was   it was already dead. A baby   sort of all dried up like,   and stuck on the bottom of a fence. And so, I just took a tooth off. That's all."

The overweight merchant leaned forward, peering hard at Joshua's neck. He had spotted Mom's fang through his unbuttoned "City" shirt. *Got cha!* Even though Joshua's plan was proceeding as he had hoped, the merchant's gaze made him feel exposed. "Well? Is that another one? There on your neck?"

Joshua tried to look sneaky. "This one is mine, but I found this place in the city foundation with a *bunch* of dead spidervipers! So I can get more ," he let the enticing implication hang in the air.

"How many?"

"A   a *lot*! Like   10, at least!" *Maybe I didn't think this through enough.   Better throw in the kicker.* "It must be like, you know, an elephant graveyard." Joshua could not read the fat man's expression. "You've heard of those, right?"

The neck rolls squeezed out rhythmically as the merchant nodded his head. "I see. So you climbed down to this...   spiderviper graveyard.... and collected these two fangs? Why not all...   10, did you say?"

Joshua felt panic rising. *Why wouldn't I get them all?* "Well, I ," he glanced around to establish escape routes, "uh, ," he looked back at the merchant, whose eyebrow lifted with his skepticism and then zeroed in on the baby fang laying on the velvet. *Maybe I can snatch it   but then word would spread   then it came to him   I'm SO stupid* "   because I was *scared*! I mean, I **was** in *The Swamp!!*"

The beady eyes bored in on Joshua. "Let me see it." He held out his hand, thick palm up.

This is not soppin' working! Joshua stepped back and grasped Mom's fang tightly. "No."

"No?   No, it's not a spiderviper fang, or no, you won't let me see it?" Before Joshua could respond, the merchant eased back into his chair with a smooth smile. "Look, Sonnie, you don't have to let me look at it if you don't want to. But if you're looking to sell *this* one to me," he held up the smaller fang between thick thumb and forefinger, "I need to see the other one to make sure they are both alike. That bigger one will give me a chance to see more detail, to *verify* that it's authentic. You understand what I mean by verify, don't you?"

"Yes.   To see the truth.   I understand."

"Ahh, an educated urchin. How refreshing!   Well, given that you're obviously a young man of some intelligence, I'm sure you understand my need to ensure these artifacts are genuine. IF they can be authenticated, I would be willing to purchase this smaller item for, say   50 UDs."

Fifty?   Joshua reached back to untie the shoe laces as the merchant picked up the loupe in anticipation. The high pitched twittering laugh of a less than sober woman echoed up from DownAve. "Come on, Sonnie Boy, there are paying customers on the way," the man gently urged. "Let's complete this transaction."

Joshua let Mom's fang drop into the merchant's outstretched hand with a swelling of unease. After examining the larger spiderviper fang for a few moments, the merchant put both fangs on the velvet and eased himself off of the tall chair. He opened the half door next to the counter. "Step right in, Sonnie, so we can complete the terms of our business deal."

As Joshua stepped into the shop, the fat man snatched his shirt in both hands and pulled him up within inches of his face. Through his astonished intake of breath, Joshua's nose pulled in a sweet orange chocolate aroma from the merchant's mouth, just before being shaken once for emphasis.

"The *terms* of our transaction are that I'm going take these fangs, which you undoubtedly stole, and out of a sense of beneficence, I will not turn you over to the enforcer over there, to be delivered to the police."

Joshua glanced over to see an extremely large man staring at him intently from 15 feet up the street. A wide vertical pink scar ran from his forehead, through his sightless milky white left eye, and down across his cheek. The world blurred and spun as his stomach rolled to sudden weightlessness, just before he thumped on his back and the rear of his head bounced off the muddy pedway. Rain drops winked into illumination as they intersected the ceiling of light from adjacent streetlamps, grew as they fell toward Joshua's face, mixing with and eventually emerging from the haze of sparkles created by the blow to the back of his skull, and finally smacking his face with distinct cold splashes. As he struggled into sitting position, Joshua pulled in enough air to point and scream,

"Those are MINE!"

"What? Did you hear that? This little beggar thief is accusing **me** of impropriety! What an absurdity! Omar! Escort this guttersnipe to the authorities!"

"Sure thing, Mr. Muldavy."

Joshua stared in disbelief at the merchant waddling back through the half door to his leather throne. Sensing an approaching mass, he turned his throbbing head to watch Omar close the distance while pulling a truncheon from beneath his slicker. *This can't be happening.* Joshua could not quite organize his body to get up and run, feet sliding back and forth over the trash and mud filled mesh of the pedway while still in a sitting position.

"No."

The statement was flat   and low   and *final*. It came from beyond the dark forest green robe that had just stepped between Joshua and Omar. The Avenue became silent. Even the tiny smacks of the falling rain seemed to fade, as if to avoid scrutiny. Joshua lifted his chin to take in the tall figure who had interceded on his behalf; it was familiar, but he could not put the pieces together. Somehow he regained his feet, and stepped to the side, but stopped when he saw the confusion and uncertainty on Omar's face.

"What are you waiting for, Omar?" The fat man turned. "Listen, what is it,   Hobo? You haven't been here long enough... to... t to...", the words stuttered to a stop as the man in green turned his head to look at the merchant. Joshua had stepped far enough to the side to glimpse the stranger's face. Its chiseled edges were not nearly as hard as the man's ice blue eyes.

"No."

They matched the intensity of the stranger's unblinking flat stare. *Green cloak   tall   Mr. Green Cloak!* Joshua had never before seen the man's face or heard him speak, but somehow he knew Hobo and Mr. Green Cloak were the same. *Maybe he'll help me get Mom's fang back!*

"He took my-," the full weight of Hobo's attention choked off Joshua's plea. While an aura of sympathy colored his deep voice, there was not a sliver of forbearance as he spoke, "You need to go. *Now.*"

The iron will contained in the last word propelled Joshua UpAve toward The Swamp. Sobs escaped as he stumbled away. There was an aching empty space on his chest where Mom's fang should have been resting. *This isn't right. THIS isn't RIGHT!*

Joshua glanced back. What he saw stifled the sob welling up in his chest and brought him to a halt. His eyes were drawn to Hobo's right forearm and hand, which seemed to be made of silver and blended in with the chrome gun that pointed at Omar. Then the bigger picture came into view, of Hobo standing in the middle of the pedway with both arms extended. The normal appearing left hand held a large pistol and it was across the sights of this gun that Hobo looked, his gaze locked with a steel grip on the merchant's eyes. Both pistols were stock still, aiming at the spot right between the eyes of the fat man and the ugly man. No longer crying, Joshua could hear Hobo's matter of fact words quite clearly in the silence of an enthralled audience.

"Now I have no desire to tangle with Omar, who looks to be a man who knows his way around a fight. Hence my little equalizer here." The gun in his silver hand jiggled a bit before it resumed its unwavering aim at Omar's brainstem. "But I realize, as Omar's employer, *you* have the final say as to how our situation ends. Hence my little persuader *here.*" The other gun jiggled. "So I would propose that *you* ask Omar to resume his prior station, the boy *continues on his way,*" Joshua knew Hobo had spoken to him and found himself shuffling backwards, "and then   *I*   will re-holster my two little companions and we can *all* enjoy the remainder of our evening. What say you?"

Fat fingers eased forward to make two small flicks to the side and Omar began moving back DownAve. Realizing that Hobo did not intend to demand his fangs back, Joshua, bleary eyed and bereft, turned his back on all three and shambled UpAve.

But before the moldering aromas of The Swamp welcomed him home, a buzzing in Joshua's inner core had replaced his tears. *I was stupid to think anybody would help me! No one does anything unless they plan on getting something out of it for themselves.   No   if I want Mom's Fang back, I'll have to get it myself.* His stride took on purpose as an image came to his mind and he decided exactly what he was going to do.

The Deepest Cut

As evening fell on the following day, Joshua walked up the middle of The Avenue, his slicker hood folded back despite the light rain. There would be little he could later recall from that walk, other than the inner buzz in his core had ebbed and flowed, but never stopped.

Only a few shop owners were out to witness the event, merchants who had finished their dinners and were hoping to catch an early adventurous customer. They would long comment on the oddity of what they saw. Most would describe the boy's expression, a strange mixture of fierce determination and barely contained glee. So transfixing was his maniacal countenance that none noticed how his left hand held the edge of a large bag into which his right arm was thrust. The undertone of reckless abandon in his wide eyes was such that even the hardened men of The Avenue took a step back from the boy's path.

There was no hesitancy as Joshua approached the fat merchant's shop. Surprise clouded into aggravation as the heavyset man caught sight of Joshua striding for his counter. He ponderously descended from his chair, opened the lower half of his shop door, and leaned out to bellow DownAve, "OMAR!" Still leaning an elbow on the flat counter top of the half door, he turned his attention back to Joshua, voice heavy with scorn.

"You shouldn't have come back, *boy*. Hobo's not around to interfere tonight."

His frown deepened, but also took on a slight ambiguity as he watched Joshua close the distance. "What do you think you're going to do, give me a good thrashing?" Not noticing that Joshua had let go of his bag, Muldavy reached forward with his left hand. "Listen runt, I don't have any prob– EEEeeeEEEEE!"

"DON'T *move!*"

Joshua grasped a fistful of silken pastel blue robe in his left hand, while in his right he held a baby spiderviper less than a foot from the merchant's multi-rolled neck, its black fang tipped tongue flicking out repeatedly, coming within inches of the quivering flesh. The man's initial shriek stretched out into a terrified mewling, eyes impossibly wide, transfixed on the real life manifestation of an icon of death, squirming furiously just out of reach. "Pp pp pllleeeesseee," he stammered out along with a splatter of drool.

"**I   want   my   fangs**."

"I I I've already sold the small one." His voice rose an octave as his trembling hand gestured toward the counter in front of his chair. "I I'll give you the money. Over there. Please, Pleeessse!"

Joshua pushed him in the indicated direction with his left hand, holding the spiderviper a bit higher. "Don't make me slip!" The fang tipped proboscis flicked out again as if in coordination with his threat.

The merchant eased his way backward, repeated high pitched squeals swelling with every step, until he reached the cash drawer under his counter and pull it open. He tore his gaze from the wriggling manifestation of death to glance at the money, paused, and then squeaked, "I I got 50 UDs for it."

"100," a low voice sailed through the absolute silence from across The Avenue. Joshua shook the spiderviper closer, whose renewed frenzied attempts to kill something, **anything**, launched an overabundance of venom out of its fang that speckled the front of the merchant's robe.

"Yes, YEEESS, it was $100. I'm sorry, I'm SORRREEeee. *Please!*"

Tearing his eyes away to look at the drawer, he dug into one of the compartments, and fumbled aside a handful of lower denomination bills, revealing only 20 UD bills. The shop owner pulled a crisp new bill from the bottom of the stack and rapidly added four more well-worn bills to it. He held out the money and his voice lowered almost back to normal as he looked at the five bills. "*Here*   take it. **Take** it!"

"Don't even **think** about moving!" Joshua waited until the big man became completely still, lifted the squirming spiderviper a bit higher, and then let go of the silk robe and snatched the money. After stuffing the bills in his slicker pocket, he again gripped the same section of wrinkled robe.

"Where's the big fang?"

The merchant, whose eyes were once again locked on the spiderviper, gestured to a display case behind him.

"*Get it!*"

They had to edge around an intermediary display cabinet to reach the one in the back of the shop where Muldavy secured the most valuable merchandize. Fat fingers did something on the far side of the cabinet, and with a click, the clear lid popped up several inches. Lifting the glass into a locked position, the merchant again pulled his gaze away long enough to locate and grab the fang before his eyes snapped back to the live spiderviper.

"Here."

Even in the face of a horrible death, the man wavered in holding out the large onyx fang, now dangling on a gold chain. But Joshua did not hesitate; he snatched the fang and dipped his head to put on the necklace.

As soon as he broke eye contact, the fat man instantly stepped back to put the middle cabinet between them. Joshua turned to find the half door, but it had closed of its own volition. Having surveyed the shop at the break of dawn by peering through the windows, he already knew its basic layout. He also knew that the back door led to an alcove with an exterior drain pipe. Aware that the back door was just behind him, Joshua rotated back to face the merchant in preparation to leave, but caught his elbow on the corner of a cabinet, forcing the baby spiderviper toward his own chest.

Joshua watched as the proboscis began to extend toward his face. He urged his wrist to twist away the spiderviper and his arm to push forward. The fang slid against the front of his slicker and then trailed behind his thrusting hand. He reflexively let go as his arm reached its full extension. The creature sailed forth from his palm and time resumed its normal pace, allowing Joshua to appreciate the full impact of the merchant screeching like a little girl as he scrambled to pull his bulk up on top of the middle counter. The baby spiderviper bounced off the far wall, but flipped catlike as it descended to land on its feet, facing Joshua, forelegs up, tongue extended and quivering, its loud piercing whistle drowning out the fat man's grunts.

"You want a fang? You can have *that* one!" *Time to go!*

Several quick steps later, Joshua's hand closed on the drain pipe behind the shop. He could still hear the inarticulate high pitched screaming even after the back door had clanked shut. He ascended to the rooftops with a huge grin, eager to return to Sanctuary and celebrate his victory.

◄7►

One more block and it's Home Sweet Home.

The next street was the last major pedway. Then he had one more dilapidated rooftop to traverse before he could drop down into the safety of The Swamp. With the lengthy pauses required to check for threats at each pedway crossing, it had taken much longer than usual to make the trip from The Avenue to The Swamp. Joshua was always cautious when approaching a pedway, but the sounds of repeated gunshots just after he had regained the rooftops behind Mulvany's shop had served to intensify his already heightened level of vigilance.

Joshua froze three feet from the edge. The sound of a steady rain faded from his awareness, allowing him to hear disparate noises much more easily. After a moment of intense listening he heard it – a hollow note to the beat of the rain that came from below. It was the sound of drops hitting the hood of a slicker *Two slickers!* Joshua's eyes swept his surroundings. The moderate rain limited visibility, but he could see nothing move on any of the adjacent rooftops. He reached the edge in a crablike crouch, pushed back the hood to his slicker, and waited. He had become very good at waiting. His head and most of his chest were thoroughly soaked when the first whisper floated up.

"You sure that thing is working right?"

"I don't know," the second whisper growled, "It looked like he was almost here, in the building across the p'dway, but now it's not moving."

"Maybe he's on the motorway below?"

"How would I haulin' know? This muckin' thing don't show elevations."

Why doesn't anyone think about up? Guess it's 'cause everyone knows, the only thing you get from looking up is rain in your eyes. In his mind, Joshua recreated the shape of the buildings below and he mentally surveyed the area. He was relatively sure they were in a deep indentation between two buildings across the pedway to his left. Already on his hands and knees, he turned his head parallel to the retaining wall and lifted his right eye up until he could see the black niche.   *There!*   An ever so faint green patch of less darkness. Joshua kept blinking the rain out of his eye, but held his head absolutely still, waiting until *Again!* Over the next several minutes of steady flashing, the shapes of two faces looking down at something coalesced. *Two men. Cops? Or worse?* Joshua now knew the role of the large menacing men who just loitered outside of shops on The Avenue, never buying anything, but always watching people. The fact that Omar had been prepared to bludgeon an 11-year-old boy when he could have removed him with one hand reflected the level of restraint he could expect from any Avenue enforcers.

The second voice cursed. "Muldavy said the tracking threads were practic'ly new. This oughta be workin'!" There was a thump.

"Well, don't break it! You know that tight fisted slag ass will take it out of the bounty!"

Another curse. "That's what's pissin' me off! If this thing ain't workin', then one of the other teams is gonna collect and then we've got nothin' but wet!"

Tracking thread? Joshua eased back and replayed the encounter with the fat man *Muldavy.* He had been looking at the $20 bills and *Not at the spiderviper!* until Joshua had taken the money. *It's in one of those bills!*

Joshua pulled out the bills, but they were just a wad of crumpled paper. He knew that even if he could examine them under a bright light with a magnifying glass, he would not know what to look for. *I don't know what a tracking thread looks like!* His shoulders slumped. *$100 I can't use.* Joshua realized that Muldavy must have previously paid for the recovery system as part of his security or the bounty hunters could not have reacted so quickly. *So Muldavy won after all.* A grim smile formed as he began crawling toward the corner of the roof. *Maybe I can't spend it, but neither will he.* Before he reached the corner the first voiced croaked, "He's moving. It **is** working!"

"Yeah? Shut up, mudbrain, peel yer eyelids back, 'n get ready t' move."

Joshua crumpled the bills into a tighter wad and dropped them into the flow of runoff rain pouring into the corner drain. A moment later, the first voice spoke out at conversational volume, "Hey! He's crossing the street, but *he's not there!*"

"He's down on the mot'rway! Hurry!"

The Deepest Cut

Joshua watched the two bounty hunters emerge from the inky recess to thump down toward the nearest interlevel access stairway. As they clanked down the metal spiral staircase, he slid down a drainpipe and made the crossing. Having bought time and knowing how hard it was to get a signal in The Swamp when it rained hard, Joshua decided to check the news before sliding down the outer pipe to the burn zone. Those earlier gunshots were worrying him.

Joshua hunched over the sheet to minimize light exposure and keep the rain from collecting on the sheet and distorting the image. The beautiful face of the lead newscaster filled the screen, "…substantiated sightings, but this time there is proof! Police have just released this surveillance video from the shop," eyes flicked down to her prompt sheet, "ah, Exotica." She shared a knowing smile, "on The Avenue, *of course*. Take a look at *this*!"

Joshua watched himself enter the upper right corner of the screen, pushing Muldavy in front of him. "Here it comes!," the woman exclaimed as Joshua's right hand came into view, and along with it, the squirming baby spiderviper. "There it **is**! In the enhanced circle!" The circle followed his progression into the shop, optics amazingly clear. Joshua did not even hear the breathless interjections of the newscaster as the video went through the sequence of events leading up to Muldavy jumping behind the center counter as Joshua put Mom's fang back on. He watched himself look to the front door and then turn and step backwards. Only the lower part of the back door was visible in the static security shot, so Joshua's right arm disappeared off the upper edge of the screen as he retreated.

The image froze and the woman's face again filled the screen, brimming with earnestness.

"And now the most terrifying part of this video, as this, this   *Viper Boy*, is not satisfied with just stealing from the owner of the shop, Mr. Mulvany, but callously seeks   to *murder* him!"

Murder?

The surveillance video resumed and Joshua looked on in horror as he appeared to throw the spiderviper at the squealing fat man, who was scrambling and clawing to pull his bulk up onto the center display case.

Joshua was only mildly surprised to see how close the spiderviper had come to getting to the rear door before he closed it. After all, he knew their capabilities fairly well by now. But he was amazed at how aggressively the small creature spun to attack the only other living creature in proximity, its fang still extended from the mouth and vibrating, eager to kill. In the wild, they were generally more cautious, first assessing threats before committing to a strike. *I guess being carried almost a mile in a bag didn't do much for its mood.*

Between the occasional intervening bulk of Muldavy, the angle of the camera, and the degree to which his slicker hood had been pulled forward, Joshua did not think enough of his face had been revealed in the video to allow recognition software to match his identity. But many people had witnessed the confrontation the day before, and just how many kids with camo slickers were out robbing shops on The Avenue? *No, everybody on The Avenue will know who did this.*

The pleading in Muldavy's voice turned to anger, drawing Joshua's focus back to the action on the screen. "All right, ALRIGHT! I'll pay it! Now GIVE IT to me!" A long dark tubular object flashed into Muldavy's out stretched hands. He wrenched his quaking mass up and stood on the case, aiming the shotgun down, frantically trying to get a shot at the skittering, circling spiderviper. BOOM! The first shot was a total miss, splintering the lower half of a cabinet door. In reaction, the spiderviper launched itself onto a nearby mid-level shelf, knocking off some glass orbs holding indeterminate shapes inside. This brought the spiderviper closer to the object of its anger, but also allowed Muldavy a cleaner shot. Squealing in terror, the merchant pulled the next shot to the left, BOOM! but at least a couple of the pellets struck the spiderviper's legs because the venomous animal spun back into the wall with a squeak. BOOM! BOOM! Small pieces of glass, wood, and globby spiderviper exploded out from the impacts of the shotgun rounds. Hysterical giggling escaped from Muldavy as he leaned over the edge of the display case to target what remained of the spiderviper's body. BOOM! BOOM! *click* Muldavy howled as he vainly tried to chamber another shell. A sob escaped when he saw there was little left to shoot anyway, and he slumped into a quivering pile on top of the cabinet, finally realizing he had just survived an encounter with the most feared creature on the planet.

The Deepest Cut

"Later the poor shop keeper shared more about his ordeal," the woman's face radiated sympathy just before it dissolved into that of Muldavy, forehead half covered with a press-on bandage. "He came out of *nowhere*, demanding my money, and I I gave it to him! What could I *do*? He was holding a *spiderviper* to my throat! But that wasn't enough for him! No! Then he viciously threw that, that, *creature* at me, *completely* leaving me at its mercy. That's attempted murder, I say, **murder**! I had to pay an exorbitant price," his eyes glanced off screen in fury, "just to obtain the means to defend myself! If I wasn't an expert shot, this could have been my last day in business!"

Too bad it wasn't! At least you pretty much destroyed half of your shop, Mr. Expert Shot.

"He spouted some story about finding the fangs in a spiderviper graveyard! I mean, who who would believe a story like that?" Muldavy pleaded to the camera, "How was I to know that this this *Devil's spawn* actually had power over the creatures? Who would *believe* that? He is *evil*! He MUST be found!" His sputtering red face faded to allow more meaningless blather from the news talking head.

Joshua blinked in dismay. No one would believe what really happened. As his finger sought the off switch, the newscaster finished explaining, "...are trying to gather evidence from the scene, but there is very little of the spiderviper left intact." The face vanished and Joshua's sense of satisfied revenge evaporated as he contemplated the silhouette of trees that formed the boundary of The Swamp. *Yeah, I got Mom's fang back, but I'm still out of money and now it looks like I'm wanted for attempted murder.*

The sinking in his stomach had nothing to do with his rapid slide down the external drainpipe to the rocks below. His descent into despondency continued as he splashed his way through the strengthening downpour back to his home.

What do I do now?

◄8►

Joshua sat on the smoke dispersing stone that covered the hole leading down to Sanctuary. He was sitting in the rain because The Perch was the best place to get PV reception for his sheet. He was waiting for the 6:00 news to begin, unaware that the drizzle had soaked his pants. The lead story for the past six days had, of course, been exclusively about him, now known as Viper Boy. The one bright spot in the coverage had occurred four days ago, when the lead story had shown Omar being arrested for interfering with a police investigation. Clearly the merchants of The Avenue did not appreciate the heavy police presence in the aftermath of the spiderviper video airing on the news. It had taken three cops with stun guns to subdue him, but eventually Omar had been led away in cuffs by the police, with more than one officer's face bruised and bleeding. Joshua grinned. *Omar didn't look so good either.*

The incident had served its purpose – the police were allowed to look as if they were doing something, but they no longer attempted to search any of the vendor stalls. They *had* searched virtually everywhere else, on both the pedway and motorway levels, even getting warrants to go into warehouses abandoned decades ago. There was endless conjecture about which dark corner Viper Boy was huddled in while he planned his next robbery. One "expert" came on with a diagram showing "the only feasible mechanism for capturing a spiderviper alive" - a box trap lowered on a rope to the foot of the city foundation. When asked by the news lead what Viper Boy might have used for bait, the expert "simply could not speculate," because it was "simply too gruesome to contemplate." Not that any of the parade of other "experts" had restrained themselves from speculation. They lined up to theorize about his motives, mental state, upbringing… *Where do they all come from? New Cincinnati isn't that big.* A particularly annoying panel guest in a bow tie and round wire rimmed glasses opined that perhaps he was the brilliant prodigy of one of the mining executives, disguising himself as an urchin, all part of a larger nefarious plan to terrorize the disenfranchised underclass. Neither this expert nor any of the other commentators ever explained the objective of such master conspiracies, but all would nod in agreement at the inevitable closing comment, "Who can understand the motives of someone who would use a **spiderviper** to rob somebody?" It amused Joshua that none of the expert commentators ever even considered *the possibility* of someone *living* in The Swamp.

What frustrated Joshua most was the manner in which The Avenue mobilized to capitalize on all of the publicity surrounding the incident. He did not resent the entrepreneurial zeal, but he watched those stories like a starving waif staring through a bakery window. Side interest stories abounded, featuring obviously manufactured spiderviper fangs being sold as "authentic." He did not even resent the cheap replicas; it was just infuriating that he could not share in the profits. The day after the real baby viper fang showed up on Ebay, the bidding reached $31,000 UDs in less than an hour. *31 THOUSAND!!!* However, the item had been withdrawn by the anonymous owner following an announcement by the police that they planned to take the fang into evidence as part of their investigation. Joshua could barely imagine how much he could have made just by creating a mold of his fang for one of the merchants to create plaster facsimiles.

Catching himself grinding his teeth at the thought of how much money was slipping through his grasp, Joshua forced himself to refocus on the PV webcast that flickered on his sheet. The adverts started to wrap up (the station always ran self-promotions of their own shows just before the anchor came on) and Joshua began breathing a bit faster in pace with the knot of tension building in his stomach. He needed to know the status of the investigation into his "attempted murder" of Muldavy, but the past two days had also been filled with speculation about whether Viper Boy was responsible for the other two recent spiderviper deaths. He had shaken with rage when a "psychiatric expert" wondered out loud whether he might be developing into a *serial spiderviper killer*. His indignation was laced with a burning guilt, the shadowy face of Uncle William lurking on the edge of his consciousness. He had resolved to turn his sheet off at the first sign of any such speculation on the upcoming newscast. *Ah, here's Miss Pretty*

Face.

"Good evening, New Cincinnati! This is Cyntheea Strom and there is Breaking News at this hour in our Ongoing Coverage of the Viper Boy!" A graphic popped up behind her large blonde hair, alerting the viewers: **CRISIS!** *Spidervipers in our Midst!!*

"We have a live broadcast from our investigative reporter, Alphred Sussmon, who is deep into UpAve to bring you the latest on this fascinating story. Alphred?"

"Yes, Cyntheea, if you can believe it, I am *so far* UpAve that I am *almost* in *The Swamp!* I am here with a Mr. Ah-berty, who claims that he has *actually spoken* with the Viper Boy!!" The young reporter turned as the view widened to include a tall thin man with a long scar across his face.

"That's *Aber-ly*, of Aberly's Curio Shop. And we are not *that* near The Swamp, although," his voice dropped and he leaned toward the camera conspiratorially, "strange things sometimes *do* happen here."

"I understand you actually had a conversation with Viper Boy prior to his attack at Mr. Muldavy's shop. What did he *say?*" Alphred asked breathlessly, obviously wanting to get right to the ratings boosting content of the conversation.

"Well, I won't say *on PV* what he purchased from me, although I must admit, it was *quite unexpected.*" Aberly gave the camera a knowing look. "In point of fact, the young man was mainly inquiring after employment. Sadly, I was not in a position to accommodate him. But it is interesting that you characterize his actions as an attack. That is *not at all* how the story is being told by those who *actually witnessed* the event."

"It's not? Where *you* there, Mr. Aferly?"

"I was unfortunately not present when the young fellow reclaimed his property. Being the sole proprietor of *Aberly's* Curio Shop, I did not have the privilege of watching the event unfold. *However,* I have spoken to *numerous* residents of The Avenue who *were* there at the time, and they provide a unanimous consensus that Mr. Muldavy had taken the boy's property without recompense!"

"So you are saying that Mr. Muldavy *did* steal the spiderviper fang!"

"Yes. Yes I am saying *just that!* Not that he will contest my assertion. The word on The Avenue is that *he has fled offplanet.*"

Alphred looked wide eyed into the camera. "That **is** breaking news,

The Deepest Cut

Cyntheea!!"

The anchor's face appeared on a split screen. "Absolutely! Terrific reporting, Alphred! Could you ask Mr. Aberly, if, during his conversation with Viper Boy, did he explain how he was able to capture a *live* spiderviper?"

Aberly laughed and looked into the camera, "Although we spoke of a number of things, *that* was not something he happened to share with me. For those who are curious enough, *and brave enough*, they can come UpAve to *Aberly's* Curio Shop and I will be delighted to speak with them further."

Alphred began to withdraw the microphone and was visibly startled when Aberly grasped his hand firmly and leaned in closer. "I *will* tell you, that **anybody**, especially a *child*, who has the unimaginable *courage* to go into The Swamp, grab a spiderviper *in his bare hand*, and carry it all the way back to the city to correct an injustice, well now, *that* person has my respect." He looked at Alphred. "Think about it, Almed, can you even *imagine* doing that?" Alphred obviously *could* imagine it and just shook his head, unable to respond verbally.

This time when he turned to the camera, Joshua knew Aberly spoke directly to him, "I don't care how desperately the police want to speak to him... **that** young man has earned standing on The Avenue." Aberly straightened up and gleamed out a welcoming smile. "If you want to hear more about this brave lad, be sure to come on UpAve, all the way to Aberly's Curio Shop and we'll have *a chat.*"

Aberly's words brought a warm smile to Joshua's lips. *I hope he gets a lot of business from this.* There was some sense of relief to discover that he might not immediately be turned over to the police as soon as he stepped onto The Avenue. But Joshua was not at all confident he could trust the denizens of The Avenue. Ever since his mother's death, the lesson had been pressed upon him over and over that most people will do only what they think is in their own best interest and that they can get away with. And regardless of his "standing" on The Avenue, the police would not stop looking for him, so he was still not sure when it would be safe to go back into New Cincinnati.

I'm in a real pickle now, Mom. No warm pulse appeared over his shoulder as Joshua made his way down to Sanctuary's entrance. He busied himself with making dinner, avoiding thoughts about the reason for her absence.

◄9►

There! And I still have some left in the can.

His new makeshift slicker now had a uniform charcoal matte finish. He would miss the extra sense of security his old camo slicker had provided, but it had become too identifiable with Viper Boy. Of course, camo slickers were everywhere! The fervor on the news had died down a bit over the past two weeks, but there were still stories related to him every other day or so. For the most part, the parade of experts had returned to their regular non-expert jobs. Press releases from City Hall saying authorities were looking into spiderviper counter-measures had been supplanted by recent statements suggesting such expensive efforts were no longer necessary given there now appeared to be only a single source for the spiderviper sightings. Not only had the public's fears died down, but most of the remaining interest was positive. In fact, Joshua had stopped making the nightly trips to the Perch to watch the news after watching a piece on how a local fashion designer was using a fang motif in her designs.

Joshua walked over to the corner between the bed ledge and oven to place the almost empty paint can with his other supplies. He squatted down to check the progress of the ironwood coals. *Just about there* It was going to be BBQ SwampRabbit pizza tonight and the oven had to be *hot* to get a good crunch to the crust. However, he really did not have to worry about making the crust soggy with excess BBQ sauce, since there had barely been enough to coat the meat. The cheese would be light as well. Joshua pushed down his rising anxiety about what the night would later bring and went about preparing his meal. *I'm not going to ruin my Welcome Home feast.*

After the escape from Bossman, he had been so focused on checking off the five items on his list that he had not fulfilled his promise to himself for a celebration of how much he appreciated Sanctuary. Having finally decided that he had to go in for supplies, Joshua had also chosen to go all out and use up what he had left to make this celebratory meal. Sure, he could survive on what he pulled from The Swamp alone, but that would not be *living*. Joshua was startled by a glow of warmth that flared behind him with the thought. He had not realized how he had missed the presence of his mother, or even that she had been absent ever since he had sought retribution from Muldavy. Hot tears of relief came with her confirmation of his decision to re-engage with people.

Early evening found Joshua chewing down his last bite of pizza. He sat beside his sheet, which had his supply list typed into a note app. It rested beside his remaining cash, *$9.37*. He did not know what he would do when that was gone, but, *as Mom used to say, Cross that bridge when you get to it.* Once the heat on Viper Boy had died down a bit more, but before interest had completely waned, he would approach Aberly about creating the "real" authentic fang replicas. *Until then...*

Joshua decided to once again visit Mom's to do his shopping. It was a smaller establishment, deeper in the NorthPoint neighborhood, and on the opposite side of The Avenue from Bossman's warehouse. He considered his approach over the roof tops and decided on a straight in, straight out strategy, minimizing his exposure time, but he would allow for some extended observation before going into the store. He did not know if they had connected him with the antics of Viper Boy, but *plan for the worst and hope for the best, right, Mom?*

Jogging up to the scree pile, Joshua stumbled and almost fell when his slicker pocket buzzed. Realizing he had never removed the flip phone, he pulled it out and saw the face screen glow with a *6 20*. It had been so long since he had even thought about Estanod that it took him a moment to comprehend the message. His eyes lifted to the looming black edge of New Cincinnati. *He wants to meet at the Shoebox. If I hurry, I'll still have 5 minutes to scope out the place.* He hurried.

Joshua peered down into the shadowed rectangle that was Rendezvous #6, slightly alarmed he could not see Estanod in the recessed doorway directly across from him. He *was* early, but then, Estanod had initiated the meeting. *I thought he'd already be here.* Joshua reached inside his slicker to touch the handle of the six-inch kitchen knife in its Shark Tape sheath. With all of the different people looking for him, he had made a harness like he had seen Estanod wearing for his gun. Somewhat reassured by the feel of a weapon, he worked his way around all four sides of the Shoebox, paying particular attention to the two entrances. *Nothing.*

After waiting several more minutes, Joshua decided it was safe to slide down to the doorway, where he would wait on the poli- *no, not anymore. But not the student either, since I guess he didn't go to Faulken to finish his school after all.* Feeling uneasy and not wanting to sit down, Joshua compromised with a squat so he would look more like a bag of trash and less like a person in the shadowed doorway. *Just in case someone comes by.* He kept an eye on the entrance across the enclosure to his left and an ear on the crevice that opened up on the wall to his right. The minutes stretched out until...

...a scuff sounded from the crevice where a dark figure was emerging. Joshua turned his head just in time to see the man rotate his hoodless head to look at him. Joshua's stomach dropped. The ears protruding out from either side of the bullet head clearly identified the arrival.

"Not who you were expecting?"

Joshua's head whipped around to confirm what the chill through his entire body already knew. Bossman strolled out from the other entrance and Joshua shivered again   Hat Man slid from the shadows right behind the drug lord. The three men spread out into a semicircle that contained the doorway. Joshua remained crouched down, painfully aware of the inadequacy of the knife hanging under his arm. He knew any sudden movements could prompt a quick, and undoubtedly painful, reaction from any one of the three. He looked up at Bossman, who regarded him through a clear dome umbrella with an exaggerated frown.

"Yeah, sorry, but my scorpion finally filtered through all of the comms traffic and isolated your stream of exchanges with Estanod." He laughed when Joshua flinched. "Yes, indeed, we figured out exactly who   The Cop   was. The use of Rendezvous numbers threw us off until we found the text where he described this place well enough so that you could find it and   what do you know? My number 1 recognized the description of the Shoebox. So,   here we are."

Bossman's demeanor shifted with his slow shake of the head, from a pouty face to a smile filled with appreciation.

"You sure had me fooled, Sonny Boy. I thought you were just a little gutter mike for the heat. But *then*   you went and   *jumped* into The Swamp! WHAT? Are you *kidding* me?   I mean, when Grimes – no, no, Big Ears, right?" Bossman's laugh was genuinely amused. "I got to tell you, Boy, he *really* dislikes that nickname you gave him. The good news is, I think you've helped *Big Ears*   get past his little stomach reaction to whacking little kids. The bad news? Yeah, I think you can guess, but I'll get back to that." The lids to Bossman's eyes had drooped into a half hooded look of anticipation, then snapped open as he continued with feigned enthusiasm, "*Any*way, ol' Grimes and Glin just couldn't stop talking about it for days, how you pushed them away, told them 'This is how a man does it!' and *then*   jumped right off the edge into a flash of lightning. We told,   gosh,   just about everybody about that, and I mean   *everybody*." The drug lord's voice flattened and his eyes turned cold, "So image my surprise,   *and* considerable embarrassment,   when the boy I told everyone we had disposed of in such dramatic fashion shows up on the evening news, shaking down some poor fat guy   with a muckin' SPIDERVIPER!!" This time the chuckle held a tone of honest regret, "Now personally, Kid, I'd really like to bring you onto Team Bossman, *but*   I can't.   Why?   Because, technically speaking, we're about to become Team Blood Star. And that Dragon Lady we talked about, remember her?"

Bossman waited until Joshua gave a single nod.

"Yeah, *her*. She still sees you as that loose end. Can you believe that?   Talk about a missed marketing opportunity!   But my negotiating ploy?   Eehhh, you might say it backfired on me. Well, mostly on Ralff and Lynyrd. *Any*way,   *now* I have to meet with the Dragon Lady's representative and-" Bossman's eyes flew wide open and he held out a hand with an apologetic shrug. "*What*   **am**   I *doing?* Of *course* you don't care about my business dealings. I'm sure you have much more immediate concerns that you would much rather discuss.   Such as   whether it will be Fenster or Big Ears who is awarded the job of ending you tonight. Right, boys?"

Big Ears' deep voice responded immediately, enthusiastically, "Right!"

Hat Man's equally succinct reply was slower and squeaky,

"Correct."

The squeaky voice made the pieces fall into place. Joshua looked at Hat Man. *That's Fenster?* He had not actually seen the man who had held the knife to his throat during his first encounter with Bossman, but now it all made sense.

Bossman looked up through the drifting water vapor illuminated by the dim security light. "And it's such a nice evening for it, *right?* Now you should know that Fenster can accomplish these tasks very quickly and painlessly, whereas, Mr. Grimes   did I mention he was unhappy with your whole   Big Ears label?   Yes?   OK, I think you get the picture. And *what* determines which fella gets the assignment, you may be curious to know? Well, Viper Boy, it all depends on whether you tell me what I want to know." Bossman's face shifted to deadpan. "Do you understand?"

Joshua nodded immediately this time.

"Where's Estanod?"

A flash of relief surged through Joshua's fear with the revelation that Estanod was not already dead. Assuming Bossman would not allow him to be killed before he had answered the question, Joshua took a chance and eased up out of his squat to allow his legs to stretch and uncramp.

"I never even knew where he lived in New Cincinnati, much less where he might go off planet."

"So he went off planet?"

Joshua quelled the lurch in his stomach. *I didn't give anything away. There are a lot of planets out there.* He shrugged helplessly. "He didn't tell me where he was going to go, but he was *really* scared, about Blood Star *and* the Mayor. He told me to lay low for a *long* time."

"He knew about the Mayor? Ooohh, she won't be happy to hear about that." Bossman's mouth twisted into a lopsided grin. "But there's a silver lining to that little association. Ms. Mayor put a sizeable bounty on your head, my friend. Unofficially, of course. There are two of them in fact, since she has offered to pay for the Estanod's CI *and* for Viper Boy. You will be proud to know that you are worth some major cashola, Boy. And I mean-" Bossman stopped smiling and frowned in the direction of the crevice entrance.

Joshua tried to pop a quick glance, so as not to lose track of the three killers in front of him, but his eyes stayed stuck on the average sized figure slipping out of the deep shadows to his right. The man was of obvious Oriental descent, except for the long bleach blonde hair, tied in a ponytail. His silk suit fit closely to his athletic body, and instead of a tie, he wore a stiff collar and short cravat with a large pearl stud pin. He was encased in a clear form fitting jumpsuit of a material Joshua had never seen before. It was so supple that there were no creases and the beads and rivulets of water on the surface testified to its ability to repel the rain. A small black umbrella with a long handle was open over his head.

Big Ears and Bossman moved back as the stranger advanced until all three of the original arrivals had pivoted to face the newcomer, who came to a stop in front of Joshua. His youth became apparent when he turned to regard Joshua with mild interest. *He's, like, a teenager!* Following a single down and up scan, Blondie looked back at the three older men, his gaze lingering on Fenster before it fixed upon Bossman. His English was perfect, his voice unexpectedly low.

"I'm sorry. Am I interrupting something?"

Bossman gave a casual shrug. "Nothing we can't handle later."

When the Oriental again turned toward Joshua, his rising hopes of a possible rescue were slammed back down to reality by Blondie's cold expression. The teen's head swiveled back and he delivered the insult as if he did not believe his listeners would understand.

"Yes. You probably *can* handle *him.*"

Big Ears' jaw clinched more obviously than Bossman's, but Fenster's face remained calm.

Joshua thought furiously, but no escape plan came to mind. Nothing at all.

"Are you accepting the terms of our offer?"

"We're talking about this in front of the kid?"

"Did you not say you were going to handle him? Did Ms. Li not make it clear *how* she wanted him handled?"

Bossman's face became stone, making obvious his difficulty in getting the words out. "Yes, it was clear and yes we *will* handle it." Pain pushed out the next words, "In the way Ms. Li said."

Joshua stood transfixed, completely dismayed at the way they were discussing his death as if it was some homework assignment. A wave of helplessness washed over him, his empty hands twitching with the realization that he had absolutely no means of fighting back. Then, a spark of anger glowed and a word formed in his mind. *Resolute.   I may not have much of a weapon, but I'm not going to just stand here and let them kill me.* He dropped his head to throw his face deeper into the shadow of his slicker hood and scanned as much of the back wall as he could without turning his head.

Bossman's words came even slower, "**And   Yes.   I   accept   the terms of your offer.**"

"Ahhh. That is good.   There *is*   one   slight   *alteration* to our agreement.   You will pay us a signing bonus of $10,000 UDs."

Joshua could only find one relevant feature on the back wall: the drainpipe to his far right. It was almost to the corner, but then, the only other pipe was on his side of the Shoebox and to the left   past Fenster. *To the right, then.*

Bossman sputtered, "I I *I'm* **paying** *you*? $10,000? *Why?*"

"As a penalty. *Reconciliation* for the dishonorable action of sending your men after me."

"**But   you killed them.** *Both.*"

"Yes.   That does not alter the fact that you betrayed our trust. And since capitalist Westerners think only in terms of money, you must make amends in the fashion most likely to dissuade you from committing a similar mistake in the future."

Exit path determined, Joshua had actually heard Blondie's last five words. He could not repress a bitter thought. *Mistake. If I had just left that soppin' flip phone in the alley, I wouldn't be here. But, **no**, I thought I might be able to use the evidence.* His breath sucked in between his lips in shock at a sudden revelation. He looked up into the sudden silence to find all four men looking at him.

Joshua pointed at Bossman. "You can't trust him. He's going to betray you again. I I have *proof.*"

Blondie's eyebrows lifted. "Oh? And what's that?"

"Recordings of him saying it. That he's going to   to *handle* the lady.

Driven to the Hilt

The lady in red."

"This is *absurd*. Fenster, dispatch the-" Bossman was silenced by Blondie's casually lifted hand.

"Where are these recordings?"

"I've got them right here." Joshua plunged his hand into his slicker pocket, but froze as everyone tensed almost imperceptibly. He brought his hand out in a very slow lift and showed Blondie the flip phone. Then he worked the front screen to pull up the correct menu and increase speaker volume to its highest level. Taking four steps forward, Joshua quickly knelt down on the fifth step to appear less of a threat. Belatedly feeling the phone in his hand, he lifted it up while keeping his head bowed. Looking up through his brows, he saw the Oriental teen's surprise and realized he thought Joshua was showing subservience.

"Just tap on the files to listen."

Once the flip phone had been removed from his hand, Joshua eased back slightly behind Blondie and turned toward Bossman in what he hoped was taken as a continued show of respect and alliance against the others. He had lowered to his left knee so he could push off with his dominant side for maximum acceleration toward the pipe. *I'm five steps closer. Now I just have to wait for the right moment   some kind of,   any kind of distraction.*

The phone's speaker made Bossman's voice sound a bit tinny, but it was loud enough for everyone in The Shoebox to hear clearly.

"Anything stirring out here?"

"No sir, ain't seen no Big Player in no red coat yet."

There was the sound of people's shuffling feet.

"You,   ah,   you were sure this   Big Player is comin' tonight?"

"*Hell* no, I'm not sure. Why do you think I keep checking with you?"

"Yessir. Got it."

After a few seconds of pattering rain, Blondie looked at Joshua with an unspoken question.

"There's more."

"Listen, surely yo-" Bossman stopped just as Big Ears' voice resumed, but before Blondie's hand had lifted, almost as if he too wanted to hear what was said next.

"So, exactly what have you heard about this Lady in Red?"

"All I *know* is that there is some woman one of my main Sector sources said was a 'Big Player' who I *really* had to meet. Wouldn't tell me why, and with this guy, I wasn't going to press. Still, he made it clear that we needed to roll out the red carpet for this bimbo."

Blondie's eyebrow lifted a fraction at Bossman's description of his superior.

"I heard she's pullin' along some slick security."

"And there you go. All of those gutter pukes strutting around thinking they are hot stuff. That's why I have to put the hurt on."

Another tiny lift of the brow.

"So, what ya figurin' to do?"

"I have to keep those little sewer roaches in line, and to do *that*, it's best to start at the top. Everyone has to learn how it works."

"Don't ya know who they are? Why, they ain't no sewer roaches, Bossman."

"Oh?"

"They are the *real* deal.   If yer not careful, they'll be in charge 'fore ya know it!"

"That's not happening."

"Are you gonna end it? Gotta say, I'd rather it was sooner than later. Course it's up ta you, Boss."

"So bottom line?   Yes. I am going to end it."

Knowing the recording had ended and wanting to forestall another objection from Bossman, Joshua spoke immediately, "That one's finished. The plan for the red lady is on file number two."

The quick interjection worked, along with Blondie's flat stare at Bossman. The second recording began with Big Ear's' voice.

"Ah-umm. So? You gonna take the deal?

"Yeah, well, the costs associated with that particular asset are looking to outweigh the benefits."

"From what I've seen and heard, she's a 'ticularly nasty one."

"Let me give you a clue on how to handle a woman like her. You have to be patient,   *enjoy* the benefits of what she brings to the table, let her assert herself on this little thing, make the decision on that little thing, feel more and more in control. You bide your time until   Bam!" Both of Blondie's eyebrows rose at the sound of a fist smacking into a palm. "You end it. After you have squeezed all you can out of the relationship, it's time to move on. *That's* how the game is played!"

"You sure know how ta work 'em, Boss!"

"*Damn* right I do."

Blondie tapped the phone face and slipped the pComm device into his pocket. He addressed Joshua while giving Bossman a flat stare, "How did you get this phone and how did you know about these recordings?"

"I was working for a cop, taking pictures of people who went to Bossman's warehouse and recording whenever they talked."

Joshua glanced up to find Bossman looking at him, his expression a strange flow of astonishment, admiration, and resignation. "I guess that jump out into The Swamp was for real."

Joshua did not see the signal from Bossman, but he noticed when Big Ears took a lazy step to the right, which made it all the more apparent that Fenster had not budged. Immediately, Bossman's eyes lost focus and dipped to his right toward Fenster, who stood looking straight ahead. When Bossman looked back up at Joshua, he had the tiny smile of a man who had just realized something   something not good. Joshua watched Bossman's eyes harden just before he shifted them to meet Blondie's smirk.

Everybody in the Shoebox understood what was about to happen. Joshua felt the weight of the knife under his left arm and he looked at Blondie's back. For an instant, a blowgun pressed against his lips and a white dart floated away from him. Then he was back in the Shoebox, looking at the other three men. Tension mounted,   and built,   and swelled   *until*

Joshua launched himself toward Blondie a second before the Oriental thug whipped his umbrella down, top forward. Both of Joshua's palms rammed into Blondie's back, *boom* shoving the teen forward and to the right while also propelling Joshua in a ricochet toward the corner drain pipe. His right foot reached for the pipe, **BOOM** step, longer step, **crack crack** lunge, lunge, **boom** lunge, leaping, **BOOM**

The Deepest Cut

grasping the pipe, pulling hand over hand, reaching, both hands gripping the lip of the wall, his feet swinging in an arc, lifting him up and over the wall. He jabbed out his feet, seeking the roof with his rubberized soles, feeling them strike the asphalt surface and his legs bunching up, absorbing his momentum.

Joshua crouched on the roof, facing back toward the Shoebox, looking down over the roof wall. For just a second, time slowed even more, and he took in the scene below: the prone form of Bossman on the ground, with Big Ears sprawled out farther behind him; Blondie standing with his umbrella held like a gun, tendril of smoke coiling up from its end; Fenster stepping past the ponytailed teen with his arm extended upward, pointing *at me!* Lunging backward, **BOOM SMACK** twisting, **BOOM thwack** slow stings to Joshua's right ear, reaching forward with his hands, scraping palms, **BOOM TWAnnnngg** digging to scramble over **BOOM THWACK** *that was closer* the corner. Sliding over the edge of the pyramid roof, **BOOM thaawhinnnne** slicker catching, ripping, and he was far enough away to bounce to his feet and run in a crouch toward the next building. Remembering the approaching gap was only a crevice, Joshua did not slow down. Terror helped him easily clear the space between buildings, torn slicker flapping behind him, and he sprinted across the almost flat roof for the next building, which had an elevated structure to his right.

It seemed forever before Joshua rounded the corner of the structure and slammed his back against its wall. Air blew in and out of his mouth in huge breaths. Seconds later, his breathing still frantic, he eased one eye around the corner in an automatic check of his back trail and his breathing stopped altogether.

There, up on the roofs, backlit by the distant lights of Sky Creek Mall, stood the silhouette of a man wearing a flat brimmed hat.

Fenster!

Joshua whipped back from the corner. Trying to quiet his breathing, he ran across the roof, keeping the structure between him and his pursuer, heading for the nearest building with another elevated structure.

Fortunately, it was in the general direction of The Swamp. It also helped that he was already in a dimmer part of the city and was moving toward the even darker backdrop of the Big Trees, keeping him from being backlit like Fenster.

Joshua finally reached the next structural cover. He immediately leaned an eye past the corner's edge to find something even more terrifying than the sight of Fenster running in his direction – he saw nothing at all. He twisted away from the corner, eyes wide. Trying to stave off the panic whirling in his gut, Joshua forced himself to look again. This time he saw several possible parallel rooftop additions that could conceal the murderer, including some pools of inky shadows tha- he sensed more than saw movement in one of those wells of blackness.

Joshua abandoned concealment and gave free rein to speed. He crammed the contents of the shredded slicker's pockets into his pants and shed the fluttering distraction. Choosing the most direct path to the closest drop into The Swamp, he began running in earnest. He fled over the slick surfaces, cut the most direct paths across roofs, flew over crevices, and ran across horizontal drainpipes with arms held wide for balance. With his rapid progression toward refuge, his confidence ticked back up a few notches. *I know these roofs* way *better than he does and I only have to make it out of the city. There is* no way *even Fenster would follow me into The Swamp.*

Finally, crouching to a stop on the other side of his exit into The Swamp, Joshua looked back over the roofs of New Cincinnati. *Nothing.* He kept looking for the few more moments it took to catch most of his breath, then flung himself over the wall and dropped down into the narrow wash way that led out into the open flats of the burn zone. He jogged through a light rain, repeatedly wiping the water from his face, stunned that he was still alive.

The black figure slid to a stop at the roof wall and looked down to the ground below. Dark eyes caught a faint heat signature and followed its progression for several seconds before it winked out. In the small amount of time provided by the limited range of the infrared lenses, Fenster estimated the heading taken by the boy. Although he could have continued the chase at that moment, he also knew he could later take up surveillance and pick up the boy when he was closer, making sure he did not lose him. *Besides, I must find out just how badly Blood Star wants this boy eliminated.*

Joshua was pleased with himself.

After only two days of isolating himself in Sanctuary, he had forced himself to return to the city. Searching dump piles as far south as Sky Creek Mall, he had finally found the item that had prompted the trip, and some other treasures as well. There was an almost intact slicker to replace the one torn in his escape from Fenster. Also, some more drab clothes that fit reasonably well, extending his options of outfits that blended into the shadows of The Swamp. And then there was the unexpected bonus   the sneakers! His form fitting Nova Clingers had become increasingly painful to wear over the past several months and he certainly could not afford another custom-made pair. Although the hightop cross trainers he had found were a garish pink and teal combination, his reserves of black paint would take care of both the slicker and shoes. The most important thing was that they fit well and had provided a reasonably good grip on his trip back across the roofs. *Speaking of which, I should probably head back up.*

He was walking the pedway because, in the euphoria of being alive and having found some useful treasure, he had gone into Mom's for some supplies. Anticipating an upcoming week of self-imposed isolation, Joshua had justified the purchase of a small cube of olive oil as necessary to help him pass the time by experimenting with recipes downloaded from the GlobalNet. Joshua felt the strap of his satchel digging into his shoulder and decided it was safe enough along this last stretch of pedway between Mom's and The Swamp. *Nobody hangs out along here.*

"Hey, Kid."

Joshua spun toward the crevice where the voice had originated, swinging his satchel to the small of his back, and ripped open his slicker to grasp the handle of the kitchen knife hanging under his armpit. He waited in a crouch, quickly deciding which nearby pipe he would break toward.

A silver hand slid out of the darkness, palm forward, fingers spread. "Take it easy, Joshua. I'm not going to do anything. I was just hoping for a little intel, that's all." The rest of the cloaked figure emerged from the blackness into the ambient grey of the deserted pedway, then slid sideways and stopped. "I'll just lean against this wall while we have a little chat, OK?"

Joshua had no reason to trust Hobo and he *definitely* did not like that the man knew his name. Not only was he nearby when bad things happened, but the encounter while retrieving the phone had been down right strange. True, Hobo had saved him from Omar, but Joshua had no idea why, and the last year had hammered in the lesson: people do not risk without expecting reward. Remembering the two guns brandished on The Avenue and noting that Hobo did not actually lean against the wall, Joshua decided running was not the best option. Even so, after Shoebox, the solid knife handle in his palm felt good.

"About what?"

"About what happened to Bossman and his men."

"Why do you think I know anything about that?"

"Good question." The tall man eased down to a squat, forearms on his knees. "You know, Oriental people are not seen around here much."

"So?"

"So, unusual things make people curious. And *that* means, when unusual people talk, other people are listening, even when they aren't the ones being spoken to."

"So?"

Hobo chuckled before replying, "So, the word on the street *oh*, I mean, the word on *The Avenue* is that a young Oriental gentleman with a blonde ponytail would very much like to speak to you before he leaves in three days." The next words were a little too casual, "Seems he's willing to pay a lot for that conversation."

Joshua pulled on the knife until it unstuck and began easing it out of the makeshift sheath *ever so slowly*. He judged the distance of the throw, doubting he could hit Hobo, but hoping it would at least make the man duck, giving him a head start for the pipe.

Driven to the Hilt

"I'm just letting you know so you can lay low until he leaves."

Joshua stopped pulling on the knife. "Why would you do that?"

The shoulders of the dark green cloak shifted up and down. "My business brings me down here every so often, so I just happened to be there when Muldavy tried to steal your *artifact*. Now, I used to be a kid on the streets, trying to survive, so that didn't sit right by me."

"Why didn't you make him give it back?"

"Like I said, I have to do business here. Most folks on The Avenue don't get riled if they see a kid get whacked in the head, but then, they don't mind if they don't. But if I'd stepped in for a street urchin and demanded property from an established member of 'the community,' *that* would have made trouble for me. *Big* trouble. And I don't need any more of that. Especially not at the moment." Another, longer chuckle. "Besides, I'd say you handled him just fine. And in such a unique and ah *dramatic* fashion."

Joshua became stock still, then quickly glanced left and right. *If he knows I'm Viper Boy, then this might all be-*

"I didn't set you up, Joshua. As I told you, I've had my own issues with the authorities from long ago."

"OK." Joshua shoved the knife back into the sheath. He straightened and took one sideways step, ready to sprint if Hobo stood up. "Thanks."

"You were there when they died, weren't you?"

The hardness in Hobo's voice reminded Joshua of how he had sounded with Muldavy. He stared into the shadowed cowl of the cloak, but only saw the sprawled bodies of Bossman and Big Ears. When his eyes refocused, the edges of his vision were blurry. He resisted the urge to wipe his eyes.

Hobo's next words were soft again, "All right, I see that you were. Mr. Ponytail took out all three?"

Joshua decided if Hobo had wanted to turn him in, he would have just grabbed him first, not started a conversation from a distance. *Besides, it's not as if he can prove I said it.* "No. Fenster turned against Bossman."

"Oh? *Interesting.* Then I suppose Fenster is the new Bossman, unless, did he survive?"

Not about to let Hobo know that he had been using the rooftops, Joshua tried to shrug innocently. "I don't know. He was standing next to Blondie the last I saw. That was a couple of days ago."

Hobo frowned at him for a long moment before, "OOOhh, I see, by *Blondie*, you mean Mr. Ponytail. Seems we both like to label people." When Joshua did not acknowledge the commonality, Hobo continued with a tiny smile, "Gotcha. You haven't seen him recently, so you don't know. Do you think Blondie might have double crossed Fenster?"

Another shrug. "Maybe." With a flush of irritation, Joshua recalled his mood before Hobo had surprised him and felt a strong desire to be back home. "Why do you care about all of this? What does it matter to you what Blondie does?"

"Let's just say we're competitors."

Joshua was shocked by Hobo's open admission. "You're a *drug lord*?"

The man's hooded head rocked back. "*What?*   No,   *no*.   Mr. Ponytail is well-known for recovering   *lost items*, just like me. In fact, I'm currently having some difficulties in that regard."

"Yeah, well, *now* he's working for a Dragon Lady from Blood Star!"

Hobo rose back up to a stand. "You're kidding!   No,   I see that you are not. Hhhhmm, that *would* explain certain unusual aspects of what I have heard."

Joshua's impatience grew. "Look, I have to go. Like *you* said, I shouldn't be hanging around so somebody can snatch me for a talk with Blondie."

Hobo gave a slow nod. "That's probably wise. I'll put out the word about what happened to Bossman and his guys. Anyone considering some quick bounty money on you will think twice about doing business with Mr. Ponytail if they know he can't be trusted."

Joshua stepped backwards toward the crevice behind him. "OK.   That would be very nice of you." He began moving more rapidly in reverse. "Thank you, Mr. Hobo." Before the man could reply, Joshua spun and sprinted into the crevice. A moment later, he turned around just beyond the roof wall and looked down to find   Hobo standing where he had left him. He did not know whether Hobo would do as he said, but he suspected that the man had some hidden agenda. Again feeling weary and just wanting to be safely tucked in at Sanctuary, Joshua turned and began jogging toward his exit into The Swamp.

Oh well, a puzzle for another day.

◄11►

A glistening black cylinder slid out from the dark hole of a slicker sleeve, followed by a figure stepping from the deep shadows of the alleyway.

"Stay right there."

Glin spun to the voice and Joshua lifted the cylinder higher.

"I mean it! Don't move!"

Glin's eyes narrowed as they locked onto the barrel Joshua had pushed out even farther into the light. "What? You going to rob me? What do you think I've got that's worth stealing?"

"Nothing." Joshua followed the gun barrel into the yellow light and pushed back his slicker hood until Glin's face widened with incredulity.

"You're *alive*?"

"Yeah. I'm alive. No thanks to you." Joshua was annoyed that Glin showed no remorse. Instead, he saw astonishment, with mounting fear tinging the edges of his eyes.

"So that *was* you with the spiderviper and Muldavy." Glin's face hardened. "And now you're going to get your payback? Is that it?"

"Maybe, maybe not. It all depends on you."

"What do you want, the code to the warehouse? Well, you can go ahead and shoot me, 'cause telling you that would kill me anyway."

"I don't want anything to do with the warehouse." Joshua was beginning to doubt the wisdom of his decision to approach Glin. He shifted to what he hoped was a more neutral topic. "Who's in charge there now?"

Glin squinted, then shrugged. "Well, ever since Bossman and Grimes were found in The Shoebox, Fenster's been giving the orders. At least until the Lady in Red showed up a couple of days ago." He gave Joshua a flat look. "She sure seemed interested in knowing about you."

"What did Fenster tell her?"

"I'm not telling you anything else." Glin's face became stony.

"Listen, like I said, I plan to stay as far away as I possibly can from you, the warehouse, and Fenster. I just want to know when the Dragon Lady and her blonde ponytail guy are in town, that's all." Joshua tried to sound inviting, "So   ah   you could let me know when they are around, I pay you some and then I just lay even lower than normal until they leave. That's a good deal for both of us, right?"

His dark face impassive, Glin flatly replied, "No. It's not." Exasperation pushed his words out, "You just don't *get it*, do you? If I cross *any* of them and they somehow find out, it's all *over.   Lights out.* And it wouldn't just be me; all the Shadow Boys would get snuffed."

Joshua now realized the magnitude of this mistake. He had confirmed for his enemies that he was still alive and that he was Viper Boy, which also indicated some association with The Swamp. Although none of the "pundits" had made the connection, it was really not a long step from there to the conclusion that he might be living in The Swamp. So, not only was Glin *not* going to tip him off about when the Blood Star operatives were onplanet, but now all of the Shadow Boys would be watching for him.

"OK. I got it. But then let me make it easy for you and your Boys. All of *you* just keep away from *me*. They aren't the only ones who can," he lifted the barrel even higher, "turn out the lights."

Glin growled, "Right. And just so *you* know, if I have to make that choice again, between what's good for me or my Boys and you, it *still* won't be you." He tore his eyes from the pistol to search Joshua's face. What happened next startled both boys.

An unspoken, but absolutely certain communication surged between the two. Glin was trying to hide his fear with defiance, but Joshua saw that and Glin's reluctance to inform on him, as well as his conviction that he would do so in order to save his Shadow Boys. Glin saw Joshua's disappointment, self-reproach, and strengthening realization that he could not safely return to the city. The odd part was that they both saw these things in each other at the same time, and *knew* that the other saw it too. The moment of mutual understanding was intense and slightly disorienting, but also created a distasteful feeling of exposure in both boys.

Glin expressed his discomfort in anger. "Just stay away from the warehouse!"

"Don't worry, I'm not going near that place. *Ever* again."

Joshua's teeth ground together in frustration. *I don't know why I*

The Deepest Cut

thought he would help me. Keeping the gun raised, he eased back into the shadow of the narrow passage between buildings. Several feet in, he stopped with a crevice on his right. He knew that to Glin, he now looked like a dark lump in the gloom. Whether the other boy could still see the gun barrel or not, the fact that he had not moved suggested he thought Joshua still had him covered. *Lucky he fell for it.*

He wanted to be looking at Glin for the last time, but he knew their world was too small. His rival's face glistened from the descending mist, expression set. *He is* Joshua grunted a small, resigned laugh *resolute.*

Joshua turned and sprinted 15 feet into the crevice, sliding the fake "gun" into the front pocket of his shirt. He had created the barrel from a short piece of plastic pipe. It was "the item" that had prompted his recent run to the dumps near Sky Creek Mall. Turning right at the T of the crevice, another 20 feet brought him to a wider alley and his objective. A quick leap to the drainpipe and he was on the roof. Joshua felt confident Glin could not have possibly followed quickly to have seen his ascent.

Well, that *didn't go like I planned, but it's not all bad.* He had confirmed that Fenster was in charge. He hoped that with the takeover of Bossman's organization, the Dragon Lady would lose interest in him. And Glin's failure to recognize Joshua's "gun" as a fake provided a possible way to get out of tight spots in the future. But as he headed for home, Joshua knew he could not count on the fake gun working every time.

The entire way back to Sanctuary, Joshua could not shake the feeling of being watched. He decided it was due to the unanswered question of whether he would be able to evade the Shadow Boys' surveillance. Hours later, a nightmare caused Joshua to sit bolt upright in a cold sweat. He had been desperately trying to make his body move, but felt as if he had been encased in swamp goo. All the while, the eyes watching him from the shadows grew and grew. *Still worried about the Shadow Boys, I guess.*

The next evening, a bleary eyed Joshua set out to speak with Aberly about creating replica spiderviper fangs and   to ask for his help.

◄12►

When the clinking of coins stopped, Joshua made a quick estimate. *About 20 percent less than last week, and that hadn't been all that much.* He looked up at his business partner.

"Yes, my lad, I'm afraid sales have fallen again." Aberly sighed. "As I feared, it didn't take long for the rest of The Avenue to create their own fang replicas off of ours. And since most people are too frightened to come this far UpAve, they never see the difference in quality. It has really cut into our sales."

"Have you been getting more requests for the real thing?"

"Forget I ever told you that. Making some money isn't worth making you dead. I'm going to meet with Harlison about offering the 'officially endorsed' Viper Boy replicas. His shop is at the mouth of The Avenue, so the increase in sales volume should make up for the amount of his cut."

"OK." Joshua was discouraged about the entire enterprise, dreams of becoming rich having given way to a fatalistic pessimism. Clearly replica fang sales were not going to lift him out of his precarious financial situation. He gave himself a mental shake and peered at Aberly. He decided he now knew the man well enough to ask, "So   do you know anything about a man named Hobo?"

Aberly's brows furled. "Hobo? Yes, a little. Why?"

"He just seems to be around every time I'm having   *problems.* Then, about three weeks ago, he stepped out at me in an alley and told me that this Oriental guy was after me, but that he'd help me by telling everybody that the guy couldn't be trusted. I haven't had any run ins with *anybody* since then, but I've been lying low too, only coming in here to see you once a week. So, I don't know. I'm asking because the guy just makes me nervous."

"Well, it's that 'Oriental guy' that *should* make you nervous. He has certainly made pretty much everyone on The Avenue nervous. After all, Ralff and Lynyrd were pretty tough guys, so, clearly it doesn't pay to step into the path of Blood Star. On the other hand, everyone knows when Blood Star is around, and none of them have been seen over the last 10 days or so."

"Yeah, well *believe* me, I'm doing *everything* I can to stay out of the path of Blood Star. But ah," Joshua squinted at Aberly, "I was talking about *Hobo* making me nervous. So, do you know anything else about *him*?"

The tall merchant slouched forward, rested his elbows on the counter, intertwined fingers under his chin, and surveyed Joshua. A moment passed before he sighed. "Nothing much, I'm afraid. Over the past couple of years, I've shared some, ah *libations* with the gentleman oh no more than a handful of times. He has always been quite pleasant, but I must say, he tends to ask more questions than he answers. Of course that could just reflect a curious and ah *cautious* disposition. Relative to his business dealings, at first he said he was 'in acquisitions,' but then later, he called it 'the recovery business.' I'm not really sure what either of those mean, since his only elaboration was that he obtained lost items of value for people for a fee. But he was quite insistent that his recovery methods were not criminal, how did he say? 'In the strictest sense of the word.' That leaves some room for interpretation, of course, but he was *very* explicit about never having *stolen* from anyone. Quite *forceful* about that, in fact. However, I must say, in as much as I can take the measure of a man in such a limited amount of time, he has always seemed to be a decent sort. And *that* is the long and short of it, my friend." Aberly pushed upright from the counter. "Not much help I fear."

Joshua's head dipped forward and back in the slow fashion of someone who is not convinced. "Ok. So you really don't know whether he can be trusted."

"Ah, well, if you *insist* upon such a determination, I would say, *yes,* I trust him."

"Oh. Ok. Well, thanks. See you next week."

"Perk up, my young man. This deal with Harlison will reap benefits, just you wait and see."

As the front door was pulled shut, Aberly let out a long, slow sigh. His words were resigned, almost sorrowful, "I'm afraid that boy isn't long for this world. One way or the other."

The fabric that hung across the back room door was silently eased to the side and a tall cloaked figure slipped into the room. He stopped just behind Aberly's back.

"Yes, my friend. The noose *is* tightening."

"Are you going to take him?"

"Perhaps. Others must be considered."

"He's the one."

"He has yet to be tested."

Aberly's statement was flat and certain, "*He's the one.*"

Hobo's reply was soft and contemplative, "We shall see."

The Deepest Cut

◀13▶

Joshua began to deflate as he climbed the slope leading to his home. The full impact of how his enterprise with Aberly was sputtering had finally settled heavily onto his shoulders. Unwilling to face more disappointment, he disregarded Aberly's optimism about the merchant at the mouth of The Avenue and decided he could not count on any more income from the fang replicas. His despondency sunk into gloom as he recalled his failed attempt to recruit Glin. *Even if the fangs were making lots of money, I'd still have to check every soppin' dark corner of every muckin' building for a Shadow Boy every single time I went in to spend any of it.*

Pushing his weary body up to Sanctuary through a medium rainfall, he sensed heavier showers were coming. As he tried to beat the approaching downpour, images from The Shoebox came to Joshua's mind: the smoldering anger in Grimes' eyes, all because of a nickname Joshua had not even meant for him to hear; the cold indifference in Blondie's face when hearing of the pending murder of a young kid; but mostly of Bossman's peculiar respect for Joshua having outsmarted him, which contrasted so sharply with his earlier mocking persona.

Finally, Joshua sludged out of the cool fall rain into The Porch and peeled off his slicker. Hanging it on the back of his wicker chair, he then shambled back, ducking at the approach of Headbanger, and-

froze.

Something was wrong. Joshua's eyes flicked about, touching on everything he could see through the narrow gap of dim light created by the glow of his soundbox control screen. A sense of urgency built as he searched for what had prompted his hesitation. Finally, it struck him. *It's the gap!* He looked *at* the gap where the wicker screen stood back a crack from the other side of Headbanger instead of through it. ***That*** *shouldn't be.* He *always* carefully pulled it all the way shut when he left, worried that leaks of light might reveal his presence at Sanctuary.

Anticipation stretched the silence until   Joshua realized what he was expecting. It was as if he was trapped in a suspense movie and this was the part where the villain stepped forth to explain how he had tracked the hero to his hide out, describing how he was going to kill the hero in the most painful of ways, ending in a rumbling evil laugh, *but*   that did not happen.

Instead, a black dot appeared along the edge of the stone wall,   and grew into a tiny triangle, which   elongated,   gently easing out   leisurely transforming   into the leading tip of a narrow thin blade.

Joshua had not felt himself transition into slowtime, but with an electrifying snap, he was no longer observing, but *understanding* that a silent death approached. He lunged backwards to the right, twisting away from what had become a hand guiding the blade closer, took one step and leapt, floating over the outer pool of water that was his wash station, falling toward the far rippling edge of the pool, to where the water rolled out of the cave mouth, hands stretching forward, reaching for the lip *splash oomph*   the shock of hitting the cold wash station water jarred Joshua out of slow time. The explosion of sound from the displaced water stunned Joshua into immobility, but his momentum slid him forward as he submerged and he felt the smooth rounded edge of stone on his palms under the rushing water. He grabbed and pulled as hard as he could, propelling himself forward, away from the death behind him and over the edge.

He felt the blade tug as its razor edge parted fabric, but from long years of experience, Fenster knew that his lunge had not scored flesh. He instantly flowed under the low rock ceiling, pulling his arm back to strike again, but instead of running for the cave entrance, his target had dived out over the exiting stream of water. He leapt forward, making it to the mouth of the cave in time to see the small dark shape slip over the edge and descend into the lifting mists of the waterfall. *What tipped the boy off? Doesn't matter now.* With practiced ease, the stiletto regained its sheath and was replaced by a large caliber hand gun. Fenster stepped out from the cave into the intensifying rain, strode to the edge of the ledge, and peered down at the pond below. *If he survived that fall, I might yet extract some info before collecting his ears for Ms. Li. If not, I'll just have to forego the*

The Deepest Cut

bonus points and settle for getting the job done.

He floated silently   suspended   arms flailing through air and
water   dropping   helplessly tumbling   *ARRUMFFF!*
After the pain of impact came the shocking embrace of cold water.
Somehow Joshua oriented himself at the bottom of his plunge and began
kicking his way in an upward direction,   hands clawing at the green
water,   scrambling frantically through the murky liquid to   break through
the surface. At first, nothing mattered more than getting air into his lungs,
but after two large breaths, Joshua wiped down his face and snapped a look
up toward Sanctuary. A black shape materialized through the heavy rain
and stopped at the edge of the overlook. There was a peculiar shape to his
head   *a hat! FENSTER!*

Joshua could *feel* the man's malicious gaze stabbing down at him. He
turned and thrashed at the water in a frenzy to propel himself to the pond's
edge. Not soon enough, his hand sunk into slimy mud and he grabbed
wildly until he latched onto some thick lichen. He reached hand over hand,
kicking desperately, until he had scrambled out of the water. He stopped on
all fours, raindrops pummeling his back, surprised he had reached his goal.

The lichen a foot in front of his face exploded at the same instant as a
cracking boom came from behind and above. A whining sob escaped as
Joshua lurched to his feet and staggered away, his water soaked clothes
feeling like ghostly hands trying to pull him back down.

Fenster's lips formed the shape of an expletive, but only a hiss came
out. It was a rare loss of self-control. He had not compensated for the
downward angle. He had not seen where the round hit, but knew it must
have been high. Despite the difficulty of seeing through the rain flowing
off the front of his wide brimmed hat, he made the elevation adjustment
and squeezed the trigger again.

Joshua lurched sideways to jump over one of the many small streams
that flowed away from The Pond. A sucking of air by his right ear came
with the second BOOM. He forced back an intense desire to accelerate and
instead cut to one side or the other every few steps. Not hearing the next

anticipated shot, he took a mad glance back toward Sanctuary. His foot struck a small growth and he fell hard.

Although the dark blot of his target was blurred by the rainfall, Fenster knew he had missed again because it still moved toward The Swamp. Flipping his lenses down, he impatiently waited the several seconds necessary for the infrared system to actuate its heads up display. Finally, he saw a flicker, and then a glimmer of heat partially masked by the cold early autumn rain. More out of frustration then with any expectation of success, Fenster lifted his hand and fired again.

boom swAATTtt! Hearing the impact just in front of him, Joshua scrambled on all fours to his right and then lunged to his feet. A whimper of terror squealed out as panic propelled him straight toward the Big Trees, efforts at evasiveness completely abandoned, all of his energy put into *escape*.

The glimmer shifted on the HUD, faded, and then was gone. Fenster experienced a rare moment of hesitation. After seven years of living in New Cincinnati, the reputation of The Swamp had sunk in deeper than he had realized. Following the shootout at The Shoebox, he had assured Ms. Li that the police informant was doomed after fleeing into The Swamp, not in an attempt to placate, but because he had been convinced it was true. However, against every expectation, the kid had surfaced again. And Ms. Li not only had no difficulty pronouncing "loose end," but had been crystal clear about that end being "tied off." *And so, here I am.*

Slamming the pistol back into its holster, he recalled the look in her eyes when she had finished squeezing Glin dry and had turned to look at him, one sculpted eyebrow raised. That was the moment he knew he was locked into a relationship with Blood Star, and that it was a bond which, even if maintained at a distance, could never be severed. He really had no choice. *I'll just have to be careful. But then, I always am.* Fenster flipped up the infrared lenses to better see the path before him and began his descent.

The Deepest Cut

Joshua narrowed his entire world to running. He tried, but could not make slowtime come back. Then he remembered his first spiderviper encounter in The Swamp and the things that had helped him escape that time, so long ago. He focused on the ground in front of him, on lengthening his stride, swinging his arms, and keeping his head down so as not to suck in so much rain with each increasingly labored breath. Soggy step after step seemed to stretch on forever. Joshua lifted his eyes. The tall gloominess of larger vegetation loomed before him *almost there!* But...

he *had* to know. Joshua threw a snap glance over his shoulder. A shifting blackness was outlined against the lightness of the waterfall. It felt like being struck by a surge of electricity and Joshua stumbled, but somehow tucked into a wild summersault and came back up to his feet, staggering to a stop while facing back toward the sight of Fenster coming for him. He heard his own strangled cry of frustration. *How! How can he follow me in the dark? In this rain?* In that petrified moment, he recalled the way Hat Man had looked directly at him as he stood in the dark alley. Then the image of Estanod's flip phone came to him and the connection clicked *infrared!*

He whipped back around and terror accelerated him toward the now nearby large clumps of vegetation. Rounding one of the big bushes, Joshua staggered to a stop, overwhelmed by a new and swelling sense of peril. He stood, cold rain drops pounding his head, and then he saw it in the distance: a large irregular puff suspended above black spikes. His terror swelled as everything came together *that's the Bluebell where I caught the baby spiderviper! Oh PLEASE let them be hunting deeper in the Big Trees!*

Joshua tried to quiet his breathing while frantically searching all around for movement. A small whine was forced out by the dread that surged from his stomach. He knew in his core that they were coming toward him. After all *I've been splashing, grunting, huffing and puffing, through their territory at night!* Then he remembered *Fenster is coming, too!* Panic final broke his frozen muscles loose and he began running toward the Bluebell silhouette.

When he reached the bottom, Fenster took the time to reactivate his infrared lenses and increase the magnification. Luckily, the rain had slackened some and a flashing signature could be discerned in the direction he had last seen the boy moving. He looked around and felt reassured that no heat signatures were between him and his designated target.

Fenster adjusted the sensitivity on the lenses and began jogging toward the wavering blob of heat. His eyes narrowed at the glimmer of misgiving that swirled in his gut as he moved closer to the inky shadows under The Big Trees. *But   that little kid has survived here for a while, so   all of those stories must be wrong.   And he doesn't have the resources* Fenster loosened the big pistol in its holster *that I have.* Feeling more confident, he accelerated toward his shrinking target.

Squish   squish   squish   *no spidervipers yet*   squish   squish squish squish   Joshua stumbled as he swatted a wet branch aside, emerged into an open area, and saw the Bluebell standing only 25 yards away. He willed his legs to pump harder,   squish   squish   before risking a final glance back. His heart skipped a beat. Through the now easing rain, he just made out a dark lump in the not far enough distance,   becoming more distinct, becoming   *a flat hat!* And it still clearly moved   *this way!*

Joshua turned back forward, heart thumping painfully in his chest; feet pounding onto the soaked lichen   splash   splash   propelling him through the easing rain to his last possible hope. *Gotta   raise*   splash   *the*   splash *leaves.* He reached for the kitchen knife in its Shark Tape sheath, but just grasped air. *It's not there!*

Realizing he lost it when he had hit The Pond, Joshua slapped his other pockets in a frenzy, seeking something else to throw   squish   squish while continuing to slog forward   squish   squish   and then he yelped as his hand felt something long and cylindrical. He pulled out the fake gun barrel and flung it at the Bluebell. Closing the distance, he saw the leaves begin to move.

Joshua summoned a final burst of energy, willing leaden legs to cover the last few yards, and launched himself feet first to the left side of the base of the Bluebell. His legs flew over the lichen-covered ground and when they hit the mud underneath the plant's canopy, he rolled across his stomach once before banging his back into the plant. He slid his legs back around the base and began clawing at the ground, scooping up cold mud and slapping handfuls of it all over himself as the long leaves began their gradual descent. *Come on   come ON!!* Smearing wet goo onto his cheeks, Joshua urgently peered in the direction he had last seen Fenster, but grey lumps of plants obscured the view. Finally, the Bluebell's leaves arched down to enclose him in darkness, but instead of feeling relief, Joshua felt   *trapped.*   His terror mounted, and even though the surroundings were blocked from view, he strangely felt more exposed than before.

Fenster stopped when the primary heat signature disappeared. Before vanishing, it had suddenly become smaller; presumably because the target had dropped to its knees to hide. *All the better. He's not going deeper into The Swamp. Now it's just a matter of finding him.* He increased magnification to try to again lock onto his target's signature. Pulling out his gun, he strode forward to close the distance to the last observed position of his prey.

Joshua's grimy hands stopped smearing a second coat of mud onto his face at the loud brushing sounds of someone shoving aside wet branches. Fenster's entry into the adjacent glen terminated his hasty efforts at concealment. He had already mounded as much cold mud over the exposed side of his body as possible. Unable to reach below his knees in the cramped space, he hoped having curled his legs back around the plant base would be enough to hide them from the infrared glasses. Very slowly, Joshua scraped aside the mud from his lids and opened his eyes. There were slivers of lighter grey through openings between the spike ends of the lowered Bluebell leaves, but he could not make out anything.

Fenster frowned. While circumventing a larger bush, he had lost the faint signal he had just reacquired and been forced to stop. He thrust aside a flush of irritation and focused on a systematic search of the intermediate vicinity as he advanced into an open area. Then he had it, a very weak signal about 30 feet to his right. With a slight grunt of satisfaction, he began moving in that direction.

Driven to the Hilt

squish   squish   Joshua heard approaching steps   squish   squish
they came closer   squish   squish   squish before coming to a stop. *This
is it, Mom.* The thought of his mother actually brought a greater calm. He
recalled her once saying that she knew she would see his father again one
day, in a better place. He had not really understood, so she had told him
everything would be explained when he was older. The memory was
unexpectedly comforting. *I'm ready for a better place, Mom.* Joshua
closed his eyes and tried not to breathe.

The signature was so partial that, even as he closed the distance, the
HUD range finder still would not engage. At six feet away, Fenster could
make out something under a bush's wide-spread, aloe-like leaves, he just
could not determine if it belonged to the boy, some small creature, or even
several smaller ones. He glanced up at the too close thick trees, the shifting
shadows under the canopy urging caution about making loud noises. And
Fenster definitely did not want to take the time to cut away the spiked
leaves to get the body out and verify the kill. *Maybe I can get a reaction-*
"Come on out, kid. There's no need to drag this out any further."

Joshua flinched at the sound of Fenster's voice. He pulled a long
lungful of air into his nose, held it, then let it ease out between his muck
covered lips. He was acutely aware of the creosote-like smell of the plant
that surrounded him, the cool, wet weight of the mud on his face and body,
and all of the variations of grey in the shadows in front of him. His next
thought was forlorn and resigned *Looks like Momma spiderviper and her
babies are somewhere else.*

"Don't make me drag you out, boy."

Joshua did not even flinch this time. He waited for the shot through the
leaves and hoped it would not hurt too much. Then he felt something
crawling up his leg.

Fenster listened and watched intently, but nothing moved. *Give me a
sign, kid.   I really don't want to have to cut you out of there in the dark.
Come on...   Give me something.* He tried to make his squeaky voice

deeper and more commanding, "Come *OUT!*" Just as Fenster was about to proceed to the next bush, he heard a small "urp" and a slight rustle of one of the leaves. *Gotcha!* Fenster took a single step forward and lifted the large pistol, but as his finger squeezed the trigger, he heard a fluttery sound from the edge of the glen. He pivoted and saw a large low shape scuttling toward him. His reaction was instantaneous **BOOM!**

Joshua's entire body spasmed at the explosion of sound. His heart had already been thumping from feeling the small Millipede exploring his leg. Now it thundered in his chest. Seconds ticked by, but he felt no pain. Even as he realized he had not been shot, he decided that Fenster had just been attempting to scare him out. The next shot would be "for real." Joshua braced himself and squeezed his eyes tight. *I'm coming, Mom.*

The big dark shape rocked to a stop with a short chirping whistle. The sound of the gunshot echoed away into an expectant silence. Fenster squinted and could just make out the spindly legs around the dark mass. His eyes widened as the legs began moving again, bringing the creature closer, the foreclaws lifting and reaching out *a spiderviper!* **BOOM BOOM** This time when the blob came to a stop a few feet away, Fenster saw the legs on either side of the bulbous body ease down in the relaxation of death. *Well, you weren't so tough after all. Mr. Spiderviper meet Mr. 357 Magnum. I guess poor old George of the Jungle just needed quicker reflexes.*

Joshua's body jerked again with each of the next two rapid shots. Then he lay frozen while comprehension seeped in that he was still alive. With another start, he realized *The spidervipers, they came!* He pressed his cheek against the slick mud so he could see more through the small gaps where the spiked tips of the Bluebell leaves touched the ground. A darker black appeared to shift and move. Shiny white dots seemed to move with the black against charcoal grey. The image resolved into something dark and solid with *reflections? Boots! Fenster's boots.*

Fenster turned and stepped back to the bush where his loose end had just revealed himself. He lifted the pistol once more, but in the lower corner the HUD came a round flash of red movement, forcing him to again pivot **BOOM!** A spray of red heat signal splashed across the HUD, out of which spun the original small red ball. When the orb came to a stop, Fenster could make out several small orange limbs sticking up *a small spiderviper. A baby?* Then one **BOOM** two **BOOM** more red balls appeared, only to go spinning away in a splattering of red spots. Fenster spun in time to see another small spiderviper only two feet from him **BOOM** but two more were closing in **BOOM** **BOOM** A third appeared contrasted against its mother's cooling yellow corpse; the pistol's sights swung onto the target click.

Joshua watched the black boots spin and step as the booms of the gun continued to shatter the sudden stillness in the night, over and over. Hope surged as he watched the small legs of a baby spiderviper come up beside Fenster's boot. Then his optimism plunged. *The slicker! Would the little fangs penetrate it?*

It took Fenster half a second to comprehend that sound and then his right thumb pressed the clip release as his left hand streaked to the replacement clip on his holster strap. It had just entered the bottom of the pistol handle when an intense burning sensation bloomed in his left calf. He managed to get the 12-round replacement clip inserted, but for some reason, his right thumb could not work the slide release. Another agonizing burn began in the front of his left leg, then one on the side of his right. Fenster was dismayed that his arms were growing too weak to hold upright, but icy fear gripped him when his legs shuddered and he began to topple. All the way down, he willed his arms to lift, his head to turn and locate targets, his body to *fight. Thump.*

His lenses flew off and the world went completely and horribly black. Fenster could feel his eyes moving in response to his frantic search for the beasts, but the all-encompassing darkness did not change. Then with sharp whistles and the skittering of feet, the black gloom eased and evolved into grey shapes, that were *advancing,* scurrying toward his now hatless head. A sharp pressure against his cheek, then a horrible burn, and as the fire spread across his face, the first dark ball was joined by a second. Flame erupted in his throat.

And then

        Fenster saw no more   felt no more.

A second group of furry feet came up to the legs. Joshua held his breath no gunshots sounded. A third set of thin legs. With a low, extended grunt, the boot heels tilted and then   a loud wet thud. Joshua watched the soles of both boots quiver and then became   *still*.

He was not sure when he began breathing again, but his overwhelming sense of relief was dowsed by a loud whistle just outside the lowered Bluebell leaves. The signal was echoed from different spots around the glen. Joshua heard the soft scrabbling of tiny claws as the baby spidervipers scurried about. His fear subsided as the movements became less frenzied. Then the questioning chirps began. During the ten minutes that the babies were reacting to their mother's lifeless form, Joshua estimated that six of them had survived. Like him, they were now motherless; unlike him, they were armed and dangerous.

The night stretched on and the calling chirps became forlorn whistles. Over time, Joshua felt less concern about being discovered and more pity for the babies as they mourned the loss of their mother. Gradually, the sad chirps and flutters diminished, to be replaced by soft rustling and slurping noises. Without warning, Joshua was standing by the front door, looking down at his mother's empty eyes, listening to wet sucking noises. His mind was numb, but his body was   cold. *That's not right.* His mother's face gave an occasional slight rock *Why?* from tugs on her leg *What?*

With a sudden understanding, Joshua again lay under the Bluebell and his guts lurched at the now unmistakable sounds of feeding. He choked down the surge from his stomach with a muffled gagging noise. The night became still. He squeezed his eyes tight and struggled to picture himself standing in the Sky Creek Mall, watching the pattern of raindrops striking one of the ion domes. He studied the small spots radiating out into circles that were then swept away by the sheet of water being redirected to the waiting fountains. The repetitious pattern was soothing and the nausea ebbed, and waned, until he no longer felt as if he was going to throw up, even after the wet gulping resumed.

Driven to the Hilt

Joshua maintained his vigil at the Mall for what seemed to be hours before he realized that all was quiet. During that time, his side had gone from painful discomfort to blissful numbness to an agonizing throb. Still, he did not move. He did look out toward the boots again, but his view of them was blocked by the resting body of a baby spiderviper. *Great! Are they just going to stay until he's a skeleton?* The cartoon image that came to mind struck him as funny and he had to close his eyes to keep from laughing. A full body shiver helped him to think of something else. He began flexing his muscles to generate heat without moving, but the shivers kept coming. He clamped his jaw tight so as not to let his teeth chatter. Finally, the shaking subsided, without attracting any attention from the baby spidervipers. Then an intense fatigue struck, and not knowing whether he would snore, he battled the desire to go to sleep. At least the torture of being unable to move helped on that score

for a while.

The Deepest Cut

◄14►

Sn n snork!

Joshua's eyes snapped open. He urgently reached out with his ears for any nearby sounds as his eyes flew to the gaps in the Bluebell leaves and he saw Fenster's boot soles! They were easier to see because the gloom had lessened. Joshua continued to listen intently. Then the predawn stillness was broken by a mournful warble. His breath immediately eased out of his mouth the sound had come from a considerable distance, as did the answering chirps and whistles. Over the next hour, the ever less frequent chirps came from farther and farther away.

When the light was as bright as could be expected under the perpetual cloud cover over New Cincinnati and silence had reigned for some time, Joshua eased his right arm forward and sank his fingers into the firm, but still damp mud that covered his chest. After forming a sphere, he did his best not to groan in pain as he flung the mud ball at the tip of one of the spiked leaves before him. It struck the underside of the leaf and nothing happened. Joshua frowned, his brain as frozen as his body, unable to think. Then he understood *I have to hit the top side of the leaves, where the sticky stuff is.* Another mud ball ricocheted off the edge of a leaf and hit the ground, but the third time proved a charm, with the ball bouncing off the underside of a higher leaf to the top of the leaf below.

As the Bluebell foliage lifted, Joshua kept completely still as his eyes flicked about, searching for any movement. Seeing none, he rolled sideways out from under his overnight hiding place. Unable to totally suppress the grunts of pain, he gritted his teeth to suppress an outright cry of pain as he sat up and spun his head as best he could on his stiff neck, looking for any approaching threats. There were none. A long breath eased out through mud covered lips *I'm alive, Mom!*

Joshua struggled not to sob at the thought of his mother. But the tears still flowed from mud encrusted eyes and he smiled as he sat, painfully rotating and stretching his arms while keeping a constant vigil for movement. Every time his gaze slid across the Bluebell, he felt a twinge of anxiety. His annoyance mounted until he stopped scanning and stared at the bush, trying to understand. At last he recalled the odd feeling of greater exposure once the leaves had descended to the ground and enveloped him. With a buzz in his core, Joshua knew he would never again choose to passively accept his fate if *any* remaining active options were available. With that realization and his decision made, the buzzing subsided.

Then he finally looked, *really* looked at Fenster, relieved to see the man was laying on his right side with his back to Joshua. The feeling of being totally helpless again came to mind, as did his just made vow to not be passive. *Okay, then. Time to back it up.* He took a full breath before easing onto his hands and knees and then inched forward to look over the man's stiff legs. Seeing that the body hid nothing dangerous, Joshua completed the climb over the dead man and crawled up for a closer look. His eyes passed over the gory mess of the stomach area and he focused on Fenster's face, seeing its left side and the entire neck were swollen and blue. Joshua's throat constricted and he looked to the ground until the urge to vomit passed. *No! I **have** to get it.*

Steeling himself, Joshua looked back down to where the babies had fed. When he saw the handle of the stiletto sticking out from the open slicker, he focused on it only and successfully snatched out the thin bladed knife. Then he stopped. Recalling how easily he had lost the kitchen knife in the fall, he forced himself to look back. Placing his total attention on the sheath, a certain clinical detachment set in and he determined that the sheath was buttoned onto the belt. Soon it was free and filled with the stiletto. Joshua secured the sheath to his belt and then his eyes fell on the pistol holster. The thought of having to roll the body around to remove the shoulder straps was allayed when he found that buttons also attached the holster to the straps. Once the holster and attached clip holders were safely in hand, Joshua spun away and searched the ground around Fenster. A moment later he had filled the second holder with the empty clip and was holding the heavy pistol.

After a quick check of his surroundings, Joshua gingerly examined the weapon. His father had impressed upon him the importance of extreme care when it came to guns. Remembering his father's emphasis about always having a safety on, Joshua carefully inspected the pistol. The first button he tried was difficult to press, so he tried a small lever behind and above the trigger. It moved with a click to cover a nearby red dot. Assuming red meant danger, Joshua left the lever over the red dot and holstered the pistol. *That's easy enough. So I just have to flip the switch and pull the trigger.* He made another 360 check before setting about a more gruesome task. Pulling out the razor sharp stiletto and keeping the pistol within easy reach on the ground, he lifted the mother spiderviper's proboscis and began cutting. The process was made much easier by the finely honed blade and not needing to avoid any swarms of Rot Eaters. Soon his pants pockets were filled with one large and six small black fangs.

Joshua set out, silently working back the way he had come when fleeing Fenster the night before. Soon he was out in the open, walking across spongy lichen and staying parallel to the monorail for safety, head bowed to the light medium rain. He realized that even if he had successfully eluded Fenster the night before, he would have been forced to abandon Sanctuary forever. He tried to come up with a viable contingency plan as he slogged through the rain towards The Pond, just in case Sanctuary was ever compromised again. But bone weary, he finally gave up, and just felt grateful that he could keep living in the one place that he thought of as home.

Despite his fatigue, while climbing the path up the slope to Sanctuary, Joshua's thoughts once again turned to people that he had known, but were now dead. **Dead**. *And, more or less, I had a hand in their deaths*. Joshua could not understand why that bothered him, since all three had threatened to kill him, but somehow   it did.

He rallied his energy as he approached The Porch, wondering whether Fenster had informed Blondie about his hideaway. He inched his way in, the large hand gun held out before him in both hands, safety off. Joshua crouched at Headbanger, and   felt none of the threat that had been there the night before. The wicker screen was lying flat on the floor, but nothing else seemed out of place. Even so, Joshua steeled himself and entered in a rush, swinging the pistol in wild arcs to cover as many shadows as possible. After several sweeps of every corner, his shoulders sagged in

Driven to the Hilt

relief. He engaged the safety, eased the pistol back into its holster, and placed the weapon on the shelf, telling himself he would Google it later to learn more about how it worked. Then Joshua shuffled over and righted the screen. He pressed it up against the entryway, knowing it could not stop anyone, but hoping it would at least make a warning noise.

It seemed that his saturated clothes were fighting him as he peeled them off, but eventually he was naked and scrubbing himself clean in the front pool. Joshua wondered vaguely why the water did not seem as cold as when he had dived into it the night before. He was so spent by the time the water ran clear and he had difficulty summoning the energy to towel himself dry. Joshua pulled on some underwear, collapsed onto his mattress, and encased himself in his blanket. He rolled onto his side, back to the wall, and struggled to hold open his eyes.

I guess I won't be seeing you as soon as I thought, Mom.

Joshua smiled when the warm glow expanded at his back and a sense of security enveloped him. He was asleep before the pulse had cooled.

Afterglow

Joshua did not register the rain anymore. Unless it was a downpour, it was just another part of The Swamp, a feature of the air that could change at any moment. On this morning, a medium drizzle came down in separate lazy sheets that drifted across his view of Bushland. So far, none of the heavier concentrations of rain had found him where he sat, feet dangling, high up on The Perch, stomach comfortably full of Orange Tater muffins. His sense of contentment from the satisfying meal had faded as he sat and contemplated many things: if Sanctuary really was one, whether he would ever have friends and whether he deserved any, if he would ever be truly safe in New Cincinnati, but mostly, *Why am I alive? Is it because I was willing to hurt people who wanted to hurt me? That I made the right decisions at the right times? Or was I just lucky?*

When his thoughts whirled past these questions yet again without any answers, Joshua gave up. Watching the curtains of rain shifting and shimmering, he tried to think about other things, simpler things. Then he recalled something his mother had often said, *'You have to take the bad with the good.'* He sighed. *Well, there is plenty of Bad...*

If he went into the city, he had to stay off The Avenue, where he was now famous as Viper Boy. Despite Aberly's assurances when interviewed on the pVid, Joshua was convinced the denizens there would either try to exploit him or turn him over to the police, seeking a reward. Speaking of which, the attempted murder charges had not been dropped, so he not only had to keep away from the Mayor's dirty cops, he had to avoid being stopped by any cop on the beat, since they would be obligated to take him in too. He still had to dodge Glin and his Shadow Boys, given Aberly's information about the changes at the warehouse. Apparently, after Fenster had been missing for three days, the Dragon Lady showed up and had some "girl talk" with Samanatha. When she left, the BossBitch was running the show at the warehouse. Based on what Aberly had somehow learned, it seemed certain that the Dragon Lady had made it part of Samanatha's mission to find and eliminate him. Joshua idly rubbed the scar on his cheek and wondered if Glen's small friend Tylir was still an official Shadow Boy with her in charge. While he thought he could avoid all of these people by using the rooftops, they were not the big threats. With their uncanny ability to appear out of nowhere, it was Hobo and Blondie who posed the greatest danger. Joshua wondered how long he could isolate himself in Sanctuary before the loneliness pushed him to make one too many trips.

But   there was also *The Good...* First, he had a plan. He would see how much Aberly could get for the real spiderviper fangs, being careful to sell them one at a time so he did not depress the market. Based upon the $31,000 offered for the first baby fang, he should net quite a sum, even after the middlemen scraped off their share and Aberly took his cut. Next, with sufficient funds, he would go to Faulken and find Estanod. *After all, he offered to let me live with him. And I know even more about biodiversity now.* He figured Aberly must know the right people on The Avenue to create a workable disguise, the necessary identification, and the proper papers for him to travel alone as a youth. *Heck, if the fangs get enough money, maybe Aberly will even pose as my dad and take the trip with me. He'd probably like to have another acting job.* So maybe, *just maybe,* if Hobo and Blondie did not interfere, he might be able to escape Cypress Grove   *if I can get enough money and if -*

Joshua straightened up and his eyes widened when the Big Trees on the far side of Bushland began to glow in a symphony of green hues. Golden sparkles leapt across the distance, even brighter from their contrast against the dark forest behind, forcing him to blink. His eyes started to follow the broad stream of light up to where it poured down from a break in the clouds over his shoulder. He had twisted halfway around when   he stopped. Turning back to face The Swamp, Joshua accepted the gift from the sun, stayed in the moment, and soaked up the transformation of the vegetation far out in front of him.

Different colors began peeking out from between the tree trunks: dots of yellow blossoms, a vertical slash of purple, clusters of blues and reds. The clouds shifted and the shimmers and sparkles moved from the inky depths to the edge of The Swamp. Joshua peered into the distance and then smiled *That's right in front of Hidey Hole #1!* The vegetation, once shrouded in a sinister gloom heavy with the promise of lurking threats, now radiated with a fireworks display of color, an exhibition of life in abundance, a wide diversity woven into an interdependent web of relationships. The grey skies moved again, pulling multiple beams of light out of the Big Trees and into the burn zone toward Joshua, marching across an ecosystem that Joshua now realized, he knew and moved in with comfort, of which he had become a part.

The bursts of light shifted and slid from the burn zone into Bushland, creating flashes of pale yellow in the Nutblossom bushes, glowing lines of pastel greens from Drooper vines in the Ironwood Trees, and shimmering blue twinkles from hanging Ice Spikes. The golden beams slowed and congregated at the juncture of the mountainside to Joshua's left, piercing the foliage that fronted the edge of the Big Trees. A ball of blue lit up and he *knew* it was the Bluebell in the glen where the baby spidervipers had done away with Fenster before he could do the same to Joshua.

His sense of awe was tinged with a deep ache that swelled as his thoughts were pulled back to the only other time he had seen direct sunlight strike the surface of Cypress Grove. Images from that day almost a year ago drifted across his mind's eye: his skipping across the street to press his nose against the glass of the new book displays; Tifinity's scream of triumph and her whisper of thanks; Mr. Donald's slicked back leers; the empty stare of his mother's eyes; the maddening feeling of helplessness; and   guilt. Joshua gave himself a shake and pushed aside the painful memories.

But I fought back, Mom. I'm like the bee and Cupid, small but with a mighty sting.

Joshua blinked away the blur in his eyes as the swath of brilliant light began to shrink, merging into a single streak of gold, moving closer, shifting and flowing across the ground at uneven pace, almost as if it was alive, a curious creature making a cautious approach. Watching it diminish as it came closer, an odd mix of emotions struck Joshua. The intense awareness that he was in an incredibly rare moment of transient beauty subsided as another, more detached part of him curiously observed the sunbeam's race to reach him before it was overwhelmed by the roiling clouds above. Melancholy swelled with the realization   *There is   no one   to share this with.   I am   alone.*

But   not *quite.*

A single pulse of warmth blazed behind his shoulder.

I'm hanging in, Mom.   I am alive.   And I won't quit.   I'll show you...

The lone remaining stream of light slid closer until it stood still right in front of him, penetrating the waters of The Pond, creating a deep, green-tinged golden glow.

I   am...   Resolute.

The sunbeam winked out.

So   you may be asking, **"What happens next for Joshua?"**

There are so many possibilities: Did he ever see Tifinity again? Did he manage to avoid the new "Bosses" of New Cincinnati's underworld? Or did he just learn to love life, alone, in the swamp? Perhaps he was able to get off the planet and forge a new life with Estanod?

All these questions, I *had* to know the answers! So, I kept writing. And if you want to know how it turns out for Joshua, please look for

Volume 2 of **Driven to the Hilt: Forging the Blade**,

which is coming soon. Keep abreast of its progress at driventothehilt.com. Sign up with your email and a notification will be sent to you when it becomes available,   *and* you'll get a discounted price!

Also, while you are at driventothehilt.com, please share your thoughts about your experience with Joshua; what you liked and what you didn't. Should Joshua feel responsible for his mother's demise or was he just guilty of being a kid? Was he justified in doing what he did to survive, or not? What was his best move and what was his greatest mistake? I would love your feedback!

Of course, if you did enjoy Joshua's story, I would also be most grateful for a rating and quick review on Amazon, Goodreads, and/or BookBub.

Acknowledgements

This book has been a family affair.

First and foremost, thanks go to my son Jacob. Why does he get first plug? Well, this book never would have been written if not for Jake. Indirectly, he is responsible for me trudging up uncounted miles of Arizona mountain sides, in 110 degree heat with a 70 pound pack on my back. As I staggered through our Boy Scout adventures, I quickly learned to lessen the pain by distracting myself. I'd like to say that I thought deep thoughts, better ways to help the brain injured clients I worked with, or magnificent concepts that would better the world in some fantastic way. Nope. But I did come up with some pretty wild stories. In my head, that is. The idea of actually writing those stories down? Phhhffffft!! Must have evaporated with those gallons of Gatorade somewhere along the dusty trail. So this is where Jake comes in again, but in a much more direct fashion. While I was lying in a hospital bed recovering from prostate surgery, he encouraged me to try my hand at creative writing. During the next several weeks of forced inactivity, he helped flesh out the initial idea, provided sensitive feedback about my initial writing style (which was horribly dry and lecturing), plot development, and pacing of the story. Then, as my original story arc kept going and going and *going*, he helped me reformat the framework of the story into an initial offering. Lastly, he helped edit the critical opening scenes to make them leaner and meaner. Thanks, Jake. I literally couldn't have done it without you.

Stop. Put your finger on this page, close the book, and soak in the cover. Take your time, I'll wait... Are you back? Quite the unique design, wouldn't you say? My daughter, Sheridan, came up with the mixture of illustration and real-life elements, chose the color palette, and combined them all into a fabulously striking cover design. Sadly, she began graduate school before she could actually create the cover, so the sloppy execution of her elegant design falls squarely on my shoulders. Sheridan also provided numerous ideas about the overall plot, which brings us to, well, Sweets, I am *so* sorry. In addition to bearing the life-long burden of being the middle child, you must now carry the guilt of a certain someone's death as well. I mean, after all, you pronounced it with such certainty *"Someone must die!"* Now how could I ignore a directive like that? Just know, I will *always* be there for you.

To my youngest daughter, Cadence: Your enthusiasm and encouragement helped get me through the early days, and even more importantly, kept me plugging away during the not-so-early months that stretched into middle years, even though the idea of 'writing a book' remained so absurd in my head (still does, actually). My Sunshine Twin came through again! And at the end, you were also instrumental in helping me *FINALLY* come up with the crucial beginning of the book, along with your Mom, of course. Bringing me to-

Tambra. Thank you for coming up with the opening line. *That* is what helped me get unstuck after how many beginnings? Also, your critical analysis, sharpened by years of theatre directorial experience, was invaluable in helping make Joshua into a *real* person. You helped me see the little details that make up the greater whole. And all of those walks around the block or through the park, with me yammering on and on? Well, I certainly know *that* couldn't have been easy. You are a patient wife to have put up with such a process, and well, *me* in general.

So. How can I possibly thank my brother, Chris? For the inestimable hours spent over the past four years providing his critical editing skills: addressing tone, character development, pacing, and plot; identifying logical inconsistencies, ill-defined descriptions, wordy passages; and of course, always with a sharp eye out for typos and missing words. He also fed me a lot of recent technological developments that then contributed to various plot devices and general futuristic world building. Most of all, his unflagging support kept me on track and made all of the difference in my decision to see this through to the end. So, while this would not have begun without Jake, it wouldn't have ended without you, Bro!

My oldest brother Pat was pretty busy being one of the best science teachers in all of Kansas (and he has the award to prove it!). So while he simply didn't have the time to work though his younger brother's crazy writing project, he has been a role model to me ever since we were kids. He was the one who organized the neighborhood football games and when we were on the ground, tears welling up from a jarring blow, he would inspire us to get up and keep playing. During the walk home from the park, he would remember some play where each of us had excelled and then describe it in passionate detail. Everyone arrived home bruised, but filled with pride. He has always been someone who strives to do his best, as a student, as a football player (to the extent you can say wide receivers actually *play* football), as a teacher, and as a man. I mean, how could I quit? After all, Pat would never quit!

Finally, I need to thank my Mom and Dad. No, they didn't encourage me to reach for my dreams of becoming an author. I never *had* dreams of becoming an author. But they provided a loving home filled with quiet expectations of their three boys, with their own attitudes and values communicated by example. To be a caring person, to be a hard worker, to be someone who does the right thing, even when it is difficult to do. In short, to be someone like Joshua. So, Mom Dad Joshua is *your* son, too. He is also the product of your parenting efforts, something of a conglomeration of your three biological sons, if you will. Flawed in some ways, of course, but also with little parts of the best of all three of us, an approximation of the ideal that you set forth when guiding our development, a goal that we continue to pursue, even now.

54192189R00184

Made in the USA
San Bernardino, CA
09 October 2017